NH: Oh my what a story, so emotional and heartfelt.

KATHARINE

By the same author

Eye of the Storm
Abortion: a woman's birthright?
Only the Best
When Suffering Comes
Laura

KATHARINE

Noreen Riols

Love and drama in war-torn Britain

Part I of the Ardnakil Chronicles

Eagle
Guildford, Surrey

British Library Cataloguing-in-Publication Data. A catalogue record for this book is available from the British Library

Published by Eagle, an imprint of Inter Publishing Service (IPS) Ltd, 59 Woodbridge Road, Guildford, Surrey GU1 4RF.

Typeset by Electronic Book Factory Ltd, Fife, Scotland.
Printed in the UK by HarperCollins Manufacturing, Glasgow.

ISBN No: 0 86347 118 8

In memory of the SOE agents who gave their lives in World War II to preserve our freedom.

TO

My son
Yves-Michel

with love

ACKNOWLEDGEMENTS: My grateful thanks to François Lebel who not only lent me his word-processor, but taught me how to use it and acted as my 'help-line' throughout the writing of this book. Not forgetting his wife, Marie-Laure, who listened patiently to my frantic telephone calls and willingly 'lent' me her husband whenever I had technical problems. To my sister-in-law, Sylvie, and our friend Pierre Yakovleff, my Russian advisers. My husband's cousin Général Jean Lamy, and his lifelong friend Commandant Georges Rolland, who shared their personal experiences of the French Resistance and the escape lines into Spain and North Africa. My brother, Geoffrey, and our old friend Lt. Colonel Jimmy Magee, my British Army and Regimental advisers. My niece Fanny Baxter for her draft cover. And lastly my husband, Jacques, for his help, encouragement and, as always, endless patience whilst these pages were coming to life.

CONTENTS

Part One

1940

Chapter 1

The ambulance siren screaming past the tube station merged with the wailing of the 'All Clear'*.

Gasping with relief Katharine scrambled breathlessly up the stairs and out into the afternoon sunshine.

As she watched the grimy white vans roar past her and over the bridge in the direction of the hospital, her tawny eyes darkened with fear. And a terrible premonition cut like a jagged knife through her slim body.

Looking wildly around, she spotted a taxi drawing to a standstill. As its lone passenger stepped down onto the pavement she ran towards the cab's open door.

'Sorry lady,' the old man crouched over the driver's wheel said wearily, removing his cap and wiping the sweat from his brow with the back of his hand. 'I've finished fer to-day.'

He painstakingly counted out some coins, as if his brain were refusing to function, and handed the change to the waiting passenger.

Katharine stopped dead, one foot inside the cab.

'Oh *please*,' she pleaded, 'please. I don't want to go far. Just to Highbury Road.'

The old man looked at her through cod-fish eyes,

* All words marked with * appear in the Glossary at the end of the book.

glazed with fatigue. Without a word he replaced his cap and jerked his head in the direction of the back seat.

''ighbury Road, you said,' he replied laconically.

Katharine nodded not trusting herself to speak. He leant heavily on the gears and pulled the cab away from the kerb in the direction of the rising spirals of black smoke.

As they turned the corner of the road, even before the pungent acrid smell of burning stung her eyes and pîerced her nostrils, Katharine knew that the house had received a direct hit. The taxi began to slow down. But she leant forward and tapped at the window.

'Can you do a *U*-turn and go to the hospital?' she choked, tears now streaming uncontrollably down her cheeks.

But the driver had already started to manoeuvre the cumbersome vehicle. He removed his cap once again then placed it back on his head, almost in a gesture of resignation. Through the dividing window Katharine sensed a current of sympathy flow from the old man towards her.

The cab slowed to a standstill under the arch in front of the hospital. Katharine's naturally pale face turned deathly white as a flurry of battered ambulances, having delivered their mutilated loads, raced past them in the opposite direction.

To her surprise, the driver heaved himself from his seat and helped her as she stumbled down the step onto the pavement.

'Want me to wait lady?' he enquired kindly, his voice strangely gentle.

She fumbled in her pocket for some coins and shook her head blankly as they dropped into his hand.

He slammed the door of the taxi and climbed wearily back into the driver's seat, his heavily jowled face grim.

'Bleedin' Jerries,' he spat, viciously crashing the gears into action as he watched her slight figure dodge between the ambulances and run towards the Casualty entrance.

The scene of frantic activity which greeted Katharine was more like something out of a horror film than one glimpsed between the grey stone walls of an old London hospital.

Nurses wearing frilly caps and doctors in white coats hurried between the lines of stretchers hastily deposited on the floor. Or rattled curtains round examination couches where bloodied bodies were lying. Mingled with the shrieks and low moans of the injured and dying was the incessant ring of the telephone.

The receptionist, seated behind a counter, looked exasperated and at the end of her tether as she attempted to cope with the flood of incoming calls and the crush of people hemming her in, frantic for news of loved ones.

The raid had been swift and severe. The casualties from Highbury Road were by no means the only ones lying in groaning heaps all around the vast echoing Casualty department.

Katharine stood helplessly in the doorway. Suddenly her eyes caught those of an elderly porter crouched in his little cubby hole beside the door.

He smiled, a thousand creases running across his face like little rivulets. In that brief instant he reminded her of her grandfather. Stumbling towards him she grabbed desperately hold of his sleeve.

He took her arm, steadying her.

'What is it little lady?' he enquired kindly. 'You looking for someone?'

Katharine nodded speechlessly.

She felt she had found a friend in the midst of this nightmare. And like a lost child she clung to him.

Unwilling to let go, lest the throttling fear which had overwhelmed her as she surveyed the terrible carnage would return.

Still clinging to his arm, he led her across the tiled floor to the reception desk.

'Just give the person's name to the lady here,' he said gently disengaging her. 'She'll help you.'

Katharine glanced at the harassed receptionist and felt her panic return. She shot a look of mute appeal at the old porter.

'Don't worry, luv,' he said reassuringly. 'You'll be all right.'

He bent down towards her and whispered.

'Her bark is worse than her bite.'

And with a conspiratorial wink he turned and forced his way through the human barrage back to his lodge.

The receptionist looked up.

'Yes?' she snapped.

And Katharine was far from reassured.

'It's my mother,' she faltered. 'I think she may be here. We live in Highbury Road and . . .'

But the receptionist cut her short.

'Name.'

'Montval,' Katharine said. 'Rowena de Montval.'

'Rowena *what*?' the receptionist barked exasperatedly.

'Montval,' Katharine stammered.

And she spelled the letters out.

The receptionist sighed and pulling a sheaf of papers towards her began running a pencil down the list.

Katharine noticed that the bright red varnish on her nails was chipped. Her lipstick smeared. And she suddenly felt sorry for the short-tempered woman. She was probably as tired and harassed as everyone else.

The thought crossed Katharine's mind that perhaps

she had someone hidden behind those jangling curtains. Someone she loved. For whom she was afraid.

And she saw the surly woman in a different light.

The rapidly moving pencil stopped and hovered.

The receptionist frowned.

'What did you say her name was?' she enquired without looking up.

'Montval,' Katharine repeated. 'Rowena de Montval.'

'Dee Mont*vale*,' the receptionist corrected, stressing the silent T. 'Yes, she's here. Take a seat over there.'

She nodded across at a crowded wooden bench.

'But,' Katharine mumbled, fear rising once again in her throat.

'Just go and sit down,' the receptionist said wearily.

Pushing the sheaf of papers away she took a gulp from a cup of what appeared to be stone-cold tea.

Katharine looked desperately round for her porter friend. But he had his arm round an elderly woman sobbing in the doorway. And, in spite of the bright sunshine flooding in through the high narrow windows, an icy sweat broke out and began to trickle down Katharine's back.

It was then that she saw Lavinia.

It would have been difficult not to see Lavinia. And impossible to ignore her.

Her tall dignified figure stood out from the crowd. There was something about her which commanded attention. Leaving the desk Katharine ran towards her great-aunt, relief flooding through her like a cascading wave. At first Lavinia did not see her. Then as Katharine literally catapulted herself into her arms, her rather haughty expression changed. She gripped her niece with a firm hand holding her tightly.

'Aunt Lavinia, whatever are you doing here?' Katharine gasped.

And dissolved into tears.

Her aunt led her to a bench in the far corner which, surprisingly, was empty. Sitting down, she snapped open her worn but still elegant crocodile handbag and, taking out a handkerchief, began to wipe away Katharine's tears.

'I came up to London to try to persuade your mother to come back with me to Goudhurst, away from all this.'

Lavinia cast her eyes round the harrowing scene.

'Unfortunately, I arrived too late,' she ended.

Katharine sat up, her face blotched with tears.

'But Mother's here,' she breathed. 'The receptionist found her name on the list.'

'I know darling,' Lavinia soothed. 'I have seen her.'

She looked down at Katharine, her slate-blue eyes guarded.

'I'm afraid your mother has been injured,' she said quietly.

A strangled cry burst from Katharine's lips and she half rose. But her aunt pressed her down onto the bench beside her.

'I think perhaps we should go and see her together.'

Katharine leapt to her feet.

'Oh *please*,' she pleaded, 'if you know where she is . . . I must see her. Is she badly hurt?'

Lavinia slowly rose from the bench, not even attempting to answer the flow of disjointed questions which were jumping erratically through her niece's brain and coming out in a series of short staccato bursts.

'Katharine,' she said, without looking round, as she led the way towards a closed door on the opposite side of the hall. 'The raid came so quickly your mother stayed under the stairs instead of trying to get to the shelter. Unfortunately, the house received a direct hit . . .'

Lavinia took a deep breath.

'Her legs have been crushed.'

Katharine stared blankly, unable to take in the full impact of what her aunt was telling her.

'I'm afraid we're going to have to be brave.'

Lavinia sighed and added grimly, '*Very* brave.'

'Oh no,' Katharine breathed, icy water beginning to trickle down her back once again. 'You can't mean . . .'

'I don't mean anything darling,' Lavinia said gently. 'No one knows. But when you see Rowena try to remain calm. You'll be shocked. But don't let her see it.'

She pushed open the door marked No Entry and walked imperiously through it into an atmosphere so diametrically opposed to the confusion which reigned in the Casualty department, that Katharine was momentarily stunned.

Here in a long straight corridor with doors leading off it on either side there was an air of cool, starched efficiency. A Sister, with stiff impeccable cuffs, wearing a tall white linen cap tied with a bow under her chin, appeared as if from nowhere. She glided towards them like a swan sailing on unruffled waters.

'This is my great-niece, Mrs. de Montval's daughter,' Lavinia said, taking the bewildered Katharine by the arm.

The Sister's non-committal expression softened as she smiled across at Katharine.

'I expect you'd like to see your mother,' she said, her voice low and modulated.

She turned and began to walk noiselessly along the corridor, pausing before a door which was slightly ajar.

Her eyes wandered to meet Lavinia's, who nodded in response.

Katharine's brain felt anaesthetised, rendering her incapable of any reaction as she and Lavinia tiptoed into the silent room.

The blinds were drawn against the late afternoon sunlight and a faint hissing noise came from a machine standing at the head of the bed. Its bulk momentarily hid the figure lying between the starched white sheets.

As her eyes grew accustomed to the half light, Katharine realised that the slight motionless hump was her mother's body. A sharp anguished cry rose unbidden in her throat and tore its way out through tightly clenched lips. She rushed forward, her eyes wide with fear.

Lavinia came quickly to her side as Katharine threw herself down on the floor beside the bed, staring in horror at the ghostly white face.

She looked up at her aunt, desperately trying to draw comfort from her But her aunt's expression was grim. As the full horror of the scene before her slowly began to seep through the numbness of her brain, Katharine realised that there was no hope.

With a low moan of despair she laid her head on the pristine sheet. Her lips brushed her mother's cold white hand as hot tears gushed behind her eyelids and began to pour down her cheeks.

The Sister appeared at the door and, crossing the room, gently raised Katharine to her feet. She allowed herself to be led, limp and helpless, from the room. Her body felt like a great weight which she was being forced to carry: an excruciating burden which she neither wanted nor had the strength to bear.

Lavinia followed them into the corridor, quietly drawing the door of the sick room to behind her.

'I'll get a nurse to bring you a cup of tea.'

Katharine heard the Sister's words coming as if from a long way off. As she turned to go, Katharine grabbed her arm.

'She's going to die, isn't she?' she whispered, her

voice an unrecognisable croak. 'My mother's going to die.'

The Sister looked down at her, her wide grey eyes now warm with compassion.

'I can't tell you,' she answered quietly. 'She's certainly very ill, but she may recover. No one can say for sure whether she will die or not. That is in God's hands.'

She gently released herself.

'Sit here in the corridor and drink your tea. Then, when you're feeling stronger you can go in and see your mother again.'

Katharine nodded bleakly.

'A cup of tea,' she whispered brokenly. 'My mother's dying, and they offer me a cup of tea.'

And, as the tears welled up once again, she covered her face with her hands and wept.

* * *

A faint whimper like the sound of a very small animal caught in a trap, pleading for its life, coming from inside the shaded room, roused Katharine from her stupor.

She glanced across at her aunt.

Lavinia was writing in a small crocodile-bound note-book, her slim black pen moving in light swift strokes across the gilt-edged pages. She seemed not to have heard the pathetic cry.

As if from nowhere, the Sister appeared in the corridor, and entered Rowena's room.

'Xavier.'

Katharine's limp body stiffened as she heard her mother call her father's name. Lavinia laid aside her pen and her face hardened momentarily.

'Xavier.'

There it was again. But this time fainter as if her

mother were already drifting away. Katharine jumped to her feet.

'She's conscious at last,' Lavinia murmured, rising and taking her niece's arm. 'But perhaps not wholly with us. Let's wait to see what the Sister has to say.'

Katharine knew how Lavinia felt about her father. Knew the anger she had harboured against him ever since he had deserted her and her mother six years ago. But she also knew that her mother had never stopped loving him, even though she rarely mentioned his name.

Katharine shook herself free and turned towards the door.

'I *must* go to her,' she cried, the tears once again pressing behind her swollen lids.

But at that moment the Sister slipped from the darkened room. Her face was grave.

'I think your mother would like to see you,' she said softly, shooting a knowing look at Lavinia as she held open the door.

Katharine stumbled across the threshold, her aunt following closely behind. She almost ran the few steps which separated her from the high bed where her mother's life was slowly ebbing away. For the first time she noticed that the the room was filled with the sickly sweet smell of fresh blood. And that the bed was flat where her mother's legs should have been.

Stifling a cry, Katharine threw herself on her knees. Her head lay on the stiff white coverlet as she took her mother's icy hand and pressed it savagely between her own, willing life back into the flaccid flesh.

Gathering together the last remaining shreds of strength, Rowena turned her head slightly on the pillow until her deep-blue eyes were level with her daughter's. Her bloodless lips turned slightly upwards in an effort to smile as her beautiful eyes clouded over and the pallor of death began to creep up her neck and around the edges of her damp blond hair.

'Go to your grandmother,' she whispered, her voice hardly more than a faint sigh.

Lavinia, standing at the foot of the bed frowned in perplexity.

Her sister-in-law, Rowena's mother and Katharine's maternal grandmother, had died six years ago. She very much feared that loss of blood had merged past and future together in Rowena's brain. And what she was trying to say could only upset Katharine even more. Lavinia moved round to the other side of the bed as Katharine raised herself on her knees and bent forwards to catch the faint feathery strokes of her mother's voice. In what was scarcely more than a distant murmur Rowena slowly enunciated the words.

'To Paris, rue de la Faisanderie. To Armelle.'

Armelle de Montval was Xavier's mother: Katharine's paternal grandmother

Lavinia found it difficult to contain her emotion.

But it was a feeling of anger which was uppermost. Anger against Xavier, and, unreasonably, against the whole Montval family who, to her mind, had ruined her beloved niece's life and now threatened to do the same to her great-niece.

She tiptoed round the bed and put an arm protectively across Katharine's shoulders.

But Katharine had understood her mother's words.

She realised that in these last poignant moments together Rowena was trying to point the way. And, although the tears were streaming down her face, and her whole being was rebelling against the injustice of her mother dying so young, somewhere in her subconscious she felt that all was not lost. Perhaps her father would one day return. Her family be restored to her.

As if Rowena could read her daughter's thoughts, a faint flutter of a smile hovered around her parted lips. And her mutilated body, which when they entered the room, had appeared rigid, seemed to relax beneath the sheets. Then, as if she had suddenly remembered something a flicker of a frown touched her brow. Rowena's lips moved again, but no sound emerged. Katharine bent even closer, her eyes never leaving her mother's face.

'The trunks,' Rowena mouthed silently.

Bewildered and confused by this last dying phrase Katharine watched, as a dull film began to slowly spread across those once brilliant blue eyes.

But Rowena appeared to be at peace.

With a last lingering whisper, hardly more than a sigh, she breathed her husband's name. Then the clammy hand held tightly in Katharine's released its faint pressure. And her life slipped away.

Lavinina gazed down at Rowena's body and couldn't take in the reality of what was before her eyes. Couldn't believe that this beloved niece, Rowena Lavinia, who had been more like a daughter, her one English bridesmaid at her glittering wedding in St. Petersburg all those years ago, was now lying lifeless, her beautiful face already beginning to take on the waxen mask of death.

And a sudden rage began to tremble inside her threatening to choke and overpower her. Futile senseless impotent anger against death, that last great enemy.

She clenched her hands into a hard stiff ball, her knuckles turning white in the lethal grip, willing herself to keep calm, to remain in control. Just as she felt that her laboured breathing must be echoing deafeningly around the entire hospital, the Sister reappeared. It was uncanny the way she seemed to sense when her presence was needed to break the unbearable tension of an emotion, a grief too heavy to be borne alone.

She gently squeezed Lavinia's shaking shoulders before walking round to the other side of the bed. Tenderly drawing Rowena's lids over her lifeless eyes, she stood gazing down at her.

As Lavinia raised Katharine to her feet, they saw that the Sister's eyes were also closed. Her lips wordlessly moving. And into Katharine's tired, bewildered brain came the answer she had given her when she had asked if her mother was going to die. 'That is in God's hands.'

And she knew that she was praying.

But the knowledge gave Katharine no comfort.

She was angry with God for snatching away her mother. And in her anger she refused the words which might have eased her pain. The Sister opened her eyes and came towards her. But, as if holding her responsible for what had happened, Katharine deliberately turned her back, and ran from the room.

'I'm afraid it's been a terrible shock for her,' Lavinia murmured apologetically, embarrassed by her niece's rudeness. 'For us both.'

The Sister placed a hand on her arm.

'One feels so helpless at a time like this,' she replied, closing the door quietly behind her. 'One wants to help but there's absolutely nothing anyone can do.'

She sighed.

'We each have to come to terms with grief in our own way. All I can do is pray for you.'

Lavinia didn't reply. Her eyes were on Katharine, standing with her back to them in the corridor, her whole body shaking. And at that moment she honestly didn't know whether it was with shock, grief or a terrible all-consuming anger.

* * *

'I do hate having to shut out the last of the daylight,' Lavinia sighed, pulling the heavy velvet curtains across the latticed windows in the hall.

She entered the drawing-room where lengthening shadows were creeping up the walls, cloaking the pictures in their heavy gilt frames.

'But I suppose if we wait any longer the fire will be reflected on the panes and we'll have dear old Mr Popham hammering on the door or blowing his whistle at us.'

Mr Popham was the Goudhurst butcher, who doubled after dark as air raid warden.

She sank into her comfortable armchair and looked across at her niece.

Katharine turned from the window, swishing the curtains into position as she did so.

Her mother had been buried that morning.

The full impact of the emotional rubble to which not only her home but also her life had been reduced had just struck her. And she had been seized with a terrible panic. A panic coupled with hopelessness and despair. And with it the dreadful realisation that she was now alone.

As she had gazed out over the garden in which late roses were jostling for place with early autumn blooms, her pain and anguish, having reached their peak of intensity, her body had taken over and brought temporary relief, dulling her senses.

In place of the overwhelming terror which had caught her in its grip, there was now just an immense sadness, an aching void which she doubted time could ever fill. The first frenzy of grief had given way to a numb acceptance. And the years stretched ahead, long dreary years of nothingness.

A log spluttered and fell into the ashes. Lavinia leant forward. Picking up the brass tongs, she retrieved it and placed it thoughtfully back onto the blaze. Outside in the hall the old grandfather clock struck the half hour.

'Katharine,' she ventured.

Lavinia had noticed the violet smudges of fatigue under her eyes. Her drawn features. The skin stretched so tightly over her cheekbones as to make her face seem transparent.

Katharine looked up.

And, once again, Lavinia was struck by the change in her niece. Her beautiful hazel eyes, once dancing with golden lights, were now dull and lifeless. She smiled. But only with her lips.

'There was a letter from Flora Hamilton in the afternoon post,' Lavinia went on. 'She's asked you to go to Scotland and stay with her for as long as you wish.'

Leaning back in her chair Lavinia studied the shadows cast by the firelight on the low beamed ceiling.

'I think you should accept Flora's invitation darling. It would do you good to get right away for a while.'

Katharine didn't immediately reply. She looked intently at her aunt. Then looked away.

'How can I go and stay with anybody,' she muttered hoarsely. 'All I possess in the world is a suitcase full of dirty clothes. There was nothing left after that direct hit. Nothing. If I hadn't been on my way home from holiday when it happened, I would only have what I stood up in.'

She faced her aunt, her mouth set in a straight hard line.

'I no longer own a single thing. Not even a photograph

of mother or Zag. Everything's gone. All those happy years in Morocco wiped out. Buried under a pile of rubble.'

And, thrusting her head in her hands, she burst into tears.

Lavinia winced.

She had never understood why Xavier had insisted on his daughter calling him by his Christian name. When Katharine was small 'Zag' was all she could manage. And, for her, Zag he had remained.

She looked across at her distraught niece.

'You're wrong in supposing you have lost everything,' she said softly. 'Whilst you were in Wales last week, your mother packed several trunks full of things she was afraid might be destroyed if left in London. They are up in the attic. We can go and look through them whenever you wish.'

For the past week Katharine had tried to shut out the agonising events of that terrible Thursday afternoon. But now, she forced herself to remember.

As her mother's dying face swam before her eyes she heard again that almost imperceptible whisper.

'The trunks.'

Katharine could not believe that, only seconds before she died, Rowena had made that superhuman effort to voice those two words if all the trunks contained were winter clothes.

And she instinctively knew that they held a secret.

A secret that would unravel the mystery which had haunted her ever since the day her father had disappeared.

In the distance she heard the thrum thrum of approaching aircraft. A fleet of RAF bombers on their way to raid enemy territory. And she shuddered. She could not face the trunks today.

Katharine

The memories were still too fresh, too raw.

But a glimmer of light had pierced the darkness which surrounded her. Beckoning her towards it from the other end of the long dark tunnel into which she had been so abruptly and cruelly thrust.

Chapter 2

Katharine left the chill sunlight of a brisk October morning and entered the grimy station.

Euston was crowded.

She had difficulty following the elderly porter, shouldering her luggage, who was pushing his way through the groups of weary-looking soldiers sitting resignedly on luggage trolleys, waiting to be shunted to their next destination.

As she threaded her way towards the platform she seemed to be surrounded by young women snuggling tearfully in a sailor's arms or entwined in a passionate embrace with a khaki-clad figure. Oblivious of the noise, the bustle, the dirt, the utter dreariness of the vast echoing vault.

The porter turned round, easing the heavy suitcase from one shoulder to the other.

'Perth you said, miss?'

'Yes please,' Katharine replied. 'The 10.20.'

She climbed into the carriage behind him and squeezed her way along the corridor. A young army officer smiled and pressed himself against the window to enable her to wriggle past.

''ere we are then,' the porter announced triumphantly, squinting down at her reservation ticket.

He entered a compartment and heaved her suitcase up on to the rack.

'Yer facin' the engine, so you can see all them 'ighland cows and things.'

He grinned at her and Katharine noticed that most of his teeth were missing.

'Be away from all them bombs up there,' he went on chattily, pushing his cap to the back of his head and passing an arm across his glistening brow.

Katharine smiled and, opening her purse, dropped some coins into his hand.

'Thanks miss,' he said, replacing his cap. 'Dinin' car's three carriages down.'

And then he was gone.

Standing on tiptoe to place the new camel hair coat which Lavinia had bought her onto the rack, she watched his thin, stooping figure trudge back along the platform. But the guard had blown his whistle. And the train, with a series of snorts and shunts, was slowly pulling away from the platform. It gathered speed as it clattered past the upturned faces, many streaming with tears, the frantically waving hands, the barrows, the lounging porters and the piles of kitbags standing, like a defeated army, at the end of the fastly receding platform.

Feeling suddenly rudderless and helpless, Katharine leant back in her seat.

For the past few weeks she no longer seemed to have had any control over her life; any say in what she was going to do. It was as if she were a pawn on a chess board, being moved around by someone else's hands.

Gazing through the tiny scrap of dirty window which was not criss-crossed with thick brown tape, she glimpsed the sordid tangle of streets, the grey washing hanging dejectedly in front of broken windows, the piles of rubble amongst which grubby children shouted and played.

And she was reminded of the smouldering ruins of her own home.

Closing her eyes tightly she fought to keep the rising tears from racing down her cheeks.

When she awoke, London had given way to lush green farmland. Stirring in her seat, she felt the soft warmth of the heather-mixture suit Lavinia had bought her, the caress of the silk blouse tied loosely at her throat. Looking down, she gazed in satisfaction at her shiny new shoes. And gradually the earlier depression gave way to a deep gratitude for her aunt and all that she meant to her.

'I'm sure there must be some of your clothes in those trunks,' Lavinia had remarked over lunch the day after the funeral. 'If you wish, we can go up into the attic this afternoon and sort through them.'

She had glanced out of the dining-room window. The overhanging sky had darkened to a gun-metal grey and heavy drops of rain were already pattering against the bottle-glass panes.

'Quite a good day for rummaging,' Lavinia had smiled, raising her eyebrows enquiringly at her niece.

But a vision of her mother's dying face rose unbidden before Katharine's eyes. And a sudden panic had seized her.

She knew she couldn't open those trunks. Not yet. Not until her emotions had settled and she could think rationally once again. She was afraid of what she might find. Or, if she were honest with herself, of what she might *not* find. What if their mothballed interiors held only winter clothes after all?

'Please Aunt Lavinia,' she pleaded, 'not today.'

'Then let's go into Tunbridge Wells and *buy* you some clothes,' Lavinia had replied serenely. 'Might be a tonic for you to have a whole new wardrobe.'

Katharine smiled to herself, remembering that rainy afternoon and relishing all the new clothes her worn leather suitcase contained.

Lavinia had spent lavishly. They had returned to Greystones laden with expensive parcels. And, despite the reason for her new wardrobe, Katharine had felt a thrill when everything had been laid out on her bed yesterday for Elsie to pack.

'Dear Lavinia,' she murmured.

Looking up, she saw the army officer she had crossed in the corridor sitting in the seat opposite. He was looking at her with an amused expression on his face.

And she realised that she had spoken out loud.

Quickly picking up the newspaper lying unopened on her lap Katharine lifted it to her face to conceal her mounting blush. Over the top of it she saw him return to the figures he had been jotting in a small notebook, that amused smile still playing around his lips.

In the distance a tinkling bell sounded. It came gradually nearer and a white-coated attendant popped his head around the door.

'First sitting for lunch?' he said, looking enquiringly round the compartment.

The elderly couple by the window kept their eyes glued to their newspapers. The middle-aged woman sitting next to Katharine shook her head. Katharine rose to her feet at the same time as the army officer. He smiled and stood aside to let her pass. Then, swaying from side to side they followed each other down the long series of corridors to the dining car.

When they entered it was almost full. The waiter, assuming that they were together, led them to a table at the far end. Katharine sat down. But the young officer stood, smiling, above her.

'May I?' he enquired.

'Of course,' she said, picking up the menu in an attempt to hide her embarrassment. He slid into the seat opposite her and flicking open the white linen napkin placed it across his knees waiting patiently for her to release the menu.

The waiter hovering above them coughed discreetly.

'I'm so sorry,' she mumbled, handing the menu across the table.

He glanced quickly down it and added his order to hers.

The waiter disappeared and they were alone, facing each other across an expanse of *LMS** glass and silverware.

'As we are to lunch together,' he said, 'let me introduce myself. Ashley Paget.'

Katharine glanced at the three shiny pips on his shoulder, denoting the rank of captain. A slight frown creased her brow. The buttons on his uniform were unfamiliar and she wondered to which regiment he belonged.

Reading her unspoken thoughts, he leant forward conspiratorially.

'Crosse and Blackwell Brigade.'*

His eyes were twinkling. And she had the distinct impression that he was laughing at her.

'I'm afraid I don't understand,' she mumbled, angry at him for laughing at her and angry at herself for letting it affect her. 'Did you say Crosse and Blackwell Brigade?'

He nodded his head, his eyes still twinkling. She noticed that they were very blue.

'But isn't that some kind of pickle?' she frowned.

'You're quite right.'

'Then how can it be a regiment?' she asked coldly, now convinced that he was teasing her.

'It's not a regiment, it's a brigade,' he corrected. 'Our

badge and buttons have the Crosse and Blackwell pickle sign on them. You know, by appointment to His Majesty the King.'

He shrugged.

'So I suppose that makes us pickles too.'

'But what sort of a brigade is that?'

'Oh, one where they throw all the odd bods they don't know what to do with,' he laughed.

He leant across the table towards her.

'Now, may I know whom I have the pleasure of lunching with?'

'Katharine de Montval,' she mumbled, still nettled.

'De Montval,' he exclaimed, and she noticed that he gave her name the correct pronunciation, not the massacred version to which she had become accustomed since her arrival in England. 'Isn't that French?'

She nodded.

'My father's French.'

'And your mother?'

'My mother was English.'

He noticed the past tense, but didn't comment.

At that moment the waiter arrived with the soup.

They sipped in silence for a few minutes.

'Did you come across after the fall of France?' he enquired, putting down his spoon and wiping his mouth with his napkin.

Raising her head, Katharine noticed the well-trimmed gingery moustache lying across his upper lip.

'No,' she said, 'I've been living here since '34.'

'It must be very difficult for your father, having his country invaded,' he pursued. 'Such a beautiful country. I went over frequently when I was at Oxford studying modern languages.'

She looked across at him, her interest growing in spite of herself.

'So you speak French?'

'I taught it for a couple of years at Rugby. Then war broke out . . .'

'My grandfather went to Rugby,' Katharine broke in.

He raised his eyebrows.

'Did he now? So did my father.'

'And you?'

'My brother and I went to Winchester.'

He gave a mischievous smile.

'I think our mother considered Rugby too tough for her little darlings.'

Katharine's expression softened and she joined in his laughter.

'Were you at Dunkirk?' she asked.

'Yes,' he answered laconically, but didn't elaborate.

For an instant his face clouded.

But at that moment the waiter placed the fish in front of them.

'Whereabouts did you live in France?' he enquired.

'We didn't live in France. We were in Morocco. As a matter of fact,' she added hastily, 'I don't really know France very well, we only ever went on holiday to visit my father's family.'

'And where was that?'

'My grandmother had a flat in Paris, near the Etoile, well nearer the Porte Dauphine really. But the family home is in the South West. They're vine growers.'

Katharine hastily reached for her glass, once again afraid, now that the memories were beginning to flood back.

'And is your father here with you in England or still in Morocco?' he pursued.

Katharine abruptly replaced her glass, panic now showing in her tawny eyes.

'I don't know where my father is,' she blurted out, 'and my mother was killed in an air-raid last month.'

She took a deep breath.

'And now, if you don't mind, could we please change the subject?'

He put down his knife and fork.

'I'm *so* sorry,' he said softly, '*do* forgive me.'

He looked straight at her and she saw that his blue eyes were no longer twinkling.

'We don't have to talk at all,' he assured her.

She glanced up and their eyes met briefly.

'No,' she faltered. 'It's perfectly all right. But let's make it more general, small talk if you like.'

She smiled weakly.

'It could be embarrassing to sit opposite each other in silence for the rest of the meal.'

He smiled back.

'Tell me how far north you're going,' he volunteered.

Then the twinkle came back into his eyes.

'Is that general enough?'

She returned his grin, strangely at ease with this unknown man now that the tension of the past few minutes had dispersed.

'To Perth,' she replied.

'Oh, so I'll be able to help you down with your suitcase. I'm going on to the Granite City.'

Katharine looked at him enquiringly.

He noticed that her lashes were long and curled up at the ends, casting shadows across her pale cheeks when she dropped her eyes.

'Aberdeen,' he smiled.

'I didn't know,' she murmured. 'But I'm afraid there's a lot of things I don't know about this country.'

He raised his eyebrows enquiringly.

'Don't you consider it *your* country?'

She shrugged her shoulders, gallic fashion.

'In the past few weeks I've begun to wonder whether I have a country. Where I do belong.'

She sighed.

'I don't think it's here, although England was my mother's home. I don't think it's Morocco any more, although I was born in Marrakesh and lived there till I was almost thirteen.'

Her finger traced a pattern on the white cloth as the waiter removed the plates.

'I think perhaps it's France,' she said quietly.

The dark shadows on her cheeks cast by the reflection of her lashes, lifted as she raised her eyes, to be replaced by a uniform creamy colour.

'Yes,' he murmured, thinking how different she was from the typical English rose. 'You're probably right.'

Katharine looked at him in surprise, but his eyes were on his plate.

'You look more French than English.'

He paused.

'And I mean that as a compliment.'

A blush rose unbidden to her cheeks and the creamy colour slowly turned to magnolia.

'Thank you,' she murmured.

And an awkward silence fell between them.

'Are you going on holiday?' he enquired after a few minutes.

'I suppose it could be called that,' she replied. 'My aunt, who is my only relative over here, well actually, she's my great aunt, thought it might be a good thing for me to get away for a while before I decide what to do.'

She shrugged.

'With the war on, I've got to do *something*.'

She cut into a slice of Cheddar from the cheese platter which the waiter was holding.

'Have you thought what you could do?' her companion asked. 'I don't imagine you're old enough to have been to University?'

Katharine shook her head.

'No, I was in Switzerland in '38, being finished off as my mother put it. Then, last year I went to Mrs Hosters.'*

She pushed away her plate and looked across at him.

He noticed how the tawny colour of her beautiful almond-shaped eyes had turned almost gold. Her delicately chiselled cheekbones, below finely arched dark eyebrows, were so high it gave her face an almost oriental look. And it fascinated him. She was quite unlike any woman he had ever met. Her beauty was ethereal and yet earthy at the same time.

'But I honestly don't think I want to be a secretary.'

She grinned ruefully.

'I don't even think I'd be very good at it. But, with the war on, I can't just sit around.'

'No, I can see that,' he remarked thoughtfully, as the waiter removed their plates and poured coffee. 'But, of course, your obvious asset, and perhaps your greatest, is your linguistic skill.'

He looked sharply at her.

'Do you still speak Arabic?'

'I haven't spoken it for years,' she demurred. 'But, yes, I imagine it would come back. After all, it was the language I was brought up with.'

'And, of course, you're bilingual, French, English.'

She nodded.

'Then I think you could be very useful,' he went on guardedly.

'In what way?'

'The British are notoriously monolingual. We just

don't make the effort to speak other people's languages. So, someone like yourself . . .'

He didn't finish the sentence.

'Please go on,' she urged.

'There's going to be a great need for linguists, and French speakers in particular. Especially in the Armed Forces.'

'I don't think that would be the answer,' she demurred. 'I'm like my father, a loner. We both hated boarding school or any kind of communal living. And although he was highly decorated during the last war, he always told me that he detested the Army and all it stood for. Very difficult considering his father was a General.'

'It sometimes happens,' Ashley agreed. 'But, coming back to you. It doesn't necessarily have to be communal living, I wasn't thinking of the ATS.'*

He refilled her cup.

'Have you heard of the FANYs?'*

Katharine shook her head.

'I daresay your aunt will have. They were very active during the last war. She may even have been one.'

'Lavinia was in Russia during the last war,' Katharine remarked.

He raised his eyebrows in surprise.

'My goodness,' he exclaimed, 'what an interesting family you are. Would it be indiscreet to ask what she was doing there?'

'My grandfather, her brother, was a diplomat. She visited him and my grandmother whilst they were at the Embassy in St Petersburg and fell in love with a young Russian Army officer. They were married just before the last war. Unfortunately Alexei was killed fighting the Bolsheviks during the Revolution. Lavinia escaped with his parents and younger sister, Tamara, to Persia. The Voronovskys finally settled in Paris, but Lavinia came back to England.'

'I imagine your aunt has some very colourful stories to tell.'

'She probably has. But although she has kept close contacts with Alexei's family, she never talks about her life in Russia. She even reverted to her maiden name when she returned.'

Katharine grinned across at him.

'Said an émigré Russian princess was out of place in a Kent village.'

'I see her point,' he grinned back.

'I may learn more about it now that the Voronovsky's are in London. They left Paris at the time of Dunkirk.'

At the mention of Dunkirk, a flash of pain once again shadowed his handsome features.

'To come back to the *FANYs*,' he said hastily. 'They wear uniform but don't necessarily live communally. In fact, quite a lot of them live at home, or independently. But even if they are away from London, they are not herded together in tin huts.'

He took out a silver cigarette case and snapping it open, offered it to her.

Katharine shook her head.

'May I?' he enquired.

'Please do,' she said. 'I quite like the smell, but I can't bear the taste.'

He selected one and, pressing his finger on the lighter, bent his head to the flame.

'Where are you staying in Perth?' he went on, leaning back in his chair and inhaling deeply.

'I'm not,' Katharine replied. 'My friends live outside Perth, in the country. A little place called Ardnatulloch.'

'Ardnatulloch!' he exclaimed.

He placed the glowing cigarette in an ashtray.

'What a very strange coincidence. That's where my mother came from. Tell me, who are you going to stay with?'

'I'm going to Ardnakil,' she replied.

'To the Hamiltons!' he exclaimed. 'It's thanks to them that I'm here.'

He grinned across at her.

'It was whilst my father was staying at Ardnakil that he met my mother.'

He reached across and stubbed out the smouldering cigarette.

'My brother and I spent many happy holidays at Tulloch House when our grandparents were alive,' he mused. 'You and I might even have met before?'

'No,' she admitted, 'I don't think so. They are great friends of my aunt's. But I've only been to Ardnakil once.'

He shook his head in bewilderment.

'This is really the most extraordinary series of coincidences. It's almost as if we were meant to meet. After all, you could have travelled on another day.'

Katharine nodded.

'But to be not only on the same train but sitting opposite each other in the same compartment . . . And both of us with healthy young appetites needing to be satisfied at the first sitting.'

He smiled roguishly.

'Do you believe in fate?'

Katharine smiled back.

'The Arabs call it Kismet.'

'Whatever it is,' he went on. 'I'm intrigued and . . . delighted it happened.'

There was a sudden silence.

Katharine looked out of the window, uncertain what to reply.

'Look,' he said, earnestly leaning across the table towards her, 'we must meet whilst you're in Scotland. I'll do my very best to get away this next weekend. Would you be free?'

Katharine nodded, her eyes shining. And she realised that this was the first time since that dreadful Thursday almost a month ago that she had felt even a flicker of happiness.

A slow blush began to creep up her neck once again. To hide her confusion she felt in her handbag for her small silver powder compact, and began dabbing at her nose with the puff.

He half turned to signal to the waiter and, as he did so, she noticed for the first time an open parachute stitched on his right arm above the elbow.

He caught her glance and smiled.

'Nothing to get excited about. I was kicked out of an aeroplane a few times, that's all.'

The waiter arrived at the table and, looking up, Katharine realised that they were alone in the dining car. The second service had come and gone and they hadn't even noticed. She glanced down at her watch.

'It's twenty to four,' she gasped. 'We must have held you up dreadfully.'

The waiter smiled.

'We'll be serving tea in five minutes. If you'd like to remain seated.'

'Oh,' Katharine protested, 'we can't. It would be unfair with other people waiting.'

The waiter glanced pointedly at the wings on her companion's arm.

'It's a pleasure madam,' he remarked. 'As Mr Churchill himself said: never has so much been owed by so many to so few.'

'In that case,' Ashley said, 'we're here under false

pretences. I'm sorry to disappoint you, but I'm afraid I'm not one of the few.'

'No matter sir,' the waiter persisted, 'if you'd like tea, I'll serve it immediately.'

'I'd like it very much,' Ashley replied.

He turned and smiled at Katharine.

'If you would.'

Katharine smiled back.

'This must be the pleasantest railway journey I can ever remember taking,' Ashley announced.

He looked appealingly at Katharine.

'May I telephone you when I get to Tulloch House on Friday evening?'

Katharine didn't answer immediately.

But her shining eyes were confirmation enough.

Chapter 3

Lady Flora was sitting alone in the drawing-room when she heard the car turn at the bend of the drive.

Crossing the darkened hall, she let herself out through the massive oak door and stood under the overhanging stone archway watching as the hooded headlights appeared, casting ghostly shadows on the trees leading up to the house. A chill sliver of pale lemon moon shone weakly through them. The autumn night was cold and Flora shivered pulling her mohair shawl more closely to her.

The car purred to a standstill. Katharine stepped down, looking diffidently around her in the misty darkness.

'How lovely to see you,' Flora exclaimed, running lightly forward and clasping her in a warm unexpected embrace. 'Welcome to Ardnakil!'

And, taking Katharine's arm, she led her towards the door.

As they entered the dark, cavernous hall, a tall stooping figure stepped from the shadows and shut it behind them. He made a slight bow in Katharine's direction then shuffled around turning on lights, and the house immediately sprang to life. A cloud of black Labradors which had been slumbering on a plaid at the bend of the great staircase leapt to their feet and slithered down the stairs yapping and wagging their tails. Katharine looked around her as two of the younger ones jumped up, placed their paws on her shoulders, and began frantically licking her face.

'Down Gus, down Reggie,' Lady Flora laughed, not in the least perturbed by their antics.

Katharine remembered that this was a regular occurrence whenever visitors arrived. Her hostess stooped to pick up a white West Highland terrier who, hearing the commotion, had waddled from a turret at the side of the door and was whining and pawing at her feet.

'They must remember you Katharine,' Flora smiled, fondling the small dog's ears.

Katharine smiled back.

She had never owned a dog, although her grandfather had kept two spaniels in his Cotswold home. But, being an only child, she had sometimes yearned for a pet. Now she knelt and buried her face in the thick hairy neck of an ageing Labrador which had painfully lumbered down the stairs after her excited yapping progeny.

'It's Hannah, isn't it?' she asked, looking up.

'How clever of you to remember,' Lady Flora exclaimed.

She put her little white pet back down on the floor. Having satisfied himself that nothing momentous was about to happen, he ambled contentedly back to his hiding-hole in the turret.

'I'll have Miss de Montval's suitcase taken up to her room,' the elderly butler said, addressing Lady Flora.

His voice was remarkably strong. It seemed incredible that it could come from such a frail body.

'I've put you in the Rose Room,' Flora went on, taking Katharine's arm and walking towards the wide oak staircase. It's in the East Turret and very peaceful. Get's all the morning sunshine.

They rounded the curve of the staircase and walked for what seemed to Katharine to be miles along a gallery whose walls were crammed with portraits of glowering ancestors. At last Lady Flora threw open a door and they entered what Katharine thought was the most charming room she had ever seen.

The bed was a four-poster with a canopy draped over it. The carpet a rich cream dotted with tiny posies of roses. Three spindly Louis XV armchairs, upholstered in a delicate rose-coloured silk, formed a semi-circle near the window, under which stood an exquisite inlaid writing-table complete with plume pen and heavily embossed inkwell. A welcoming log fire glowed in the grate.

Flora pressed Katharine's arm affectionately.

'I want you to feel at home here,' she said softly. 'Don't hesitate to ring if there's anything you need . . .'

* * *

As they sat together after dinner in a companionable silence, the leaping flames roaring up the vast chimney lit up the gracious room, sending shadows creeping across the worn carpet and round the clusters of elegant and comfortable sofas and chairs.

Katharine lay back contentedly, casting an appreciative eye around her.

'This is such a beautiful room,' she breathed.

She closed her eyes and relaxed against the deep cushions of the sofa, completely at peace.

'You will probably be my last guest to enjoy it until this ghastly war is over,' Flora remarked.

Katharine opened her eyes and looked across at her hostess in surprise.

'The house has been commandeered by the Army,'

Flora went on. 'They are going to turn it into a convalescent home for wounded Allied officers.'

'Oh no,' Katharine groaned. 'What a *pity*.'

Flora smiled at her.

'I don't think so,' she remarked. 'In fact, I think it's a very good idea. Ridiculous my being here alone with the children when it could be put to so much better use.'

She leant forward and, opening an engraved silver box from the low table between them, offered it to Katharine.

She shook her head.

'I don't smoke either,' Flora smiled, replacing the box. 'How alike we are Katharine. It's so unusual for young women not to smoke nowadays.'

Katharine nodded.

'But do tell me more about this convalescent home.'

'There's not really very much to tell,' Lady Flora remarked. 'All sorts of official people have been here during the past few months, sizing up the floors, counting rooms, jotting lots of things down in notebooks. They'll probably take over early in the New Year. Then I shall move with the children into the West Wing. Or wherever they ask me to go.'

Flora shrugged.

'It will just be a question of getting used to not having the whole house, that's all. I really don't mind at all.'

'But what does your husband think about it?' Katharine queried.

'Robert?' Flora said vaguely, as if her guest had just asked her for news of the man in the moon. 'Oh Robert isn't here. Didn't I tell you? He and his brother Hamish are back in the Army. They were called up.'

She smiled mischievously at Katharine.

'. . . Or volunteered. They are both over age. But the Army had been their career for many years. I imagine they'd have felt they were missing something if they hadn't gone.'

'So you really are all alone here,' Katharine commented.

'Yes my dear, that's why I'm so pleased that you have come to keep me company. I do hope you'll stay for as long as you wish. For the duration of the war if you'd like to.'

Katharine smiled, but said nothing.

Outside in the hall an old grandfather clock began to wheeze then ponderously struck eleven.

'Katharine,' her hostess exclaimed. '*DO* forgive me. You must be aching with tiredness and simply longing to go to bed.'

She got to her feet and held out her hand.

'Goodnight my dear,' Flora said softly as they reached Katharine's bedroom door. 'Please don't get up in the morning. I know the terrible strain you've been under. Just ring when you're ready for breakfast.'

She leant forward and kissed Katharine's cheek.

Then she was gone.

Katharine opened her door and entered the firelit room, a pot-pourri of strange new emotions billowing round and round in her mind.

She had been deeply touched not only by Lady Flora's welcome but also by her warmth.

Until then she hadn't realised how much she had missed the spontaneous shows of affection so natural to the Latin temperament. And seemingly so foreign to the Anglo-Saxon race.

Her father had always been generous with his hugs, his kisses, his praise, his bubbling delight in her. Which she had believed to be normal, until she had come to her mother's country.

Katharine had been thirteen.

Still under the shock of leaving Morocco.

But above all leaving Zag.

Settling into this northern clime, where the vivid colours, the sunshine, the noise and the laughter which had surrounded her since her birth appeared to have been washed away by the incessant rain, her demonstrative nature and natural warmth had been quickly dampened by the reserve of those with whom she came in contact. And, bewildered, homesick for Morocco, she had retreated into a cocoon which, over the years, had gradually hardened into a protective outer shell.

But Lady Flora had been different.

And she warmed to Flora as she had not warmed to any other person since the day she had last seen Zag.

Walking across to the window Katharine pulled aside the heavy pink damask curtains and stood looking out into the night.

The dark shapes of the distant mountains seemed to be gliding towards her beneath a sky in which stars flashed fire and ice, turning the dew shining on the lawn strangely phosphorescent; the few remaining roses clustered together beneath her window, a milky white.

The stillness and peace of the moonlit garden belonged to another world. A world far removed from the tension and the pain, the turmoil and the anguish which she had lived through in the past weeks.

Suddenly Zag's laughing face appeared, filling the space between the mountains. His smile beaming towards her through the mist rising up from the dark garden. She gasped and reached out to him. But, as suddenly as it had appeared, his face was gone mingling with the spirals of vapour curling upwards to merge with the endlessly shifting clouds.

The curtain dropped from her hand and she turned

from the window back into the darkened room, her father's face vividly before her.

At that moment, Katharine knew that he was alive. And that someday, somewhere they would be together again.

* * *

When Katharine opened her eyes the morning was already far advanced.

She blinked drowsily as the pale northern sun filtered through the half-open windows. Raising herself up on one elbow, she shook her head in an effort to rouse herself from her deep sleep.

As consciousness came flooding back, so did Zag. And she remembered that she had dreamt of him for the first time in years.

Slowly surfacing, her eyes gradually focused on the things around her: the large old-fashioned bedroom filled with the mellowness of beautiful faded silk, its furniture shining with the polish of centuries, the wide open curtains.

And she knew that it had not been a dream.

She had been awake. Looking through the mullioned window at the night sky when his face had appeared somewhere out there between the tall dark mountains.

Propping a pillow behind her head Katharine sat up, willing him to reappear.

But the mountains were now heather-tipped, bathed in purple and deep green as they rose skywards into a pastel-shaded mist.

Katharine sighed.

But it was sigh of deep contentment.

That peace and hope which had flooded through her the night before was still with her. Smiling to herself at the recollection, Katharine stretched luxuriously and tugged at the tassled rope hanging beside her bed. For the first time in over a month she was feeling very hungry.

When she returned from a relaxing soak in the large antiquated bath, standing sedately on four lion's paws below a shelf of glass bottles and jars full of sweet-smelling bath salts, her breakfast had arrived. It was set on a low table which had been drawn up in front of the freshly lit fire.

Katharine sank happily into the armchair and, lifting a cover, discovered a bowl of steaming porridge, a small silver jug of what looked like fresh cream standing beside it. Next to it was a boiled egg wearing a knitted hat to keep it warm and, on the hearth, covered in a damask napkin, she glimpsed the crusts of freshly toasted bread.

'Gracious,' she said to herself, pouring a cup of tea. 'If I carry on like this I shall *waddle* back to London.'

But, all the same, she poured the cream over the porridge and, sprinkling it liberally with crunchy brown sugar, plunged her spoon into its glutinous depths.

The Scotsman lay folded beside her plate. Finishing her breakfast, Katharine nestled back in her chair and started to rustle the pages.

But gradually her eyelids drooped. The newspaper fell from her hand. And Ardnakil began to weave its spell around her.

London's bomb-racked streets, endlessly wailing sirens, shrieking ambulances, tired-looking khaki clad figures crowding the railway stations; the frenetic activity which everyone seemed to be engaged in either to further the war effort or forget that there was a war on at all, now seemed to belong to another world. And the tensions of the past few weeks, which had twisted her already taut nerves into tightly wound coils just waiting to snap at the slightest pressure, slowly evaporated.

She couldn't understand this sudden peace and happiness which seemed to be seeping into her every pore.

Was it really only yesterday she had left London?

'Twenty-four hours ago I was in the train,' she mused.

At the remembrance a strange current which she had never before experienced raced through her slim body, flooding it with warmth and an intense excitement. And she began to tingle from head to toe.

Bewildered and ill at ease she got up and stood looking pensively down at the fire, one foot resting on the shining brass fender. Ashley Paget's face seemed to smile up at her from the leaping flames.

'This is ridiculous,' she exclaimed, shaking her head in annoyance.

But that warm tingling feeling would not go away. And she knew that part of the intense happiness she had experienced in the few hours she had been at Ardnakil had not only been because of the magic of the old house. There had been another dimension. An awakening of her womanhood.

Until that moment Katharine had never desired a man.

Her sheltered life had permitted her to meet only what her mother had laughingly called 'Hooray Henrys'.

But her companion on the train had been different.

Behind his twinkling eyes she had sensed a seriousness, a maturity which had been lacking in her former acquaintances. And, without realising it, she had been captivated by his charm.

She thought back to their conversation in the dining-car. And was struck by the many coincidences.

The small marble clock on the mantlepiece tinkled

and chimed the half hour. Shaking herself free from her thoughts, Katharine looked up at it. Half past twelve.

As she slowly removed her foot from the fender and placed the guard in front of the fire, there was a smile on her lips and her heart was singing.

It was Wednesday.

He had asked if he might telephone her when he arrived on Friday evening.

Only two days to wait.

She smiled in excited anticipation and her whole body thrilled at the thought. That same voluptuous feeling which she had experienced only a few minutes before swept through her once again. And this time she didn't deny it.

She wondered what would happen when his call came through.

How she would react.

The forty-eight hours passed with Katharine in a state of suspended animation, not understanding what was happening to her. Not understanding anything. Just living for Friday evening when she would hear his voice again.

But Friday evening came and went.

And he didn't ring.

She went to bed telling herself that he had been delayed. He would telephone to-morrow. But when on Sunday evening the telephone still remained silent, she knew that he would not call. And her spirits which had been at fever point all weekend, dropped to zero.

* * *

Katharine awoke on Monday morning to hear rain splashing from the gutters and hammering against her bedroom window. November had arrived in full force.

As she rang for breakfast she told herself miserably that she had behaved like a dewy-eyed adolescent.

But the intense feelings she had felt a few days before would not go away. Only now the anticipation, the thrill had gone and been replaced by anger. Even a kind of contempt against herself for being so easily duped.

Flora had noticed Katharine's shining eyes and heightened colour when she had come down to lunch the day after her arrival. And had realised that they were not due solely to a good night's rest. She had also noticed how Katharine had become progressively more pensive as the weekend progressed. And she had wondered what was behind these changing moods.

* * *

'Are the people living at Tulloch House particular friends of yours?' Katharine enquired with forced casualness.

She and Lady Flora were sitting in front of the fire after lunch on the Monday, drinking coffee and listening to the rain patter incessantly against the drawing-room windows.

'The Farquharsons?' Flora answered. 'Oh yes. Great friends. Dorothy and I see a lot of each other. Especially since we've both become grass widows.'

Katharine raised her eyebrows enquiringly.

'Fergus is now in the Army. Their son Colin is the same age as Alasdair so they often meet to play together. He'll be joining Alasdair and Graeme in the schoolroom here after Christmas. But tell me, what made you ask?'

She picked up the coffee-pot and refilled Katharine's cup.

For a moment Katharine hesitated.

'Oh nothing really,' she said, taking a lump of sugar

and dropping it thoughtfully into the cup. 'It's just that I met a young army officer on the train coming here.'

Flora smiled encouragingly.

'We happened to be sitting opposite each other in the dining-car,' Katharine hastened to add. 'He asked me how far I was going and it turned out that he is related to the Farquharsons . . .'

'How interesting,' Flora cut in.

'Yes, he even knew Ardnakil quite well.'

'I wonder who he was,' Flora puzzled. 'Did he tell you his name?'

Katharine nodded and looked away.

'Ashley Paget,' she finally blurted out.

And hated herself for the blush which began to creep slowly up her neck and flood her cheeks

Flora noticed it but said nothing.

'Paget, Paget,' she repeated to herself pursing her lips in concentration. Then suddenly her brow cleared.

'Of course,' she exclaimed, smiling across at Katharine. '*Now* I remember. His mother must have been Catriona Farquharson, Fergus' aunt. She married an Englishman, an Anglican clergyman. I believe he's a bishop now.'

Her face clouded.

'*Such* a tragic family,' she murmured, shaking her head sadly.

'What do you mean?' Katharine frowned.

'Oh, a horrible series of terribly sad events,' Flora went on. 'Catriona had a sudden heart attack and died last July. And Guy, her elder son, was killed at Dunkirk.'

Katharine remembered Ashley's brief non-committal reply when she enquired whether he had been at Dunkirk. And she mentally shrivelled remembering how cutting she had been with him when he had gently tried to pry into her past. Convinced then that she was the only person who was suffering.

'But the other son, Ashley, the one I met, was also at Dunkirk,' she faltered. 'Or, at least, that's what he told me.'

'Was he?' Flora replied vaguely. 'Possibly. I know he was in Norway, some sort of Commando expedition which was landed there just before. I remember Dorothy saying that his mother was extremely worried. Dorothy even said that it was a good thing it was the unmarried one who was doing such dangerous things.'

Flora sighed.

'And then it was poor Guy who was killed.'

'I think he got a medal for bravery,' she added as an afterthought.

She looked across at Katharine.

'But I'm sure his wife would rather have had her husband than a posthumous decoration. She's left alone now with two little boys.'

Flora picked up a tasselled silk cushion and began idly straightening out the silken threads.

'I'm so glad I married an older man Katharine,' she said quietly. 'I don't think I could have borne to have to tell the boys that their father was dead.'

She looked up and Katharine saw tears glistening in her hostess's deep grey eyes.

'And now from what Dorothy told me last week Ashley, the younger son, is doing top secret dangerous things. Jumping out of aeroplanes and goodness only knows what.'

She sighed.

'Do you understand war Katharine? I'm afraid I don't.'

Katharine didn't answer.

Her heart had lurched painfully, then begun to beat with excitement at Flora's announcement that Ashley was up to something dangerous, on some top secret mission. It made her think that, perhaps, it had not been entirely his fault that he hadn't telephoned.

She looked across at her hostess, who had risen to throw some extra logs onto the fire.

'He mentioned during lunch that he would be visiting the Farquharsons for the weekend.'

She paused and breathed deeply.

'He . . . he asked if he might telephone me here.'

Understanding dawned in Flora's eyes, confirming her earlier suspicions. And her heart went out to this young guest of whom she had grown fond during the few days they had spent together. Katharine had been badly hurt. She was very vulnerable. She hoped that the brief encounter on the train had not meant as much to her as it appeared to have done.

'I promised Dorothy we would go over for lunch whilst you're here,' she said brightly. 'She left it to me to choose the day.'

Flora raised her eyebrows enquiringly.

'I could telephone her now and make arrangements.'

Katharine started to protest but Flora silenced her.

'Life is very quiet here at the moment,' she said. 'All our husbands have gone and I daresay the Army will be taking over Tulloch for something or other before very long. So we may as well make the most of it whilst we can. *And* whilst there is still some food to be had.'

Flora picked up the lovely gold fob watch hanging on a chain round her neck and gazed down at it.

'My goodness, how the time does fly,' she exclaimed. 'I'll telephone Dorothy and then, if you'd like to, we can go up to the nursery and have tea with the children.'

Katharine picked up a glossy magazine and idly flicked through it as she waited for her hostess to return. Within a few minutes Flora came back into the room.

'Dorothy is *delighted.* Wants us to go to lunch tomorrow with the children. Colin is apparently very miserable and it will cheer him up.'

She sat down on the arm of Katharine's chair.

'His father was home on leave for a few days last week but had to return to his unit on Friday morning, since when Colin has been inconsolable. Dorothy was hoping that one of Fergus' cousins who was in Aberdeen last week would be coming for the weekend. Colin needs some masculine company. But, unfortunately, he had to cancel at the last minute. He'd been recalled to London urgently.'

She got up and held out her hand to Katharine.

'Ah, this war,' she sighed. 'When is it going to end? It's upsetting so many lives.'

Flora smiled innocently down at her and Katharine smiled back.

But her hostess hadn't fooled her.

Katharine knew that this was her tactful way of telling her that Ashley hadn't forgotten. He hadn't telephoned her simply because he hadn't been able to.

'And now let's run up to the nursery,' Flora concluded, 'before it's too late. I hope you like marmite sandwiches?'

'Love 'em,' Katharine laughed, springing to her feet, her heart suddenly lighter.

Chapter 4

'Who,' said Katharine, walking unannounced into Lavinia's bedroom, 'is that strange woman I've just seen crossing the garden with a dead Christmas tree in her hand?'

Lavinia looked up from the suitcase which she was busy unpacking.

'Oh, that's Myrtle, Elsie's sister.'

She brushed a wisp of hair, which had escaped from her immaculate chignon, away from her face.

'Whilst you were away, the bombing over London became horrific and poor Myrtle lives near the East India Dock which was a prime target. So, when her son Bert was sent overseas, Elsie persuaded her to pack up and come down here.'

'So she's with us for the duration?' Katharine enquired.

'I imagine so,' Lavinia replied, peering into the old fashioned three-sided mirror on her dressing-table and gently patting her hair back into place

'Where's Bert gone?' Katharine enquired, sitting down on the pale blue satin coverlet on Lavinia's bed.

'Goodness only knows,' her aunt remarked. 'It's always to an unknown destination. Probably Alexandria or Cairo, or somewhere in Egypt. Myrtle was in a terrible state. First time she and Bert had ever been parted. He worked as a gas-fitter and even came home for lunch.

I don't know what she'd have done if she hadn't had Elsie.'

'Or you,' Katharine put in, smiling across at her aunt.

Lavinia shrugged and picked an imaginary piece of thread off her immaculate skirt.

'Don't make me out a heroine darling, I really had no choice. Myrtle lost her husband in the last war and she's convinced the powers that be organised this one in order to kill Bert as well. I'm afraid her cockney sense of humour was sadly lacking when she arrived.'

She walked over to an inlaid mahogany chest and slid open the top drawer.

Katharine lay back against the mound of soft pillows on her aunt's comfortable bed listening to the gentle rustle of tissue paper as ivory and pale coffee-coloured slips and nightdresses, frothing with matching lace, slithered from Lavinia's hands and coiled themselves voluptuously into the rose scented drawer.

She inhaled deeply as the delicate perfume lingered in the tastefully furnished room, leaving an imperceptible scent of summer

It was early January.

They had returned the day before from Ardnakil, where Lavinia had joined Katharine for Christmas. But a heavy attack by German bombers on the outskirts of London had delayed their train by two hours. So that by the time they finally reached Goudhurst it was almost midnight and only the faithful Elsie was still waiting up for them.

Katharine placed her hands behind her head, her eyes wandering across the low-beamed ceiling. She realised that she had been away for almost two and a half months.

And she was not sure why she had come back. Why she hadn't capitulated to Lady Flora's pleas to spend the war with her, in Scotland.

It would have been so easy.

And, at times, Katharine had been sorely tempted.

She sighed.

Lavinia looked round, closing the drawer as the last of the exquisite garments slithered into place, and raised her eyebrows enquiringly.

'Oh,' Katharine said, stretching luxuriously. 'Just thinking about my future.'

'I imagine there will be any number of things for you to do at Ardnakil now that the house is going to become a convalescent home.'

Lavinia straightened up.

'You could always train as a VAD.*'

'That's what Flora suggested.'

Katharine drew her brows together in concentration.

'Aunt Lavinia,' she said slowly. 'Just what is the connection between us and Ardnakil? I know we're not related to the Hamiltons, but there's some strong bond there.'

Lavinia bent her head and began fumbling amongst the tissue paper.

'The two families have known each other for a very long time,' she answered vaguely. 'My great-aunt Henrietta Stanhope was a lady-in-waiting to Queen Victoria with Robert Hamilton's grandmother.'

'But that's an awfully long time ago,' Katharine protested.

'And my two brothers who were killed in the last war were both at school with Robert's elder brother Alasdair. In fact, Clifford and he were especially friendly. Alasdair often spent holidays at Abbott's Priory when I was a young girl.'

'And?' Katharine prompted, sensing that there was more to the story than her aunt had so far revealed.

'He came to my coming-out ball in 1909,' Lavinia went on, her head still buried in the drawer. 'Everyone expected us to marry.'

'Why didn't you?'

Lavinia shrugged.

'Oh, a strange combination of circumstances. Just before we were to be officially engaged Alasdair's father was killed in a hunting accident and, as the eldest son, he had suddenly to take over the estate. I was staying at Ardnakil at the time. In those days, there was a very long period of mourning, at least a year, and no question of any engagement until it was over. So Great-Aunt Henrietta, who was my guardian, packed me off to St. Petersburgh to stay with my brother and his wife, your grandparents. Richard was Chargé d'Affaires at the Embassy at the time.'

'And you met Alexei?'

'Yes.'

'Please go on,' Katharine pleaded when her aunt stopped and seemed disinclined to continue the conversation.

'It was a coup de foudre,* as the French say. Alexei was unbelievably handsome and charming and it was all very glamorous. I'd never met anyone like him in my sheltered English life, and was completely bewitched.'

'So,' Katharine mused, 'had his father not been killed you would have married Alasdair and been mistress of Ardnakil, not Flora.'

'I suppose so,' Lavinia replied shortly. 'And Alasdair would have been alive today.'

She straightened up.

*Love at first sight.

'When the Revolution broke out he went off to Russia with a special task force to try to rescue me and bring me back. But we had escaped by another route into Persia.'

'And he was killed?'

'Yes. They nearly all were. Two hundred men went and only twenty came back.'

'What a story,' Katharine breathed. 'He must have loved you very much.'

But Lavinia made no reply.

'It's a wonder the Hamiltons even speak to us now, let alone invite us after what happened.'

'They're a wonderful family,' Lavinia said quietly. 'Perhaps it would have been different had Alasdair not left a letter for his Mother asking her to look after me should he not come back. Great-Aunt Henrietta had died during the Spanish flu epidemic and he knew that I had no family in England.'

'And she did?'

Lavinia nodded.

'Isobel was a wonderful woman. She welcomed me to Ardnakil and nurtured me until I was strong enough to come back to Greystones and remake my life. We remained friends until she died in thirty–one.'

Lavinia sat back on her heels and pushed a wisp of hair away from her face.

'She must have been a wonderful person,' Katharine breathed.

Lavinia nodded. And a silence fell between them.

'Do you have any regrets?' Katharine asked after a few moments.

'Regret, my dear Katharine,' her aunt answered softly after a slight pause, 'is perhaps the most futile of all human emotions.'

The little gold clock on the mantelpiece tinkled and struck one.

And, suddenly, inexplicably, Lavinia's manner changed. It was as if that chime had brought her back to the real world after the journey into nostalgia of the past hour. Or perhaps her natural reserve had taken control and she realised that she had revealed too much of herself. Had stirred up memories best left buried. She shut the drawer firmly and rose swiftly to her feet.

'And now, young lady,' she said briskly, glancing at the clock which was preparing to strike the quarter hour, 'if you don't want to risk incurring Elsie's wrath by being late for lunch you'd better stop asking questions and hurry down to the dining-room. Mr. Tutt dug up half the lawn last spring to plant cabbages and Brussels sprouts, so we might as well eat them.'

She smiled mischievously as Katharine swung her shapely legs over the side of the bed.

'He said he was digging for Britain!'

* * *

'Aunt Lavinia,' Katharine announced after lunch, placing her empty coffee cup back on the silver tray, 'I've decided to go through those trunks in the attic.'

They were sitting cosily in front of the drawing-room fire.

Lavinia glanced up from sifting through the pile of letters which had accumulated while she'd been in Scotland. Katharine noticed that her aunt looked desperately tired. There were dark shadows under her eyes and the lines round her mouth were more deeply etched, giving her aristocratic face a faded look.

'Oh darling,' Lavinia pleaded. 'Do you *have* to do it today?'

Katharine got up from the sofa and walked across to her aunt's chair.

'Yes Aunt,' she said softly, placing an arm round her shoulders, 'I do. And I can easily manage on my own. I don't expect there's anything very exciting in them. Most things are still in the country, at grandfather's. Mother didn't have the heart to go through everything after he died last year, and now that the house has been requisitioned, we'll have to wait till the war's over. You can help me sort out trunks when it comes to clearing up Abbotts Priory after the war.'

Lavinia laid her head back against the embroidered cushions of her wing chair. And she suddenly looked very old.

'What a dreadful few years this has been Katharine,' she said quietly. 'I'd almost forgotten Richard's death.'

She sighed.

'We could do with him now, couldn't we? He was always so wise.'

Katharine nodded. She had been very attached to her grandfather.

For a moment, neither of them spoke.

Then a log dropped lazily into the ashes breaking the silence which had fallen between them.

'I've just got time to open the trunks before tea,' Katharine smiled. 'How many did you say there were?'

Lavinia frowned.

'I really can't remember,' she murmured. 'Perhaps three, maybe four. But it will be dark in less than an hour.'

The morning had dawned grey and overcast, with a damp clinging mist hanging over everything. But as the day advanced a stifling yellow fog, like a thick flannel blanket, had gradually crept towards the house. Now it was barely possibly to see beyond the clumps of rhododendron bushes growing close to the drawing-room window.

Lavinia glanced out of the window at the thick menacing fog. But she also saw the determination on Katharine's face.

'At least it will keep the bombers away,' she sighed. 'Can't imagine anyone sending them up in this. Even Herr Hitler.'

She lay back in her chair and closed her eyes, fatigue finally overpowering her.

'The keys are in the bottom drawer of my desk. The ring has your grandfather's initials on it,' she said softly. But her speech was already slow and slurred.

Katharine tiptoed lightly across the room, a strange excitement masking her fatigue. Her heart was beating loud staccato notes, like the throb of the tom-tom coming ever nearer, slowly at first then with a rising crescendo until she thought her eardrums would burst.

Opening the door into the kitchen passage she crept along its narrow length. The smell of cabbage and lino struck her nostrils as she felt her way to the key cupboard.

It would have been so easy to switch on a light but she knew that not only Elsie and Myrtle but also Mrs. Smithers were sitting around the large old fashioned kitchen range drinking tea and knitting acres of khaki scarves and balaclava helmets.* A light would have had them scuttling to her aid. Which was the last thing she wanted.

Slowly opening the key cupboard, she felt amongst the serried ranks until she found the one to the attic. Then, carefully closing the door, she walked swiftly back along the twilit passage, the cold heavy key clasped in her hand.

Once in the hall, she took the stairs two at a time then ran without stopping until she reached the small back staircase leading to the attic.

But when she inserted the key into the lock it remained stuck.

Katharine stamped her foot in impatience.

The light was already beginning to fade. Holding the heavy key in both hands, she twisted it frantically this way and that. Finally there was a creak and a groan, followed by a noise like the clanking of chains. And the heavy door swung open.

Mounting the last step, her fingers felt for the light switch. She blinked as the semi-gloom was suddenly crudely lit by a single naked light bulb hanging from the raftered ceiling.

And Katharine entered Aladdin's cave.

Pushing her way between dusty tailor's dummies, a silk upholstered recamier sofa with the stuffing hanging out, a large regency sideboard, two brass bedsteads, broken dining-room chairs, tables with only three legs, ornate vases and chamber pots piled up amongst old lamps, broken fuses, mountains of yellowing newspapers and magazines all stacked higgledy-piggledy amongst other discarded pieces of furniture and overflowing cardboard boxes, her eyes suddenly fell upon what she was looking for.

Standing in a corner far from the swinging light bulb, were three humpbacked leather trunks.

Katharine picked her way warily across the uneven floor and, lighting a match, knelt down beside them. As the flame leapt and quivered, she lowered the match and saw neatly painted onto the front of the trunks, her grandfather's name. R. H. Brookes-Barker.

Passing her hand lovingly across it, she trailed it downwards until her fingers were able to trace the letters.

'Richard Henry Brookes-Barker,' she breathed, her eyes glistening in the semi-darkness.

Tears splashed down onto the trunk's raised hump as she felt in her pocket for the keys and placed one in the nearest lock.

It slipped easily into place and turned smoothly. Katharine bent to lift the heavy lid. But, at that moment a loud commotion rumbled up the stairs followed by heavy feet lumbering along the passage.

Mrs Smithers and Myrtle arrived in panting convoy outside the open attic door. And instantly everything was plunged into darkness.

From outside an angry male voice shouted:

'Put out that light. Don't you know there's a war on!'

'Oh Miss Katharine,' Mrs Smithers wheezed. 'Mr Popham's ever so cross. He says he's going to report us.'

Katharine turned away from the trunks, refraining from asking who to.

She could just make out the women standing glaring at her, their outsize bodies like two overstuffed cushions tied in the middle with string, bristling with indignation.

'I'm so sorry,' she said contritely.

Although they were all three now standing in total obscurity, Mr Popham's war cry, several octaves higher and angrier than ever, hurled itself upwards in a series of mounting arpeggios.

''e won't never give us no extra sausages now,' Myrtle forecast dismally.

'No,' Mrs Smithers chimed in, her voice full of gloom and doom. 'An' 'e let us 'ave a lovely bitta streaky off the ration last week too.'

Katharine picked her way towards them.

'Don't worry,' she soothed, stepping down from the attic. 'I'll go and apologise.'

The two middle aged women looked at each other.
'Won't do no good,' Myrtle said encouragingly.
Katharine sighed, irritated and bitterly disappointed.
'I can but try,' she flung over her shoulder.
And, with the two of them clucking indignantly behind her, she slowly walked back along the passage and down the stairs, fighting to control the further untapped depths of the river inside her which was threatening to overflow once again.

* * *

Katharine looked up from the letter she was reading as Lavinia walked into the dining-room the following morning.
'You'll never guess who this is from,' she burst out, waving the thick sheets of linen writing paper in front of her aunt. 'Your other niece, Tatiana! She's inviting me to a ball for Russian New Year. It could be fun.'
Lavinia picked up the heavy silver teapot and poured herself a cup.
'Interesting, exotic, exciting yes, my dear Katharine. But fun, no. At least, it is hardly the word to use for something which almost outdoes the former Imperial Court Balls. Do accept darling. You'll have a splendid time.'
She reached for the marmalade.
'It was at a diplomatic ball for Russian New Year that I met Alexei.'
Katharine nodded her head absently, her eyes still scanning the heavily-embossed pages.
'Tatiana has given me the names of some of the people who will be there. All enskys and itzines and ovs,' she said. 'Can't pronounce any of them. One or two sound like a disease!'

'Katharine,' her aunt reproved. 'You are going to meet the cream of the old Russian aristocracy, and creamier than ever now since most of them, like the Voronovskys, lived in France until last year.'

She smiled across at her niece.

'It will be a lovely excuse for me to buy you a splendid new ball gown.'

'That might not be necessary darling,' Katharine said brightly, hastily folding her napkin and replacing it in its silver ring. 'I may find that the trunks are full of evening dresses. I think I'll go and get started on them now.'

She felt in her pocket for the keys and, leaving the dining room, ran quickly across the hall and up the stairs.

Entering the dusty attic, which she had left so abruptly the evening before, her nostrils were attacked by a multitude of smells rising from the toppling stacks of old yellowing newspapers and the forlorn looking heaped-up piles of long discarded furniture.

She idly picked up one of the newspapers and shook her head in amazement. The headlines glaring up at her announced the relief of Mafeking! Katharine wondered what other historian's treasures were hidden beneath the decaying rubble.

But quickly, her eyes sought out the particular treasure she had come to seek. The three heavy leather trunks standing in splendid isolation on the far side of the attic.

Stumbling over scattered objects in her haste to reach them, Katharine dropped to her knees before the largest. Placing her hands under the hump she lifted the lid.

It was surprisingly easy and swung up under her grasp, creaking slightly, a faint odour of cedarwood rising from its depths. Removing the empty top tray, and placing it carefully on the floor beside her, she peered inside.

Her first impression was of layers of tissue paper. But speedily removing these, her fingers closed over rich, thick velvet. Plunging into the depths of the lightly packed trunk she drew out a royal-blue satin housecoat which she had often seen her mother wear. Placing it on top of the tray she felt again. But as her arms dug deeper and deeper her disappointment mounted.

The trunk was full of clothes. Not romantic gowns belonging to another age, or even bustles and ostrich feathers. But winter coats, tweed suits, the smart little black dress which had been her mother's uniform on her rare ventures into society.

Katharine felt the scratchy green moiré silk lining at the bottom of the trunk and knew that she had emptied its contents. The one naked light bulb was behind her, her body shielding the contents of the trunk from its glare. So she leant to one side, hoping desperately that in the glimmer now released, she would find what she was seeking.

But all the light revealed was the trunk's musty depths.

And Katharine felt cheated.

Sitting back on her heels, she looked at the clothes scattered around her.

They were all useful, practical, everyday garments.

Discouraged, she gathered them up and stuffed them back into the trunk, wondering whether it was worth opening the others. If this was all they contained, there was really no hurry.

But something drove her on. And, moving over, she put the key in the second lock.

The second trunk swung open with a creak much as the first had done. Inside the tray there was a sheet of paper with something written on it in her mother's handwriting.

Katharine picked it up and hurried over to the light, her heartbeat quickening. Perhaps this was the key to the answer she had been seeking. She held the paper under the bulb. 'My fur coat is in storage at Harrods for the summer', she read. Clipped behind it was the receipt.

Her hand dropped to her side. A terrible wave of disappointment swept through her and she almost switched off the light and left the attic. Then her father's infectious sense of humour revealed itself, and she suddenly started to laugh at the absurdity of the whole situation.

How could she ever have been so naive as to imagine that the trunks held some wonderful secret just waiting to be revealed. She had stopped believing in fairy tales a long time ago.

Stuffing the receipt into her pocket she returned to the trunk and lifted out the tray. More clothes! Household linen. Beautifully embroidered sheets which had belonged to her grandmother. Enormous monogrammed damask tablecloths. Katharine grimaced.

'How exciting!' she murmured ironically.

Yet her mother's dying words kept coming back to her and she delved deeper until her hands once again felt the rough moiré silk at the bottom. And she knew that this trunk held no secrets either.

She sat back on her heels and pushed her hair away from her face with a dusty hand. The floor around her had begun to look like the old clothes counter at a jumble sale.

Rising stiffly from her cramped position she stuffed the things back in the second trunk in the same disordered fashion with which she had replaced the others. Then, slamming down the lid, walked dejectedly towards the door.

As she raised her hand to flick off the light it was almost as if it were arrested in space. And she found herself turning round.

The third trunk was standing there beside the others, just as it had been when she first arrived. But now she noticed that it was different. It was larger than the other two and flat, not hump-backed, with brass studs around the edges.

'Strange,' Katharine mused. 'I could have sworn they were all three identical.'

And, in spite of herself, she walked back into the attic and stood staring thoughtfully down at it.

Taking the keys from her pocket, she inserted one in the lock, but it remained stiffly in position.

She selected another one, but the same thing happened. She frowned slightly, intrigued. The same key had fitted the locks of the other two. What was different about this one?

Jiggling the keys around on the ring Katharine picked out a carved bronze one and fitted it into the lock. It turned smoothly.

At first sight, the trunk appeared to be filled with blankets.

And a terrible desolation swept over her: to be quickly replaced by anger. She felt duped and cheated and, slamming down the heavy lid, scrambled furiously to her feet.

Yet, as she turned to go, it was as if something were pulling her back, willing her to look further beneath the dull grey outer covering. Reluctantly, she lifted the heavy studded lid again and removed the first layer. Underneath was another grey blanket. Katharine drew in her breath in exasperation. Then, flinging the one she was holding in her hands onto the dusty floor, determined to rid herself of this feeling once and for all, she grabbed the second blanket. But it resisted and, dropping to her knees, she carefully unfolded it.

A small ormolu clock revealed itself.

The one she had remembered from her mother's bedroom at Abbotts Priory.

Placing it carefully on the floor on top of the two discarded blankets, she dug further, and other objects which they had brought to London from her grandfather's house, ornaments, small paintings, trinkets which he had collected from all over the world, slowly surfaced.

And with them mementos of their London home.

Tears came into Katharine's eyes as one by one these treasures which she had thought lost came to light. She gasped with pleasure as a domed box covered in rich red velvet, standing on four tiny gold feet surfaced. She knew that it contained her grandmother's jewels.

Scrambling amongst the blankets and the thick protective paper with which everything had been wrapped, she reached the last layer. There, lying flat on the bottom of the trunk, were the precious photograph albums which had once belonged to her grandfather. And she knew that inside them were not only a history of her grandfather's and her great grandfather's colourful diplomatic careers, but also her memories of Morocco, of Zag, of their house in the Palmeraie, outside Marrakesh. And their villa by the sea at Mehdiya. But above all, the precious reminders that they had once been a happy family.

Clasping them to her, Katharine resisted the urge to sit on the dusty floor and go through them, and bent to close the trunk. As she did so, she noticed a small gilt-edged black box lying in a corner on the bottom.

In her excitement at discovering the albums she had almost missed it.

Carefully placing the books of photographs onto the floor, she reached down and picked it up.

For such a small box it was surprisingly heavy.

Opening the lid, she took out a faded piece of paper.

It was her birth certificate.

Zag and Rowena's marriage certificate, issued by the French authorities in Casablanca, was attached to it.

She put them aside and fumbled quickly through the rest of the papers, most of which belonged to her grandfather.

At the very bottom, she came across an envelope addressed to her in her mother's handwriting.

Frowning, Katharine stared down at it.

Why should her mother have written to her?

With shaking hands, she withdrew several sheets of paper.

The letters had not been written by Rowena.

But by Zag!

At first Katharine imagined that they were old love letters from her father to her mother. But the ink was fresh, the paper unfaded.

Walking over to the bulb dangling from a rafter she started to read.

But the light was dim in the musty attic.

It was not easy to decipher the closely written pages. Frustrated, not even bothering to replace all the precious treasures which she had uncovered, Katharine crossed the littered floor and walked quickly back down the attic stairs and along the passage.

As she entered her room, a pale wintry sun was attempting to warm the damp earth after the fog of the previous day. Its yellow filtered rays were shining on a patch of carpet near the latticed bay window. Drawing an apple-green velvet bergère into the circle of sunlight, she sat down and, raising her face to its warmth, slowly removed the precious letters from her pocket.

Chapter 5

'My dearest darling,' she read. 'It is such a long time since I held you in my arms and whispered those words to you. And I do not know whether I still have the right to do so. Although you have never ceased to be it for me.'

Katharine smiled.

Her father had never used the contracted form. Which made his perfect English almost too perfect.

'I do not know whether I shall even send this letter. I have written you so many in the years since I last saw you both. All of which have been destroyed in frustration and disgust at my inability to express what I mean.

'My precious Rowena, if only I could be beside you and explain. Hold you close to me. Feel your soft body moulded with mine. Show you not by empty words on a page but by my hunger for you, my longing for your tenderness how my love is still as vibrant as when we first met.'

'Can you believe me when I say that I cut myself off from you thinking it was in your interest? I wonder now if I was not wrong.

'After you lost the baby which we both so ardently desired, I sensed a great sadness in you, a longing to return to your roots. And I knew that in your roots there was no place for me.'

Katharine's brows drew together in surprise.

She had not known that her mother had been expecting another child.

She thought back.

Rowena had been taken ill that winter before they returned to Paris. And for many weeks afterwards had been pale and depressed, lying for hours on the shaded terrace of their villa, gazing out over the tops of the palm trees at nothing in particular.

Katharine's eyes misted over.

The memories were so strong that, for a few seconds, the closely-packed words on the page before her were blurred. And she wondered whether, had the baby lived, things might have been different.

As her vision cleared, her eyes returned to Zag's letter.

'Had there been the slightest hope that there could have been a reconciliation with your father,' he had written, 'That he would have forgiven me for eloping with you, I would have taken you home. But he had made it clear that he would never accept me.

'And so, my darling Rowena, I left. It seemed at the time to be the only solution. I thought that if you could believe I had abandoned you both, you would be hurt, but you would go back to England and find happiness with Harry Fairfax.'

Katharine looked up, frowning.

Who was Harry Fairfax? Surely her mother hadn't been involved with another man!

The clouds in her brain shifted slightly and she remembered a Mrs Fairfax, a distant cousin of Rowena's, whom she had met for the first time at the funeral. And she wondered whether there was any connection. But she dismissed the thought and returned to her father's letter.

'You had been so disinterested in life, even in our love, after we lost our baby. So often in the warm dark nights I had yearned for you, reached out for you – I still do, my darling. Just to feel your beloved body so near set mine on fire. But the passion which had always flared between us at the slightest touch seemed to have been extinguished. And you turned away, cold and lifeless. I had thought that our visit to Paris might revive your spirits, but you remained listless . . . until the day Fairfax arrived to take up his position at the Embassy. I knew you two had been childhood friends so I was not surprised when, soon after his arrival, he became a frequent visitor to the house.

'Until that day at Bagatelle.

'I had spent the afternoon at Longchamp with my old friend Hubert de St Aubin and his wife. I did not press you to accompany us knowing that you did not particularly enjoy racing.

'Afterwards we were all three having an apéritif at Bagatelle when you arrived. I had not noticed Fairfax sitting at a table on the terrace. You went straight up and joined him. We were inside and Hubert and Clothilde had their backs to the terrace but I was facing it, and I saw you. You were your old animated self, the depression which had crushed you since the baby died, gone. You were both laughing and seemed to be so happy to be together.

'Fairfax ordered champagne, which I found surprising. Then he took a small box from his pocket and snapped it open. There was a flash of diamonds. You put the ring on your wedding finger to admire it. But it was too big. Fairfax put it back in his pocket and you raised your glasses to each other.

'It was as though I had been winded. I did not know what to do. I felt as if a heavy rock had crashed on my hand leaving me reeling and in agony. You got up to go and he was holding your arm. You seemed so right together I could not bear to look at you. The pain was too intense. I decided that I had no choice but to give you your freedom and, I hoped, give you back your happiness. I could not bear to share your life, my darling Rowena, believing that you longed only for another man's arms.

'We left shortly afterwards and I walked up and down the alleys in the Bois it seemed for hours, not knowing what to do, trying to come to a decision.

'When I returned to the rue de la Faisanderie, it was late and you were already dressed. We were going to the Opera with Lavinia who was in Paris for a few days on her way home from Nice. The Finch-Grants and Fairfax were in the box with us, so I was unable to say anything to you. But I determined to talk to you on the way home.

'It was a beautiful June evening. Do you remember Rowena? After the Opera we all had a late supper together at the Café de la Paix and you mentioned going to England for a short holiday. It was then that Fairfax suggested you leave the following Friday when he would be travelling and could accompany you. You smiled at him and he smiled back. I knew then that you intended to leave me. And I decided to give you your freedom.

'We took a fiacre home and you fell asleep. You looked so young and beautiful, my heart almost broke with love for you. Late that night I packed a bag and took the early morning train for Marseille, and the first boat to North Africa. I could not think what else to do. I loved you so much I could not bear to think of you being unhappy.

'I walked out of your life believing I was doing it for the best. That now you could return to your roots and marry the man who had brought the laughter back to your eyes, who seemed so right for you.

'But it has not happened my darling. What went wrong? You never asked for a divorce. Which has puzzled me because what finally convinced me to leave was so that you could be free to marry him. Does that mean that I can still hope? That perhaps you and our precious Katie still love me enough to forgive me?

'As you know my first marriage was a failure in spite of the church bells, the choirs and the splendid reception. You may remember my telling you, my dearest, that when I was younger I wanted to become a Catholic priest. But when my father heard about it, he immediately sent me to Saumur and, from there, straight into the Army. And to thwart any hopes I might still be cherishing of later following my calling he saw to it that I was safely married off to Ghislaine de Condé as soon as I was commissioned. We never loved each other, we merely did as we were told. I am sure Ghislaine was only too pleased to divorce me and find happiness elsewhere, this time I hope with a man of her choice.

'I think that is why I never wanted little Katie to call me Papa, my relationship with my own father had been so cold and distant. In actual fact, I disliked him intensely.

'If I was highly decorated during the war it was not out of bravery. But because I was so disenchanted with life that I thought running into danger would be the best way to end it, with the least trouble to anyone. Isn't it strange how fate plays tricks? So many of my fellow officers, who unlike me had so much to live for, were killed. And I was spared.

'I wondered why. Until I met you my darling.

'And that is why I insisted on leaving France, and going where I hoped you could not be trapped by the social structure I had come to loathe. And you agreed.

'Life was beautiful for us. You captivated me, Rowena, and I was your willing slave, happy only in your arms, wanting nothing other than to be with you, nothing more than our love. That love which deepened and grew more beautiful, as you did my darling, as the years went by. Until that visit to Paris in '34 when Harry Fairfax appeared. I was sure that if I stayed it would be the end of our happiness.

'I couldn't bear to go back to Morocco. So I went to Algiers and offered my services to the Pères Blancs.* They were helping the poor and the outcasts and I worked with them for a while. Until I learned that you had gone back to England, and I believed that you were happy. Now I wonder.

'I have heard that your father has died and I know what a sorrow this must be for you. But may I take care of you both once again? Will you have me back Rowena?

'Please answer me my darling. Even if the answer is no. I shall understand.

'Kiss our Katie for me.'

It was signed 'Xavier.'

Katharine let the letter fall on to her lap. Then sat for a few minutes staring at the opposite wall.

She felt totally drained.

Her father's letter had been so packed with revelations that she was finding it difficult to take it all in. And she wondered why her mother had not told her about it.

She frowned.

Perhaps Rowena had kept the news from her because she had not wanted to renew contact with the husband who had so inexplicably deserted her.

And then she remembered her mother's voice on that grim Thursday afternoon when she and Lavinia had sat helplessly beside her, watching her die.

She had called for her husband, and her voice had been full of joy. As if Rowena had seen Xavier. And he had come to fetch her.

At the remembrance a cold hand squeezed Katharine's heart. Could that mean that her father was also dead?

'Oh *no*,' she cried in anguish. 'No, God, you couldn't be so cruel.'

She stopped, startled, realising that she had invoked the name of the God she wasn't even sure she believed in.

The clutch of closely-packed sheets of writing paper had fallen to the floor and, picking them up, she saw that there was another page.

It was her father's answer.

'My darling,' she read, 'your letter arrived this morning. I hardly dared open it. I know I wrote that I would understand. But would I? No, I would have been even more desolate than I have been all this time without you.

'Thank you Rowena for explaining everything.

'Oh, what wasted years. What terrible heartache I could have spared us both had I only told you of my fears, instead of packing up and running away. If only I had known that Fairfax was unofficially betrothed to your distant cousin, Julia Chetwynd. And that he had let you into the secret and shown you the ring he intended to give her when the engagement was formally announced. *That* was why he was such a frequent visitor and why you appeared to have so much to discuss. You were the only person in Paris he could talk to about his plans and his beloved. What a stupid, hot-headed jealous idiot I have been. Can you ever forgive me?

'Thank you for your gracious, loving spirit. Thank you for being yourself, for not having changed, for still being the beautiful girl I fell in love with over twenty years ago. Thank you for still loving me.

'I am on my way, my darling. I do not know how long it will take me to get to London or even how I shall get there. But I'm coming, my precious Rowena, I'm coming to take you home. Is your hair still the colour of primroses in spring? Your eyes like deep sapphire pools? My whole being trembles at the thought of holding your beautiful body in my arms again, of kissing you. I shall never want to stop. One day soon we shall be together in our little villa in Mehdija: listening to the sea whispering beneath our window as we lie entwined in each other's arms happy and replete, satiated with love.

'Till then, my heart overflows with love for you,

'Your Xavier.'

Katharine leant back in the chair and closed her eyes.

She didn't know whether it was to prevent the tears gathering behind them from overflowing, or whether it was from sheer exhaustion. But whatever it was, for the moment her emotions could take no more.

* * *

When she finally stirred, the patch of weak sunlight had disappeared and the room was bathed in the cold grey light of a winter morning.

Picking up her father's letters once again Katharine re-read the last paragraph. 'I am on my way,' he had written.

She frowned. Then where was he? Why hadn't he appeared?

Idly turning them over she saw the date on the

first one. October 1939. The war had just started, the phoney war which had since become so real and violent. And she wondered how long it had taken for the letter to reach her mother. The second one was dated, Alexandria, 30th April 1940.

And she immediately understood.

By the time her mother's answer had reached him, the phoney war had ended and the fighting begun in earnest.

Now half France was under the German heel. Crossing it to get to England would be impossible and other routes by sea from North Africa would be blocked with military convoys heading for the battle zones.

As these thoughts crossed her mind, a feeling of utter desolation swept over her.

She had been so excited, so thrilled at the thought of being reunited with Zag that she had completely forgotten the 2,000 miles which separated them. 2,000 miles fraught with danger and endless difficulties.

And a tear stole slowly down her dusty cheeks.

Chapter 6

In the soft glow of the droplets of light falling from the glittering chandelier, Tamara's green eyes were sparkling: her high Slavic cheekbones tinged with unusual colour. Her emerald silk gown, the exact colour of her eyes, swished its train across the parquet floors as she glided between the adjoining rooms exclaiming over Katharine and Tatiana as they each prepared for the New Year's Eve Ball.

She bent over her daughter to pat a stray hair into place then stood back to admire Katharine as she put the finishing touches to her make-up.

'*What* a beautiful gown,' she breathed, the Russian inflexion in her voice always more exaggerated when she was excited, slurring voluptuously over the adjective.

Katharine dabbed her mouth with a last touch of lipstick, smiling at her hostess in the dressing-table mirror as she pressed her lips together.

'Another present from my generous aunt.'

'Ah, Lavinia,' Tamara murmured.

And there was deep affection for her brother's widow in her voice.

'She must be so pleased to have you to spoil Katharine.'

She placed her hands on Katharine's shoulders and their eyes met in the bevelled mirror.

'Then she's certainly having a great deal of pleasure at the moment,' Katharine laughed.

She stood up and the shimmering gold satin slithered over her slim hips.

'Your dress matches your eyes,' Tamara glowed.

She turned her head from side to side.

'I cannot decide,' she frowned. 'Are they brown or gold?'

'It depends on how you look at them.' Katharine smiled. '*And* on the light.'

She gave a final pat to her thick chestnut hair.

'I think tawny is the usual description.'

'Ah yes,' Tamara breathed. 'I see now. Tawny.'

She pronounced it 'Tony.'

'Beautiful!'

And once again Katharine noticed the delightfully sensual sound she gave to the word.

'Come Katharine, let us go into the drawing-room. Tatiana,' she called through the half-open door. 'You are ready?'

'Coming Mamenka,' her daughter replied as she joined them wearing a full skirted cream lace dress, dotted with tiny rosebuds.

'Otets,'* Tamara called, her tiara glinting and flashing on her smooth dark hair. 'Come see what beautiful young ladies you have to escort you.'

Katharine gasped as the Prince's tall frame appeared, silhouetted in the drawing room door.

He was wearing the full military dress regalia of the old régime. A sword hanging at his left side; his chest bristling with decorations.

'Oh, Prince . . . General,' Katharine cried not sure by which of his titles to address him. 'You're magnificent!'

His eyes lit up and he bowed.

'Why don't you just call me Deduschka like Tatiana does,' he said softly. 'It's Russian for Grandfather.'

Taking her hand, he raised it solemnly to his lips.

Katharine's eyes misted over as his trim white beard brushed lightly across her fingers.

It was the first time her hand had been the kissed. In France the *baise-main* was reserved for married women. But she had also been deeply moved by his words. They had touched a need inside her making her feel loved and wanted, part of a family again.

As Tamara ushered them into the drawing-room, the door bell rang.

'That will be your escorts,' she said her eyes shining.

Katharine looked in surprise from mother to daughter.

'Our escorts?' she echoed. 'But I thought *you* were escorting us.'

'Oh yes,' Tamara, purred. 'Papa and I.'

She laughed.

'But we are your *chaperones*. You must have handsome young men to escort you. Young men whose families come from the old Russian aristocracy.'

Katharine sat down on the sofa beside Tatiana, not knowing what to expect.

Her mind was by now so dazzled that she wondered if the unknown young men would be wearing black astrakhan hats and flowing embroidered trousers tucked into high cossack boots.

The drawing room door opened and Olga announced two unpronouncable names. Katharine wasn't sure whether she was pleased or disappointed when their escorts walked in, soberly attired in white tie and tails.

As they seated themselves, Olga returned carrying a heavy silver tray on which were glasses of vodka and, to Katharine's wide-eyed astonishment, small fragile cups of steaming consommé.

Nobody seemed to think it at all odd.

Seeing her surprise, Tatiana leant towards her.

'Mamenka and Deduschka haven't yet realised that we're not going out into the freezing wastes to be drawn to the ball on a horse sleigh in temperatures twenty degrees below zero.' She giggled behind her dainty ivory fan.

Katharine looked down at the floor, trying not to laugh.

Tamara rose to her feet and the two young men shot from their seats as if there were fire crackers under them. The Prince offered his daughter his arm and, in solemn procession they all moved towards the door.

Katharine had difficulty containing her laughter. It was exactly like a scene from a Chekov play.

* * *

'Wasn't it a *lovely* ball,' Tatiana yawned, kicking off her shoes and collapsing fully dressed onto her bed.

She looked across at Katharine who was walking towards the dividing door

'Did you enjoy it?'

Katharine turned, her hand on the knob.

'How could I not,' she breathed. 'I've never known anything like it.'

Tatiana stretched and yawned again.

'The Russians certainly knew how to enjoy themselves in the old days.'

'It seems they still do,' Katharine put in.

'Oh, according to Mamenka, nothing like it used to be. How did you like Dmitri Ivanovitch?'

She sat up and began peeling off her stockings.

'He was charming,' Katharine smiled. 'And Sergei?'

'Oh, I've known them both since I was in the cradle,'

Tatiana replied offhandedly, throwing a stocking nonchalantly across the room to just miss the chair.

Katharine stooped and picked it up.

'There was a huge White Russian colony in Nice. We met each other all the time.'

She threw the other stocking. And this time aimed correctly. Then flopped back on the bed, her hands locked behind her head, abandoning any further attempt at undressing.

'Who was that distinguished-looking Englishman who was talking so earnestly to you during supper?' Katharine enquired. Tall, dark . . .

'Oh I know who you mean,' Tatiana broke in. 'But how did you know he was English? We spoke French all the time.'

'It was obvious,' Katharine laughed.

'Perhaps,' Tatiana said reflectively. 'I had no idea who he was, but he came up and introduced himself to me. Now what was his name?'

She tapped her teeth reflectively with her forefinger.

'Oh, never mind. He gave me his card and asked me to contact him if ever I felt like working, furthering the war effort or something.'

She sat up and looked across at Katharine, her hands clasped around her knees.

'Now what do you think he meant?'

Katharine shrugged.

'I've no idea.'

'Do you think he was a recruiting officer for the ATS?' Tatiana giggled

'Hardly likely,' Katharine replied. 'I very much doubt whether they'd choose a man. And it's even more unlikely that he'd have been invited to the Ball.'

'True,' Tatiana conceded. 'But you must admit it was very strange.'

There was a light tap at the adjoining door and Tamara walked in.

'You are not in bed yet?' she exclaimed. 'I could not believe my eyes when I crept into Katharine's room and found it empty. Do you know that it is after four o'clock?'

Tatiana shrugged.

'What does it matter Mamenka, we don't have to get up in the morning.'

'But that is where you are wrong,' Tamara exclaimed. 'I have just found this message which Olga left by my bedside lamp.'

She held up a piece of paper.

'It is for Katharine,' she went on. 'Somebody telephoned her this evening . . .'

'Who?' Katharine interrupted, 'nobody knows I'm here except Aunt Lavinia.'

'It is not Lavinia,' Tamara went on. 'But a young man who is very anxious to speak to you. He says it is urgent and asked if he could telephone at nine in the morning.'

Katharine frowned.

'But what young man?' she puzzled.

Tamara squinted down at the paper in her hand.

'It is . . . Captain Paget,' she read.

She handled a scribbled message to Katharine.

'I hope Olga spelled it correctly.'

Katharine looked at the paper in bewilderment. Then recollection suddenly dawned.

'Captain *Paget*,' she breathed.

And those strange emotions which had stirred in her at Ardnakil when she believed she would see him again slowly began to trickle through her body leaving a tingling pathway in their wake.

'I will wake you when his call comes through,' Tamara assured her.

'Oh no,' Katharine began to protest, not knowing whether she wished to take the call or not. She pressed her lips tightly together, trying to suppress those throbbing emotions. But they would not go away.

'Don't worry,' Tamara soothed. 'I shall be up. My father always wakes very early and he likes me to have breakfast with him. I will take this call myself so that Olga does not get it all wrong.'

She patted Katharine's arm.

'Now, darlings, you really must try to get some sleep.'

Katharine noticed again how her deep voice slurred over the r, making it sound rich and vibrant.

'Don't keep Katharine up talking any more Tatiana,' her mother chided.

There was such love in her voice as she spoke to her daughter that a lump rose in Katharine's throat.

Tamara turned and saw her standing in the half-open doorway, watching them. Crossing the room she put her arms round Katharine brushing her lips lightly on both cheeks.

'Good night darling,' she breathed.

She stood back and held her at arm's length, looking down at her.

'Deduschka has adopted you as his second granddaughter,' she smiled. 'So please consider us as your family, as we still consider dear Lavinia part of our family. And this your home whenever you need it.'

She drew Katharine to her in a warm embrace, then walked swiftly and lightly from the room.

* * *

As Katharine shuffled sleepily towards the telephone a few hours later her heart was beating a rapid drum beneath her warm dressing-gown.

Tamara held out the receiver, then pushing a chair beneath her, walked swiftly away.

'I *do* apologise for telephoning you at this hour.'

The voice coming down the line was the one she had waited and longed to hear at Ardnakil a few months before.

'But how did you get this number?' Katharine cut in, slowly returning to consciousness.

'Quite a circuitous route really. I rang Flora Hamilton. She said you were with your aunt in Kent and gave me her number.'

He laughed suddenly.

'When Miss Brookes-Barker had proved to herself that I was bona fide, she told me where I could get hold of you. But by the time I got through you had just left. I had to try to explain to some dear old dodderer who appeared not to speak any known language.'

Katharine couldn't help smiling.

'That was Olga,' she remarked. 'She's Russian.'

'I see,' he answered reflectively.

'But I really don't see why you went to all that trouble,' Katharine flashed coldly, remembering the torment she had endured waiting for his call at Ardnakil. 'Why exactly are you telephoning me?'

She almost added, two months late, but refrained.

'I'm sorry,' he admitted, sensing the coldness in her tone. 'It must seem very odd. I wanted so much to meet you whilst you were at Ardnakil. But something happened which was quite beyond my control I'm afraid, and I was recalled to London urgently on the Friday morning.'

She remembered that Friday and the following two days, the disappointment she had felt. And she did not reply.

'Katharine,' he pleaded.

She was shocked and then thrilled that he had called her by her Christian name. And all those strange emotions which had resurged the night before began racing through her body once more.

'I do want to see you. I want to very much.'

He sighed.

'But in the midst of this war, I can't always do as I would like.'

She didn't reply. She couldn't.

But again he mistook her silence for coldness.

'Please believe me,' he pleaded.

Katharine took a deep breath and pressed her lips tightly together.

'Is that why you had to telephone me urgently at nine o'clock in the morning?' she enquired.

'One of the reasons,' he answered. 'For me, the most important one. I'd like to be able to explain the rest but I can't. I've been away for two months. Only just got back and I have to leave again in an hour.'

He sighed.

'I don't know when I'll be back. But when I do we *will* meet I promise you. I want to so very much.'

There was an abrupt silence, when the line seemed to crackle with suppressed emotion. She thought they had been cut off and panicked.

'Hallo,' she called, 'hallo, hallo.'

'I'm still here,' he replied quietly. 'I was just wondering how to tell you the rest.'

He paused.

'Do you remember when we had lunch on the train you said you needed to do something but didn't know what?'

'Yes.'

'I mentioned then that your languages would be invaluable.'

He took a deep breath.

'If you really want to help your country, and I don't mean England, I mean France, the country you consider as yours . . .'

He paused again.

'Have you a pencil and paper?'

She leant forward and took a well-sharpened pencil out of a tall heavy silver jug standing at her elbow.

'Yes,' she went on, drawing a red leather jotter pad towards her. 'I'm listening.'

'Then take down this telephone number and ask to speak to Colonel Masters.'

'Have you got it?'

'Yes.'

'Would you mind repeating it. It's very important.'

She repeated the number.

'If you're serious,' he said gravely, 'ring him today, now, when you put down the receiver. He's expecting your call.'

She started to protest, but he cut her short.

'Please Katharine,' he pleaded, 'there really is no time to lose. I have to go. I'm sorry but when I get back it will be different. I promise. Goodbye for now . . . and God bless you.'

Without thinking, she repeated his last three words. Then there was a click and the line went dead.

Her mind in a daze, Katharine looked down at the pad and, without knowing why she was doing it, picked up the receiver and dialled the number he had given her.

'Masters,' a deep male voice answered.

And she did not know what to say.

'It's . . . it's Katharine de Montval,' she stuttered at last.

'Miss de Montval, how good of you to telephone,' he

said smoothly. 'Captain Paget has spoken to me about you. Perhaps we could meet?'

But she remained tongue-tied.

'Would lunch to-day be possible?'

Still bewildered, and understanding nothing, Katharine heard herself agreeing.

'I suggest a quarter to one at the United Hunts Club if that would be convenient for you?. The address is 17 Upper Grosvenor Street. I look forward to meeting you then.'

As Katharine replaced the receiver, Tamara walked quietly out of the dining room.

'How are you feeling darling after your short night?' she purred. 'Would you like to go back to bed and try to sleep or shall Olga bring you your breakfast now?'

Katharine looked at her and everything seemed unreal.

She felt as if she had been bumped back and forth between several spinning planets and then left standing on her head looking at the world from upside down.

'I'd like to have breakfast now if I may Mrs Wellesley.'

Tamara laid a hand on her arm

'*Not* Mrs Wellesley,' she chided. 'Please call me Tamara.'

She smiled sweetly at her and Katharine thought how beautiful she looked, standing there in a crimson velvet housecoat with her shining dark hair hanging loosely down her back.

'Oh, really,' Katharine stammered '. . . I couldn't.'

'Then call me *Aunt* Tamara,' she smiled. 'You are my family.'

Katharine smiled back. And, once again that warm, secure feeling pulsated through her.

'I will tell Olga to bring you your breakfast and then you can perhaps sleep a little?'

'Oh no,' Katharine babbled, 'I forgot. That telephone call. I've been invited to lunch.'

'But how lovely,' Tamara cried. 'By the mysterious Captain Paget? How romantic.'

Katharine said nothing.

There didn't seem to be any point in trying to explain something she didn't understand herself. And, after all, Tamara had got it partly right.

It was not Captain Paget who had invited her. But it was certainly mysterious.

* * *

The porter ushered Katharine into the small dark lounge of the Club some three hours later.

It was empty save for a tall man in uniform standing looking down into the fire, his elbow on the high mantlepiece, one foot resting on the brass fender.

The porter coughed discreetly.

'Miss de Montval, sir,' he announced.

The man removed his foot from the fender and turned round. Katharine stood, transfixed, her eyes wide with disbelief.

The officer facing her, wearing on his uniform the same Crosse & Blackwell Brigade markings as Ashley Paget, was none other than the mysterious Englishman who had talked so earnestly to Tatiana during supper the evening before.

Part Two

1942

Chapter 7

Lawrence Masters shuffled the papers on his desk together and, looking up, smiled across at the young woman sitting facing him. She was wearing FANY uniform.

'I must say you've surprised me,' he remarked.

Katharine raised her dark eyebrows enquiringly.

'In what way?'

'Oh, in a most agreeable way. When we first met, how long ago was it?'

'Over a year ago,' Katharine commented.

'That's right.'

He grinned down at her.

'Just after the Russian New Year.'

'Where you cleverly caught two fish,' she teased.

Tatiana was now wearing the same khaki uniform, with the distinctive maroon buttons and voluminous beret, as Katharine.

'How right you are,' he replied smoothly, affecting not to notice the unaccustomed familiarity between a Lieutenant Colonel and a very junior FANY.

She leant forward, a puzzled frown puckering her brow.

'But why have I surprised you?'

He came round towards her and perching nonchalantly on the side of his desk, opened a leather cigarette box and offered her one.

Katharine shook her head.

'My goodness,' he remarked, 'even after all these stressful months you still manage to resist. I congratulate you.'

He took a cigarette and raised an eyebrow at her.

'May I?'

'Please do,' Katharine nodded. 'And there's no need to congratulate me. I can't bear the taste.'

Lawrence Masters snapped his lighter shut and inhaled deeply.

'But you still haven't told me why I surprised you,' Katharine pursued.

Twin jets of smoke belched from his nostrils as he laid the glowing cigarette in an ashtray on his desk.

'Paget had been very enthusiastic about you. But when we first met I thought he'd made a big mistake. I never dreamt that under that frail exterior was hiding someone who could not only stand up to the rigours of our SOE* training and be suitable as an undercover agent. But also be prepared to parachute into occupied France.'

He scrutinised her through half closed eyes.

'Quite an undertaking for a girl of your age and sheltered background,' he went on. 'Are you still willing to accept the risks involved . . . and keep your mouth shut?'

Katharine nodded, looking him straight in the eye.

'I presume you have kept your mouth shut? Your aunt believes that you have been on different FANY courses, but has no idea what they involved?'

'She knows nothing,' Katharine said tightly.

'Good,' he nodded. 'Paget was right. You're tougher than you look.'

Katharine's gaze dropped to the floor. Was *that* what Ashley thought of her? Someone tough! Could that be the impression she had given him? She had imagined that the tingling excitement which had swept through her whole body when she had heard his voice had been mutual.

She pressed her lips together and a feeling of disappointment swept over her.

Lawrence Masters' eagle eyes observed her change of mood. But he said nothing.

He merely noted it in that compartment of his mind where he had an extraordinary capacity to observe and store endless seemingly useless snippets of information. Information which could not only one day prove interesting but, more importantly, decide the success or failure of a mission. And even the life or death of those taking part.

'And I was wrong,' he concluded 'You still look frail, but you've toughened up quite a bit. And . . .'

He picked up the file on his desk and flicked through the pages.

'Your instructors don't agree with my first impressions at all. They've nothing but praise for you.'

Katharine raised her eyes as a flush of pleasure stained her ivory cheeks to that entrancing magnolia.

'So you see,' he smiled, stubbing out his dwindling cigarette. 'First impressions can be very wrong.'

'And Tatiana?' she enquired.

'Ah,' he said, his expression changing as he slipped off the edge of the desk and walked back behind it. 'Tatiana will work here in Baker Street, or at one of the Groups. There is no question of her being infiltrated into France.'

Katharine opened her mouth to protest, but his look, which had hardened, silenced her.

'I'm sorry Katharine, but as you know, we owe nobody an explanation as to why we accept one and not another. Tatiana has done very well and can continue to do very good work here in London.'

A smile broke across his lean, aquiline features.

'There's no disgrace in not getting past the final hurdle,' he chided. 'Many very worthy people don't even get chosen for the first.'

He paused and idly selected another cigarette.

'And you're not home and dry yet.'

Katharine glanced across at him, the reflection in her tawny eyes shining golden in the shifting winter sunlight seeping in through the office's dirty window.

'You've still got to get through Group R.*'

He bent his head towards the flame.

'Obviously, if you have got this far the chances are that you will not be turned down. But you could be refused.'

He looked up and smiled.

'Somehow, I think it very unlikely.'

Katharine returned his smile.

Opening her file he suddenly became business-like.

'You leave for Group R this afternoon?'

She nodded.

'What's it like there?' she asked. 'Not more crawling about under barbed wire in the pouring rain at three o'clock in the morning. Or having people bursting into your room in the middle of the night pretending to be the Gestapo?'

He laughed in spite of himself.

'No, not at all. Group R is quite different. Very much more civilised.'

'But what else must I learn before I can be dropped and start working in earnest?'

'Well, for one thing, how to pick a lock. Once you're in the field* you're not going to have a front-door key to everywhere you need to go.'

'I realise that,' she said testily.

'We've got a splendid fellow down there. Was in the field himself until very recently. Now blown* unfortunately. Name of Mann, Charlie Mann. Tremendous sense of humour. You'll like him. He goes around carrying a door with every conceivable type of lock on it and by the time he's finished with you you'll be able to pick any one of them in a matter of seconds.'

Katharine's eyes widened.

'Then you'll have outings round and about to the outlying towns, all very charming places, where you'll be taught how to detect someone who's following you and how to throw them off. How to spot contacts and pass messages to them without anyone who might be watching realising what's going on. Once you've been dropped everyone you meet will be a potential enemy.'

Katharine nodded.

'By the way, can you speak without moving your lips? It's quite an art.'

Katharine stared at him blankly.

'You'll have mastered it, together with countless other little tricks, by the time they've finished with you.'

He leant back in his chair and smiled at her.

'You'll enjoy Group R. Most relaxing after what you've been through.'

He glanced down at her file again.

'So,' he reflected, his brow rutted in concentration. 'All that's now left to be done is prepare your cover story, find you a code name, get you false papers and drill you about where you're going to be dropped. They'll do that very thoroughly at Group R. And we'll give you a final grilling here before you're actually dropped.'

He looked up at her, a mischievous grin on his handsome face.

'Do you enjoy parachuting?'

Katharine grimaced.

'Can anyone in their right mind *enjoy* being heaved out into space?'

'Good answer,' he flashed back. 'Had you made some poetic statement about the beauty of floating between earth and sky watching the buttercups rise to meet you, I'd have failed you on the spot . . . No matter what your instructors said.'

He stubbed out his half-smoked cigarette and looked intently at her.

'How well do you know Paris?' he asked.

Katharine shrugged and he suppressed a smile. It was such a typically gallic gesture.

'My grandmother lives near the Etoile, well, nearer the Porte Dauphine really. In the rue de la Faisanderie. Or she did. I've no idea what has happened to her since the Germans invaded.'

'And the rest of your family on your father's side?'

'They mostly live in the Aude. My great-grandmother has an estate down there, not far from Narbonne.'

'And you know that area well?'

Katharine spread her hands, gazing down at her small slender fingers as the memories came flooding back.

Montval. Its old houses clustered round the ferruginous water spring which bubbled in the middle of the cobbled square. That sleepy, picturesque village. which seemed only to waken to the sonorous clanging of the Angelus echoing from the mediaeval church with the creaking door, its dim interior heavy with the smell of incense.

And Casterat, her father's family home, standing

beside it. Its towering wrought-iron gates opening onto a long alley of plane trees leading to the wide stone archway through which, in former days, carriages jolted into the inner courtyard.

There, sheltered by the east and west wings of the rambling stone house, a fountain splashed and tinkled throughout the sultry summer days. The shaded park, the lawn perpetually watered to keep it from drying in the intense heat. The lake where Zag had taken her boating. And the acres and acres of vineyards stretching, as far as the eye could see, down to the Canal de la Robine.

She sighed softly and Lawrence Masters did not interrupt her dreaming.

She was remembering her mother, swinging lazily in a hammock in the shade of early evening. Or sitting sewing in the cool shuttered music room on hot summer afternoons, listening to Zag's Uncle Armand playing Beethoven sonatas on the black Bechstein grand.

Her great-grandmother, presiding every morning over the immense table in the summer dining-room, her younger grandchildren and great-grandchildren around her. Katharine smiled as she remembered the unwritten rule that parents never appeared at breakfast. Eight o'clock each morning was the one moment of the day when her great-grandmother had exclusive rights over her numerous young progeny.

What a long way away those happy, carefree holidays now seemed.

And she wondered whether she would ever again see Casterat, that house full of uncles and aunts and cousins and laughter and memories.

'Katharine,' Lawrence Masters said gently.

She came to with a start, realising that she hadn't answered his question.

'I'm sorry,' she said. 'What was it you asked me?'
'Where were you?' he smiled.
'At Casterat,' she mused. 'Back in those sunny days before the war when life seemed so simple.'
'They will return,' he affirmed.
And there was an unusual gentleness in his voice.
She flashed him a surprised look.
'Do you *really* think so?' she pleaded.
'I know so,' he replied.
One of his rare smiles crossed his lean features, changing his whole expression.
'But not unless we do something about it,' he went on briskly.
And the smile disappeared.
'Dreaming, I'm afraid, will *not* win the war.'
He looked up sharply, as if afraid that the smile had betrayed him.
'I asked you how well you knew that area around Narbonne.'
'Oh very well,' she enthused her face lighting up. 'Much better than I know Paris. We always went to the rue de la Faisanderie when we arrived from Morocco, but we spent very little time there.'
'I see,' he said reflectively.
'And your family?'
Her brow creased in a puzzled frown.
'What do you mean?'
'I mean,' he said abruptly. 'Can they be trusted?'
For a moment Katharine was speechless.
'How can you say such a thing,' she burst out at last, her eyes dark with anger. 'My uncles were all in the 1914 war, most of them decorated. And I'm sure my cousins aren't just sitting around waiting for the rest of France to be occupied by the Germans!'
Her voice faltered and for one awful moment he

thought she was going to burst into tears. But she shot him a venemous look and pulled herself together.

'You don't know my great-grandmother,' she said through clenched teeth. 'This is the third time in her life that France has been invaded by the Germans.'

Katharine's chest was heaving and her breath came in short sharp gasps, as she began gesticulating with her hands.

'She lost two grandsons and a son-in-law in the last war. Not to mention countless other members of her close family. And heaven knows what damage they'll do this time. How *can* you suggest that they can't be trusted.'

Lawrence Masters put up his hand to silence her.

He realised that Katharine still had a lot to learn not only about self-discipline but about provocation. Still, he admired her pluck and her loyalty to her family. Group R would be the final test and show him whether the other instructors had been right to recommend her for work in the field.'*

And he realised that his words to her about the last dice not yet having been thrown had more than a grain of truth in them.

'All right Katharine,' he said firmly. 'We've established your family's patriotism and loyalty.'

He raised his eyebrows enquiringly.

'But what about the servants, the workers in the vineyards?'

'But they've been there for *years*,' Katharine burst out. 'They all know me.'

'That,' he cut in tartly, 'is the problem. We can hope that your own family would not betray you but . . .'

He looked up at her.

'Servants and workers on the estate are another matter. Especially if they are hungry.'

He leant across the desk towards her.

'It's only a matter of time before the whole of France is occupied. People living in occupied countries are going to be very hungry before this war is over, even starving. And under great pressure if one of their own family members is threatened. What will happen then?'

His dark eyes seemed to look straight through her.

'We can vouch for everything, organise everything . . . except, sadly, human nature.'

His eyes narrowed.

'*No one* can be trusted when pushed to the limits of endurance.'

Katharine's hands lay clenched together in her lap, knotted into a tight little fist.

But she didn't reply.

'Schemes, courses and exercises are one thing,' he said quietly. 'But reality is another.'

He fiddled with a brass paper-knife for a few seconds. Then, placing it carefully on the blotter in front of him he looked across at Katharine, willing her to meet his gaze.

'You do realise don't you, just what you are getting into?'

Katharine sighed in an exaggerated fashion.

'*Of course* I do,' she expostulated. 'It's been drummed into me almost hourly ever since I started training.'

'I hope it has also been drummed into you that there is no disgrace in changing your mind, even at the last minute?'

'I have no intention of changing my mind,' she answered tightly.

'Then let us go on to the next point.'

He glanced down at the folder on his desk, more for the form than anything else. He knew without opening it every scrap of information it contained.

'You have been trained as a courier?'*

She nodded.

He lifted his finely-arched eyebrows in an expressive gesture.

'A very dangerous job. Next to the W/T operator,* with whom you will be working in very close contact, possibly the most dangerous.'

Katharine kept her eyes fixed to the floor and did not reply.

'You also know, I'm sure, that should anything go wrong you will be on your own. We shall not be able to help you?'

He banged his fist on the desk.

'Katharine please answer me!'

There was a hard authoritative edge to his voice which made Katharine look up in surprise. He was staring straight at her, his face unsmiling.

'Yes,' she said quietly. 'I know all that.'

'I hardly need to tell you that capture and interrogation by the Gestapo are not pleasant experiences. But that is what you might have to face. In which case, death could be a relief . . .'

Lawrence Masters leant back in his chair and watched her through half-closed eyes.

'A relief which they rarely grant.'

He paused ominously.

'Or, if they do, only by slow agonising means.'

'You put it so charmingly,' Katharine remarked drily.

He suddenly dropped the paper-knife which he had been balancing between two fingers and leant forward, his eyes piercing hers.

'Is the reality of what you are volunteering to do clear in your mind?' he rasped. 'Because if it's not, if it's only a vague theory taught by your instructors or some romantic notion, then we'd better rethink this whole thing. It's not only your life which will be at risk should such an eventuality arise, but the lives of countless other people as well.'

He carefully studied the flaking ceiling.

'As I said before Katharine, there's no shame in having second thoughts.'

But his tone had softened.

Katharine's head shot up and her steady gaze caught and held his. He could see the stubborn set of her chin, the determination in her unusual eyes.

'I haven't changed my mind,' she replied haughtily. 'And, no matter what happens, I never will.'

The flash in those captivating, long-lashed eyes seemed to have spilled over onto her cheeks, flooding them with angry colour.

And he was satisfied.

He had set his trap, played his little game.

And she had won.

'Good for you,' he said, getting up from his desk and reaching for his cap. 'And now, if you have no other plans before leaving for Group R, why don't you let me invite you to Richoux's? After today, it may be some time before you'll be able to sample their delicious French cakes.'

Katharine jumped to her feet as he held the door of his office open for her.

'Oh, by the way,' he remarked casually as they walked into the long dusty corridor, 'I let Ashley Paget know that you have almost completed your training.'

He glanced down at her out of the corner of his eye as she scrambled along beside him in an attempt to keep up with his long strides. Their eyes met his and he saw the question in hers.

'He asked me to give you his love.'

Katharine stopped dead.

'Where is he?' she faltered.

'Oh,' Masters replied vaguely, putting on his cap and opening the swing door to let Katharine out into the noise and bustle of Baker Street. 'He's around.'

And, falling into step beside her, he left it at that.

Chapter 8

'Here comes Aunt Lavinia,' Tatiana yawned, stretching her arms lazily above her head as she turned towards the house. 'And she's waving something in her hand.'

Katharine stirred in her deckchair and half opened sleepy eyes.

It was a glorious mid-May afternoon. The late spring sunshine was casting lengthy shadows across the grass and dappling the overhanging branches of the trees above them with ever changing flecks of light. Katharine shaded her eyes against the golden rays until they focused on Lavinia walking towards them, elegant as ever in spite of her WVS* uniform.

'She wears it as if it's Coco Chanel's latest creation,' she mused, getting up to meet her aunt.

'Don't disturb yourself darling,' Lavinia called gaily. 'I'm on my way to a WVS meeting but I'll be back for dinner. I thought you might like to have this letter from Flora Hamilton which has just arrived by the afternoon post.'

'Aren't you having any tea?' Katharine enquired as Myrtle came up behind her aunt with a tray.

'No, darling, I can't stop or I'll be late. And, anyway, one is always plied with endless cups of a good strong brew at these affairs.'

Lavinia smiled mischievously.

'Enjoy yourselves. Ah, I see that Myrtle has surpassed herself and made one of her splendid seed cakes for you.'

And flashing one of her special smiles at the simpering Myrtle she walked swiftly away.

Katharine yawned and sat up.

'I was flat out,' she remarked lifting the heavy silver teapot.

'Haven't you been sleeping very well?' Tatiana enquired.

'No, not very. How did you know?'

'Just tried to put myself in your shoes. It must be like having a terrible sentence hanging over you.'

'It is,' Katharine mused, handing her the cup and digging a knife into the seed cake.

She shovelled thick slices onto delicate Victorian flowered plates, then lay back in her deckchair again thoughtfully licking her fingers.

'I'm *so* pleased you managed to wangle these few days off Tatiana. I think I'd have gone mad just sitting here thinking, with absolutely no one to share with because no one is allowed to know.'

'That's probably why they didn't make any fuss when I asked for a long weekend,' Tatiana confided. 'They know the strain you're under, the strain every bod* is under just before they leave. But when an op* has been cancelled at the last minute, it is rather like the postponement of an execution just as the prisoner puts his head on the block.

Katharine shuddered and momentarily paled. Then, raising her eyes, watched the midges hovering in the sun's warm rays,

'It's such a joy having you here.' she said slowly. 'You're in the racket*, you know what's going on. So I don't have to pretend I'm on stupid courses or driving

Generals round to highfaluting meetings, like FANYs are supposed to be doing.'

'Or *say* they're doing,' Tatiana put in. 'It's not quite the same thing.'

Katharine bit into a slice of cake.

'Were you terribly disappointed not to finish?' she enquired.

'Not really,' Tatiana mused. 'I realised when they told me, that it wasn't for me. They're pretty astute you know, Masters and his gang, they know what they're looking for and they can see right through people and out the other side.'

Tatiana placed her cup on the grass beside her.

'It's different for you Katharine,' she went on, linking her hands together behind her head. 'You consider yourself French. But even though I lived in France all my life I never *felt* French. And I think they realised that. As it turns out it's probably a blessing in disguise.'

Katharine put down her plate and looked across at her friend.

'What do you mean?'

'Well, think of my family situation. An only child with an elderly, doting, stateless Grandfather. And poor Mamenka who has spent her life, since she left Russia, caring for everybody. My father was ill for a very long time before he died.'

She looked up at the fluffy clouds sailing serenely past in a pastel coloured sky.

'I'm glad the final decision was out of my hands.'

Katharine gazed straight ahead of her.

'Whereas I have nobody who cares whether I live or die.'

'Oh Katharine,' Tatiana chided. 'Stop feeling sorry for yourself. It doesn't suit you. Read your letter instead.'

Katharine grinned at her. And pushing her finger

under the flap of the envelope, pulled out several sheets of thick linen paper covered in Flora's sprawling hand-writing.

'Flora's wonderful,' she smiled, her eyes rapidly skimming the pages. 'She writes just as she talks.'

Suddenly the smile froze on her face and she stared in disbelief at the lines in front of her.

'Is something the matter?' Tatiana enquired gently.

Katharine looked vacantly across at her friend.

'Listen to this,' she said hoarsely after a few seconds of silence, broken only by the distant whirr of a lawnmower.

'William Paget came to spend a few days after Easter at Tulloch House. Oh dear, as I said before, what a tragic family. His other son, Ashley, is now missing.'

Katharine's voice quivered to a standstill.

Then, pulling herself together, she continued reading.

'I believe you knew him, didn't you? Wasn't he supposed to telephone you whilst you were here? He's not missing in the way one would think, not killed in action or anything,' Flora ran on in a woolly-headed fashion. 'His father hasn't heard from him for some time and has no idea where he is. But apparently the War Office sends William an official communication about once a month stating that his son is well. That's all the news he has. Very trying for him.'

Katharine put the letter on her lap and looked across at Tatiana.

'Isn't that what we do?' she enquired, drawing her brows together in concentration. 'Send official blurbs to the family every now and then?'

'Yes,' Tatiana replied, without elaborating.

'So,' she said, pursing his lips. 'He's probably in the field.'

Tatiana shrugged but made no comment.

'He was a fluent French speaker. In fact the few words he spoke to me were flawless. So he's probably one of ours. What do you think?'

'I don't think anything,' Tatiana said, leaning forward and pouring herself another cup of tea.

Katharine looked at her strangely for a few minutes.

'Tatiana,' she said, carefully avoiding her eyes as she placed her cup on the tray. 'Could you find out for me?'

'Why do you want to know?'

Katharine shrugged.

'No special reason.'

'Then why bother?'

'Because,' Katharine insisted, her colour rising. 'I once met him . . . and I like him. I'd like to know what's happened to him.'

Tatiana leant back in her deckchair and contemplated Katharine intently.

'I think you more than *like* him,' she remarked. 'Wasn't he the man who telephoned you after the New Year's Ball?'

Katharine nodded.

'Then you'll find out for me?'

'I don't think it would be a very wise thing to do.'

'Why *not*?' Katharine flared, two crimson spots of anger staining her creamy cheeks.

'Because, my dear Katharine, you're about to go into the field yourself. And the less you know about other people working there the less information you'll be able to give away should you ever be captured. Which heaven forbid you should be.'

She looked pleadingly across at her friend.

'You know how, for security reasons, every circuit* is kept absolutely watertight. Be sensible Katharine, it wouldn't be in your interest, or his, to know.'

Katharine lay back in the deckchair and closed her

eyes to prevent the tears of anger and frustration, which had gathered behind them, from spilling over and pouring down her cheeks.

'Yes,' she said at last. 'You're right.'

She got up from her seat and started pacing up and down the lawn.

'It's just this interminable hanging around.'

She struck her palm with her clenched fist.

'Can you imagine what it's like Tatiana? I was all keyed up, ready to go. I'd had my cover story drummed into me day after day inside out, upside down, backwards until I could repeat it standing on my head. I no longer *was* Katharine de Montval. I had become Ginette Leblond.*

'Everything was set.

'I'd changed into my supposedly "made in France" clothes. They'd checked that I wasn't wearing a Marks and Spencer's vest or hadn't left a Woolworth's lipstick or a box of Swan Vestas or an empty packet of Woodbines in a pocket. Or even a *shoelace* which could have been identified as "made in England." I knew where I was to be dropped, who the reception committee would be, the pass words, what to do if I landed wide of the mark. It had all been hammered and rehammered into my head. Then at the last minute, everything was cancelled.'

'*What happened*?'

'I can't tell you,' Tatiana replied. 'But there must have been some very good reason.'

Katharine snorted exasperatedly.

'The Germans may have got wind of the drop,' Tatiana said thoughtfully. 'All I know is that the op was suddenly called off because it was too dangerous.'

She looked accusingly at Katharine, who was still boiling with rage.

'You weren't the only one going you know. There are three others who must be just as frustrated as you are.'

Katharine's taut features relaxed.

'I know,' she conceded.

She grinned down at her friend.

'And if Lawrence Masters could see me at this moment, I wouldn't be allowed to go at all.'

'That's possible,' Tatiana smiled.

'I must pull myself together,' she declared through gritted teeth, sitting down in the deckchair once again. There's nothing anyone can do now except wait for the next moon in three weeks time.

She reached across and squeezed her friend's hand.

'Bless you Tatiana,' she breathed. 'You've kept me sane . . . or almost.. And you're probably right to refuse to find out about Ashley Paget for me. What good would it do to know? At the moment I've got to concentrate on the job in hand, and leave all romantic notions till the war is over.'

Tatiana smiled across at her.

'So there *were* romantic notions?'

But Katharine only grinned in reply.

Chapter 9

Lawrence Masters passed a hand over his face in a gesture of utter exhaustion.

Apart from a quick trip to the basement at half past midnight, when the air raid siren had sounded, he had scarcely left his office for twenty-four hours. It was eight o'clock on a sunny May morning and his handsome features were drawn with fatigue.

Suddenly, the door burst open and a short sturdy man with wisps of reddish hair straggling across his balding pate strode in. He too was in his shirt sleeves, his tie awry, his uniform creased and crumpled.

'What is it Alan?' Masters enquired wearily, looking up at the intruder.

Alan Tait placed a sheaf of papers on the desk.

'Bristol caught it again last night,' he remarked as his superior drew the papers towards him.

'It's this top one which I thought would interest you.'

Tait leant forward and stabbed it with his forefinger.

'Somehow, I don't think you're going to be very pleased.'

Lawrence Masters picked up the signal,* his eyes running swiftly down the sheet. A momentary look of annoyance swept across his lean features, but otherwise his expression didn't change.

'It came from the Cairo Office?' he enquired, without looking up.

Tait nodded.

'Who's the girl mentioned?'

'Gisèle,' Masters replied laconically.

Alan Tait let out a long, low whistle.

Gisèle* was Katharine's code name.

'That's a pretty kettle of fish!'

'To put it mildly,' Masters said acidly.

'Where do we go from here?'

Masters didn't immediately reply.

His stroked his stubbly chin thoughtfully as his gaze once more travelled over the words typed on the flimsy sheet of paper in his hand.

'Gisèle not repeat not to join Barnyard.* Security risk for Louis.'

'So the old man found out,' Masters murmured to himself.

Tait shot an enquiring look in his direction. But Masters didn't elaborate.

'Isn't Louis organiser of the Wanderer circuit?'

Masters nodded absently.

'Then what the . . .'

'He's also Xavier de Montval . . . Gisèle's father.'

'Strewth!' Tait expostulated. 'I thought she was an orphan.'

'So did everyone,' Masters replied, his eyes still on the signal. 'Her mother was killed in an air-raid during the Battle of Britain. She hasn't heard of her father since '34.'

Masters sighed.

'It suited us to assume he was dead.'

He passed a hand wearily across his unshaven face again.

'Now, there's not a great deal we can do.'

'But she has the makings of a damned good agent,' Tait expostulated, his ruddy face becoming even redder with anger.

'Louis has already *proved* himself to be a damned good agent. He's also the organiser of a circuit which is working very well . . . and growing. The General's probably right.'

'But how the hell did the old man find out?' Tait exploded angrily. 'And why did the signal come through Cairo?'

'The General's in Cairo at the moment. He went off on this secret mission to see how things were being organised over there.'

Masters sighed.

'And Louis was recruited in Cairo.'

He shrugged his shoulders in a gesture of resignation.

'He was trying to get to England in 1940 when France fell so he went back to Egypt, where he'd lived for some years, and somehow contacted the Cairo set-up. He was infiltrated into France by submarine. Landed at Saint Pierre on the south west coast, an area he knows like the back of his hand since his family comes from Narbonne. Then made his way across the unoccupied zone to Montbéliard where he set up the circuit.'

'So he wasn't trained here?'

'He wasn't really trained anywhere,' Masters said drily. 'He's a former Spahi officer, highly decorated in the First World War, who refused to offer his services to his old regiment because he was in total disagreement with the Vichy government. So, not finding any action with the French Army in North Africa, he was contacted by the Cairo office when they set up shop.'

He shrugged.

'What training he had came from them.'

Masters pushed the leather cigarette box across his desk towards Tait before selecting one himself.

'I think he's a bit of a law unto himself,' he reflected, leaning back in his chair as smoke streamed from his nostrils.

'So you knew of the family connection?' Tait queried.

'Yes, I knew. But only at the very end of Gisèle's training. Just before she left for Group R as a matter of fact. I grilled her then on every side to see if she'd capitulate. But nothing would make her change her mind about dropping and, after the glowing reports I'd received from her instructors, I wasn't prepared to start stirring up trouble. Good women couriers don't exactly grow on trees.'

He shrugged.

'And if the watertight conditions we impose on the circuits in theory worked out in practice, they'd never have come across each other.'

Masters leant forward and stubbed out his cigarette.

'But there appears to be have one hell of a breakdown somewhere.'

He leant back in his chair and looked thoughtfully at the ceiling.

'Could come from Montval choosing that damned silly false name,' he mused. 'I know the Free French can't keep their own names because of possible reprisals to their families left behind.'

Masters sighed exasperatedly.

'But Jean Dupont sounds as phoney in French as John Smith would in English.'

He spread his hands on the desk in front of him and looked thoughtfully down at his fingers.

'The General may have smelt a rat. Or he may just have been poking around in the Top Secret files in the Cairo office and made the connection. The Montvals are a very well-known family and Gisèle was a protégée of the old man's. He'd apparently known her grandfather quite well.'

Tait took a last long draw at his dwindling cigarette, staring intently at the smoke as it jumped and twirled around them.

'But what about Gisèle?' he asked at last.

'The General's no doubt right. There's no question of her being dropped for the moment. If ever she discovered her father was working in the neighbouring circuit, the urge to contact him might be too great.'

Masters opened a drawer and selected a file.

'No, we'll just have to come up with another plan for Mademoiselle de Montval for the time being.'

Tait took out a handkerchief and wiped pearls of sweat from his glistening forehead.

'Rather you than me after that fiasco of last week. She was practically on the plane when the op. was cancelled.'

'Yes, it was most unfortunate but a mercy also. Barnyard is on the run at the moment. Baptiste, their W/T operator was captured. If those three had dropped*, they'd have walked straight into the Gestapo net.'

'But she'll expect to be sent to another circuit. They're crying out for couriers.'

Tait rocked his chair slowly back and forth on two legs, scrutinising Masters through half-closed eyes.

'Are you going to tell her *why* she can't go?'

'There's no question of that,' Masters said curtly. 'She's no idea her father's in the field and we'd better see to it that she doesn't find out. We may need to use her later on.'

He leant forward staring intently at Tait.

'Imagine what would have happened yesterday if Baptiste had known the names of the members in all the neighbouring circuits. The Gestapo would have had a field day. As it is, even under torture, he can't give away information he doesn't have.'

The two men were silent for a moment.

'Then you'll tell Gisèle?' Alan Tait ventured.

'I'll tell her,' Masters replied. 'And now, do you think someone could rustle up some tea?'

'I saw Caroline getting out of the lift as I was coming along the corridor,' Tait volunteered, rising heavily to his feet.

'Caroline,' Masters frowned. 'What's she doing here this morning?'

Caroline was his devoted FANY assistant. Sometimes too devoted for his liking.

'Search me. She knew you were under pressure and would be working today so I imagine she came to give you a hand.'

Masters nodded then rose to his feet and stretched.

'I think I'll go out and get a breath of fresh air. Maybe the Dutch Oven can give me breakfast. Do you know if it's open on a Sunday morning?'

Tait grimaced.

'I've no idea but I doubt it. London on a Sunday . . . even in wartime. Still, you can always try. And if you don't find anything open I'm sure the resourceful Caroline will manage to provide something.'

'I'm sure she will,' Masters put in drily.

He shrugged himself into his tunic and, picking up his cap, walked from the room, his mind on Katharine.

When he returned an hour later, tired and hungry after an unsuccessful search, the news had worsened.

Tait followed him into his office, carefully closing the door behind him and walked towards the desk where Masters was standing, reading the signal on his blotter.

Without raising his eyes he opened the leather box and absently placed a cigarette between his lips.

The door opened quietly and Caroline appeared carrying a tray holding two thick white steaming cups and some rough cut slices of bread and marg. She jerked her head towards the signal in Masters' hand and raised her eyebrows enquiringly at Tait as she placed the tray on Masters' desk.

He pursed his lips and slowly nodded his head.

'I've made coffee,' she mouthed. 'Thought it would have more pep in it than tea.'

Tait smiled his approval. And she slipped from the room.

Masters put the paper back on his desk and, walking to the window, stood looking down at the street below.

It was usually noisy and full of people. But this morning it was bathed in an eerie Sabbath calm, deserted except for the odd churchgoer strolling by, prayer book in hand.

He drew deeply on his cigarette, gazing at nothing in particular.

Tait coughed discreetly.

But Masters didn't turn round.

He stirred uneasily in his chair.

Alan was used to his boss's taciturn moods, his paucity of emotion. Masters wasn't a man given to over-sensationalism. And although Tait knew that the news he had just brought him would affect him, he hadn't realised quite how deeply.

Leaning forward he took one of the thick cups from which steam was no longer rising and began to sip the rapidly cooling brew.

'I advise you to drink the coffee before it gets cold,' he ventured, in an attempt to break the electric silence.

Masters turned round and Tait saw the terrible strain etched on his face.

The lines around his mouth now seemed to have been dug out with a sharp heavy tool, not lightly chiselled as they had been earlier in the day. The creases on his brow had deepened and his dark eyes were almost black and smouldering with anger or distress. Tait couldn't tell which.

He hurriedly rose to his feet and passed a cup across to his superior.

Masters took it and sat down heavily behind his desk.

'You've read this of course,' he enquired, holding up the flimsy piece of paper.

Tait nodded.

'It arrived just after you left.'

'I see.'

Masters passed his hand resignedly through his thick dark hair and, picking up the coarse cup, drank thirstily.

'So, Thursday night's hash-up is worse than it at first appeared?' he remarked looking at Tait over the rim.

'It seems so.'

Suddenly Masters put down the cup and thumped the table with his fist, rage now masking any other emotion in those smouldering eyes.

'What the *hell* was Paget doing in the Barnyard circuit?' he thundered. 'He's the organiser*for Carousel and supposed to stay there.'

'He went to warn them Lawrence,' Tait put in. 'As far as I can gather, his courier somehow got wind that the Gestapo had found out about the drop. I don't know how. And as she had already been tailed there was no question of her going. So Blaise went himself.'

In his anger, Masters had used Paget's real name and

not his code. He realised his slip and it calmed him down, chastened him momentarily. He admitted to himself that, under stress, anyone can make a mistake.

'And fell into the Gestapo's net,' he added icily.

'Yes, but the other members of the circuit got away. Blaise was able to warn them. Then he stayed and covered Baptiste whilst he was transmitting the message.'

'He knows perfectly well that it needs at least two people to cover for the W/T operator whilst he's transmitting,' Masters exploded. 'Or did he imagine that he has superpowers enabling him to look in every direction at once?'

Masters rose abruptly to his feet, knocking over the cup as he did so. A sticky brown drizzle spread slowly across his blotter.

'He'd no business taking matters into his own hands,' he thundered again. 'I'll have him court-martialled if ever he gets back.'

'If he hadn't done it Lawrence, the four agents due to drop, one of whom was Gisèle, would have been caught immediately . . . as well as most of the Barnyard circuit. As it is, they're still here and over there only Baptiste has been caught.'

'And what about Carousel?' Masters eyed him coldly. 'What's going to happen to them? They've got no organiser now.'

Tait looked at his feet, squirming in his chair.

He had never before seen his superior so angry, although he had been the butt for his sarcasm many times.

Masters had a quick brain and a lightning impatience to go with it. And he didn't suffer fools gladly. Or anyone, for that matter, whose intelligence wasn't as sharp as his own. But this steely cold anger was something Tait had not experienced before. And he didn't know how to deal with it. He especially didn't know how to inform him of later developments.

'Shall I ask Caroline to bring in some fresh coffee?' he enquired, playing for time.

Masters shook his head and angrily tore up the stained blotter.

'There has been a further development Lawrence,' he said diffidently.

Masters looked up.

'Louis, the organiser of Wanderer, has moved in and joined Carousel and Wanderer together.'

He paused and breathed deeply.

'So, for the moment, until another organiser can be sent out, the circuit is intact, working under Louis.'

He thought Masters was going to explode.

His usually suave, slightly mocking, features suddenly turned puce. Clenching his fists on the desk, his whole body shook with a seemingly uncontrollable rage.

'What the . . .' he spluttered, half rising to his feet.

Then, as suddenly as his rage had boiled up it fizzled out and died. And he slumped back in his chair like a limp, lifeless rag doll.

Tait sat watching him, not daring to move.

Masters seemed to have run through every known gamut of human emotions in the past few minutes and Alan waited, holding his breath.

The heightened colour in Lawrence's face gradually faded and a dull grey corpse-like mask took its place.

As the large, ugly, black clock on the opposite wall slowly ticked away the passing minutes, and still no word or sign from Masters broke the ominous silence Tait began to feel distinctly uneasy.

Suddenly, Masters looked up and gazed past him, as if seeing through him. Then to Tait's utter surprise he threw back his head and broke into peal after peal of loud crackling laughter.

Completely disconcerted, Tait sat squirming in front of the desk watching what he thought was a total breakdown in his superior officer. He wondered how long it would be prudent to wait before calling for help.

But, as suddenly as the laughter had erupted, it ceased. Masters mouth closed in a straight hard line and he looked at Tait, anger still blazing behind those expressive dark eyes.

'These damned undisciplined Frenchmen,' he hissed. 'How the hell can we ever expect to organise any kind of valid resistance if they spend their time playing Robin Hood, ignoring even the basic rules of security? Louis may be a flaming good agent, but he's impossible. Flaunting every rule and completely oblivious of the danger he's putting not only himself into, but everyone else as well.'

He threw up his arms in a hopeless gesture

'Not only *one* circuit blown, but now *three*. And all through that idiot's lack of discipline.'

'But Lawrence,' Tait intervened.

'There's no but about it,' Masters flashed back. 'Barnyard's blown, Carousel's blown and now Wanderer. The biggest rout we've had . . . and with what loss of life?'

His lips tightened.

'MI5* are right to want to have us closed down as a bunch of incompetent amateurs. We've played right into their hands. That's exactly what this fiasco will have proved us to be.'

Caroline glided in and put a piece of paper on the desk in front of him. Seeing the expression on Masters face, she grimaced at Tait on her way out. He shrugged helplessly in reply.

Masters glanced down at the flimsy paper and once again passed a weary hand through his hair.

'Another signal?' Tait ventured.

Masters passed it across the desk to him.

It was from Wanderer's W/T operator.

'Barnyard members in hiding. Stop. Will attempt escape via Switzerland. Stop. Blaise not Baptiste in Gestapo hands. Stop. Carousel bods safe. Lysander* rescue not advisable. Terrain watched. Stop. Louis.'

Tait put the paper back on the desk, glancing up at Masters from beneath his gingery lashes as he did so.

But Lawrence's face had resumed its usual impenetrable mask. All past emotion seemed to have been wiped away, leaving only dark shadows under his eyes and the heavy lines of extreme fatigue as evidence of the immense strain he was toiling under. Tait did not know what avenue to take: just how to approach this new turn of events without provoking yet another terrifying outburst.

'In a way Lawrence, it's good news,' he murmured at last. 'Only one agent, not two, in German hands and . . . the others all safe.'

He refrained from adding, for the moment.

Masters lifted heavy-lidded eyes, as if the effort was almost too much for him.

'If you say so,' he replied wearily.

'Wanderer is still transmitting,' Tait went on, encouraged by the lack of emotion Masters had displayed. 'And Louis seems to have everything under control.'

Masters shot him a withering look. And he mentally crumpled.

Tait had been in the field himself until very recently. He knew the almost unbearable strain agents were under. And he also knew that theory learnt in a classroom or on the streets of a quiet English town, where the only real danger was being picked up by a friendly bobby for loitering, could not be compared with operating in the field.

There the constant danger, the suspicion and fear that every person, friend or foe, could be a German sympathiser, waiting for the chance to denounce one to the authorities: the omni-present threat of capture by the Gestapo lurking around every corner day and night lent an edge to life and created a tension which sometimes caused strange reactions. Reactions which simply could not be understood from the relative safety of a London office.

Masters had been a diplomat before the war.

He knew and loved France well. But he couldn't even begin to comprehend the feelings of those who had volunteered to be parachuted back: were now living in subversive conditions, with false identities, pretending to go about their everyday business, but always under the watchful eyes of the Gestapo. Yet at the same time having this secret double life which generated a perpetual tension, a perpetual fear, not only of betrayal and capture but fear of how they would react were such a thing to happen. The dread of possibly betraying those who trusted them, simply because they could bear the torture no longer.

As these thoughts went through Tait's mind and he relived his own time under the occupier's boot, he realised that the mental gap between himself and Masters was too wide.

Lawrence could never fully understand what it was really like.

Masters looked up at the clock on the wall.

The hands pointed to ten minutes to one.

He rose wearily to his feet.

The midday sun was pouring in between the strips

of thick brown paper which criss-crossed the dirty windows, pinpointing the dust on the furniture, the stained paintwork.

The whole effect was one of unutterable dreariness.

'Unless someone has any more pleasant surprises in store for me,' he said caustically, his old composed self once again, 'we may as well try to find something to eat.'

He stretched his tired limbs.

'Collect Caroline and I'll take you both out to lunch. When we come back we'll probably see things in a different light. And, who knows, there may even be good news waiting for us.'

He picked up his cap and brushed the crown thoughtfully.

'Heaven knows, after these last few days, I could do with some.'

'But then,' he went on almost as if he were talking to himself. 'I daresay those poor devils over there could too.'

He anchored his cap in position and straightened his shoulders as he fastened his Sam Browne* around his narrow waist.

'Maybe we *could* arrange for a Lysander to pick up the Barnyard agents,' he mused.

And for the first time that day he smiled.

Chapter 10

'What on earth's going on?' Tatiana said, throwing her khaki beret down onto the desk as she entered the office on the Tuesday morning. 'I thought I was early, but by the look of things my watch must have stopped.'

She glanced down at the small gold dial on her wrist.

'No, you're on time,' Caroline answered briefly. 'There's a bit of a panic on at the moment that's all.'

Tatiana raised her eyebrows.

'Don't take your jacket off,' Caroline said briskly as Tatiana began undoing the buttons. 'And you'd better retrieve your cap. I want you to take this over to the signals room immediately.'

She leant forward across her desk holding out a piece of paper on which figures had been hastily scribbled.

'But what . . .' Tatiana began as she took the paper from her hand.

'Oh, don't ask questions now,' Caroline spluttered. 'Just take the signal across. And come back immediately. We've been flat out since Sunday and it's not likely to let up.'

Tatiana opened her mouth to speak then thought better of it and, quickly adjusting her beret, walked swiftly from the room and down the stairs. As she left the building and rounded the corner towards Montague

Mansions, the sedate block of flats standing in the quiet side street behind, she noticed that there was an unusual amount of coming and going everywhere. All the doors leading to the various offices were open and, even at this early hour of the day, there seemed to be a bustle of activity coming from every room.

More intrigued than ever, she skipped down the stairs to the basement, the hum of transmitters rising to meet her at each step.

Handing the signal to the sergeant in charge, she leant against the long table which ran down the centre of the room.

'What's going on?' she enquired.

He glanced at the paper briefly, then handed it to a corporal for coding.

'Where've you been?' he smiled, removing a cigarette from behind his ear and placing it in his mouth.

'Had a few days leave,' she remarked.

'Oh, so you haven't heard the news?'

She shook her head.

He struck a match and, cupping his hands round the flame, inhaled deeply.

'Been a real 'ow's yer father,' he announced as curls of smoke streamed from his hairy nostrils.

He glanced across at the corporal sitting in front of a complicated instrument.

'That another signal?' he shouted.

The corporal removed his ear phones and nodded.

'Get it decoded pronto,' the sergeant barked.

He turned to Tatiana.

'Hang on a sec, miss, and you can take it back with you.'

Tatiana looked at him and suddenly remembered Caroline's parting shot.

'I'd better not wait,' she said, slipping from the table.

'I was told to go straight back, there seems to be a panic on over there.'

'That's putting it mildly,' the sergeant said, his cigarette dangling precariously from his lower lip. 'OK you buzz off, I'll see this gets over in double-quick time.'

When Tatiana walked back into the office, Lawrence Masters was deep in conversation with Caroline.

He frowned slightly as she entered, as if not quite sure who she was, then his brow cleared and he gave one of his slow smiles.

'Come along to my office,' he said straightening up.

Caroline looked up from her desk and pursed her lips.

She was thirty-one years of age and it was obvious to all but the person concerned that Lawrence Masters was her raison d'être. And younger FANYs presented a threat. Especially pretty ones like Tatiana.

'We're run off our feet at the moment,' she said sharply. 'And I need Tatiana.'

'I know,' Masters replied. 'I won't keep her for long.'

Caroline bent her head and began writing furiously as Masters crossed the room and opened the door for Tatiana.

'I believe you have some kind of family connection with Katharine de Montval,' Masters said, motioning Tatiana to a seat as they entered his office.

He raised his eyebrows enquiringly.

'We share an aunt,' Tatiana smiled.

'I see.'

Masters reached across his desk and, offering her a cigarette from the leather box, flicked his lighter into action as she bent her head to the flame.

'And you've just spent the weekend with her?'

Tatiana nodded.

'How did she feel about the op. being cancelled?' he enquired, perching on the edge of the desk as he lit his own cigarette.

'Well, obviously, she wasn't very happy about it,' Tatiana demurred.

'Naturally,' he said.

'She's just waiting now for the moon to be right,' Tatiana volunteered.

Lawrence Masters removed his cigarette from between his lips and stared intently at the glowing tip.

'I'm afraid,' he said quietly, 'as far as Katharine is concerned, there won't be a next moon.'

Tatiana sat straight up in her chair.

'I don't understand . . .'

'Had you been here yesterday, you would have. The circuit she was assigned to has been blown, together with two other circuits.

He laid his cigarette in an ashtray and looked intently at her.

'But there are other circuits,' Tatiana burst out. 'They're crying out for women couriers.'

Masters didn't reply.

'She'll be so disappointed,' Tatiana exclaimed. 'Shattered, in fact. She's been on edge all weekend.'

She paused and bit her lip.

'But to be told it's off for good.'

She looked up at him pleadingly.

'Is there *no* hope of Katharine being dropped at a later date . . .?'

Her voice trailed away.

'None at all,' he replied curtly. 'At least, not in the foreseeable future.'

'I don't know how she'll take it,' Tatiana ended, her voice almost a whisper.

Master turned and walked back behind his desk.

'We must just find something else to keep her occupied,' he said, sitting down heavily in his swivel chair.

He looked directly at Tatiana.

'I'm thinking of sending her to Group R. They're expanding and they need women there permanently. She could be very useful helping in exercises in the local town. In fact, doing all the things men simply can't do.'

He leant forward and stubbed out his cigarette.

'There's a small cottage at Group R, next to the main house. A housekeeper has already been installed and we need two FANYs there permanently, possibly three.'

He folded his hands on the desk and smiled across at Tatiana.

'Would you like to go as well?'

Tatiana gasped.

'I'm not trained . . .'

'We'd train you,' Masters cut in.

He gave her one of his rare smiles.

'I think you might even enjoy it,' he went on. 'More exciting than Baker Street.'

He paused. But Tatiana didn't react.

'These students on their last lap before being sent into the field need to be thoroughly tested. And that's where you FANYs would be used. As decoys. You'd be playing the enemy. The students wouldn't know you, or even suspect they were being watched when they were let loose for a few hours in a neighbouring town. There they would be expected to make contact with other prospective agents, leave and collect messages placed in telephone booths, between the pages of a newspaper left lying casually on a park bench amongst other places. Meet contacts in cinemas and cafés and get messages to them without a sign of recognition or a word passing between them. And you would be somewhere around. Watching to see that they were able to do all those things without arousing suspicion. A woman having a cup of tea in a café, sitting on a park bench, gazing into shop windows or strolling along carrying a shopping basket is much less conspicuous than a man. You'd also have to follow them, check whether they have found out they are being followed, can spot you and give you the slip. Once they're dropped they'll be constantly rubbing shoulders with the enemy and need to be on their guard twenty-four hours a day.'

Masters looked at her intently. But still she made no move.

'You'd also have to see if you could make them talk,' he said slowly.

At that, Tatiana raised her head, a panic-stricken look in her eyes as visions of Mata Hari* flashed through her mind.

'Don't worry,' he smiled. 'You'd be protected. The meetings would always be arranged with one of the instructors from Group R around. Although it might seem like it to the students, you wouldn't be alone.'

He leant back in his chair and played idly with the paper-knife.

'But it would be up to you to try to make them talk. To get them to tell you what they were really doing. A man who cannot resist boasting to a pretty face, no matter how well he has come through all the other parts of his training, would be a danger in the field, not only to himself, but to others.'

There was suddenly a deep silence between them.

'Well?' Masters enquired after a few seconds, broken only by the rhythmic tick of the clock.

Tatiana did not know what to say.

She was thinking of her mother, her grandfather, who doted on her. But she also knew that she had no choice. In spite of the way Masters had framed the question she realised that it was not a suggestion he was making. But an order he was giving.

She sighed.

It made it easier in a way. There were worse places than Group R to which she could have been sent. And for Katharine it would help to have her there.

Tatiana kept her eyes on the tip of her shiny laced-up shoes as these conflicting thoughts raced through her mind.

'I could, of course, oblige you to go,' he went on smoothly.

Tatiana didn't reply.

'But I'd much rather you went voluntarily.'

He paused, his brilliant dark eyes searching her face. But still Tatiana made no sign.

'That's settled then,' he said briskly. 'I'm sure Katharine will appreciate having you with her. You would, of course, have a weekend every month when you could come up to London if you wished. There's a young South African FANY who has just joined us whom I'm also considering sending. I'm sure you'll all get on splendidly.'

One of his rare smiles broke slowly across his taut features.

'And Miss Ricks, the housekeeper, is a splendid cook.'

At last Tatiana raised her eyes and met his gaze.

'Has all this something to do with the general panic there seems to be at the moment?'

Masters nodded.

'When is Katharine due back?'

'Tomorrow afternoon,' Tatiana answered.

'Then perhaps we should make arrangements for you both to go down to Group R on Thursday. We're going to have an influx of agents within the next few months and the sooner things get moving the better.'

He reached for a file.

'As you so aptly said, there's a general panic on at the moment and Caroline made it plain that she needed you. You'd better nip back pretty smartly.'

Tatiana gathered that the interview was over.

'Will you tell Katharine?' she murmured, rising to her feet.

'Yes, of course,' he answered, unscrewing the cap of his fountain pen. 'Ask Caroline to come and see me will you?'

Tatiana walked unsteadily across the room, feeling slightly punch drunk, and almost collided in the doorway with Alan Tait. He burst into the room waving a piece of paper.

'Louis has managed to get all the Barnyard bods. down to the plateau at Marchaux, near Besançon,' he shouted excitedly, throwing the signal onto Masters' desk. 'He intended smuggling them into Switzerland, but had to abandon the idea. The Germans are patrolling every inch of the border.'

Tait leant over and stabbed the signal with his forefinger.

'He wants to know if we can arrange for a Lysander pickup, to-night if possible. Apparently the courier is wounded. He's sent the message for the BBC.'

'Yes, yes I can see,' Masters cut in testily, his eyes on the paper in front of him.

He leant back in his chair, and picked up the telephone.

'Can you get on to Jennings at the Air Ministry, Alan?'

he said, putting his hand over the mouthpiece. 'I think he's our only hope for getting a Lysander at such short notice. And even so . . .'

He broke off and spoke into the receiver, giving rapid instructions.

'Will do,' Tait answered, jumping to his feet.

Masters put down the phone, then started dialling again.

'And let me know as soon as you hear anything,' he said as the familiar dring dring came down the line.

'Nothing about Blaise on the signal?' Tait enquired turning in the doorway on his way out.

Masters shook his head without looking up.

Tait sighed as he left the room. Paget and he had been friends in training. But he was becoming used to living with bad news. Though it didn't make it any easier to bear.

'Colonel Masters is sending me down to Group R,' Tatiana announced as she walked back into the office.

Caroline's head shot up from amongst a pile of papers.

'When?' she barked.

'On Thursday.'

Caroline flung herself out of her chair and glared at Tatiana, as if it were all her fault.

'Oh no he's not,' she choked. 'Not with this crisis on our hands.'

She threw up her arms in a gesture of defiance and despair.

'I'm already working seven days a week,' she exploded. 'How the blazes does he think I'm going to manage if he filches my staff?'

She had omitted to mention that if she was working at such a pace it was by choice. No one had asked her to spend her weekend catering to Lawrence Masters' supposed needs.

Tatiana suppressed a smile.

'I'm perfectly happy to stay here,' she said sweetly.

'And I'll jolly well see that you do,' Caroline thundered, reaching for the phone.

'Blast,' she said, 'occupied.'

She shrugged.

'Might have guessed it though, after that signal.'

'Did the signal mention Blaise?' Tatiana enquired, remembering her conversation with Katharine in Lavinia's garden only a few days before.

She had known then that Ashley Paget was in the field but had been unable to share the information with her friend. Now, remembering Katharine's shining eyes when his name had been mentioned, the news of his capture struck an almost personal blow.

Caroline shook her head, crashing the receiver back in place.

'I just thought,' Tatiana put in, 'since Louis seems to be able to perform miracles, he might have engineered Blaise's escape as well.'

'Not so far,' Caroline said shortly, picking up the telephone again.

'Oh *no*,' she groaned. 'Still engaged. I'll just have to go and see him.'

And she slammed out of the office.

The day was hectic.

The corridors seemed to be perpetually full of dishevelled young officers in shirtsleeves, ties askew, rushing in and out of open office doors with bits of paper in their hands.

Many of them had already spent time in the field and were blown or had been returned to base for some other reason.

But they all knew the dangers facing those in hiding from the Gestapo or trying to escape: the fear and tension they were living under. And there was an air of quiet desperation about them, their minds constantly on their comrades on the other side of the Channel.

Lawrence Masters didn't leave his office all day. And was hardly off the telephone. He looked up only to issue curt staccato orders or bend his head to the lighter flame as he kept himself going on cigarettes and the black coffee which the faithful Caroline regularly placed in front of him.

'There's no hope of a Lysander for tonight,' Tait said grimly, walking into Masters' office at about four o'clock. 'But it might just be possible to-morrow.'

Masters clicked his tongue in annoyance.

'Sorry Lawrence,' Tait said wearily. 'I've tried every avenue. The poor devils are doing their best. But there's this big campaign over Cologne which has just started They're planning to bomb every important German city like blazes in the next few weeks . . .'

'I'm not asking for a *bomber*,' Masters bellowed.

'I know,' Tait soothed. 'Did Louis give a message to send in advance?'

Masters shovelled the pile of papers round on his usually tidy desk and finally picked one out.

He held it out to Tait.

'Are you *sure* about tomorrow?'

'As sure as one can be about anything in this adjectival war,' Tait grimaced.

'Right, well, get on to Bush House* and make absolutely sure they broadcast this Message Personnel* on every one of their evening news bulletins . . .'

'Unless,' he sighed. 'Louis signals us that there's been a change. With the Germans hunting them down, I doubt whether even *he* can keep them hidden for long.'

Tait glanced down at the paper Masters had just handed him.

'The cherries in Louis garden are not yet ripe,' he read. 'OK I'll see this goes out on every French Service news bulletin this evening.'

He stretched and stifled a yawn.

'By the way,' he remarked, helping himself to a cigarette from the leather box on Masters' desk. 'Jacques' wife had twin boys during the night. How the devil do we phrase that one?'

Masters frowned.

'How were we supposed to?'

'Well, we were supposed to say "Jacques ressemble à son père" if it was a boy, or "Jacqueline ressemble à sa mère" if it was a girl.'

'So, where's the problem?'

'As I said, dear boy, twins.'

Tait tapped a pencil against his teeth, frowning in concentration.

'I suppose we'd better say "Les deux Jacques ressemblent à leur père." He wasn't expecting a double ration, only hope he'll understand.'

Tait grimaced.

'As they already have two boys . . . he could have arranged it better.'

Masters looked up briefly.

'Oh, just do as you think fit,' he said disinterestedly, scribbling something on the pad in front of him. 'But make doubly sure that that message for Louis goes out whatever else has to be sacrificed.'

He tore the sheet loose and handed it to Tait.

'Here's the message for tomorrow evening which must also be broadcast on every French bulletin.'

He passed his hand wearily across his face.

'Always supposing that we get the Lysander.'

'We will,' Tait soothed as he took the paper.

'God,' he said, rising heavily to his feet. 'I'm tired. Getting too old for all these crises.'

Masters ignored the remark and Tait hobbled stiffly out of the room.

Chapter 11

Tatiana walked down the crowded platform at Waterloo Station beside a rebellious Katharine.

'Here we are,' she said brightly, as the porter opened a carriage door and shuffled along the corridor till he found an almost empty compartment. 'Good thing we came early, you've got a window seat and can enjoy the scenery.'

Katharine handed over some loose change to the porter, and tossing her gloves onto the seat, sauntered moodily back into the corridor.

'Come on Katharine,' Tatiana chided, as her friend stood gazing down at the criss-cross of tracks and the motley assortment of travellers standing in groups or sitting on their suitcases on the opposite platform. 'You'll probably enjoy Group R once you get there.'

'You seem to have forgotten that I've already *been* there,' Katharine replied wearily.

'Look, I know you're terribly disappointed,' Tatiana floundered. 'But it's no one's fault your drop was cancelled at the last minute.'

She now knew that the chances of Katharine being dropped in the near future were slim. And she was at a loss to know how to cheer her up without raising false hopes.

But she need not have worried.

Katharine's good nature suddenly surfaced.

'I'm sorry,' she smiled, threading her arm affectionately through her friend's. 'You're quite right. I'll probably enjoy it once I get there. And you'll be coming soon, won't you?'

Tatiana smiled back at her, then looked away.

There had been so many orders and counter orders in the past few days that her head was swimming. Officially, from today, like Katharine she was supposed to be part of the FANY set-up at Group R. But Caroline had won and Tatiana's transfer was now in abeyance until the present crisis was over. With things as they stood at the moment, anything could happen.

She glanced quickly down at her watch to prevent any further questioning on Katharine's part.

'Gracious,' she exclaimed, 'I *must* go. Just slipped out during the lunch hour and it's already almost two. If Caroline's back I'll really be in for it.'

She hurriedly kissed Katharine on the cheek.

'The train leaves in ten minutes,' she said encouragingly.

'I know,' Katharine sighed.

Then she suddenly grinned.

'Give my love to Larry boy.'

Tatiana grinned back and squeezed her arm.

'I'll ask Caroline to do that for you. She'll leap at the chance.'

And, on that lighter tone, she jumped down onto the platform and was soon swallowed up by last-minute passengers hurrying in the opposite direction.

Half an hour later Tatiana gingerly pushed open the door of her office, peered round it, then sighed with relief when she saw Caroline's empty chair. Only Nadine was there, typing noisily at her little desk in the corner.

'Hasn't she got back?' Tatiana enquired.

Nadine shook her head without turning round.

'Nope,' she answered above the din of her machine. 'After the hysteria of the last few days it's all quiet on the Western Front.'

She grinned at Tatiana.

'Absolute bliss, they all seem to have scooted off to Orchard Court.'*

'All of them?' Tatiana queried.

'Well, all the bigwigs. Luscious Larry and Co. Caroline must be in seventh heaven having the Loverboy almost to herself for the day.'

Nadine laughed and leant back in her chair to retrieve a packet of cigarettes lying on Caroline's table. She selected one and tossed the packet to Tatiana.

'Whilst the cat's away . . .' she grinned. 'May as well make the most of it before another crisis occurs.'

Tatiana sat down at her desk opposite Nadine and for a few seconds they competed with each other as to who could blow the biggest smoke rings.

'No more news?' Tatiana asked.

The Lysander had finally left the previous evening to pick up the party on a plateau near Marchaux where they had been in hiding.

It had been a dangerous touch-and-go operation and everyone had felt the strain. Only on its arrival would they know if the rescue operation had been successful.

Masters had scarcely left his office until it was time to meet the returning Lysander in the early hours of the morning. And the faithful Caroline had hovered in the background all night waiting to jump to his call.

After the recent frantic activity, the sudden lull and unusual quiet were unnerving. And Tatiana suddenly felt very tired.

Nadine pursed her lips and shook her head.

'Nothing from Louis if that's what you mean. After all his heroics of the past few days, I should imagine that he and his W/T operator are lying pretty low.'

She stubbed out her cigarette and swivelled round in her revolving chair.

'My, what a man he must be,' she drooled.

She winked impishly across at Tatiana.

'Wouldn't mind meeting him, would you?'

Tatiana smiled but didn't comment.

'Now, that's a *Frenchman* for you,' she exulted. 'Can't imagine why my mother went and married an Englishman when she had all of la belle France to choose from.'

'Nadine,' Tatiana chided.

'Well, would you?' Nadine teased.

'I don't know,' Tatiana demurred. 'Depends who you fall in love with I suppose.'

Nadine swung her chair round and round roaring with laughter.

'I wouldn't have any difficulty falling in love with the gorgeous Louis,' she chortled. 'Worth ten of Luscious Larry any day.'

'Oh Nadine stop it,' Tatiana said impatiently getting to her feet. 'And anyway, how do you know?'

Nadine helped herself to another of Caroline's cigarettes and, breathing out spirals of smoke into the dusty atmosphere, went off into peals of laughter once again.

'I'd better see about the Messages Personnels,' Tatiana murmured, sorting through a pile of papers on Caroline's desk. 'Did she say anything about them before she left?'

'Only the confirmation of the gang's arrival. It's on the top of the pile over there. "All the cherries in Louis garden are now very ripe." And the one for Jacques about his twins which has to go out three nights running. Let's see, Tuesday was the first time, so this will be the last.'

Nadine grinned across at Tatiana.

'Wonder what he makes of it? Hope it clicks. Otherwise it'll be an awful shock when he gets back and sees two little Jacques instead of one. I've heard they're identical.'

Tatiana looked at her watch.

'I wonder when they'll be back?' she queried. 'They may have news of Blaise.'

'You seem to be unusually interested in Blaise,' Nadine teased, hacking away at her machine again. 'That's the second time you've mentioned him since you got back.'

Tatiana shrugged.

'Aren't you?'

'I suppose so,' Nadine sighed. 'As much as one dare become interested in anybody in this benighted war.'

Tatiana looked up. A solitary tear was trickling down Nadine's cheek. She walked across to where she was literally bashing the daylights out of the old Remington.

'Nadine?' she said gently, placing a hand on her shoulder.

Nadine angrily brushed her arm across her face.

'Don't take any notice of me,' she faltered.

'I can't help it,' Tatiana soothed. 'What's wrong?'

Nadine's hands fell from the keyboard and she gazed dully at the ancient machine. Then suddenly, inexplicably, she burst into tears.

'I'm not as blasé as I seem,' she sobbed. 'Sometimes I've seen you looking at me Tatiana, when I've said something outrageous, as if you couldn't believe your ears.'

She looked up, the tears running in little winding streams down her pale face.

'Pretending I don't care is the only way I can cope.'

Tatiana pulled up a chair and sat down beside her.

'Cope with what?' she asked softly.

Nadine stared blankly in front of her for a few seconds before replying.

'Life,' she said dully. 'And death.'

She turned towards Tatiana, the tears now drying on her face causing black streaks to run in every direction.

'I joined the FANYs to get away from the war. They said they wanted women drivers to cart Colonels and above off to meetings and things.'

She shrugged expressively.

'Then when they discovered my mother was French and I was bilingual I found myself here. Or more correctly in training.'

She sniffed and fished up her khaki sleeve for a handkerchief.

'I was quite pleased at the idea of going back to France. I used to spend all my holidays there and could easily pass for French. But . . .'

She shrugged again.

'I didn't pass the test.'

'Me neither,' Tatiana soothed. 'It's no disgrace. Much better to find out one's not suitable *this* side of the Channel.'

'I suppose so,' Nadine sighed.

'Why did you want to go so badly?' Tatiana urged, sensing that there was more to Nadine's tears than this simple explanation.

'Because I wanted to do something. I wanted to get my own back on the Germans.'

Tatiana creased her brow but made no comment.

'I was engaged,' Nadine breathed, almost in a whisper 'in July '39. We were to have been married before Christmas.'

'What happened?' Tatiana urged.

'Peter volunteered for the Navy when war broke out.'

She smiled wrily.

'Wavy Navy* the regular officers called them.'

'And . . .' Tatiana prompted.

Nadine took a deep breath which ended in a shuddering sigh.

'He went down in the *Glorious* off Narvik in June '40.'

For a few minutes there was a deep silence in the stark dusty room.

Tatiana felt not only a dreadful weariness overwhelm her but a helplessness, a deep engulfing despair.

The past months had been so weighed down with pain, other people's pain, beginning with her meeting with Katharine just after her mother died, that she felt totally lost and helpless. Unable to cope in the face of so much grief.

'Nadine,' she whispered at last, finally breaking the silence. 'I'm so sorry. I didn't know.'

Nadine reached out a hand and squeezed Tatiana's.

'Nobody knows,' she said tightly. 'That's why I joined the FANYs, not the Wrens*, like most of my friends did. To try to get away from everything that reminded me of Peter.'

She smiled sadly at Tatiana.

'And he was English. So you can see what twaddle I talk can't you, in an effort to forget.'

She scrubbed her hankie across her face and then fiercely blew her nose.

'And, now, if you don't mind I'd rather not talk about it any more. I don't know about you but I've had about as much emotion as I can take in the past few days.'

She pushed her hankie back into her sleeve and

jumped up. As she smoothed down her khaki skirt, a smile creased her tear-streaked face.

'How about a cup of tea?' she chirped over-brightly. 'I'll go and tidy up before Caroline comes back or else she'll think I've been weeping for her Larry boy. You do the honours.'

Slamming open a drawer she took out a toilet bag and, ostentatiously humming a popular tune, walked purposefully down the corridor to the cloakroom.

When she returned, all traces of her tears now erased, Caroline was sitting at her desk, an ashen look on her aristocratic face.

Behind her back Tatiana motioned to Nadine to keep silent.

Placing a cup of tea on the desk in front of Caroline, Tatiana quietly handed one to Nadine then went to sit at her own desk, her hands cupped round the steaming brew.

Caroline looked up and patted the papers piled up on the desk, searching for her sadly diminished packet of cigarettes. Blindly finding it, she extracted one and placed it between her lips.

'Have the Messages Personnels been sent?' she enquired.

Tatiana got up and went over to Caroline's desk.

'There's just these two as far as I know,' she demurred.

She glanced at her watch.

'It's only a quarter past four. We've got another hour before they need to be at Bush.'*

She bit her lip and looked down at Caroline, hidden behind swirls of blue smoke.

'Do you think there'll be any more?'

'I don't know,' Caroline replied absently. 'Get hold of Major Tait, he'll be able to tell you. And if not, see that those two get over there straight away.'

She raised her eyes and Tatiana saw the strain etched on her face. Her lips were blanched and her eyes seemed to be rimmed with charcoal. And she wondered what else could have happened.

'Hang on a minute,' Caroline frowned. 'Maybe Colonel Masters has some others which need to go out to-night.'

She picked up the telephone, then slammed it back into place.

'Engaged,' she muttered. 'I'm not surprised.'

She pushed the papers away from her and rose to her feet.

'I'll go along and see.'

'Would you like me to go for you?' Nadine enquired sweetly.

Caroline shot a look in her direction as she fiercely stubbed out her half-smoked cigarette. But Nadine's face revealed nothing but demure innocence.

'No, it's all right, I'll go myself.'

As the door slammed behind her, Nadine and Tatiana burst into uncontrollable giggles.

'You really are the end,' Tatiana tittered, recovering herself at last. 'Poor Caroline, you shouldn't tease her like that.'

'She sure has got it bad,' Nadine announced, affecting an American drawl and rolling her expressive brown eyes. 'Fancy falling for Livery Larry. He's such a cold fish.'

'How do you know?' Tatiana frowned.

Nadine grinned.

'Must be, to remain immune to my charms.'

And the two of them went off into peals of laughter again. Nadine had become her old self once more.

'Pleased someone seems to be happy.'

They were brought back to earth by the entry of a young lieutenant carrying the inevitable piece of paper.

'Oh Hugh,' Nadine said. 'You're just the person we need.'

He raised his eyebrows enquiringly.

'Are those Messages Personnels for the BBC?'

'Yes.'

'Hand 'em over. I've got some others to send across to Bush. Is that the lot for this evening?'

'As far as I know.'

He perched on the edge of Tatiana's desk.

'But do tell me why I'm in such demand. I'm flattered.'

Tatiana and Nadine exchanged glances.

'And I'd also like to share the joke,' he went on. 'There doesn't seem to have been very many of them around these last few days.'

'There isn't any joke Hugh,' Nadine said contritely. 'Just a release of nervous tension I think.'

She paused and studied her finger nails intently.

'I don't suppose you were at Orchard Court to interrogate the bods who came back by Lysander last night?' she queried, looking intently at him from under her eyelashes.

'Not high enough up the social ladder,' he grinned.

'But perhaps you know what happened?' Nadine urged.

The young lieutenant took out a monogrammed cigarette case and passed it round before taking one himself.

As they all drew deeply and rather nervously on their cigarettes he heaved himself more comfortably on to the desk.

'What don't you know?'

'We don't know anything,' Nadine replied. 'Except that Caroline came back looking like a ghost.'

'She didn't tell you what's happened?'

'She hardly spoke,' Tatiana put in. 'Seemed terribly

preoccupied and upset and immediately went back to see Colonel Masters.'

'I suppose they're all trying to work out some plan of action,' he said.

'But what's happened,' Nadine pursued. 'I thought all the bods got safely back.'

'They did,' Hugh said quietly. 'Unfortunately they brought back bad news of Blaise.'

Tatiana's heart missed a beat.

'But we knew he was in Gestapo hands,' Nadine interrupted.

'It's much worse than that,' Hugh said slowly.

He drew heavily on his cigarette before crushing it viciously into the ashtray. Then, rising from the desk, he walked over to the spattered, brown-papered window and gazed down into the side street below.

'Blaise was being transferred under armed guard to Paris, to La Santé Prison. Somehow, he managed to jump off the train at a bend near where he knew, if he made it, there would be wooded cover where he could hide. He's very familiar with that part of France. Apparently, he rolled down the bank and got into cover of the trees with only minor cuts and bruises. Of course they stopped the train and there was a general hoo-hah whilst the guards went in search of him. But everything was in his favour as the train had run several miles along the track before it could be halted. Then, as luck would have it, he ran into a routine German patrol.'

Hugh shrugged his shoulders and turned back into the room to face the two girls who were hanging on his every word.

'Scruffy, no papers . . .'

He raised his eyebrows expressively.

'What hope did he have?'

'And where is he now,' Tatiana whispered.

'No one really knows. We'll just have to wait and see.'

There was a sudden silence in the room; the only sound the monotonous buzzing of a wasp trying to escape.

Tatiana got up and walked across to open the window. As the distant hum of traffic drifted up from the street below, the wasp hovered uncertainly for a few seconds then took its leave.

'The four who got back have an incredible story,' Hugh went on as Tatiana closed the window and the buzzing and the hum receded. 'Apparently Louis is an amazing man. But there's a limit to what even he can do.'

Nadine shot an amused yet triumphant glance at Tatiana.

'And for the time being he's lying very low, in hiding somewhere. He's apparently on tremendously good terms with the Germans. Almost enough to make one think he could be a double agent.'

'Oh *no*,' Tatiana burst in.

The young officer shot her a curious look.

'I don't think for one minute he is . . . and neither does the hierarchy. But he's got enough cool to freeze the Sahara, otherwise the others would never have got away.'

'How *did* they get away?' Nadine put in.

'Through Louis' bluff and know-how,' Hugh remarked, settling himself once more on the edge of Tatiana's desk.

'He realised that it was hopeless to try to get them into Switzerland as the Germans were patrolling all along the border. So he did the opposite of what the Germans expected. Took them further inland . . . to Besançon. He had a contact there, a priest whom he'd known in Algiers when he was working with the Pères Blancs. And through him Louis had the whole lot hidden in . . .'

A smile broke over Hugh's handsome face.

'. . . a convent of all places.'

Both girls began to giggle, but more from nervous tension than anything else.

'It was the priest who drove the van which took them to the landing-site. Louis was sitting in the front seat playing hail-fellow-well-met with the Germans they ran into on the way. Luckily only local patrols, not Gestapo, or they wouldn't have stood a chance. His cover story*is that of some kind of travelling salesman. So he moves around more freely than most people and gets to know everyone, including the Germans.'

Hugh let out a long low whistle and sat swinging his legs backwards and forwards for a few minutes.

'But for cool and courage, he really takes the ticket. They made the journey to the landing ground in daylight, because of the curfew, and anyway they would cause less suspicion than doing it after dark. Then he holed them up in the crevices I think they said, some kind of caves which pot the area, until the Lysander arrived.'

'What a story,' Nadine breathed.

'I reckon the pilot could tell a story too,' Hugh grinned. 'From what they said, he barely touched down. The whole operation was so dicey, don't think he even stopped. Louis and Co. just chucked the bods in through the door and off they went. But Louis fears it must have created some kind of stir so he's holing up for the moment. With the result that until he surfaces, we're not likely to have any news of Blaise.'

He stopped swinging his foot and gazed thoughtfully at the wooden floor.

'Poor devil, he may make it. But I don't hold out much hope.'

'Oh, there *must* be some way,' Tatiana cried. 'I'm sure Louis . . .'

'There's a limit to what even *Louis* can do,' Hugh clipped in. 'He's not God Almighty.'

He sighed and passed a hand through his thick fair hair.

'And, personally, I can't say I believe in miracles.'

He looked at Tatiana with a wry smile.

'But if you're one of those who does, I advise you to start praying. That's all that'll save him now. Pray either for escape or a quick death.'

Tatiana and Nadine blanched. And for a moment an uneasy silence hung over the dreary room.

'Oh, that's where you are!'

Alan Tait walked into the room, his face grey and his moustache bristling with anger.

Hugh Barrington leapt smartly off the table.

'Just coming,' he replied. 'Delivered the BBC messages as you said.'

'As I said at least half an hour ago,' Tait put in tartly. 'Please don't let me interrupt anything important, but when you've finished your social chat perhaps you'd care to wander back to the office . . . there *is* work to be done.'

Nadine swivelled quickly round on her chair and began typing furiously as Hugh Barrington reddened under the snub. She was taken aback by Tait's outburst. He was one of the more informal easy-going officers and it was most unlike him to be unpleasant. Tatiana fiddled nervously with the papers on her desk, embarrassed for Hugh, and not quite knowing what to do. She looked up at him surreptitiously from under her eyelashes.

'Where's Caroline?' Tait barked, catching her eye.

'She's with Colonel Masters,' Tatiana stammered.

'No, she isn't,' Tait snapped. 'I've just been to his office and it's empty.'

Nadine stopped typing and the two girls looked at each other.

'Would you like me go and look for her?' Tatiana ventured.

'No,' Tait said exasperatedly. 'Stay where you are.'

He turned angrily on his heel, then paused and looked over his shoulder.

'As soon as she comes back . . .'

'We'll tell her you want to see her,' Nadine cut in.

Tait nodded curtly, and walked swiftly from the room.

Hugh Barrington had already taken the opportunity to slip away and the two girls were left alone to digest the information they had received.

'I'll see that these messages get over to Bush,' Tatiana said getting up, happy for an excuse to leave the room.

But when she returned the whole situation had changed.

Tait brushed past her in the corridor as if he hadn't even noticed she was there. And the silence of the earlier part of the day was broken by a hum of activity coming from every office.

Opening the door, she saw Caroline scribbling something on a piece of paper, Lawrence Masters tapping one foot impatiently beside her.

Nadine signalled Tatiana to keep quiet. So she slipped behind her desk and tried to look occupied.

But within seconds both Caroline and Masters had rushed from the room and other footsteps were heard hurrying along the corridor.

'Whatever's happened?' she said as soon as the door slammed behind them.

Nadine looked up from her typewriter, her usually impish face white and drawn.

'It's Blaise,' she said, a break in her voice.

Tatiana's hand gripped her pen more tightly.

'What about him?'

'They've just had word that he's been sentenced to death.'

Nadine's voice broke.

'He's to be executed on Saturday morning,' she choked. 'That's why no one could find Caroline and Masters. They'd rushed off to see the General.'

'But what can *he* do?' Tatiana whispered.

Nadine shrugged and a lone tear stole down her cheek.

'Not much. But I suppose it's easier if someone else takes the responsibility. That's probably why Alan Tait was in such a foul mood, Blaise was a friend of his. And I believe he was a friend of Masters too.'

Nadine looked across at Tatiana, her expressive brown eyes large and frightened.

'Oh Tatiana,' she cried. 'I *hate* this war, don't you?'

Tatiana nodded.

'Did you know Blaise?'

'No.'

'He was a super chap,' Nadine went on. 'Young, handsome, charming. He had everything going for him.'

'Perhaps Louis will do something,' Tatiana faltered.

Nadine gave her a withering look.

'You still believe in Father Christmas I suppose!'

Tatiana looked up and smiled weakly.

'Maybe,' she said. 'My grandfather is very devout and he believes that God is Sovereign in everything in our lives. He says that he never abandons his children in their hour of need.'

She looked across at Nadine, her beautiful green eyes sparkling with tears.

'Perhaps God doesn't want Blaise to die yet.'

Nadine snorted.

'Perhaps pigs can fly,' she said, turning back to her desk and beginning to pound the keys.

Tatiana gazed at her shoes, but didn't reply.

'Grow up Tatiana,' Nadine bellowed angrily, raising her voice to compete with the din. 'You're living in cloud-cuckoo-land.'

'I still think there's hope,' Tatiana said softly. 'Whilst there's life, there's *always* hope.'

Nadine's face, usually dimpled with smiles was set in a hard line.

Looking at her, Tatiana realised that with each crisis, each death, Nadine was reliving her own personal tragedy: that she had never come to terms with her loss and had no anchor to cling to, no faith which could have sustained her.

Tatiana's faith was minimal.

But at that moment of stress and pain, pain for the anger and the hurt she saw in her friend's face, she realised that the strong faith with which she had been brought up, was indeed a bulwark. She had a rock to cling to when the storm raged. And she wished she could have passed some of her Grandfather's strong belief in a loving God on to Nadine.

With a sigh she picked up her pen and began to sort through the accumulation of work.

But it was hard to concentrate.

Caroline appeared half an hour later to say that she and Masters would be working late but that there was no point in the two of them hanging around.

Tatiana thankfully put the cap back on her pen and slithered into her jacket. Anchoring her large khaki beret firmly on her curls she walked out of the dreary office into the warm May evening, telling herself that sufficient unto the day was the evil thereof: words she had been obliged to learn by heart during her childhood, but which had never meant anything to her, until now.

She hoped against hope that news of Blaise's fate had not filtered down to Group R. But she doubted it. And her heart ached for Katharine, for Nadine, for all those innocent people who were suffering because of the war.

As she came up from the tube at South Kensington station and started to walk towards her home, she felt stunned and bewildered.

She could not believe that it was only a week ago that Katharine's drop had been cancelled at the last minute. Only six days since they had gone together down to Goudhurst to stay with Lavinia. It seemed that up till then it had been for her the age of innocence when, as Nadine put it, she had still believed in Father Christmas.

But since her return to the office, two days ago, she felt that she had grown up. She was suddenly much older. And the weight of the years and the succession of dramas she had lived through, albeit only as a bystander and not as an active participant, seemed to be dragging her down.

With these thoughts tormenting her already overtaxed sensibility, Tatiana turned the corner into her quiet road. She knew that something had changed inside her, something radical, and that whatever happened in the days to come she would never be the same again.

Chapter 12

It was Tamara's evening for fire-watching duty at the local ARP Post.*

By the time Tatiana arrived home her mother, armed with tin hat and whistle, had already left. So she and her grandfather dined alone.

Tatiana was strangely silent during dinner. The Prince noticed it, but made no comment until they were sitting opposite each other in the ornate, old fashioned drawing room.

'How are you enjoying your work at the Foreign Office?' he enquired, as Tatiana lifted the heavy silver samovar to pour his tea.

Tatiana looked down at the worn Persian rug beneath her feet. She was feeling drained and sore inside after the buffetings of the past few days.

'Its . . . very interesting,' she managed to articulate at last, plopping a sliver of lemon into the tall steaming glass in its silver holder, before handing it to him.

'Then tell me what is upsetting you.'

For a moment Tatiana was so taken aback by her grandfather's direct remark that she almost blurted out the truth. But she remembered Lawrence Masters warning to her before she had joined the staff.

'No one, I repeat no one must know what you do here. Not mother, father, brother, sister, fiancé or anyone else.

As far as the outside world is concerned you're working in a Government office doing a routine, rather boring nine to five job.'

He hadn't exactly made her sign the pledge. But almost.

Tatiana looked across at her grandfather, tranquilly sipping his tea.

They had always been very close in spite of the enormous age gap. It would be so healing to pour out all her misery to him, tell him just how she was feeling. He would have the words to bring her hope and comfort.

She pressed her lips tightly together to prevent them betraying her.

Her grandfather's kindly eyes focused on her for a few seconds. Then wandered across to the window through which the late evening light was already beginning to fade. Above the rooftops the sun was slowly sinking, dyeing London a warm apricot as the opal twilight flecked the sky with the last gold of the day.

Tatiana rose to her feet.

'Perhaps I should put up the blackout?' she said diffidently, for want of something better to say.

'Call Olga,' the Prince smiled 'And then, my dear, if I were you I'd go to bed. You look worn out. And we don't know how long it will be before the Germans pay their nightly call.'

Tatiana walked over to his chair and bent to kiss his withered cheek.

'Whatever it is that is upsetting you,' he comforted, squeezing her hand, 'lying awake worrying about it cannot do any good.'

She looked down at him and a great surge of love swept over her.

'I am so lucky Deduschka,' she whispered.

He looked up at her in surprise.

'I've got so much, you and Mamenka. I'm surrounded by people who love me.'

Her brilliant green eyes suddenly clouded with anguish.

'Katharine has so little. Her mother's dead and she doesn't know where her father is and now . . .'

Suddenly Masters' penetrating dark eyes blazed accusingly in front of her face.

'And what now?' her grandfather gently prompted.

But she didn't finish her sentence.

The anguish in her own eyes was replaced by tears, sparkling like raindrops in the gathering gloom.

'Oh, why is life so unfair!'

'I don't know Tatiana,' her grandfather said sadly. 'But the Bible tells us that the rain falls on the just and the unjust. Perhaps that is the explanation.'

He reached up a hand and stroked her face resting close to his.

'Which makes us realise that there will be a reckoning one day. That there is a God, a Supreme Being, who will stand in judgement on all those who have committed these terrible crimes.'

He smiled up at her.

'Otherwise life doesn't make any sense does it?'

As the light slowly faded from the room, casting grey shadows on the heavy old furniture, they remained close together in a companionable silence.

'Darling Deduschka,' Tatiana faltered at last, leaning over the back of his chair and twining her arms round his neck. 'What would we do without you?'

* * *

Tatiana's heart was much lighter when she skipped down into the blackness of the underground station at South Kensington the next morning.

She had slept well. And, having been able in an oblique way to share her burden with her grandfather without betraying the trust placed in her by Masters, had removed an immense weight from her shoulders.

The Prince's calm had helped her to remove her emotions from boiling point and enabled her to face the painful situation more dispassionately.

Remembering their brief conversation as the crowded train jolted over the rails, hissing to a stop at littered stations then groaning on on its eternal round, Tatiana felt comforted.

But when she left the lift and walked along the corridor to her office, it was a different story.

Caroline's desk was cluttered with papers. But her chair was empty.

Nadine was piling an assortment of dirty mugs and cups onto a tin tray. She pushed aside a wire basket overflowing with papers and dumped the tray in its place on the table as Tatiana entered.

'Hallo,' she said without looking round, leaning across the desk to retrieve an ashtray.

The room had a dusty unwelcoming look. The sun never even attempted to pierce through the grimy patched-over window panes before late afternoon. But this Friday morning it reeked of staleness and tobacco smoke.

Tatiana's nose twitched in disgust. The overall effect was that of a bar parlour on the Sunday morning after the Cup Final.

'They've been at it all night,' Nadine remarked, emptying the last ashtray into the wastepaper basket.

The grey dust fluttered up and floated around her, increasing the musty smell.

'Caroline looks a wreck.'

She dimpled.

'And I don't mean what you think I mean.'

'I didn't think anything,' Tatiana replied. 'Where's Caroline now?'

'Gone over to the Dutch Kitchen with Luscious Larry to get some breakfast.'

Tatiana tossed her cap onto her desk and began unbuttoning her jacket.

'It's funny isn't it,' she remarked pensively. 'We're going through this awful drama and yet, as I came up in the lift, the other Sections are carrying on as if nothing has happened.'

'Nothing has happened for them,' Nadine remarked practically. 'For us, it's a bit like a death in the family.'

Tatiana winced at the word.

'Well, it's true,' Nadine said belligerently. 'When Peter went down, it seemed like the end of the world for me. And yet for everyone else I met life went on as usual.'

She shrugged her shoulders.

'Same thing for the other Sections. They certainly have their dramas and crises, but we aren't involved. So, not knowing anything about them, for us it's business as usual.'

'I suppose so. But . . .'

She never finished her sentence. The door burst open and a dishevelled Hugh Barrington strode into the room.

'Can you take this across the road,' he flashed. 'It's almost time for the Powerhouse sked.*'

He flicked a piece of paper onto Tatiana's desk.

'What can *they* do?' she enquired, getting up.

'Nothing,' he barked, flying back through the open door. 'But life can't stand still. We have enough problems as it is without asking for more from the other circuits.'

The door banged behind him.

Nadine looked up from her typewriter and grimaced. 'They're all their usual charming selves this morning I see.'

She sniffed.

'But one can generally count on Hugh for a bit of a giggle.'

'I expect they've been up all night and are feeling the strain,' Tatiana replied, wriggling herself back into her jacket.

The door opened again and Alan Tait, looking as worn and weary as his assistant, walked into the room.

He raised his eyebrows towards Caroline's desk.

'Gone to get some breakfast,' Nadine shouted in answer to his unspoken question, her usually chirpy voice fighting a losing battle with the rattle of the Remington.

He frowned and walked out without replying.

'Looks as if we're in for a jolly day,' Nadine declared. 'Heigh ho, what a luvverly war.'

But the day was far from jolly. Even Nadine's efforts to present the light touch fell flat. And, in the end she abandoned any attempt and joined in the prevailing tension and gloom.

At six o'clock a weary Caroline, who had hardly spoken all day except to blare a few orders, said there was no point in the two of them staying on.

'You're not going to spend another night at the office are you?' Tatiana demurred as she fixed her beret in front of the scrap of spotty mirror hanging beside the door.

'Oh, do mind your own business,' Caroline snapped.

Then instantly regretted it.

But she was too weary even to apologise as Tatiana tiptoed from the room in an effort to avoid another explosion.

Regaining the familiar security of her pretty blue and white bedroom as soon as dinner was over, she fell swiftly and deeply into an exhausted sleep.

For once the night was undisturbed by the wailing siren.

But, as the dawn chorus broke, Tatiana opened her eyes and was instantly awake.

Slipping out of bed she drew back the heavy blackout curtains and leant on the window-sill, gazing down at a sleeping London.

The street below was grey and deserted, the unlit lamp-posts, standing like tired sentinels, a dreary reminder of Britain at war.

But, in stark contrast, birdsong trilled from every budding tree lining the pavements. Backwards and forwards it went, rising and falling between the leafy branches as night faded and a glittering May morning shimmered around the sun, bursting from the sea of deep blue into its full rounded glory.

Tatiana gasped, spellbound by the sheer beauty of the dawn.

It contrasted strangely with the starkness of the city's ruins lying like jagged broken teeth across the skyline.

Then, suddenly, she remembered. And her heart, filled with joy at the morning splendour only seconds before, suddenly turned cold.

It was Saturday. The day Blaise had been sentenced by the summary German court to die at dawn.

She thrust her head into her hands, her heart heavy and swollen with anguish at the thought of this man, whom she had never met, but about whom she had heard so much, standing perhaps at this very moment, blindfolded before an enemy firing squad. And, as if to confirm her worst fears, in the distance it seemed that she heard the rapid, staccato crack of far away bullets.

* * *

Norgeby House* was bathed in its customary weekend calm when Tatiana walked along Baker Street and entered it a couple of hours later. Yet, as the lift stopped at her floor, although there was not the usual bustle and noise, merely a subdued hum of voices coming from behind closed doors, she knew instinctively that most of the offices were occupied.

To her surprise Nadine was there, standing gazing out of the window at the trickle of traffic cruising along the street below.

'I didn't expect to find you here,' Tatiana exclaimed. 'Isn't it your wekend off?'

Nadine nodded, without turning round.

'I couldn't stay away,' she murmured. 'Couldn't settle to anything in the flat.'

She turned and gave Tatiana a rueful smile.

'I share with two girls from the Min. of Ag. and Fish.* It was bad enough last evening when they were getting ready to go out on the tiles with a couple of dashing fighter pilots.'

She looked across at Tatiana, her usually laughing grey eyes dull with misery.

'I felt so isolated Tatiana. I couldn't share with them. Couldn't identify with their giggles. Do you know what I mean?'

Tatiana nodded.

'Couldn't you have gone home?'

'I could have but I didn't want to. My parents moved down to Bath with the Admiralty.'

Nadine shrugged.

'I think that's why Peter opted for the Navy. Thought it would impress Pa, and change his way of thinking, even though he was only Wavy Navy.'

'Why, didn't your parents approve?'

'Oh yes, they approved. But Pa is of the old school. Thought we should wait to get married until we had an olde-worlde cottage in a leafy lane with a blasted horse poking its head out of a paddock. He considered that at twenty-three, Peter was far too young.'

Nadine smiled to herself.

'Now I think he's sorry. So he tries to make up for it by being too sympathetic every time we meet, which is awful. Just makes me feel worse.'

'What a pity,' Tatiana commisserated.

She slung her jacket over the back of her chair.

'I suppose there's still no news?' she asked tentatively.

Nadine sat down at her typewriter and removed the cover.

'Not that I know of. But I must say, I haven't seen anybody, except a rather bad-tempered Caroline.'

She looked over at Tatiana and shivered.

'It's eerie, isn't it? I know everyone's here, but there's hardly a sound.'

She picked up a sheaf of papers and shuffled them together before propping them up on a stand in front of her.

'Might as well do something,' she said practically. 'The time will go quicker. Oh, *how* I wish it was Monday morning. Then perhaps we could all get back to normal again.'

And she banged away at the rattling old keyboard as if her life depended on it.

Tatiana looked down at her desk and tried to concentrate.

But her mind kept wandering.

And if ever she did manage to align her scattered thoughts for more than two minutes, she found herself suddenly jolted back by a terrible crack of bullets ringing in her ears.

Lunchtime came and went.

And still Caroline didn't appear.

Tatiana and Nadine decided to go to Richoux's.

They neither of them felt they could stomach lunch, but they needed to get away from the sinister atmosphere hanging over the office. Papa Richoux's cream cakes were the obvious solution.

They could stop when they felt sick or even *be* sick without it causing too much comment.

But once there, they were both restless and anxious to return to the ominous silence and gloom.

Yet, back in the office, nothing had changed.

Doors were still being opened and closed quietly and footsteps muffled in the long echoing corridor. The friendly noisy everyday chaos was strangely absent.

And they steeled themselves to face a long, hot, tense afternoon.

Caroline had obviously come back during their absence. There were signals for coding left on Tatiana's desk. So, grateful for something to do, she set off down the stairs and round the corner to Montague Mansions.*

As she was about to return, the sergeant laid a hand on her arm.

'Can you hang on a minute?' he said. 'They've been trying for days to get Wanderer up at his sked time but without any luck. But he's just come through.'

He took the dead end of a cigarette, which had been lolling perilously at the corner of his lip, out of his mouth and stuck it behind his ear.

'I expect Colonel Masters will be anxious to have it.'

Tatiana's throat went dry and her tongue felt as if it had swollen up and now filled the entire cavity of her mouth.

'Wanderer was Louis' reseau!*'

She tried to force words past this gigantic blockage. But not even a croak came.

'You all right miss?' the sergeant said, catching sight of her face which had become chalk-like.

She nodded, still unable to speak.

'It's this bleedin' cellar,' he went on, 'if you'll pardon my French. What with this 'eat and the electric light, it makes some people come all over queer. You nip off. I'll see this gets over toot sweet.'

Tatiana smiled at him gratefully, and stumbled back up the stairs and out into the sunshine.

By the time the lift door had clanged behind her, her tongue had shrunk back to its normal size, but her heart was still jumping erratically. Small beads of cold sweat clustered on her chin and forehead and tickled their way down her spine.

What was it her grandfather had said the other evening? There must a Supreme Being who sorts out all the injustices in the world.

Tatiana had always gone with her family to the Russian Orthodox Church, though she had never been sure whether her mother went out of faith or duty. But, remembering her grandfather's words, she longed for him. He would have found a way to still her wildly-pulsating heart, to stop this terrible cold chill from creeping down her spine. He would have known how to talk to this Supreme Being.

She sighed deeply.

He would have shown her how to pray.

'Oh God,' she implored. 'Please do something. Please save Blaise.'

Then she stopped.

It was too late.

She should have prayed before.

Perhaps that was why she had awakened so early, before it was light . . . before dawn.

At the ominous word, a lobster's claw seemed to take her in its grip.

God had awakened her so that she could plead for Blaise's life before it was even light, knowing that afterwards it would be too late. Now Wanderer was taking the tremendous risk to get through, perhaps for the last time if Louis were in hiding, only to confirm the execution.

A choking cry escaped her lips. And Tatiana stumbled along the corridor to her office blinded by fear and tears of remorse.

Then, out of the corner of her eye she saw the lift rise slowly and stop at the floor. A young corporal holding a signal in his hand got out and walked past her. Her glazed eyes followed him until he reached Lawrence Masters' office.

He raised his hand to knock on the door.

And Tatiana watched, unable to move.

* * *

Caroline looked up from her desk as Tatiana tumbled into the office.

'What on earth's the matter with you?' she frowned.

'Caroline,' Tatiana gasped, 'it's . . .'

But at that moment the telephone rang.

Caroline picked it up.

'I'll come right away Lawrence,' she answered.

And replacing the receiver, she got to her feet.

'Should anyone want me,' she said briefly, 'I'll be in Colonel Masters' office.'

'But Caroline,' Tatiana cried, catching hold of her sleeve as she brushed past her.

'For heavens sake Tatiana,' Caroline said testily. 'Stop behaving like a prima donna. Say what you have to say and get it over with.'

'It's Louis,' Tatiana whispered. 'Wanderer came up on the sked. when I went over with the signal. And the corporal has just come over with the message. Do you think . . .'

Nadine abruptly stopped typing.

She put a hand over her mouth to stifle a cry rising in her throat then, leaping from her chair, upsetting the paper holder propped on her desk, she ran across to where Tatiana was standing.

Caroline turned round on them.

'Whatever's got into the pair of you?' she said furiously. 'And to answer your question Tatiana, I don't think anything. Now for goodness sake control yourselves.'

'But Caroline,' they both pleaded at once.

And then suddenly stopped.

The steely glint in Caroline's blue eyes was cold and angry.

'There's some work I've prepared for you on your desk Tatiana,' she said, frostily. 'And you, Nadine, sort out that awful mess you've managed to scatter all over the floor, and get back to your typewriter.'

She paused in the doorway and looked them witheringly up and down.

'*Why* I have to be lumbered with mongrels I don't know,' she exploded. 'No one would believe you had English fathers. You're both behaving like a couple of ill-bred hysterical Continentals!'

And with that scathing parting shot, she stalked majestically through the door, slamming it loudly behind her.

Tatiana collapsed in a heap onto a chair.

'She's under great stress,' she bleated feebly, seeing the angry glint in Nadine's eyes.

Nadine bent down and swept the jumble of papers into her arms.

'She's a bitch,' she grated through clenched teeth.

And thrusting herself in front of her typewriter she pounded the keys as if all the devils in hell were howling at her heels.

Tatiana picked up her pen.

But she couldn't concentrate, just sat, like a lifeless doll, staring blankly at the opposite wall.

Suddenly the oppressive calm was broken by a door banging somewhere down the corridor, followed by another and then another. Hurried feet ran agitatedly past the door.

She looked enquiringly across at Nadine.

But she was still hammering at her typewriter, her face set in a hard mask.

As quickly as it had started, the frantic activity outside ceased. Tatiana sighed and picked up her pen again.

But at that moment the office door crashed inwards and Hugh Barrington burst into the room.

'Have you heard the news?' he shouted.

He was in his shirtsleeves, his usually immaculate hair falling across his forehead in a loop almost masking one eye.

Nadine's fingers dropped abruptly from the keys and the sudden silence was unnerving.

In one bound Hugh was across the room and, grabbing Tatiana's hands, almost lifted her from behind her desk.

'He's been rescued,' he exulted. 'Blaise has been rescued. Louis's done the impossible!'

Nadine leapt from her chair and ran across to join them.

'They managed to make contact with Wanderer after all these days,' Hugh continued. Wouldn't be surprised if Louis didn't send the signal himself, the old devil. He's the sort who wouldn't risk his W/T's life with the Gestapo on their heels.'

'But what happened?' Tatiana gasped. 'Is Blaise *really* safe or just in hiding.'

'*Really* safe,' Hugh echoed. 'Don't ask me how Louis did it, another one of his bluffs no doubt. We'll have to wait to hear the details till Blaise gets back. All Louis said was that he'd been smuggled across the Demarcation Line* and is now in hiding with Louis' family somewhere near Narbonne.'

'But I thought Narbonne was the unoccupied zone?' Nadine frowned.

'It is,' Hugh grinned. 'But there are plenty of informers *and* the Milice around. And, don't forget, there'll be a price on Blaise's head.'

He paused for breath as the two girls hung on his every word.

'Someone will be arranging for his escape, either across the Pyrenees or some other way if he's not in shape to tackle that mountain walk.'

'Why wouldn't he be in shape?' Nadine demanded.

Hugh looked at her pityingly.

'Would *you* be after spending a few days as guests of the Gestapo?'

'But what other way would there be for him to get away?' Tatiana asked seriously.

'Dunno exactly,' Hugh reflected, thoughtfully stroking his chin. 'Perhaps by boat from Marseille to North Africa. Though I imagine all passengers are pretty thoroughly checked and scrutinised. *Or . . .'*

He pursed his lips reflectively.

They might just infiltrate a submarine to one of the beaches in the area, Gruissan or St Pierre. There are dozens of small beaches along that coast, and it could be done . . .'

He paused, nodding his head thoughtfully.

'Yes, I imagine that's what they'll probably do.'

He jumped off the edge of Tatiana's desk and slapped his thigh.

'But, whatever happens, we're not likely to see him around here for some time. If he crosses into Spain over the Pyrenees, they'll probably shove him in quad.* And if he's landed in North Africa, he's not exactly home and dry.'

'But he's alive,' Tatiana broke in, her eyes shining. 'And we none of us thought he would be.'

'That's for sure,' Hugh agreed. He grinned downed at her. 'You must have prayed.'

The three of them were standing together in a huddle, tears rolling down the two girls' cheeks, when Caroline walked in holding a cup in her hand.

She looked completely different.

Gone were the tetchy lines of irritation and fatigue. Even the charcoal shadows beneath her eyes seemed to have faded to a pale shade of grey.

And she was smiling.

'I've come to fetch you,' she beamed.

She glanced at Barrington.

'I thought that's what *you* were supposed to be doing Hugh.'

He passed his hand through his hair, restoring order.

'Yes well . . . I was just about to bring the two of them along.'

He wrinkled his nose at her.

'We were merely having our private celebration first.'

'Well collect some cups or mugs or anything you can find,' Caroline chirped brightly. 'Lawrence has opened a bottle of champagne.'

She glanced across at Nadine, who had turned her back and plonked herself down in front of her typewriter the instant Caroline appeared. But Nadine kept her eyes steadfastly fixed on the keys.

Caroline walked over to her.

'Come on, Nadine,' she said, putting an arm tentatively round her shoulders. 'You're invited too.'

Nadine shrugged her arm away.

'I hardly think the illustrious Colonel's party is for mongrels,' she retorted stiffly.

Hugh raised his eyebrows questioningly at Tatiana.

'I've collected all the cups we have,' she said hurriedly. 'Let's be off Hugh. Caroline and Nadine can catch us up.'

He took the tray from her hands and held open the door.

'I'm sorry, Nadine,' Caroline said softly as it closed behind them. 'Mongrels are usually much better natured, and much more fun to be with than thoroughbreds . . . who can be unreasonable at times . . . and *very* bad tempered.'

For a few seconds Nadine didn't react, merely kept staring at the black lines on the page in front of her. Then she dimpled.

'One all,' she laughed, jumping up from the chair.

And they left the room together, their laughter echoing down the corridor.

Part Three

1943 – 1945

Chapter 13

Katharine stamped her frozen feet as she lifted the latch and entered the warm cottage.

It was the end of January.

More than eight months had passed since her departure from London for Group R after the abortive attempt at being parachuted into France.

At the time she had accepted, albeit with bad grace, the explanation given her that her circuit was blown and until she could be drilled for another one, there was no hope at all of her joining the resistance fighters.

Apart from a new identity, she would need to have a thorough knowledge of the geography and local habits of the area to which she was being sent: an area in which she was supposed to have lived. And all this would take time. But as the months passed, she slowly came to realise that nothing was being done.

At first, she had fumed and fretted. But gradually the routine of her new life, shared with Nicola, the FANY from South Africa whom Lawrence Masters had mentioned, and Anne from Montreal had lulled her restless spirit into a kind of limbo.

When, at the end of August, Tatiana had at last joined them, her friend's quiet calm and gentle spirit had finally managed to deflate the remaining shreds of Katharine's rebelliousness. And she had accepted that, for the time being, for reasons unknown to her, HQ had decided to leave her on this side of the Channel.

Even coming into daily contact with agents who were about to be dropped into France no longer caused resentment and anger to flare up inside her.

The glorious beauty of the early autumn countryside and the cosiness of the old timbered cottage had wound their spell around her and she at last felt at peace.

'Brrrrr,' she shivered, pulling off her thick woollen gloves and tossing her beret onto a small dark oak settle sitting primly just inside the door. 'Wouldn't be surprised if there was snow in the offing.'

She sniffed appreciatively as she unwound her scarf and struggled out of her heavy greatcoat.

'Rickie,' she called. 'Whatever are you cooking? It smells delicious!'

A plump, rosy-faced woman appeared at the kitchen door.

'Steak and kidney pie.'

'Steak and kidney *pie*,' Katharine hooted following her back into the kitchen. 'Rickie, you're a marvel! However do you do it?'

Eleanor Ricks turned round from the stove and smiled.

'Got friends in high places,' she winked.

'Oh yes,' Katharine said. 'I forgot. You used to live near here.'

'And hope to again one day when all this nonsense is over.'

'Don't we all,' Katharine laughed.

She pulled out a stool from under the kitchen table and sat down.

'Rickie,' she said pensively, gazing at the back of Eleanor's matronly figure as she returned to the stove.

'I can't think why you never married. You'd have made a wonderful wife and mother.'

Rickie shrugged without turning round.

'It just never happened,' she remarked. 'I was part of the generation which grew up before the last war.'

She paused.

'By the end of 1918 all the eligible young men were dead. Or all those I had known.'

Miss Ricks turned and smiled impishly at Katharine.

'Or else married to someone else.'

She picked up a beater and started to swish it round a bowl until a thick frothy yellow mass rose to the surface.

'My two brothers were killed in the last war and my father had died in 1913. So, by the time it was over, with the terrible burden of three lots of death duties one after the other, my mother and I were reduced to what is politely called genteel poverty.'

'Was it your mother who taught you how to make those wonderful dishes?'

Rickie threw back her head and laughed.

'My mother never lifted a saucepan lid in her life,' she elaborated. 'No, it was force of circumstances. We could no longer afford a cook. So it was either learn how to do it myself or starve.'

She poured the finished custard into a bowl then bent and placed it in the Aga to keep warm.

'And, as you can see from my ample form,' she twinkled, 'I enjoy my food.'

'And so do we,' Katharine smiled. 'But however did HQ manage to find you? Just imagine, if they hadn't, we might have been landed with some terrible old harridan who served us soggy cabbage and chips!'

'Oh, Lawrence Masters thinks far too highly of you all to do such a thing.'

Katharine's eyes widened.

'You *know* him?'

'I've known him since he was a baby,' Rickie said smoothly. 'As a matter of fact, I'm his godmother.'

'I can't imagine Lawrence Masters as a baby,' Katharine mused.

'I can assure you he once was,' Rickie smiled, 'And a delightful one at that.'

'Is that how you come to be here?' Katharine enquired.

Rickie stirred thoughtfully with a large wooden spoon.

'I imagine so. Lawrence contacted me about it. For obvious reasons they couldn't put an advertisement in the newspaper. And it couldn't be just anybody. It had to be a person they knew, who was aware of what was going on here and could be trusted to keep her mouth shut.'

She pushed the saucepan to a back burner and her face broke into her incredibly youthful smile.

'. . . and who enjoyed cooking!'

Out in the hall the telephone rang. Slippered feet slithered along the worn polished parquet floor as their owner went to answer it.

A few seconds later, Anne's face appeared round the kitchen door.

'Oh *there* you are!' she exclaimed. 'I thought I heard you come in. Guess what?'

'What?' Katharine replied disinterestedly.

'That was Harry on the 'phone. You'll never believe who's here.'

'Father Christmas,' Katharine volunteered.

'Idiot,' Anne laughed.

'How about Ali Baba then?'

'Wrong again. No, no more,' she interrupted as

Katharine opened her mouth to offer another suggestion. 'You'll *never* guess right.'

She paused for dramatic effect.

'It's Blaise!'

Katharine's forehead wrinkled.

'Blaise?' she puzzled.

'Oh don't pretend you can't remember,' Anne chided. 'You know very well who he is. Even down here in the dense jungle of the New Forest the news seeped through.'

'Yes,' Katharine frowned, 'now I remember. Wasn't he the bod who had that amazing escape from the firing squad?'

'The very one,' Anne sparkled.

'What's he doing here?' Katharine queried. 'Shouldn't have thought we could teach him anything.'

'We can't,' Anne laughed. 'But he's just got back and has come down to talk to the students* who are leaving tomorrow. Probably to give them tips on how to outwit the Gestapo.'

'Only just back?' Katharine queried. 'I thought he escaped last summer.'

'He did,' Anne said patiently. 'You must know his story. It's almost a legend. Escaped from France by walking across the Pyrenees with a Basque guide. What a hike that must have been, dodging border patrols all the way. Then after all that the poor guy was picked up by the Spanish police soon after he crossed over. He was hiding in a so-called safe farmhouse, but they must have denounced him. Anyway, the police carted him off to Barcelona or somewhere and finally imprisoned him at Lerida.

'But the wonderful Louis had given him the name of an aunt of his who had married a Spaniard. Her husband was dead but as he'd been Spanish Ambassador to France in the early thirties, she still had a bit of weight to throw around with the authorities.'

'My father's aunt was married to a Spanish diplomat who was Ambassador to France in '34,' Katharine mused as Anne paused for breath. 'I remember her well. Tante Solange.'

'Was her husband also a marquis or some kind of Spanish grandee?' Anne interrupted.

'Uncle Octavio? Yes, I believe he was,' Katharine replied vaguely.

'Probably the very one,' Anne chortled triumphantly. 'My, don't we move in high circles!'

Katharine smiled but, strangely enough, did not make the connection with her father.

'*Anyway*,' Anne continued. 'Through her influence, your Auntie Mabel's that is . . .'

She grinned across at Katharine.

'After a few months Blaise was released. Jolly lucky as otherwise he would probably have been sent to the Miranda concentration camp, which wouldn't have been funny at all. Finally he reached Malaga, and from there got a boat to Casablanca and then back to HQ in Cairo.'

'You *have* learnt your lesson well,' Katharine said disnterestedly. 'Do you always tell people's entire life story all in one breath?'

'OK? Katharine,' Anne clucked. 'So what's biting you? You must have had a bad day to be in such a foul mood. But whatever sourpuss attitude you take you won't dampen my enthusiasm.'

'But how do you know all this about him?' Katharine insisted.

'I spent my last weekend off in London at Nadine's. Blaise had just got back and she went with the bigwigs to Orchard Court to his Y9.'*

Anne's eyes sparkled.

'Apparently they have the most marvellous black marble bathroom there. Did you know?'

'I did, as a matter of fact,' Katharine answered drily.

Anne realised that she had touched a sore point.

'Gee Kath, I'm sorry,' she said contritely.

But she soon bounced back again.

'I can't wait to meet Blaise,' she breathed, her eyes glistening with excitement.

'Are you likely to,' Katharine remarked, 'if he's come to speak to the students?'

'Yeah,' she said triumphantly. 'That's why Harry rang.'

Harry was the Major in charge of the students.

'It's probably against all security rules. But as it's rather a special occasion and the students are leaving tomorrow anyway . . .'

'I thought Blaise was supposed to be speaking to them tomorrow,' Katharine cut in.

'No, he apparently arrived last night and has been with them all day, or most of it . . .'

She paused, her eyes bright with suppressed excitement.

'Harry suggests we have a knees-up round at The Vineyard.'

The Vineyard was where the students were housed, deep into the woods away from the main buildings.

'A knees-up?' Katharine frowned.

'Oh well, a hop then. You know . . . Well, you obviously don't, but what Harry suggests is that as one of his corporals plays the piano and another the saxophone, we all go over to The Vineyard and have a little jig to celebrate.'

'I don't see what there is to celebrate,' Katharine said coolly.

The unoccupied zone of France had been taken over by the Germans only a few weeks before, and the news had affected Katharine more deeply than she realised.

Anne cast her eyes to the ceiling in exasperation.

'Well, Blaise's escape and the students' final haul . . . But if you don't wanna come.'

Katharine got up from her stool.

'I don't see the point,' she said. 'There's only *four* of us. Who's everyone going to hop *with*?'

'There *are* some women students,' Anne said patiently. 'And, anyway, most of the men will only want to prop up the bar, so there'll be no problem.'

She looked pleadingly at Katharine.

'So what's biting you?'

'I had a ghastly afternoon,' Katharine shrugged. Aftermath of the exercise we went on yesterday.'

Anne propped her elbows on the kitchen table.

'C'mon, tell auntie,' she wheedled.

'Do you remember that Danish student I had dinner with last night,' Katharine began. 'The one you and Rollo were trailing round Bournemouth all afternoon?'

'Sure I remember,' Anne cut in enthusiastically. 'A gorgeous blond Viking who passed with flying colours.'

She grinned across at Katharine

'Gave me the slip in Plummers all right. Walked up the stairs and completely disappeared. Instead of taking the lift at the first floor, as I'd expected him to do, he whipped off his hat and mac and shot down the other side. So even though I looked amongst the crowd before rushing to the lift I didn't spot him. His back view had completely changed.'

Anne shrugged expressively.

'Same thing happened in the Pier Gardens. Rollo was in the phone box pretending to make a call and I was standing at the bus-stop, right opposite our blond Adonis. We both watched him like hawks. But neither of us saw him slip a note to the bod reading a newspaper at the other end of the bench. Goodness knows how he did it. I thought he might have rolled it up and left it in the cigarette packet – he lit up before leaving. But he put his fags back in his pocket and strolled casually off as if he hadn't a care in the world.'

Anne made a thumbs up sign.

'Ten out of ten for the Viking!'

'If only it had ended there,' Katharine groaned.

'Why, what happened?'

'Charlie had arranged to meet him for dinner in the Royal Bath Hotel. They were in the bar when I arrived "by chance" and was hailed by Charlie as an old friend he hadn't seen for ages. He invited me to join them and we all decided to have dinner together. Of course, no sooner had we settled in the dining-room than Charlie had an urgent telephone call. He apologised profusely saying he had to leave but would be back as soon as he could and, as prearranged, didn't return until we were in the lounge having coffee.'

Katharine spread her fingers thoughtfully on the old wooden table.

'By which time I'd managed to persuade the poor student to tell me what he was doing over here.'

Anne whistled.

'So he's had it?'

''Fraid so.'

'Oh well,' Anne shrugged, 'better now than once he's in the field. If he can't keep his mouth shut here he won't be able to once he's dropped. And it wouldn't be only *his* life that'd be at stake either.'

'That's what the Colonel said.'

'So what's the problem?'

'I'd have thought it was obvious,' Katharine wailed. 'He's failed at the last ditch. And he's furious!'

'Whose fault is that? If he can't resist boasting to a pretty face . . .'

'But it's what he *said* . . .' Katharine broke in.

Anne raised her eyebrows enquiringly.

'The Colonel confronted him with me this afternoon. He realised that he'd been lured into a trap. And, by that one slip had lost any chance of returning to Denmark as an undercover agent.'

'Well, what *did* he say?'

Katharine took a deep breath.

'You *bitch*!'

Anne laughed and pushed back her chair.

'Oh, is *that* all. I've been called much worse. It's what you have to expect in this cockeyed job. Don't let it get you down. It probably won't be the last time. And all the more reason why you should come to the hop tonight and take your mind off things.'

She grinned impishly at Katharine.

'Don't be a spoilsport and stay behind and sulk just because of the Viking.'

Katharine grinned back.

'Oh, all right, I'll come. What time?'

'8.00, 8.30, as soon as we've finished dinner.'

Anne winked.

'And had time to put on our war paint.'

'If you don't get out of my kitchen,' Rickie interrupted, 'there won't *be* any dinner.'

* * *

As Katharine started to pile the dirty plates and dishes onto a tray, Rickie laid a restraining hand on her arm.

'You leave all this to me this evening,' she smiled. 'Off you go and make yourself beautiful.'

Katharine turned slowly towards the stairs. She was not very enthusiastic about the evening but felt she couldn't let the others down. It was true, women were at a premium at Group R. And a celebration of any kind was so unusual.

Opening the little corner cupboard in her low-ceilinged bedroom with the sloping roof and small casement window, she swished the few clothes she had brought with her back and forth, her head on one side, her lips pursed. Suddenly she caught sight of a dress Myrtle had made for her a few months earlier which she had never worn.

It had been fashioned from a bolt of Indian shot silk which she had discovered in one of the trunks stored in Lavinia's attic. Katharine smiled as she remembered Myrtle balancing on her knees, her mouth full of pins, tutting and purring around her.

She took it down and held it against her. The silk shimmered as she twisted this way and that in front of the mirror. The soft pale green contrasting beautifully with her chestnut hair.

Tossing it on to the bed Katharine shivered. The bedroom was none too warm and tiny goose pimples began to prick her arms as she climbed out of her uniform.

'Only hope they have a good fire going over at The Vineyard,' she grumbled. Otherwise I shall be waltzing in my greatcoat.'

'Kaaaaaatharine,' Anne yelled up the stairs. 'Do get a move on. We're all waiting for you.'

Rickie, proud as a mother hen, was hovering in the hall to brush non-existent dandruff off their collars, twitch scarves into place and generally fuss over her brood before letting them out into the cold night air.

When they entered what had once been the impressive drawing room at The Vineyard, the party was in full swing.

Harry hailed them from across the room, threading his way towards them through the clustered dancers as the band blared 'We're gonna hang out the washing on the Siegfried Line.'*

'Some hopes of that,' Katharine thought grimly.

'Come along girls,' Harry barked jovially. 'We've all been waiting for you. It's really the answer to a maiden's prayer this evening: at least three to one.'

His jovial red face broke into a round smile, his laugh, like the crackling of dry leaves, bellowing out around him.

Katharine stood a little to one side to survey the scene. Anne had been right, most of the officers were propping up the bar. But whether by choice or because of the paucity of women she didn't know.

Catching sight of a tall blond man standing on the other side of the room talking to Charlie Mann she frowned, not recognising him. Perhaps this was the famous Blaise.

The two-piece makeshift band drifted hauntingly into 'We'll meet again'. And at that moment the man across the room laughed at something Charlie was saying. Then he turned round.

It was Ashley Paget.

Katharine gasped, took a step forward, and abruptly held back.

What on earth was he doing here? Suddenly the tune the band was playing seemed prophetic and she didn't know what to do. Her instinct told her to run away and hide. Hide somewhere out of sight until the evening was over and she could safely regain the security of the cottage. But her legs refused to move.

At that moment he looked up and saw her.

A flash of recognition lit those sparkling blue eyes she remembered so well. Putting down his glass he threaded his way deftly through the dancers to her side.

'Katharine,' he said softly.

Taking her hands in both of his, he looked down into those tawny brown eyes which were gazing back at him in a kind of terror.

'I've waited so long to see you.'

Katharine just stood looking at him, not believing, not understanding, not knowing what to say.

'But,' she stumbled at last. 'What are you doing here?'

He shrugged, not understanding either. They seemed to be talking at cross-purposes.

'I was asked to come and talk to the students before they left,' he answered.

Katharine's mouth opened and shut, but no words came. She just kept gazing at him with that terrified look in her eyes.

'I don't understand,' she stammered at last, as they stood there, hands locked. 'You're . . . you're . . . Blaise?'

The word came out in a prolonged whisper.

He looked surprised.

'Didn't you know?'

'How could I know?' she cried.

He dropped her hands and, taking her arm, led her to a sofa which had been pushed against the wall.

'So you had no idea why I didn't get in touch with you as I promised I would?' he enquired sitting down beside her. 'You didn't know I was in the field?'

She shook her head dumbly.

'Oh, *Katharine*,' he groaned. 'What sort of heel must you have thought me?'

Tatiana, circling the floor in her partner's arms looked anxiously in the direction of the sofa.

She had been in two minds before dinner whether or not to reveal to Katharine Blaise's true identity. But they had never been alone. Seeing them sitting together on the sofa, she felt reassured.

The music stopped and the dancers dissolved to the sides, clapping enthusiastically. But Ashley and Katharine didn't appear to hear. They just gazed at each other in disbelief.

A white-gloved soldier glided towards them, a tray of drinks in his hand.

Ashley looked up.

'Just a minute Bombardier,' he said, reaching into his breast pocket.

He drew out a small notebook, tore off a page and quickly scribbled something on it.

'Give that to the pianist will you?'

The soldier took the paper and, wending his way through the dancers, held it up in front of the band. The saxophonist nodded towards the pianist, who struck a few resounding final chords, then slid gently into 'All the things you are.'

Ashley looked down at Katharine and smiled.

'It seems we've got a lot of catching up and straightening out to do.'

He rose to his feet and held out his hand to draw her up beside him.

'Let's dance. This tune says it all.'

A blush slowly crept up her neck and tinted her creamy cheeks as he led her across the rolled-up carpet to the tiny scrap of parquet floor, and held out his arms.

She slid effortlessly into them. And when they closed around her, she suddenly felt as if she had come home.

It seemed so right to be there. She fitted so easily, so rhythmically in with his steps as they gently swayed, moulded together, scarcely moving, oblivious of the other couples whirling around them.

And once again that wonderful voluptuous feeling she had experienced when waiting for his telephone call at Ardnakil thrilled through her. Yet this time it was more powerful. Shaking the very fibre of her being, because he was there and she was in his arms, listening to the steady beat of his heart as her head nestled in the hollow beneath his shoulder.

The pianist leant towards the microphone and began to croon the words of the song.

'The dearest things I know are what you are' floated across the room.

She closed her eyes in a kind of ecstasy.

'Someday my happy arms will hold you . . .'

Katharine felt his arms tighten round her. She inhaled the faint odour of his hair cream as he bent his head and let his cheek rest softly, caressingly, against hers. The room slowly swam round and round as ripples of passion which had begun to pulsate through her at his first touch now throbbed in every nerve, completely taking control.

'Someday I'll know that moment divine,' crooned the throaty voice of the pianist, as his fingers tripped up and down the keyboard and the saxophone moaned sensually in the background. 'When all the things you are are mine.'

Katharine trembled. Her whole body felt jelly-like and totally out of control.

But at that moment the saxophonist, who was doubling as MC,* leaned towards the microphone and announced a Paul Jones.

Immediately there was chaos.

Someone grabbed her hand. Ashley was dragged off in the opposite direction and two concentric circles of dancers began to race crazily around the room.

The music stopped abruptly and she found herself facing Charlie Mann.

He grinned and immediately whisked her into a quick step.

Out of the corner of her eye Katharine saw Ashley dancing with Anne. And she felt a stab of jealousy. Anne had been particularly anxious to meet Ashley. And she wondered what would happen when this mad whirl was over.

But before she had time to think or Charlie had time to get back his breath, the music changed again and they were all hurtled back into their wild circular gallop.

At last it ended. Everyone limped from the floor and collapsed on to sofas, helpless with laughter.

Immediately Ashley was by her side.

'Aren't you thirsty?' he enquired, leading her towards the bar.

'Let's hope that's the end of those antics,' he smiled, raising his glass to her.

'Here's to us,' he said softly.

And she didn't know what to reply.

Harry dawdled up and stood beside them.

'See you've got yourself a pretty partner,' he cackled, his laugh crackling out again.

Ashley nodded.

'Yes,' he said. 'We've met before but we haven't seen each other for a long time. Got a lot of catching up to do.'

But Harry didn't take the hint.

'Three to one this evening old boy,' he winked. 'Let the others have a chance.'

And he took Katharine's arm.

'I want you to meet . . .'

Harry's voice was lost in the saxophonist's announcement that the next dance would be a Ladies' invitation. Katharine turned to look helplessly over her shoulder at Ashley. But Anne, seizing the opportunity, had rushed across the room and was triumphantly leading him on to the dance-floor.

As the silent Belgian Harry had introduced her to propelled her, wooden faced, round and round the room, Katharine was in agony She felt sure her partner would rather be drinking beer with his friends. And when she suggested it, he immediately dropped his arms and agreed.

Ashley was still dancing with Anne, who was looking up into his face, talking animatedly. Knowing that she wouldn't let him go without a struggle, Katharine turned and wandered miserably to the door leading to the hall. But at that moment the music stopped and a few seconds later she sensed Ashley behind her.

'It's impossible,' he said, slipping an arm lightly round her shoulder. 'There's no way we can be alone, or even talk if we stay in there.'

'We can hardly go into the garden in this weather,' Katharine murmured, hearing the diamond-cutting wind which had risen during the evening rattle every window-pane in the old house.

'Katharine,' he murmured. 'There's so much I want to say to you.'

He turned her around to face him.

'Actually the one tune we were allowed to dance to said it all.'

Looking up at him in the dimly-lit hall, everything else seemed to dissolve and fade away. All she could see was his face. The strong jaw, the firm mouth. She knew that those intense blue eyes were sparkling down at her in the gloom. His head bent slowly towards her and she felt drawn as if by a magnet.

'Ashley,' she murmured, closing her eyes, calling him by his name for the first time.

'Come on, you two!'

Harry's voice brayed through the half-open doorway.

'Don't hog the pretty girls, Paget. Let someone else have a chance. Be the last waltz in half-an-hour and there are dozens of handsome young men waiting to partner Katharine.'

Ashley's arms dropped to his side. Katharine looked down at the floor, tears of frustration rushing up behind her eyelids.

Harry looked from one to the other and suddenly realised he had made a blunder.

'I say old boy, frightfully sorry and all that. Didn't mean to disturb anything. Forgot that you two were old friends.'

He coughed apologetically, suddenly ill at ease.

But Ashley immediately retrieved what could have been an awkward moment.

'You're quite right Harry,' he smiled. 'I mustn't hog Katharine. She and I can catch up on our news another time.'

'Well, if you're sure that's all right . . .' Harry demurred.

Ashley took Katharine's arm and gave it a reassuring squeeze.

'Quite all right,' he affirmed.

And they all three returned to the dance floor.

When the last waltz was announced, before Ashley could get to Katharine's side, she had already been claimed.

He stopped halfway across the floor and smiled

resignedly as she shrugged helplessly and slipped into the arms of her waiting partner.

Once it was over and the National Anthem had been played, Harry grabbed the four FANYs. Bundling them into their greatcoats, he hurried them to the jeep waiting to take them back to the cottage.

Katharine looked desperately around for Ashley. He had been cornered by the Colonel, and they were deep in conversation. She tried to catch his eye but to no avail.

She almost wept.

Chapter 14

Katharine slept badly that night and didn't appear for breakfast.

'For someone who didn't want to go to the knees-up,' Anne teased during lunch, 'you didn't waste any time once you got there making a bee-line for the star performer.'

Katharine didn't reply and Tatiana looked across at her anxiously.

'He's gorgeous, isn't he?' Anne went on rolling her eyes expressively. 'Hope he's on the train going up to London this afternoon.'

Katharine looked up abruptly.

'Why, when's he leaving?'

'Today, I guess. After all, he's done what he came to do. With any luck the jeep taking us to the station will pick him up on the way.'

It was Anne's weekend off and the jeep always dropped them at the station in time for the three o'clock train to London.

'What's the betting I get him to date me tonight?' she said archly.

'Might even persuade him for the whole weekend,' she provoked.

'Anne,' Tatiana reproved. 'I thought you were staying with Nadine?'

'Oh, she'll understand if I change my plans,' Anne said nonchalantly. 'A la guerre, comme à la guerre, n'est-ce pas?'

Katharine had never understood Anne's outrageous behaviour, or what appeared to her to be outrageous. And she was not at all sure how much was bluff and how much truth. Normally she was merely amused by it, but today she felt something tighten in her chest, and she wanted to be sick. Quickly excusing herself, she got up from the table.'

'And anyway,' Anne prattled on, 'Nadine's got other fish to fry. Didn't I tell you, Tat, she and Hugh Barrington are going great guns? He's due for a transfer and I wouldn't be surprised if they don't become engaged, or even get married.'

Anne's chirpy voice faded into the distance as Katharine made for the stairs.

Tatiana quickly excused herself and followed her friend.

Katharine was lying on her bed staring at the ceiling.

'Don't take any notice of Anne,' Tatiana soothed, poking her head round the door. 'You know what she's like. It's more talk than anything else.'

Katharine smiled, but didn't reply.

Tatiana walked in and sat down on the bed.

'I'm all right, honestly,' Katharine said. 'Maybe I drank too much last night.'

Tatiana didn't comment. But she knew this wasn't true. Katharine hardly ever touched alcohol.

'You go back down and have your pud.' Katharine urged. 'Tough on poor old Rickie if everyone walks out. I'm just going to rest till it's time to go back.'

'Perhaps I will,' Tatiana murmured, rising to her feet. 'Nicola's not feeling too well. Got a cold coming on and hasn't much appetite. And, as you say it's tough on Rickie. She goes to such lengths to feed us.'

Katharine waited anxiously for the telephone to ring.

But when the jeep came to pick up Anne at 2.15, she knew that Ashley wouldn't call her now. If he had wanted to get hold of her before leaving he would have done so earlier.

For the hundredth time that day she relived the events of the previous evening, wondering what would have happened had Harry not interrupted them in the hall. And she couldn't understand why Ashley had seemed so pleased to see her, if all he was going to do was walk out of her life once again without even saying goodbye.

After dinner that evening Rickie bundled them out of the kitchen, saying that they must be tired after their late night and she could very well manage the washing up on her own. Nicola retired to bed with three aspirins, two hot-water bottles and the promise from Rickie of milk and honey later in the evening. Katharine and Tatiana settled down drowsily in front of the roaring fire.

The biting wind had dropped in the night and the morning had brought a powdering of snow which had gradually deepened as the day wore on. It was now snowing heavily and bitterly cold outside.

Tatiana looked up from the newspaper she was glancing through.

'Did you hear footsteps?' she enquired.

Katharine opened one eye, half comatose.

'Didn't hear a thing,' she yawned, and closed her eyes again.

But at that moment there was a knock on the door.

Tatiana looked up.

'Told you so,' she triumphed. 'Whoever can it be, coming out on a night like this?'

They heard Rickie bustle out of the kitchen to open the door followed by voices in the hall.

'Katharine,' Rickie said, putting her head round the door. 'You have a visitor.'

And Ashley Paget walked in.

Katharine sat bolt upright.

She noticed that there was snow on his gingery moustache.

'I'll go and see if Nicola wants anything,' Tatiana mumbled, scrambling hastily to her feet. 'She might be ready for her hot milk.'

Katharine just sat staring, not saying a word.

'May I sit down?' he smiled.

His voice brought her back to earth.

'Oh, I'm so sorry,' she stammered 'Yes, please do.'

He sat on the sofa and held out his hands to the fire.

'How did you get here?' she murmured.

'I walked.'

'*Walked*. But it's about five miles.'

'I know,' he smiled. 'And five miles back. But if I wanted to see you, I had no option.'

He leant forward.

'And I very much wanted to see you.'

He patted the sofa.

'Won't you come and sit over here? You're so far away.'

Like a sleepwalker Katharine got up and sat down beside him.

'I don't understand,' she murmured, passing her hand wearily across her eyes. 'I thought you'd left on the afternoon train.'

His brow furrowed.

'Who told you that?'

'Anne.'

He laughed.

'She would have liked me to. Tell me, is she really the tramp she makes herself out to be?'

'No, I don't think so. It's all an act.'

Katharine paused.

'Would you like a drink? Perhaps something hot after your long walk in the snow?'

'All I want,' he said softly, putting his arm round her shoulders and drawing her down on the sofa until her head was resting on his shoulder, 'is you.'

Katharine lay back and closed her eyes.

'But,' he said gently brushing her hair with his lips. 'It seems to be very difficult.'

He raised his head and looked towards the door.

'How long before Tatiana pops back in? Or Miss Ricks comes to tell you it's time for bed?'

Katharine laughed.

'Somehow, knowing Tatiana, I don't think she *will* pop back in. And Rickie's a born matchmaker, she'll keep very much out of the way.'

She suddenly realised what she had said and sat up in confusion.

He smiled at her from his corner of the sofa and held out his arms.

'Come back,' he whispered. 'It feels so right to have you here.'

Ashley looked at her and a flash of lightning shot between them, quivering on the electric air.

Katharine allowed herself to be drawn back into his arms and, as she did so, she felt the tickle of his moustache brushing against her face. For a brief moment he caught his breath. And then he was holding her close to him, drinking in the tantalising scent of freshly fallen rose petals which clung to her silky skin.

And once again that wonderful feeling went racing

through her like sudden successive flashes of lightning on a hot summer night plummetting through the sky to pierce her slim young body. Her dormant unawakened emotions roared to the surface causing her to tingle and tremble in every nerve. And all resistance left her.

She leant towards him, her eyes closed, her lips parted expectantly. His mouth was firm and cool as it gently enveloped hers. His slow-moving kisses a drugging delight which rippled, quivered through her as she floated blissfully on a warm caressing sea of love. And the world narrowed down to just the two of them.

'Oh Katharine, Katharine,' he murmured. 'If you knew how many times I've dreamt of this moment.'

He drew her closer until it seemed that they were breathing as one person. And, as he did so, his kisses became more forceful, more passionate, leaving Katharine gasping at their intensity, all her emotions unleashed.

After what seemed to her to be a lifetime they drew apart.

Ashley sat up, smoothing down his hair and gazing into the fire. Katharine remained where she was, her head resting on the back of the plump sofa breathing in the faint perfume from his hair which clung to the worn fabric.

For a few moments the only sound was the hiss of the fire as a log dropped further into its depths.

Ashley felt in his pocket for his cigarettes. And then decided against it. He appeared to be ill at ease and Katharine reached out towards him, wondering what was wrong.

He turned and smiled at her in a strange detached fashion. Then, as if taking his courage in both hands, took a deep breath.

'There's something I want to say to you,' he said.

She looked at him, not understanding his sudden change of mood.

He tapped the pockets of his tunic again; pulled out his pipe, then replaced it. And sat staring intently into the fire, his hands clasped tightly together between his knees.

'This is going to sound very strange,' he said, nervously clenching and unclenching his fists. 'In fact, I've no idea how you're going to take it. It's almost Hollywoodian in its brashness.'

He paused and took a deep breath.

'But I'm terrified of someone doing a Harry on me again and you being snatched away for good this time.'

Katharine was by now completely bewildered.

Suddenly he turned and looked her straight in the eyes.

'Katharine,' he blurted out. 'Will you marry me?'

She was so stunned she was unable to reply. But he mistook the meaning of her silence.

'I know it's ridiculous,' he said. 'In fact it's lunatic.'

He unclasped his hands and spread them in an expressive gesture.

'But everything that's happening at this time is lunatic. Normally I'd get to know you, woo you, have an engagement, do things properly. But there just isn't time.'

He took hold of both her hands in his and squeezed them until she almost cried out in pain.

'I don't want to go away again until I know that you're my wife. That I've got you to come back to when all this carnage is over.'

He loosened the terrible pressure on her hands and smiled down at her.

'Then we can have a proper wedding if you like; page-boys, bridesmaids, the bells ringing at St Margaret's.'

Ashley put his head on one side pleadingly.

'But in the meantime could we just get married as quickly as possible. I seem to have waited so long. All those months since I was arrested it was your face which was there in front of me, willing me to come through.'

He smiled ruefully and released her hands when she made no reply.

'I know what you must be thinking,' he said quietly, once again gazing into the fire. 'We hardly know each other. But I've thought about you so much . . . and longed for you. I seem to know you so well.'

'Ashley,' Katharine cried, cradling his face in her hands. 'I don't want a wedding at St Margaret's. I only want *you*.'

For a split second he looked at her as if he couldn't believe what he was hearing. Then a cry, almost a whoop, of joy tore from his lips and he pulled her towards him.

In the hall the telephone rang. But they didn't hear it.

A few minutes later there was a gentle tap on the door and Rickie, muffled in her old red flannel dressing-gown, a hot-water bottle dangling from one hand, popped her head round.

'That was a call for Major Paget,' she beamed. 'He's to ring The Vineyard when he's ready to leave and a jeep will come and fetch him.'

Ashley smoothed down his hair and straightened his tie as he hurriedly jumped to his feet.

'But how did they know I was here?' he enquired.

'I've no idea,' Rickie twinkled. 'But I imagine the proverbial little bird must have told them.'

They grinned at each other across the room and an instant rapport sprang up between them.

'But do tell me,' Ashley queried. 'What did Harry say when he telephoned? I presume it *was* Harry?'

'You presume right,' Rickie beamed. 'To give you a verbatim report, Harry said: "Tell that ass Paget to ring for a jeep when he's ready to come back. He's no longer a boy scout and he's past the age of playing Rudolph the Red Nosed Reindeer."'

They all three burst out laughing.

'It's time I went,' Ashley said.

He smiled at Rickie, silhouetted in the doorway.

'Would you mind awfully telephoning for a jeep?'

'I didn't congratulate you on getting your majority,' Katharine said prosaically as the door closed behind Rickie's ample form

'Promotion comes quickly in wartime,' Ashley grinned.

He drew Katharine to him

'I have to leave tomorrow,' he murmured into her shining chestnut hair. 'But I should be back in London by the end of the week.'

'Where are you going?' she cut in.

He looked down at her and tweaked her nose.

'Ask no questions and you'll hear no lies.'

Then seeing the sudden panic shadow Katharine's face, he smiled.

'Don't worry, it's nothing exciting. Quite routine in fact. Can you come up to London next weekend, or shall I come down here?'

'It's Tatiana's weekend off,' she demurred. 'Mine's the week after.'

Ashley's brow furrowed.

'Do you think . . .'

But Katharine put a finger on his lips.

'I don't think, I know. Tatiana will change with me.'

'God bless Tatiana,' he smiled, sighing with relief.

'God bless her indeed,' Katharine breathed.

He walked across the room still holding tightly to her hand.

'I must go,' he said. 'Not fair to keep the driver out on a night like this.'

'Katharine,' he breathed, turning round and taking her in his arms again. 'I can't believe it.'

She closed her eyes and snuggled close to him, content just to feel his strong arms around her.

'Neither can I,' she murmured.

In the distance the crunch of a car's wheels against the snow came nearer.

He shrugged himself into his British warm* and picked up his beret. It was maroon-coloured.

'You're no longer with the racket?' Katharine enquired wide-eyed. 'I thought you'd be having a safe job down here or somewhere now that you're blown.*'

He smiled down at her.

'Don't be too impressed by the beret. I've been seconded to the Airborne Forces for a while.'

But Katharine was not impressed. She was afraid.

'Ashley,' she cried, grabbing hold of his lapels.

'It's all right,' he soothed, gently disentangling her. 'I'm a survivor. Haven't you noticed?'

But she wasn't convinced.

'You can tempt fate once too often,' she beseeched.

'I'm not tempting anything,' he whispered. 'Not now that I've so much to stay alive for.'

They looked at each other for a long minute, oblivious of the jeep's engine throbbing outside in the snow.

'Our tune is right,' he whispered at last.

She looked up at him in surprise. The jeep's engine stopped and a soft tap sounded on the front door.

'Last night,' he smiled. 'Our first dance together.'

'The dearest things I know are what you are,' he sang softly.

He held her close, his hand stroking her hair.

'Very soon my darling "I'll know that moment divine when all the things you are are mine." Nothing else matters.'

And, swiftly kissing the tip of her nose, he switched off the light and walked out into the cold, starry night.

Chapter 15

They were married a month later.

After his departure from Group R, Ashley followed up his sudden proposal of marriage with no less than five letters, within as many days, each one repeating and confirming his love for her. And his joy at their approaching marriage.

Katharine was so full of this newfound happiness, so much in love that when she arrived at Goudhurst for her weekend leave, on the Friday following her meeting with Ashley, Lavinia knew immediately that something had happened. Her niece was completely transformed. Wisely, she did not immediately comment.

But as soon as Elsie left the room after serving dinner, Katharine, unable to contain herself any longer, shyly told Lavinia that she was going to be married.

Her aunt stopped serving the vegetables, the spoon arrested in mid-air.

'Darling, that's wonderful,' she breathed.

She placed the spoon back in the dish and handed Katharine her plate.

'But to whom?'

'Ashley Paget,' Katharine said shyly.

Lavinia raised her eyebrows enquiringly. The name meant nothing to her.

'Do you remember I told you I had met a young

officer on the train going to Perth? He telephoned me here a few months later. His family are friends of the Hamiltons.'

She paused and looked across at her aunt, her face radiant with happiness, a soft lustrous light shining in her beautiful eyes.

'It was the evening of the Russian ball. You gave him Tamara's number and he telephoned me there the next morning.'

Lavinia's brow creased.

'Yes, now you mention it, I do remember something . . .'

She looked up sharply.

'Katharine, have you been seeing this young man for the last two years without any of us knowing anything about it?'

Katharine looked down at her plate in some confusion.

'He's been abroad and only just got back.'

Talking of her romance with Ashley like this, with someone who'd never met him, made the whole thing sound preposterous. And she knew what must be going through Lavinia's mind.

'We met again . . . and he's asked me to marry him.'

'But darling,' Lavinia cried. '*When* did you meet again? You didn't say anything about it last month when you were here.'

Katharine didn't immediately reply. She knew that what she was going to say would sound the height of lunacy to her aunt.

'Last week,' she whispered.

Lavinia laid down her knife and fork and leant back in her chair, eyeing Katharine strangely.

'And you've not seen him in between?'

Katharine shook her head.

Her aunt leant forward.

'Darling, do you *really* think that two meetings are sufficient basis for a marriage?'

Katharine bit her lip tightly in an attempt to control the tears squeezing themselves behind her eyelids.

'No,' she whispered. 'Not when one thinks about it logically.'

She looked up and Lavinia saw her sudden pallor, the gold in her eyes dampened by the glistening tears.

'But nothing's logical at the moment. *Nothing.*'

She rubbed a hand across her eyes.

'Ever since that day in the train I've not been able to get Ashley out of my mind. I've tried to, Aunt Lavinia. I've met other men. But no one matched up to him . . . And apparently it was the same for him.'

She sniffed and fished in her pocket for a hankie.

'When we met again last week after all this time . . .'

She rubbed the hankie round her face and blew her nose.

'It just felt like coming home.'

'I see,' Lavinia said picking up her knife and fork. 'And when do you intend to be married?'

Katharine smiled.

'As soon as possible,' she breathed, the beautiful golden light returning to her unusual eyes. 'Ashley is coming to London this weekend and we're going to make arrangements. He'll telephone me as soon as he arrives.'

'Shall I be allowed to meet him?' Lavinia teased.

Katharine leapt from the table and ran round to her aunt's side.

'Oh darling,' she cried, throwing her arms round her neck. 'Of course you will.'

She leant her cheek against Lavinia's.

'And I know you'll love him just as much as I do.'

Lavinia looked up at Katharine's radiant face and knew that there was no more to be said.

Ashley rang at ten o'clock that evening.

Katharine had been sitting on tenterhooks in front of the drawing-room fire, pretending to read a book for the past two hours.

She leapt to her feet and, without waiting for Elsie or Myrtle to shuffle from the kitchen and answer the call, rushed into the hall and picked up the receiver.

As soon as she heard his voice, that same wonderful feeling swept through her body, setting her pulses racing.

'Darling,' Ashley breathed.

But she was so breathless with excitement, that no words came.

'Katharine,' he said anxiously.

'It's me,' she babbled, grammar going to the wind.

He laughed.

'For a moment, I was beginning to wonder. Look, I only have a few minutes. I shan't be in London until after lunch. Can you meet me at Gunter's for tea? I'll do my best to be there by four, maybe even a little earlier.'

'I'll be waiting,' Katharine breathed, her eyes shining in the darkness of the hall. Oh . . . Ashley.'

She could feel him smiling down the line.

'Love you Kate,' he whispered.

And then the line went dead.

She stood leaning against the wall for a long time, the receiver clasped to her chest, his last three words ringing in her ears.

The only other person who had ever called her Kate was her father.

* * *

As the light from the short winter's day gradually faded on that damp January afternoon, Ashley gave her a ring.

They were sitting in the window at Gunters sipping China tea, looking out on the bare trees in Hyde Park and watching the Saturday afternoon crowds sauntering down Park Lane, when he snapped open a small leather box to reveal a hoop of diamonds.

'Do you know what it means?' he asked, holding the little blue box on the palm of his hand.

Katharine had shaken her head, too numb with happiness to reply.

In the language of diamonds, each one represents a word: 'will you be my wife?'

He put a finger under her chin and forced her to look at him.

'Will you?'

Still unable to speak, her eyes spoke for her.

He slowly removed the ring from its box and picking up her left hand placed it on the third finger.

'I know I asked you before,' he whispered. 'But I just wanted to be absolutely sure.'

He closed his hand over hers and they sat there, oblivious of the waitresses gliding quietly by on the thick carpets, trays of tea and hot scones in their hands.

'And it even fits,' he laughed at last.

He felt in his pocket and looked at her with a mischievous grin.

'I got this at the same time,' he went on. 'Just in case your answer was still the same.'

He snapped open an identical square blue leather box and there, nestled in its bed of velvet, was a plain gold band.

Ashley grimaced.

'I'm afraid there wasn't much choice,' he added. 'No frills in wartime. We can only have what they call utility wedding rings in nine carat gold.'

He gently took her hand again.

'But never mind. After the war I'll take you to Cartiers and you can choose whatever ring you like. And we'll get married all over again.'

Katharine's eyes filled with tears.

'I don't think I'd ever want to change my wedding ring, Ashley,' she choked. 'There'd be too many happy memories attached to it.'

She looked lovingly down at the slim gold band, the unshed tears sparkling at the corners of her eyes. Ashley noticed that her thick dark lashes curled up at the corners like a gull's wing.

He shook his head unbelievingly.

'I can't believe it's really happening,' he murmured, smiling across at her. 'I've imagined this so many times . . . and now it's actually come true.'

Walking out beside him into Park Lane Katharine felt as if she were living a dream. She gazed up adoringly at the tall handsome man at her side, wearing his maroon beret at a jaunty angle, and almost burst with pride.

Ashley hailed a taxi and, as they drew away from the kerb and bowled down Park Lane in the direction of Piccadilly, she removed her glove and held up her hand, admiring her ring.

He smiled down at her fondly. Then taking her face in his hands gently brushed her soft lips.

'Did I ever tell you that your mouth looks like a full-blown rose,' he whispered.

Katharine closed her eyes, and clung to him. But they had arrived outside Lillywhites and the taxi rumbled to a stop.

As they strolled towards Eros, an old flower seller

sitting on the stone parapet surrounding the statue, her basket by her side, held out a posy.

'Violets sir,' she pleaded. 'Lovely violets. Buy a bunch for the pretty lady.'

Ashley felt in his pocket for change and, taking the flowers, pinned them to Katharine's coat.

'Just right for later on,' he said.

'Why,' Katharine enquired. 'What's happening later on?'

'I've got tickets for the theatre.'

'Lovely,' she enthused. 'What to see?'

'As a matter of fact, I've got a box. Thought it was worth seeing it in style, the title's so appropriate.'

'But what *is* it?' Katharine pleaded.

'A Ralph Lynn Robertson Hare comedy called *Is your honeymoon really necessary*?'

They looked at each other and burst out laughing.

By the time he finally dropped her in Kensington it was well after midnight.

'I won't come in,' he said as he put her key in the lock and opened the door. 'And I promise I'll put on my best bib and tucker tomorrow to meet your family.'

Katharine clung to him as the waiting taxi purred outside.

'It's not for much longer my darling,' he whispered, gently disentangling her. 'Then we won't have to say goodnight ever again.'

And, bending, he kissed her closed lids.

* * *

Lunch the following day was a sumptuous affair. Olga really surpassed herself, in spite of the rationing.

Lavinia travelled up from Goudhurst and by the time it was over and Ashley and Katharine were preparing to leave, he had won the hearts and approval of them all.

As he propelled her along the crowded dimly-lit station at Waterloo to catch her train back to Group R that evening, a dreadful feeling of desolation swept over her.

Stark evidence of war was everywhere.

Weary soldiers and sailors, kitbags slung across their shoulders, slouched along the platform, some with tearful girls clinging to their arms. In the relative privacy of dark corners couples were locked together in what for some could be their last embrace. Others hung awkwardly around open carriage doors, longing for the train to go. Yet terrified of the emptiness the back of its clacking carriages, pulled out of sight by the trail of smoke, would leave behind.

People were laughing too loudly, mechanically, saying anything which came into their heads. Stupid, inane things. Meaningless phrases spawned by the war like 'ta ra' or 'atta girl'. Banalities such as 'might even snow' or 'looks like rain'. Anything which would keep away the terrible spectre of imminent parting. No one daring to voice their innermost thoughts, much less pronounce the ominous word 'goodbye'.

Katharine clung to Ashley's arm as he gazed up at the departure board then, with a purposeful step, threaded his way to the platform and walked along its length, peering into the overflowing compartments in an attempt to find her a seat.

'Ah, here we are,' he said at last, triumphantly throwing open a compartment door. 'Just one seat left.'

He looked up at the window and grinned at her.

'It's a non-smoker too.'

Taking her gloves he placed them on the empty middle seat.

A crusty old Colonel, furiously rustling the pages of *The Sunday Times*, which he was incapable of reading in the dim blue light, glared at them both.

'He didn't look very pleased,' Katharine whispered as Ashley jumped down on to the platform.

'No, he didn't,' Ashley grinned, 'perhaps he was reserving that seat for his feet.'

She giggled, and felt for his hand.

'Still got ten minutes,' he said, peering at the station clock.

They meandered in silence for a few seconds, weaving their way through the crowds lingering, dawdling or hurrying to find a seat.

'I like your Aunt Lavinia,' Ashley said at last.

'Yes, she's sweet,' Katharine replied. 'Actually she's my great-aunt, my only living relative on this side of the Channel. I'm an only child and my mother was too, so I don't have any aunts and uncles over here.'

Ashley squeezed her hand.

'But where do the Wellesleys come in, and General Voronovsky? I was completely lost. Are they part of your family?'

Katharine smiled.

'No, not really. The Prince is Lavinia's father-in-law and Tamara is her sister-in-law, so Tatiana is her niece.'

Ashley let out a low whistle.

'So she's not Miss Brookes-Barker?'

'Oh, it's all very complicated,' Katharine murmured.

Ashley grinned.

'So it seems.'

'She preferred to revert to her maiden name after the Revolution. I'll explain it all to you some other time.'

Ashley's brow rutted.

'But why does the General refer to you as his granddaughter?'

'After my mother died he asked me to consider him as my grandfather. That's why I call him Deduschka, like Tatiana does.'

'Complicater and complicater,' Ashley murmured. 'I *have* got myself an interesting wife.'

He smiled down at her.

'He was really touched when you asked him to give you away.'

'Yes,' Katharine smiled dreamily.

She turned impulsively towards him.

'Oh Ashley,' she breathed. 'In less than a month we'll be married.'

They stood facing each other and the dreary, poorly-lit station, the crowds pushing past, the porters' hoarse shouts, the rattling barrows, the hisses of steam from the waiting engine disappeared. And all they could see was the other's face.

But at that moment a raucous voice shouted 'All aboard' and the hissing became more insistent and prolonged.

Ashley bent towards her and she stood on tiptoe, eager for his embrace. He kissed her hungrily with hard, almost cruel passion.

But the guard had blown his whistle and was now raising his flag.

Dragging her arms from around his neck Ashley grabbed her hand and raced back to her compartment just as a porter slammed the door in their faces. Tugging it open, he pushed her inside. The train snorted and began to slowly draw away from the platform, its windows crammed with heads and furiously waving arms.

Katharine dragged frantically at the worn leather

belt and the window slammed down. Leaning out, she grasped his hand and he ran a few steps along the platform holding tightly to hers. But the crowd, frantically waving or standing stiff and lifeless, blank misery written on their faces, was too dense. And he had to let go.

The train gathered speed, its engine belching out acrid black smoke which coiled backwards then fanned out behind it momentarily enveloping him.

Katharine panicked. She knew he was there, but she could no longer see him. Then, as suddenly as it had blotted him from her sight, the smoke cleared and she caught a last glimpse of him, his hand raised to his beret in a half salute.

She remained standing at the window, a terrible loneliness enveloping her like the dirty grey cloud which had swallowed up Ashley, until the train clattered round a bend and the station was lost in the smoke's thick black blanket. And the inky darkness of wartime London was all that was left.

Katharine slowly pulled the strap and the window creaked into its closed position. As she fell listlessly back on to her seat, the air-raid siren wailed. The dull boom of ack-ack* fire echoed in the distance. And the feeble blue light in the compartment was immediately extinguished.

Chapter 16

Katharine's prediction had come true.

Lavinia was charmed by Ashley. And, all misgivings thrown to the winds, entered into preparations for the wedding with great gusto.

Ashley and Katharine had at first thought of having a small London wedding, no veil, no bridesmaids, no fuss, at the King's Chapel of the Savoy.

But after their Sunday lunch with the Voronovskys, Lavinia took over and decided that it would be at the old church in Goudhurst with a reception at Greystones afterwards.

'A country wedding with the wedding breakfast at home is so much less formal,' she insisted. 'And you must wear your great-grandmother's wedding dress.'

'But what if it doesn't fit?' Katharine wailed, when faced with the *fait accompli.*

'Myrtle will see that it does,' Lavinia remarked blithely. 'She's a very able seamstress.'

She smiled pleadingly across at her niece.

'Can you imagine how disappointed Elsie and Myrtle would be if they weren't able to help with your reception?'

And Katharine capitulated.

The day before the wedding, Katharine was introduced to her future family for the first time.

The Wellesleys and the Prince were staying overnight with Lavinia and Katharine at Greystones where Elsie, Myrtle and Mrs Smithers were in their element, bustling about preparing the next day's wedding breakfast.

Lavinia had booked six of the eight rooms for Ashley and his guests at the picturesque Golden Eagle next door to the church, And had also arranged for a family dinner party to be held there on the eve of the wedding.

The Golden Eagle was reputed to have been a monastery in the fourteenth century, and a meeting place for smugglers four hundred years later. It was now a low-ceilinged, cosy, country hotel with creaking floors, a large open fireplace and blackened beams both inside and out.

When Katharine walked down the stairs that Friday evening, her only piece of jewelry a small gold Croix de Lorraine* pinned to the collar of the simple lime-green silk frock, which she had worn to the "knees up" on the evening she and Ashley had been reunited, he was waiting for her.

His eyes misted over as he held out his arms.

Elsie and Myrtle, who had been eagerly awaiting their first glimpse of the bridegroom, ogled approvingly from behind the half-closed door leading to the kitchen.

But, as she slid happily into his embrace, Katharine did not even notice them.

She had eyes for no one but Ashley.

Ashley's father was to marry them in the little village church the following morning.

'Isn't he a bishop or something?' Katharine had enquired with awe.

'Or something would be more accurate,' Ashley had laughed. 'No, my precious love, he's not a bishop, and I very much doubt that he ever will be. He's the Rural Dean, Rector of a string of country parishes in Buckinghamshire. And that's the way he likes it.'

'So I don't have to kiss his ring or call him my Lord?'

Ashley roared with laughter.

'You do have some very strange ideas about the Church of England. Are you sure you wouldn't be more at home if we got married in the French Church in Soho?'

His eyes twinkled.

'Or even the Russian Orthodox Church?'

Katharine shook her head.

'I'm marrying an Englishman. I'm going to be English from now on.'

'Please don't,' he said suddenly becoming serious. 'It's because you're so different that I love you.'

And he had folded her in his arms and kissed her with such passion that she was left gasping.

That evening before their wedding, he kissed her in just the same way.

'My family is waiting to meet you,' he whispered. 'And I can't wait to introduce you.'

He released her and held her at arm's length.

'I'm so proud of you.'

* * *

'I *do* like your father-in-law,' Lavinia enthused as they all walked into the drawing-room to review the evening before going to bed. *Such* a charming man.'

She threw a couple of logs on to the dying embers, stirring the fire into a comfortable blaze.

'And what a pleasant person Ashley's sister-in-law is. How *very* sad that she lost her husband. She tells me she has two little boys.'

'Yes,' Katharine replied. 'They're quite young. I believe Ashley said they were four and five. Guy and Hope came over from America in the summer of '39 to introduce the boys to their English grandparents. Then war broke out, Guy joined up and was killed at Dunkirk. And now poor Hope is stuck here.'

'What was Ashley's brother doing in America?' Tamara enquired.

'He was studying for his PhD at Harvard. Hope's father is a professor there. That's how they met. I imagine she'll go back to Boston to her family once the war is over.'

'And who is Colonel Masters?' Lavinia continued. 'Why has Ashley chosen him to be best man? Is he an old friend?'

Katharine and Tatiana exchanged looks.

'I think he's a very good friend of Ashley's,' Katharine answered evasively. 'Had Guy not been killed he would have been best man.'

'Of course,' Lavinia acquiesced.

She looked over to where the Prince was sitting bolt upright in his chair, his hands folded on the silver knob of his cane, his head nodding jerkily as he fought against sleep.

'Good gracious me,' she exclaimed, getting up. 'We must all go to bed. We don't want the bride looking washed out tomorrow.'

And she began shooing everyone in the direction of the stairs.

But, for Lavinia, the day began earlier than she had expected.

At ten-past seven the telephone rang.

'Darling Lavinia,' an excited voice echoed down the line. 'I'm at the Ritz. I've just arrived by the night train and I'm going to have breakfast and change into all my finery. But *do* remind me what time the wedding is.'

Only one person could ring out of the blue like that,

not announce herself and expect whoever answered the telephone to immediately know who it was at the other end.

'Flora?' Lavinia groped sleepily.

'Yes,' Flora babbled on. 'Isn't it thrilling. I'm *so* excited and *so* happy for Katharine. To think that this beautiful romance all began at Ardnakil . . .'

'But Flora,' Lavinia, now wide awake and sitting up, cut in. 'We never expected you to make that long journey.'

'Oh Lavinia, you couldn't keep me away. Dorothy Farquharson would have come too, after all Ashley is Fergus' cousin, but she's just had another baby, two weeks ago. A little boy, absolutely adorable.'

'Katharine will be delighted to see you,' Lavinia cut in again. 'The wedding is at 11.00 at the church in Goudhurst.'

'Splendid,' Flora enthused. 'I'll get a taxi.'

'I very much doubt that you'll get a taxi to bring you out here,' Lavinia demurred.

Though knowing Flora she wouldn't have been surprised if she managed it.

'Better take a train, there's one which arrives just before ten. I'll arrange for a taxi to meet you and bring you to the house. How long can you stay?'

'Oh, I shall probably take the night train back. Just a rush visit to see my dear Katharine married. I can't stay away from my darling little baby for too long.'

Flora had given birth to a daughter just before Christmas.

'Lavinia you *must* come to Ardnakil and meet Cristobel. She's *gorgeous*, so different from the boys as babies. And please persuade Katharine to come with you.'

Flora appeared to be totally oblivious of the fact that there was a war on.

'Oh, just *look* at the time. I must go or I'll never be ready. Goodbye darling, see you very soon.'

The phone clicked and went dead.

As she replaced the receiver there was a tap at the door and Myrtle entered with a tray of tea.

She looked the picture of gloom.

'Whatever's the matter?' Lavinia asked, propping herself against her lace-edged pillows and reaching for her bed-jacket, as Myrtle went to draw the curtains.

Myrtle turned round, one hand on the tasselled cord.

'It's raining Madam,' she wailed as if she were announcing that they'd all been swallowed up in the night by an earthquake.

And with a dramatic gesture she tugged at the cord and swished back the curtains.

A lowering grey sky, hung with sullen milky clouds sprang into view. And a white layer of mist, lying over the garden, pressed against the wet window panes.

Lavinia glanced up at it disinterestedly.

'Oh, is that all,' she remarked, pouring out her tea.

Myrtle stood rooted to the spot, her wide-open mouth like a question mark.

'But Madam,' she mooed at last.

'Come now Myrtle,' Lavinia chided. 'Let's be sensible. It *is* the last day of February, we can't expect a heat wave.'

'But Miss Katharine's wedding . . .' Myrtle bleated.

'Miss Katharine will get married whether it rains or shines,' Lavinia cut in briskly. 'And *that*'s all that matters to her.'

Myrtle's face, still full of doom, framed against the drizzly grey morning was the colour and texture of raw tripe. Her overall expression suggested that she had spent the night sipping bismuth in an attempt to come to terms with an acute attack of indigestion. Looking at her, Lavinia wondered how Myrtle had ever managed to produce someone as cheerful and presentable as Bert.

She glanced down at the little gold carriage clock on her bedside table.

Only another three hours.

'Come along now, Myrtle,' she said crisply, 'off you go, otherwise you won't be ready in time to go to the church. And you never know, Miss Katharine's dress might need a stitch or two at the last minute.'

When it had been removed from the layers of tissue paper, in which it had been lying for years, the veil had disintegrated. But the resourceful Lavinia had unearthed a white lace mantilla mellowed with age, like the beautiful hooped satin dress, to a soft shade of cream. And, to hold it in place, Tamara had lent a small pearl and diamond tiara. It exactly matched the tiny garlands of pearls holding the flounces of the lace overskirt.

As the clock in the hall at Greystones struck 10.30, a starry-eyed Katharine walked carefully down the stairs, a posy of tiny white winter rosebuds clutched in her hands.

She looked round at the little group gathered in the drawing-room to greet her.

Tamara was wearing a lilac velvet gown under her sable coat, a swathe of feathers wreathing her head. Lavinia was also wearing furs, though with a more classical cloche hat. And Flora, dear Flora, was splendid in a sweeping maroon picture hat and dress to match under a stark black coat with a flutter of diamonds pinned to her lapel.

Realising how much love and care had gone into the preparation of this her wedding day, Katharine's eyes misted over as the Prince, magnificent in his full regalia as a general in the old Imperial Russian Army, offered her his arm.

The village had turned out in force and the little church was full.

Mr Popham, who besides being the local butcher and ARP chief was also church warden, had forgiven Katharine's blackout offences and, donning black coat and striped trousers, had shut his shop for the morning.

When Katharine entered, diminutive on the Prince's arm, a subdued gasp rippled through the assembled congregation. The old general marched, upright and firm-footed, looking neither to right nor left until they reached the altar where Ashley was waiting for her.

She turned and handed her little posy to Tatiana, who had followed her down the aisle in the white satin dress, dotted with rosebuds, which she had worn to the Russian New Year's ball.

The organ sighed to a stop and, with a rustle, the congregation sank down on to the old polished pews.

Ashley's father gave her a beautiful smile, and the short simple service began.

Katharine realised later that she remembered very little about her wedding.

Her responses and vows were uttered in such a low whisper that her father-in-law had to bend his head in order to hear them.

Ashley's responses, on the other hand, rang out loud and clear.

Once or twice he looked anxiously down at her. But she smiled radiantly up at him, teardrops glistening like diamonds on her dark lashes.

She was so overcome with emotion that she was unable to join in the hymns. Though she did recall Ashley singing in a deep, strong voice 'The King of love my shepherd is', which he had especially asked for because it had been his mother's favourite. Lawrence

Masters had read something from the Bible about God wanting us to know how broad and high and deep His love is.

And then, as if he were speaking just to the two of them, Ashley's father had echoed the Bible's words in his address saying that even the terrible carnage of man fighting man could not separate us from the love of God, as long as we believed and trusted in him.

When she left the church on her husband's arm the drizzle which had greeted them when they arrived had turned into a downpour.

But she hardly noticed.

Ashley had put the thin utility nine-carat gold ring on her finger thereby making her his wife. She had gladly, if slightly inaudibly, promised to love, honour and obey him until death should part them. And he had promised to love and cherish her.

Nothing else mattered.

They stood in the church porch, their guests and family crowding around them, smiling, congratulating, embracing. Then, with the rain lashing down in great sweeping brooms, Ashley caught his wife round the waist and, heading into it, ran swiftly with her to the waiting car.

Leaning forward to wave as they splashed away from the church porch, Katharine suddenly felt overwhelmed with such an immense happiness that she laid her head back against the car's leather cushions and laughed hysterically out of sheer joy.

It was only later that she realised that, in the hasty whirl of preparations, one detail had been forgotten.

There had been no photographer present.

Those beautiful, unforgettable moments, heavy with emotion and meaning, had not been recorded. In less than an hour it was over, vanished like a puff of wind.

And there was no tangible reminder, except in her heart.

At the time, they had laughed.

It hadn't seemed important.

Nothing mattered beyond the fact that they were married. They were together and had been given three days during which no one could separate them, no one could tear them apart. When there would be no good-byes.

Three days and four nights of complete happiness. Of unclouded rapture made all the more precious because it was snatched out of the ugly mire of blood and fear and slaughter which dominated England.

But, looking back in later years, Katharine was to wonder if that simple oversight on her wedding day had not, perhaps, been an omen.

Chapter 17

'Are you going to spend the whole night wandering round the room in that luscious negligé?'

Ashley was lying on the bed, his hands clasped behind his head, watching Katharine with amusement.

She coloured and sat down on the little stool in front of the dressing table. This was the first time she and Ashley had really been alone together. And she suddenly felt embarrassed and shy.

Ever since they had left Greystones after the wedding breakfast Katharine had been floating on cloud nine.

It had been a beautiful wedding.

Everything had been perfect. From the time she set foot inside the old church on the Prince's arm to the moment she walked back down the aisle as Ashley's wife.

She smiled to herself, reliving that wonderful day once again in her mind.

'Dear Flora, how good it was of her to make that long journey from Perth just to be there.'

And she felt overwhelmed, almost choked by so much love, so much happiness.

'Darling,' Ashley said, getting up from the bed in concern. 'Whatever's the matter? You're not going to cry are you?'

She shook her head, unable to speak.

He leant his cheek against hers and looked at their reflection in the mirror.

Katharine reached up a hand and touched his.

With infinite tenderness he slid his fingers beneath her hair and undid the clasp of the single row of perfectly-matched pearls, which Lavinia had taken from her own jewel-case that morning and fastened round Katharine's neck.

She shivered as the pearls slid smoothly across her skin and snaked silently downwards, coiling sensually into her outstretched palm. His touch had sparked that same thrill, and it shuddered voluptuously through her.

Ashley gently lifted her from the stool and drew her towards him. His hand caressed the back of her neck and then slipped downwards slowly rotating over her shoulders and back.

'I must say,' he whispered into her hair, 'I much prefer you like this to when you're in uniform.'

He moved his fingers caressingly towards her shoulders, then carefully peeled off the negligé. It slithered down her body to lie a pool of shimmering satin at her feet.

'You're so beautiful,' he said hoarsely, as she stood there before him in her flimsy nightdress. A froth of ribbon and lace moulding the contour of her young breasts.

He picked her up in his arms and carried her to the bed. Then stood gazing down at her.

And suddenly, Katharine was no longer embarrassed, no longer shy, no longer afraid. She felt as if she had known Ashley all her life, knew everything about him and was already a part of him. Holding out her arms, she raised her face expectantly to his.

When she awoke she could not at first remember

where she was. Raising herself on one elbow, her mind still clogged with sleep, in the half-light she saw Ashley's blond head on the pillow beside her. Remembrance came flooding back, and with it the knowledge that they still had three whole days before them.

She lay contentedly beside him, watching him as he slept. Recalling the tender moments of their hours together, the emotions he had awakened in her which still lingered like the scent of a beautiful perfume lingers after the person has gone.

He had been so patient, so loving. Gently leading her along paths of previously unexplored rapture. Awakening sensations in her which she had never known, never even dreamed existed. There had been no hurt, no fear. Only a tender rippling joy as a new love between them awakened and blossomed. And she had felt herself floating away on a sparkling sea of pure delight.

They had come into possession of an enchanted garden far from the war-torn world outside. A place where they both had so much to give, to discover about each other. A place where words were superfluous.

Katharine nestled back into the shelter of Ashley's arms and gazed at the stars glittering in the dark night sky. They were unusually bright and looked as though they had slid down from the heavens to be a little closer to them. She felt completely happy, with a happiness which many never discover, as she lay beside him listening to the steady beat of his heart, warm and replete in the afterglow of love.

She sighed deeply shutting her mind to the future, refusing to think beyond Wednesday when the gates of their enchanted garden would clang shut and they would find themselves back on the outside. For the moment she was content to know that he was there. That she could watch him as he slept, and hear his voice when he wakened.

Over the years she had ached for Zag, for Rowena, for Morocco. But now her longing was over. She had found in Ashley all that she could ever have wished for. She knew that whatever pain or anguish the future might hold, she had touched the summit of perfect happiness. And even if her life were to end tomorrow, she would die content.

Katharine moved slightly and felt his arms tighten around her. She gingerly turned her head and watched him sleep, trying to imprint on her mind every angle of his face. To record every inflection of his deep voice so that she could store them, sharp and distinct in her memory. Never forget one detail, but always have them before her through the long bleak days and weeks when she knew he would not be there.

The blackness which had dyed the night sky was fading, leaving behind a faint mist floating off the sea like a diaphonous chiffon scarf.

As the dawn merged sea and sky together in a clear translucent grey light, he stirred in his sleep then awoke.

Katharine lay back in his arms, her hand slightly raised, gazing in wonderment at the pale-orange band on her finger, the outward symbol of her marriage to Ashley.

'I'm Katharine Paget,' she breathed.

Ashley turned over and smiled at her.

'Like my mother,' he said.

Katharine frowned.

'But her name wasn't Katharine.'

'No,' he smiled. 'It was Catriona, which is Scots for Katharine.'

Katharine smiled dreamily.

'If we have a little girl I'd like to call her Catriona,' she murmured. 'It's such a pretty name.'

'We can have several if you wish,' Ashley grinned. 'Starting now.'

He sat up and leant over her.

But she caught his face in her hands.

'It's strange to think I'm not Katharine de Montval any more. All that is now behind me.'

He propped himself on one elbow and looked down at her quizzically.

'No regrets?'

'No regrets,' she whispered, drawing his head back onto her shoulder.

A tremor went through her as she felt the weight of his body upon her, the deep-gold hair on his chest brushing her bosom.

'Ashley,' she murmured.

'Yes, Mrs Paget.'

His voice came in a stifled whisper.

'There is just one regret. Everything would have been perfect yesterday if only my parents could have been there.'

He rolled on to his side and cradled her head in his arms.

'I know my mother couldn't have been with us, after what happened. But my father could have.'

Ashley gently stroked her cheek.

'I'm sure he's alive somewhere and that he will come back, in spite of what everybody says.'

She turned towards him pleadingly.

'I want him to know you Ashley. I want him to share my happiness.'

For a moment he remained silent. Then, to her surprise, got out of bed and walking across to the window stood looking thoughtfully down at the gardens below.

The mist was drifting lazily across the damp, black earth. It rose in graceful curls above the trees to finally merge with the grey-tipped clouds into the rainbow-coloured dawn.

'Your father does know me Katharine,' he said quietly.

She sat straight up in bed.

'What do you mean?'

'I met him before the war when I spent a year in North Africa doing relief work after I left University.'

Katharine frowned.

'But why didn't you tell me before?'

'Because I didn't know. In Algiers, he was Brother Xavier, working with the Pères Blancs. Not Xavier de Montval.'

Katharine fell back on her pillows.

'So it *was* true what those letters said,' she breathed.

Ashley turned away from the window and lit a cigarette.

'I don't know what the letters said,' he went on, coming to sit on the bed beside her. 'But now you're my wife I think you've a right to know.'

He inhaled deeply before stubbing out his half-smoked cigarette. Then taking her hand, fondled it gently.

'It was only when I asked Lawrence to be my best man that he told me whose daughter I was marrying.'

Katharine looked at him, her beautiful eyes clouded in bewilderment.

'What is this all about Ashley,' she pleaded. '*Please* tell me.'

For a brief moment his blue eyes locked with hers.

'Your father is alive darling,' he said at last. 'And, I hope, well.'

He took a deep breath.

'I owe my life to him.'

Katharine looked at him unbelievingly. Then, suddenly, as the truth dawned on her, she paled.

'You don't mean . . . you *can't* mean . . .'

He nodded slowly.

'Louis,' he declared, 'is Xavier de Montval.'

She fell back on the pillows, deathly pale.

And for a moment he was afraid, fearing something terrible had happened to her.

'Darling,' he said anxiously, taking her in his arms.

'It's all right,' she gasped, pushing him away, as if she needed all the air she could get. 'It's going to take me a few minutes to get used to what you've just told me, that's all.'

He said nothing, just sat gazing at her, willing her to look at him, to say something.

At last she raised her head.

'And Lawrence knew all the time?'

'Of course.'

She thrust her face in her hands and burst into tears.

'How could he,' she sobbed. 'How could he have been so cruel!'

Ashley sat in silence, waiting for the storm to abate.

'I can understand how you feel darling,' he said softly, after a few minutes. 'But try to see it from his point of view. You were supposed to be dropped into the sector next to your father. You would probably never have met. But had you known he was there you'd have tried to get in touch with him, now wouldn't you?'

Katharine shook her head

'I don't know,' she whispered.

'Oh you would, you'd have been unnatural if you hadn't. And Lawrence simply couldn't risk that happening. Neither could he risk telling you the truth in case you were to be sent into the field later. That's why the reason for your being sent to Group R was rather blurred. He needed time to make up his mind whether or not to drop you to another circuit. In the end, he decided that the risk was too great.'

Ashley sighed.

'You believed your father was dead, Katharine. Knowing the dangerous work he was doing, Lawrence thought it would be cruel to enlighten you, only to have to tell you later that he had been killed.'

He gently tried to remove her hands from her face. But she resisted him and turned away.

'Katharine,' he said patiently after a few more minutes. 'We only have three days. Are we going to waste them quarrelling over Lawrence?'

When she made no response, he got up and walked back to the window and stood looking out at nothing in particular.

The grey clouds of early morning had disappeared. A pale lemon sun had left the horizon and was now climbing high in the sky giving promise of a fine day. He shrugged miserably, cursing himself for having told Katharine the truth.

Suddenly he felt a light touch around his waist and, looking down, saw his wife's slender arms encircling him. He slowly turned round and she lifted her face to be kissed.

'Come back to bed,' she whispered. 'It's cold out here. My father didn't save your life so that you could die of pneumonia.'

With a quick intake of breath, he bent and picked her up in his arms.

* * *

The three beautiful days of their honeymoon, which had seemed like a lifetime when they set off from Greystones, were coming to an end.

Katharine remembered glowing with happiness when Ashley had told her of this wonderful bonus.

'We're so lucky,' she had exclaimed. 'Dickie only had forty-eight hours when he and Harriet got married just before Christmas.'

'That's all I expected,' Ashley had smiled. 'But almost four days is a gift from heaven.'

Katharine wasn't sure that she believed in heaven. But she was grateful for the gift, whoever it came from.

On the Tuesday afternoon they travelled up to London.

Ashley had to leave early the following morning. And, as Katharine wasn't due back at Group R until later in the day, he did not want to leave her stranded on her own in their honeymoon hotel, miles from anywhere.

That evening they dined at the Savoy, listening dreamily to Carroll Gibbons lazily crooning popular tunes as his fingers raced up and down the keyboard.

Slipping as smoothly and as easily into Ashley's arms as she had done on that first evening at Group R, they once again swayed together on the dimly-lit dance floor, almost motionless, their bodies pressed close, moulded into one. Ashley's cheek rested lightly against her hair as she nestled closer to him breathing in the scent of his masculinity, that special smell that was his.

'It's just the nearness of you', a man's voice throbbed over the microphone.

Katharine looked adoringly up at her husband and his arms closed even more tightly around her slim body. 'It's not the pale moon that excites me, that thrills and delights me . . .' the voice crooned on.

Ashley's breathing quickened.

The song ended but they remained locked in each

other's arms on the tiny patch of dance floor. The band slipped into another air and the same husky voice whispered 'What'll I do when you are far away . . .'

It was too much for Katharine's taut nerves, strung into a tight coil in anticipation of their goodbye. She looked up at her husband, her eyes glistening with tears. Putting a protective arm round her, he led her through the dancers swaying all around them and out of the ballroom.

The following morning it was Katharine who was standing on the station platform waving Ashley goodbye.

He had tried hard to persuade her to stay in bed.

'I'd much rather kiss you goodbye here darling,' he'd pleaded. 'Railway stations are ghastly places, especially in the early morning. You just turn over and go back to sleep. You're not expected at Tamara's for lunch until 1.15. And tomorrow morning you'll be back at Group R and have to get up.'

But Katharine had insisted on accompanying him.

'I want to stay with you until the very last minute,' she faltered, as she packed his few possessions, her eyes puffy from lack of sleep.

They stood together on the littered platform in the early light of dawn. The engine began to make preliminary snorts and snuffles, then rumbled as its steam hissed up into the dirty mosaic of the ceiling, sending out spirals of smoke into the cold morning air.

It began to pant, then whistle, then whistle again.

They looked at each other. For the moment all passion spent, not daring to touch, or even draw close. A hasty kiss would be worse than no kiss at all: almost an insult after the precious days they had just shared.

Then as the hands of the station clock moved relentlessly on and the engine ground its teeth and prepared to tear them apart, they avoided each others eyes. Each seeing the terrible void which was gradually opening up between them. Dreading having to say goodbye.

But as the guard blew his whistle and the engine gave a final snort before chunting off into the distance, a kind of panic seized them both.

He leant dangerously far out of the compartment window and reached for her hand.

But it was too late.

The train was already gathering speed. She just stood there as the carriages rattled past, her eyes dark with pain and fear, rooted to the spot. Unable to move, unable to run, to cling for one last desperate minute to that outstretched hand. His body became smaller and farther away and finally disappeared from view.

Katharine stumbled out of the station as if in a daze.

An old man was sitting propped against the wall playing a mouth organ, the strident notes trembling on the chill morning air.

She looked down at him through glazed eyes. Then fished in the gas mask slung over her shoulder for some coins and dropped them into the cap lying on the pavement beside him.

'Thanks miss,' he said, removing the mouth organ and shaking it to get rid of the spittle.

When she walked back into the hotel half-an-hour later, early risers were just beginning to appear.

She asked for her key and went back to their empty room. Throwing off her coat and kicking her feet out of her shoes she lay down on the dishevelled bed.

But she couldn't sleep.

Ashley's presence was everywhere.

Everything reminded her of him and of their love.

Without him, the room was an empty shell, accentuating her loneliness even more cruelly. Mocking her in her misery.

She rolled over and hugged his pillow close to her heart, breathing in the distinctive scent of his hair cream which had lingered for so long on the back of the sofa in the sitting-room at Group R. And tears, once again stretching her eyelids in their haste to be released, gushed forth and streamed down her pale cheeks.

As she lay there, rocking miserably backwards and forwards, his pillow clutched in her arms, she knew that she was simply not interested in a wonderful post-war world. The land fit for heroes which had been promised before and had become a cliché once again. Frothy words slopped about by bigwigs in chairborne jobs in order to glorify war, sanctify killing and being killed. Instead of revealing the murderous war for what it really was.

She didn't want a dead hero for a husband. Or a medal in a velvet box, a name on a plaque to be read out on Remembrance Sunday. She wanted Ashley in her arms now, at this very moment, warm and young and vital, throbbing with life and love for her in battered, war-torn London. Not some future pie-in-the-sky paradise.

'Ashley, Ashley, where are you?' she sobbed. 'Why did you have to leave me?'

The only reply came from the sudden blare of the air-raid siren shattering the silence with its melancholy wail, and the distant drone of approaching aircraft.

Doors opened hurriedly and footsteps raced down the corridor past her room.

But Katharine didn't care.

Pulling the rumpled bedclothes over her head she

hugged her husband's pillow even closer and sobbed herself to sleep.

* * *

It was nearly three months before they met again.

Although they tried to write to each other every day, at times there were days, even a week, when Katharine had no news from Ashley, then several hastily scribbled notes would all arrive at once.

She knew that he was on manoeuvres in the very north of Scotland instructing or being instructed, she didn't know which. But she had learned not to ask questions. Occasionally he managed to telephone, but these precious contacts were rare.

Late one night, towards the end of June, a call came through to the cottage for her.

'Can you make yourself free next weekend?' he enquired. 'I'll be in London on Saturday, have to leave Sunday night, but . . . if you could come up?'

'I'll manage somehow,' Katharine exulted.

'Meet me at the Savoy sometime in the afternoon. I'll book a room so just go up and wait for me. I'm afraid I can't give you an exact time, but it won't be till after lunch.'

'It doesn't matter darling,' she had sung. 'I'll be there.'

She hesitated.

'What is it?' he asked anxiously.

'I was wondering,' she demurred. 'Do you think that we ought to spend the weekend in Buckingham? Your father's seen so little of you and I know it would please him. Hope has kept in touch with me, and she told me . . .'

But Ashley interrupted her.

'Darling,' he pleaded. 'Could we make it next time? It's sweet of you to suggest it but . . . I haven't seen you since our honeymoon . . . nearly four months.'

His voice dropped to a whisper.

'I just want to be alone with you. Is that too much to ask?'

Katharine smiled, willing her love for him to flow down the crackling telephone wires.

'No, darling, of course not,' she whispered back. 'That's all I want too.'

When she arrived at the Savoy, Ashley was waiting for her at the reception desk.

'Beat you to it by three minutes,' he announced.

She held up her face to be kissed.

'Just had time to dump my stuff and place a posy on your dressing-table,' he murmured, encircling her tiny waist with his arm and drawing her to him as the lift glided upwards.

Katharine gasped when he threw open the door.

It wasn't a room. It was a whole suite.

'Ashley,' she bleated, wandering from one room to another. 'Why ever did you book a *suite*?'

He was lolling against the doorpost separating the bedroom from the sitting-room, grinning at her.

'Had no choice. By the time I got round to booking, that was all there was left.'

Katharine sat down on the wide double bed.

'But we didn't have to stay *here*,' she chided. 'There *are* other hotels in London.'

'*Are* there?' he teased, raising an amused eyebrow. 'You find 'em. Since America came into the war hotel rooms in London are scarcer than kangaroos at the Café de Paris.'

He stood up and removing his Sam Browne belt threw it on to a chair.

'Unless, of course, you'd prefer a bed and breakfast in Wapping. I'm sure that could be arranged.'

She laughed and shook her head as he walked across the room towards her.

'Anyway, I know you like those gooey swan meringues they still manage to rustle up for tea in the River Room here. So, I really didn't have any choice, did I?'

He looked down at her, and she saw his eyes darken with love.

'No,' she said weakly, as he sat down beside her on the bed and gently slid her back against the pillows.

'But I don't want tea just yet,' he whispered hoarsely. 'Do you?'

She didn't answer. Just mutely shook her head.

His strong arms closed around her, her lips parted and she closed her eyes her whole body trembling, every nerve alive and throbbing with love for him.

They never did have tea.

In fact, they didn't do any of the things that Ashley had planned for that evening. The theatre tickets remained in his wallet. The table he had booked at the Hungaria was cancelled. And dinner was served in their sitting-room. Just the two of them, with a bottle of champagne to celebrate.

When the long summer evening began to fade, they sat close together in that warm aftermath of sunset. That moment when all the shades of earth and sky mingle into a brief rainbow twilight and the first stars begin to swim in a cool green sky. As she snuggled in the crook of his arm watching the sky over London change from pink to indigo through purple to a deep midnight blue, the night seemed to be wrapped in an eternal magic. And it was impossible to believe that England was at war.

Ashley gently rubbed his cheek against hers as Carroll Gibbons' lazy voice filtered over the hotel wireless.

Then, without even pausing to draw the blackout curtains, he picked her up in his arms and crossed over to the bedroom.

* * *

'When shall I see you again?' Katharine asked anxiously as she clung to him on the platform at Waterloo just before her train was due to leave.

The station didn't seem to be any less dreary in the streaming sunlight of a late June evening than it had done in January. Then it had been dimly lit with a biting wind sucked into it from outside whirling round like a vortex: whipping up the day's debris and the loose papers scattered everywhere.

Katharine realised that whatever the weather, whatever the day or the time of year, she would never get used to these endless partings. This terrible feeling of emptiness, of utter desolation which wormed itself into every fibre of her being every time she had to say goodbye to Ashley.

His arms tightened round her and he gently stroked her hair.

'I don't know darling,' he said sadly. 'I only wish I did.'

'But you'll be here, in Scotland, won't you?' she said anxiously. 'You're not going overseas?'

'Not for the moment,' he answered evasively.

And, with that, she had to be content.

Chapter 18

Ashley remembered his promise, and the next time he had a weekend's leave, caught the night train down to London and was waiting for Katharine when she arrived at Waterloo.

It was a glorious morning in early October as they travelled up to Buckingham together. The drab desolation of London and it's bomb-torn suburbs gradually gave way to lush fields and woods. Trees with brilliant autumn tints, flashes of gold and red and green which looked as if they had been slashed onto them by an enthusiastic artist, gone wild with his brush.

By the time they arrived the sun was shining brightly, if somewhat crisply, in a clear blue sky. Philip, hopping about on the station platform as their train chunted in, went wild with excitement when he saw Ashley. And, had it not been for his mother's firm handling, would have commandeered his uncle for the entire weekend.

'He's starved of young male companionship,' Hope confided to her sister-in-law as they left the station. They both are.'

Ben and Philip were dancing around Ashley like a couple of young puppies, hanging on to his hands, both jabbering at once.

'Father's sorry he couldn't come to meet you himself,'

Hope went on. 'But he's taking a wedding service at the moment.'

She grimaced at Katharine.

'A young village couple marrying by special licence on forty-eight hours embarcation leave. I suppose the bridegroom's off to the Western Desert.'

She linked her arm in Katharine's as they strolled down the lane together.

'It's terrible, isn't it? What's forty-eight hours? Couples need that just to get over the strain and fatigue of the wedding. But that's all they get nowadays and it may be years before they see each other again. Embarcation leave means either North Africa or India.'

Hope sighed.

'These two are so young. I met them when they came to see Father last night. She doesn't look more than eighteen, and he's only a year or two older.'

She shook her head.

'Just think how people can change at that age.'

Katharine nodded.

'We were so lucky,' she whispered. 'Ashley and I. We had almost four days.'

When they arrived at the Rectory, the wedding party was just leaving the church. And a few minutes later Ashley's father, still wearing his cassock, came into the house. His joy at seeing them was so overwhelming that any slight feelings of jealousy, which had plagued Katharine in the train at the thought of having to share Ashley during their precious moments together, immediately vanished.

That afternoon, Ben and Philip scarcely left Ashley's side.

Hope and Katharine lay idly back in deckchairs in the sheltered garden, soaking up the last rays of the sun, hearing in the distance the boys' enthusiastic shrieks as Ashley coached his nephews in the art of rugger tackles.

But, after lunch on Sunday, when both boys approached Ashley with the same determined gleam in their eyes, Hope intervened.

'That's enough,' she said briskly. 'This afternoon you're going to take a nap.'

They opened their mouths to protest. But a look from their mother silenced them.

'And, if you're very good, after tea I'll finish reading *The Wind in the Willows* to you.'

She winked at Katharine as they left the room.

'I think I'll follow the boys' good example,' William Paget said. 'And then I must collect my thoughts for Evensong. We have it earlier nowadays you know, not at six-thirty as before. In the winter, with the blackout and the fear of air-raids, people prefer not to be out after dark.'

He smiled across at Ashley and Katharine.

'I'm sure you two can amuse yourselves. Such a glorious afternoon.'

Katharine detected a twinkle in his eyes as he got up and walked towards the door.

'There are still bicycles in the old shed if you want them.'

Ashley grinned across the table at Katharine.

'Do you want to have a bicycle race?' he teased.

She shook her head.

'Let's walk then. There's some beautiful countryside around here.'

They found themselves alone in a sun-dappled wood.

Ashley threw his tunic down on a grassy knoll under a huge canopy of trees. The afternoon sun was glinting through the leaves, sending shifting shadows dancing across their faces.

'You look as if you've been tattooed,' he laughed, pulling Katharine down beside him.

They lay there, fingers entwined, their heads propped against a fallen tree trunk, not speaking, perfectly content just to be in each other's company, to feel the other one close.

'Ben and Philip seem to adore you,' Katharine ventured at last.

'I'm a substitute for Guy I suppose,' Ashley said laconically, plucking at a blade of grass and twirling it between his teeth. 'Poor little chaps. And there must be thousands like them.'

He sighed.

'Ashley,' Katharine said pensively. 'What *is* the point of war?'

'I wish I knew,' he murmured. 'Hitler had to be stopped. But I sometimes wonder whether there wasn't some other way.'

He shrugged philosophically.

'All we can do is live through it the best we can and try to make things different once it's all over. Make sure this time it *doesn't* happen again. Otherwise, what's the point?'

Katharine didn't attempt to reply. And they lay for a few minutes in silence while the shifting sunlight flitted across their upturned faces.

'Have you thought about after the war darling?' he enquired, turning on one elbow and looking down at her.

Katharine opened her eyes in surprise.

'No, not really. What is there to think about?'

'Well . . . us.'

She half sat up.

'You'll go back to Rugby I suppose and be a housemaster again, won't you?'

'That's what I want to talk to you about,' he said quietly, pulling her back into his arms.

'I've changed Katharine,' he said after a few minutes. 'War does change a man. I'm no longer that idealistic young University graduate I was before all this started.'

He threw away the blade of grass he had been sucking.

'I've grown up, I suppose.'

'What do you mean Ashley?' Katharine said hesitantly, bewildered and not a little afraid by his remark.

'I mean that I've no desire to go back to being a schoolmaster.'

'Then what *do* you want to do?'

He looked up and saw fear widening her beautiful almond eyes. They were clouded. Yet there was a strange light glowing through them from behind, like the sun shining through a soft sea mist.

He pulled her back into his arms.

'I've never seen anyone with eyes as beautiful as yours,' he whispered hoarsely.

And, holding her tightly captive he began to kiss her with a passion which increased her fear.

'Ashley, no,' she cried, struggling free. 'You must tell me now you've started. What *is* it you intend to do?'

For one awful moment she imagined his future did not include her. She looked down, pressing her tightly closed lips together, as tears began to gather behind her eyes.

'Am I part of that future?' she choked at last.

He looked at her in stunned surprise. Then, quickly recovering himself, folded her back into his arms.

'Darling Kate,' he murmured, rocking her gently backwards and forwards as he would an unhappy child. 'Of *course* you're part of that future. You *are* my future. Without you, everything is pointless.'

She relaxed and gazed up at him.

'Then it doesn't matter to me what you want to do. As long as I am part of it, that's all that matters.'

He relaxed his hold and leant back against the log once more, looking thoughtfully up through the trellis of red and gold leaves to the patch of sky above.

'I think it was my father's sermon this morning which confirmed it,' he said reflectively.

'Oh, wasn't it *wonderful*,' Katharine breathed. 'He speaks so simply yet with such strength . . . and such love. What was that text he used? It didn't sound biblical at all.'

Ashley smiled down at her.

'But it was. Taken from the Old Testament, from Ecclesiastes to be exact. It's one of Dad's favourites. "I know there is nothing better for men than to be happy and do good while they live."'

He paused.

'That's what I want to do,' he said at last. 'Help people as he has done, as he's still doing and no doubt will continue to do as long as he lives.'

Katharine's brow furrowed.

'It was when I was in prison, about to be executed. I began to question life and wonder what I'd done with it. And I came to the conclusion that I'd done precious little of any worth. I made a vow to God then that if I lived I would serve him.'

He took a deep breath and carefully selected another blade of grass.

'I wanted to live to see you again, and I told him so. But I wasn't sure whether God would grant my request. I'd been brought up by my parents to worship him but, like a lot of young men, I'd wandered away. Thought I knew it all. Those days in that terrible prison taught me otherwise. I realised how impotent we are faced with the really important issues of life.'

'But where is this leading?' Katharine queried.

'When the war is over, I want to take Holy Orders,' Ashley said quietly.

Katharine gasped.

'Become a *Monk*?'

'No darling,' he laughed, drawing her to him once again. 'I want to follow in my father's footsteps. Train for the Anglican ministry.'

He stopped laughing and looked down at her, his blue eyes serious, piercing through her.

'But I can only do it if you are willing. If you are with me.'

Katharine remained cradled in his arms. She didn't know what to say.

'It's a double ministry,' Ashley went on. 'My parents formed a splendid team. My mother was behind my father in everything he did. But, if the wife is an unwilling partner, it simply doesn't work.'

'And you don't think you can serve God by being a schoolmaster?' Katharine enquired at last.

'No,' he said firmly. 'Not in the same way. But Kate, if you're not happy about it . . .'

'I'm happy about it,' she broke in. 'Whatever you choose I'll be behind you.'

She looked up at him, her eyes full of love.

'All I want is to be with you Ashley.'

'Kate,' he said hoarsely. 'Oh Kate.'

And his voice almost broke as he gathered her back into his arms.

They were brushing the grass off their clothes and preparing to return to the Rectory when Katharine shyly placed a hand on Ashley's arm.

He stopped shaking out his tunic and looked at her enquiringly.

'There's something I've wanted to ask you ever since that first morning of our honeymoon,' she said diffidently.

'Ask away,' he smiled.

She frowned slightly, as if not sure how to begin.

He buttoned up his jacket and carefully replaced his maroon beret.

'Let's walk,' he said gently, 'perhaps you'll find it easier then.'

He took her arm and, twining his fingers in hers, led her out of the leafy glade back onto the deserted path.

The sun had now completely disappeared and a slight breeze had sprung up. A sudden eddy caught her hair and lifted it as she walked along beside him, swinging her khaki beret in her free hand.

He stopped and looked down at her.

'Did I ever tell you you're beautiful?' he murmured.

She smiled happily.

'Standing there amongst the trees with the breeze in your hair, you're just like one of those impressionist paintings in the Jeu de Paume.'*

He caught hold of her hand again and walked along swinging it backwards and forwards between them.

'Didn't you have something you wanted to ask me?' he teased.

'It's just . . .'

Katharine stopped, not knowing how to go on. Not wanting to break the wonderful web of happiness which seemed to have been woven around them.

'Just what?' he smiled.

'Oh Ashley,' she cried.

And then it all came out in a rush.

'I've wanted to ask you this ever since the morning

after our wedding when you told me that Louis was my father. But I was afraid talking about him might cause tension between us like it did then.'

She raised her eyes, blurred with love, to meet his.

'These meetings we have are so rare . . . and so precious. I don't want *anything* to cast a shadow over them . . . Not even my father.'

'Why should your father?' he asked.

'Ashley,' she blurted out. 'You knew him. Tell me, what sort of a person is he? What is he *really* like? It's almost ten years since I saw him and . . . I've heard so many conflicting stories.'

Ashley kept walking, his eyes fixed steadily on the road ahead.

'I don't know what stories you've heard,' he said slowly. 'And I don't know what you remember of him. But, all I can say is that he's the most courageous, unselfish . . . one of the most wonderful men I've ever known. And that's not just my opinion. All those who've worked with him in the field think the same.'

He paused and, taking his pipe from his pocket, tapped it against the heel of his shoe.

'Your father is not an ordinary agent,' he went on. 'He's a double agent. The Germans think he's working for them. That's why he's so valuable and how he managed to engineer my escape.'

He thoughtfully pressed the tobacco into place.

'How he's still alive escapes me, he takes the most horrendous risks.'

Ashley grinned.

'*And* breaks all the rules.'

He lit a match and cupped his hands round the bowl.

'I only hope,' he said puffing steadily as the pungent smoke rose and spiralled into the overhanging foliage, 'that I can be worthy of being his son-in-law.'

He took his pipe out of his mouth and looked down at her.

'You have a father you can be very proud of darling.'

* * *

They left the next morning after breakfast.

As the tranquil countryside receded and the train began to meander through the battered ruins of outer London, Ashley felt Katharine stiffen at his side.

He took her hand and squeezed it affectionately. But she remained tense and on edge, knowing that their short idyll was coming to an end.

'Shall I ever get used to saying goodbye to you?' she whispered brokenly as the train drew into Euston.

'We're not saying goodbye yet,' he grinned. 'I'm going to take you to lunch at Quaglino's first.'

* * *

'Have you thought about Christmas,' Katharine enquired, as they sat at a secluded table in the dark, intimate restaurant.

'Many times,' he teased.

'Idiot,' she smiled. 'What I mean is . . .'

'I know exactly what you mean,' he cut in quietly. 'Shall I have leave?'

'Yes.'

'I hope so,' he went on. 'It would be wonderful to spend our first Christmas together, wouldn't it?'

'You must be due for leave soon,' Katharine pleaded.

'I am,' he sighed. 'Overdue, as a matter of fact.'

He smiled wanly.

'In wartime one can never be sure of anything. But yes, let's say we'll spend Christmas together. Where would you like to go? Paris, Vienna, Berlin? I believe the music is wonderful in all of them.'

He grinned across at her.

'Especially military bands at the moment.'

She looked at him and their eyes met and locked together each hungry once again for the other's touch.

'Anywhere, as long as you're there,' she whispered at last.

He reached across and took her hand, squeezing it tightly in his own. Gazing at her with a terrible longing as if trying to memorise every feature, every line and contour of her face.

'Do you think we should spend it with your father?' she murmured, disentangling her hand as the waiter glided by.

Ashley grimaced.

'You've obviously never spent the festive season in a Rectory. If you had you'd know it's not exactly hilarious. By the time Christmas lunch is over, Dad's comatose. Knocked out by dozens of nativity plays, not to mention several hundred carol services. Got any other suggestions?'

'It might be a good idea if we did go to Buckingham,' Katharine persisted. 'For Hope's sake.'

'What about Lavinia? Wouldn't she feel left out?'

Ashley's mouth twitched mischievously.

'I suppose she could always come as well and referee the backstage fights between brawling shepherds and howling angels.'

'She usually spends Christmas with the Voronovskys,' Katharine smiled. 'At least, we have done since my mother died.'

He grinned at her once more across the table.

'I honestly don't think Buckingham could cope with a Russian invasion, not at the moment. The General turning up in full dress uniform, plus clanking sword, might be just too much for rural England.'

'Well what . . .'

'You decide darling. I'll fit in with whatever you choose.'

As the waiter bent to brush away the crumbs, Katharine looked down at the pristine table cloth and began tracing squares on it with her finger nail.

'What is it?' Ashley enquired. 'Penny for 'em.'

'I was just thinking about last Christmas,' Katharine murmured, without looking up. 'You were in Cairo, weren't you?'

'Nope,' he replied. 'I didn't arrive until just before the New Year.'

He put a finger under her chin and forced her to look at him.

'So what?'

'We heard that you were fêted as quite a hero out there. Lots of beautiful women . . .'

Ashley threw back his head and roared with laughter, causing couples at surrounding tables to look enquiringly in their direction.

'So *that's* it. You wouldn't be jealous by any chance?'

A blush crept slowly up Katharine's cheeks.

He dropped his bantering tone and suddenly became serious.

'There were dozens of beautiful women out there, Egyptian, French, Lebanese, Armenian. There was one, a Levantine princess, or so they told me. An incredible creature: jet black hair down to her thighs, eyes like two outsize green marbles. She had all the young bloods, and not so young bloods, dancing round her, falling down like nine pins at her feet. What was her name? Ashra, Amra, something like that.'

Katharine looked up at him.

'And were they hanging around you too?' she enquired. 'The women, I mean.'

'You bet!'

His eyes sparkled across at her.

'I was a novelty. The conquering hero, something new to chase after. They were all angling for a husband or an escort. They didn't seem to mind which.'

'And . . .'

'And . . . I remained a spectator, albeit an amused spectator. If I'd escaped from the Gestapo, it wasn't to fall into that net.'

He reached for her hand once again.

'I came home for you.'

Their eyes met and locked across the table.

'Oh Ashley,' Katharine breathed. 'I love you so much.'

* * *

'Do you feel like a walk, or shall we take a taxi?' Ashley enquired, when they finally left the restaurant and wandered down St. James in the sparkling sunshine of that October afternoon.

'Why? Where are we going?'

'Regent Street.'

'What for?'

'Surprise,' he grinned. 'Come on, we'll cut across the park to Piccadilly. Then if you're tired, we'll get a taxi the rest of the way.'

They turned into Swallow Street and crossed into Lower Regent Street. Two buskers were standing on the corner playing 'Something to remember you by'. Pushing open the door of the Goldsmiths and Silversmiths, Ashley ushered her inside.

'I want a Pegasus brooch for my wife,' he announced to the assistant who came forward.

He chose a small discreet model set with tiny diamonds and held it against Katharine's tunic.

'Like it?' he enquired.

'It's beautiful,' she breathed as the diamonds sparkled up at her.

'Those buskers said it all,' he whispered. 'I want you to have something to remember me by.' As Katharine's eyes filled with tears he grinned down at her. 'What better than my regimental brooch? You can pin it on your shirt, next to your heart.'

'Violets, lovely violets,' the old flower seller chanted as they left the jewellers and passed by Eros.

They looked at each other in amusement.

'I think this is where we came in,' Ashley smiled.

Chapter 19

During the golden autumn days which followed, Katharine was bathed in an unaccustomed serenity. An immense feeling of well-being enveloped her like a soft cashmere shawl.

She wondered whether it had something to do with their weekend in Buckingham. Her blossoming friendship with Hope, William Paget's sermon or even Ashley's revelation that he wanted to follow in his father's footsteps and serve full-time this God whom they all three worshipped.

Whatever it was, she revelled in her new-found peace. This freedom from fear and the constant anguish which had invaded her whenever she allowed herself to dwell on the possibility of her husband not returning from the war.

Eleanor Ricks noticed the bloom on her face, the new depth to her eyes and a curvaceousness to her slim figure which had not been there before. It was as if Katharine had suddenly awakened, shed her girlish coil and blossomed into womanhood.

Others at Group R noticed it too.

And envied Ashley Paget.

As October drifted into November and the weather became cloudy and overcast, the nights cold and frosty, Katharine began counting the days until Christmas.

Ticking them off on a small calendar standing on her bedside table next to Ashley's photograph.

'Only another six weeks,' she exclaimed excitedly one morning.

She sat up in bed and reached for her pencil. As she did so, a sudden feeling of nausea swept over her. She lay back against the pillows, gasping at its intensity. But it didn't abate and, groping blindly for her slippers, she rushed to the bathroom.

It was Sunday, the one day in the week when rationing allowed Rickie to prepare a cooked breakfast. But, as she dressed, the smell of sizzling bacon wafting up from the kitchen caused the nauseous sensation to rise in her throat again. And once more she found herself in the bathroom, retching violently.

Tatiana discovered Katharine lying white-faced on her bed when she popped her head round the door to find out why she hadn't come down to breakfast.

'I must have eaten something which has disagreed with me,' Katharine said weakly. 'I feel ghastly. I'll sleep it off and be right as rain by lunchtime.'

Tatiana looked at her wan face and wasn't so sure. But, true to her word, Katharine came down to lunch in fine spirits.

Eleanor looked at her sharply across the table, refraining from comment.

But, when Katharine began leaving for the office each morning without breakfast, she drew her aside.

'Don't you think you should see a doctor?' she suggested. 'Apart from this nausea, you're looking awfully tired.'

'You're right,' Katharine admitted, flopping back on the sofa with a yawn. 'I *have* been feeling dreadfully sleepy lately.'

It was Sunday afternoon, two weeks later.

Nicola and Tatiana had gone for a walk and Anne was in London for her weekend off. Katharine and Rickie were alone together in front of the sitting room fire.

Rickie put down the khaki balaclava helmet she was knitting and crossed over to the sofa.

'Katharine,' she said gently. 'Have you any idea why you are feeling like this?'

Katharine shrugged.

'Need some leave I suppose.'

She stretched and yawned again.

'But I keep putting it off,' she went on wistfully, 'saving it for Ashley.'

She looked at Rickie, her eyes shining.

'He's promised me he'll have leave for Christmas . . . he might even manage a whole *week*.'

She sat up and grabbed the older woman's hands, her face radiant.

'Just think Rickie. A whole *week*.'

Rickie smiled.

'Then you'd better be well enough to enjoy it, hadn't you?' she said briskly.

'Oh, I shall be,' Katharine breathed. 'I've been feeling wonderful ever since our last weekend together.'

She gazed at the leaping flames.

'I've had a peace, a kind of glow that seems to come from inside me these past two months.'

'Have you noticed anything else?' Rickie probed.

'No,' Katharine puzzled. 'What?'

'It obviously hasn't occurred to you that you could be pregnant,' Rickie replied practically.

Katharine looked across at her, her eyes glowing with a soft golden light.

'I had wondered,' she whispered. 'But I didn't dare believe it.'

She paused, as if afraid to voice her desires.

'Do you think . . . Could it possibly be . . .'

'I don't know. There *are* other signs of course. That's why I asked if you'd noticed anything else.'

Katharine coloured.

'Well . . . yes. But I kept telling myself it was probably due to the emotional upheaval, all the wonderful things which have happened to me this year.'

She looked down at her hands, and her colour deepened.

'It does sometimes happen doesn't it? Nicola said it happened to her when she left Durban. Things didn't sort themselves out for nearly six months.'

'Yes,' Rickie continued. 'It *can* happen? But that *plus* morning sickness, sleepiness and . . . well just the way you look. Pregnant women often have this feeling of well-being. And you're absolutely blooming.'

Katharine lay back against the sofa.

'Oh Rickie,' she murmured ecstatically. 'Do you really think it could be? But, isn't it too early to be sure?'

'When are you next due for a weekend?' Rickie enquired.

'In three weeks. Well,' she dimpled, 'two and a half now.'

'If I were you I'd make an appointment to see a gynaecologist then.'

'All right, I will.'

Katharine stretched luxuriously.

'By that time it will be almost Christmas and Ashley will be coming on leave.'

She looked thoughtfully across at Rickie who had returned to her armchair and was placidly knitting.

'Do you think I should tell him now?' she queried.

'There's nothing to tell at the moment,' Rickie reminded her. 'Wait until you're sure.'

She stopped counting the stitches clustered on her needle and smiled fondly at Katharine.

'It'll be a lovely Christmas present for him.'

* * *

But Ashley's Christmas leave never materialised.

He telephoned a few days before she was due to go to London on her weekend off, asking her to stay with Tamara for the Saturday night.

'I'm going to try to come to London,' he said. 'I'll telephone you there if I can make it.'

He sounded ill at ease.

'Is something the matter?' Katharine asked.

There was a pause and she thought they had been cut off.

'Ashley,' she cried.

'I'm here darling,' he soothed. 'And I heard what you said.'

He paused again.

'The only thing the matter is that I love you so much it's become a kind of constant ache.'

He could hear her breath coming in short, excited gasps.

'So do I darling. But it's not long now till Christmas. Oh *Ashley*, I can't *wait*.'

'Katharine,' he cut in, and his voice sounded crisp and curt, almost business-like. 'I've got something to tell you . . .'

'And I've got something to tell *you*,' she interrupted joyfully. 'But let's both keep it till Saturday, shall we?'

He didn't reply.

'You'll ring me at Tamara's?'

'I'll ring you,' he said.

And the line went dead.

Katharine shook the receiver, but there was only a long low buzz. With a shrug she put it down. Ashley had sounded strained but it was probably because he was overtired.

She arrived at the Wellesleys after lunch on the Saturday to wait for Ashley's call.

Katharine didn't need to tell Tamara anything.

As soon as she saw her face, she immediately guessed. And insisted that she accompany Katharine to her appointment with the gynaecologist on the following Monday morning.

Saturday afternoon dragged by.

Sensing her anxiety, the Prince suggested a game of cribbage. But Katharine was unable to concentrate. It seemed to her that the hands of the clock never moved.

When they stood at eight o'clock she became distinctly restless.

'Come and have dinner,' Tamara pleaded. 'If Ashley telephones, you can rush off. Your bag is all packed.'

Katharine sat at the table and toyed with the food, her eyes constantly on the clock. Each time it struck it sounded like a death knell pounding on her heart.

Coffee was just being served when the telephone finally rang.

It was a quarter past nine.

'I've just arrived,' Ashley said. 'Can you meet me at Victoria Station? I think that's the simplest thing. I'll grab a taxi and we should both arrive at about the same time.'

'Yes darling,' Katharine breathed, tears of relief streaming down her face. 'But why Victoria? Wouldn't it be simpler if I went straight to the hotel? Where are we staying?'

There was a pause. And she anxiously called his name.

'I'm afraid I'm just passing through, Katharine,' he said tautly. 'Don't bring a case. I can't stay.'

'Can't *stay*!' she cried.

'I'm sorry,' he went on miserably. 'I didn't want it to be like this. I'd hoped I could explain things to you quietly. But there's been a change of plans.'

His voice took on a desperate note.

'Grab a taxi darling. Victoria in, hopefully, about fifteen minutes.'

Stunned, Katharine put down the receiver.

Tamara was hovering in the drawing-room doorway. She had heard the anguished high-pitched note in Katharine's voice and sensed that something was wrong.

'Can you ring for a taxi please,' Katharine said limply. 'For Victoria and . . . I'll be spending the night here.'

Wisely, Tamara made no comment.

'Please Katharine,' she said, as she accompanied her to the door. 'Do take this tin hat, it's the one I wear for fire-watching. If there's an air-raid you may not be near a shelter.'

Katharine shook her head.

But Tamara was adamant.

Feeling she had not the strength to argue, Katharine stuck the cumbersome hat into the strap of her gas mask.

When she arrived Katharine looked anxiously around her. But she couldn't see him. And an awful panic gripped her.

Suddenly she caught sight of a tall officer in battle dress standing with his back to her. Her heart leapt and she ran forward.

But it wasn't Ashley.

Jet black hair curled out from under his maroon beret.

As she pulled up sharply he turned round, his eyes

screwed up as if searching for someone. Then, his expression cleared and he ran towards her.

Katharine gasped.

His moustache had gone, and dark tufts of hair curled above his ears.

'Katharine,' he breathed hoarsely, coming to a stop in front of her.

She stared up at him, her mouth open, her eyes wide with disbelief.

Taking her arm he walked with her along the platform.

'Ashley,' she burst out. 'What's happened? Your moustache . . .'

'And my hair?'

She nodded mutely.

But at that moment the air-raid siren set up its mournful wail.

'Oh *no*,' he groaned. '*now* where can we go? I've got very little time.'

Everyone on the station was being herded into the underground.

They looked at each other in dismay. Catching hold of her hand he ran with her to the other end of the platform into the relative shelter of one of the side entrances.

As they stood there in the dirty draughty doorway, listening to the scuffle of feet outside as the siren's wail slowly groaned to a halt, he pulled her to him.

'I should take you to safety down that blasted tube,' he said fiercely.

'I'm not going,' she shrieked, her voice rising almost to a scream.

'All right, all right,' he soothed, 'we'll stay here. It's sordid, but at least we're alone.'

'Ashley,' she cried, catching hold of his lapels. 'What's happening? Why this disguise?'

Their eyes met. And the awful truth hit her.

'You're going back,' she gabbled, drawing away from him, her eyes almost black with anguish and fear. 'You're going back into the field.'

He nodded slowly. She crumpled against him as if someone had struck her a terrible blow.

'Oh no,' she moaned, 'You *can't*. You're blown. You won't stand a chance.'

'Darling,' he said gently, his face against her hair, his hand slowly caressing her back. 'You didn't recognise me . . . and you're my wife. Neither will they.'

But Katharine wasn't to be consoled.

'If anything happens to you,' she sobbed. 'I'll *kill* Lawrence Masters. I swear I will.'

'Lawrence had nothing to do with it,' he replied. 'The decision was taken at a much higher level.'

He pulled a handkerchief from his pocket and tenderly wiped her tear-streaked face.

'Things are happening Katharine,' he said urgently. 'The war can't go on much longer. We've reached a turning point and now it's a downhill battle for the enemy. I don't imagine I'll be away very long and then . . . I promise you, I'll never leave you again. No matter what happens. Please try to understand.'

He looked down at her. Then placed his hand under her chin, forcing her to meet his eyes.

She sniffed, holding back tears which were bursting for release.

'All I understand,' she said brokenly, 'is that you're going. I can't see beyond that. And . . . I'm afraid.'

He held her tightly to him.

'Don't be, my darling,' he soothed. 'I've told you before I'm a survivor. And now I've got someone to survive for.'

She looked up at him, her eyes glistening with unshed tears.

'Is that what you had to tell me?' she asked.

'Yes. Now you see why I couldn't break the news on the telephone.'

He looked around the deserted station.

'Though it might have been preferable to here.'

He cradled her head beneath his shoulder, lovingly stroking her hair.

'But didn't you have something to tell me?'

At that moment, there was a terrible thruuuuump, followed by another, then another. What looked like a firework display could be seen lighting the dark night sky as the sudden rattle of fire engines clanged past the deserted station.

'Heavens,' he said drawing her closer to him. 'That was near. I'm taking you into the tube.'

'No,' she shrieked. '*No*.'

How could she tell him her wonderful news sandwiched in between hundreds of sweaty bodies, with children crying and bawdy songs being sung all around them?

She opened her mouth, searching for the right words. But another deafening thruuuuuuump was followed by an ear-splitting whistling as the engines of death hurtled down from the sky.

Ashley noticed the tin hat crammed beside her gas mask. He pulled it out.

'Here,' he said, 'put this on.'

She put up her hands to prevent him.

'Katharine, I insist,' he said sternly. 'I'm already risking your life by not forcing you into the shelter. Now, do as I say, and put this thing on immediately.'

She had never known him so authoritative before. And meekly submitted as he clamped it firmly over her khaki beret.

'You look like a garden gnome hiding under a

toadstool,' he smiled, tweaking her nose. 'Now, what was it you had to tell me?'

She looked up at him and saw the laughter in his eyes at her clownlike appearance.

This was not what she had imagined. This wasn't the romantic evening they were to have spent together.

How many times in the past two days had she planned it all. Dreamed about the exact moment she would tell him, lying in his arms in the wonderful afterglow of love.

A fan of searchlights swept across the sky illuminating the grimy archway under which they were standing. In their brief glare she saw Ashley's lips twitch with amusement at her vaudeville headgear.

She looked away, her lips trembling as the tears threatened to overflow.

How could she tell him now, standing in a sordid doorway, wearing a ridiculous tin hat!

Clamping her lips tightly together in order to hold back the tears, Katharine shook her head.

'It wasn't anything important,' she whispered sadly. 'It can wait.'

He looked at his watch.

'Darling,' he said urgently. 'I only have another five minutes.'

She clung to him, terror back in her eyes.

'What do you mean?'

'I've been at Orchard Court all day for briefing . . . and this.'

He smiled and touched the hair peeping out from under his beret.

'It wasn't easy to persuade them to bring me here so that I could see you and explain . . .'

'So you rang from Orchard Court, not from Euston?' she cut in.

'Yes, I'm being picked up at half-past ten.'

Katharine felt as if her legs had suddenly turned to jelly.

'When are you going?'

'Soon.'

There was an eerie silence. The bombing appeared to have stopped for the moment.

She looked up at the sky. A bright moon. Ideal conditions for a drop.

And she suddenly felt sick.

'I intended to take you back to Kensington,' he said. 'But with this raid on you *must* go down into the tube until it's over.'

Katharine shook her head.

'I'll get a taxi back to Tamara's, whilst there's a lull. I'd rather be there, under the Morrison* table.'

He guided her along the empty platform to the main entrance.

'Everything seems quiet for the moment, perhaps we'll be able to get a taxi,' he said briskly.

It was the deathly hush before the next wave roared over.

'Ashley,' she suddenly cried, clinging to him.

He held her tight.

'It's going to be all right darling. I promise you.'

A taxi drew to a standstill beside them.

He bent his head and kissed her gently. Then, as if no longer capable of controlling his emotions, he crushed her to him and kissed her passionately, hungrily. Unable to stop.

A car glided up to the kerb, a few feet away and stopped, its engine throbbing.

Ashley looked up, tenderly wiped the tears from her face and, picking up the tin helmet which had fallen to the ground in the heat of their emotion, handed it back to her.

She climbed into the taxi without a word being spoken. As it drew away, she saw the other car cruise towards Ashley.

Her last glimpse of her husband was of him standing in the bright moonlight outside the dark station, his hand raised to his beret in a half salute.

Chapter 20

Katharine didn't keep her appointment with the gynaecologist.

In the deathly stillness which hung over London after the bombers had departed and the screech of ambulances and clang of fire engines had finally ceased, she was seized with violent abdominal pains.

As the grey dawn crept eerily over the shattered city, she tried to get out of bed. But collapsed on the floor, a sticky pool of dark red blood widening at her feet.

Tamara, awakened by her agonised shriek, immediately telephoned for an ambulance and went with her to St George's Hospital.

When she drowsily regained consciousness later that morning, a nurse was standing beside her, taking her pulse.

'The baby?' Katharine asked weakly.

'The doctor will be in to see you later,' the nurse smiled, and passed on to the next bed.

'We are not sure you were pregnant, Mrs Paget,' the doctor said early that afternoon, sitting down beside her bed.

'But all the signs,' she protested.

'Your desire for a child could have produced them,' he replied kindly.

Katharine looked away, too tired and dispirited to argue. To explain to him that her husband was her whole life, all she wanted. The desire for a child had not even crossed her mind.

'You must rest here for a few days,' the doctor went on. 'We will inform the authorities of your accident and arrange with them for you to have convalescent leave.'

He looked down at the notes in his hand.

'I see you live in Kensington.'

Katharine hadn't the energy to explain. What did it matter where she lived? Ashley had gone. And she'd lost the baby. Whatever anyone said, she was now convinced that it had been a baby.

'Have you friends or family in the country where you could rest for a week?' he droned on.

Katharine's thoughts immediately turned to Flora.

She had written so enthusiastically after the wedding inviting them both to come to Ardnakil whenever they had leave and felt they would like to get right away. And, suddenly, she longed for Ardnakil. For its peace, the security she had found inside its old stone walls. In less than a week it would be Christmas, when her leave was due. She could go to stay with Flora almost until the New Year.

'Yes,' she replied. 'I can go to Scotland.'

'Splendid,' he beamed and looked down at her kindly.

'Don't worry about this Mrs Paget. You're young. You've got plenty of time.'

And, with a brief nod, he passed on to the woman in the next bed.

Katharine's eyes filled with tears, that awful fear gripping her once again. She had plenty of time but . . . had Ashley?

* * *

As the car turned the corner and slowed down at the approach to Ardnakil drive Katharine had a shock.

The immense wrought-iron gates were no longer there. They had been taken away to be melted down and used for cannons and aeroplane parts. The waving canopy of trees bordering the drive had great gaps where many had been felled. As the house came into view she saw that the wide sweep in front of it was peppered with ambulances, jeeps and an assortment of official cars and other Army vehicles.

Flora was waiting for her at a little side door, the imposing front entrance having been taken over by the Army. Running forward as the car hummed to a standstill, she wrenched open the door and wordlessly embraced Katharine.

'I'm afraid you haven't got the canopied bed this time,' she said as they mounted the unfamiliar stairs. 'That's been commandeered. But I'm sure you'll be comfortable here.'

She threw open a door and showed Katharine into a low-ceilinged, daintily furnished room with Flora's own distinctive imprint on it.

Katharine gazed round the pretty room, then looked longingly at the bed.

Flora had been shocked by Katharine's ashen features and she intercepted the look.

'These all-night journeys are exhausting,' she remarked. 'Why don't you have a bath and go to bed for the morning? I'll have breakfast sent up to you. I want you to really rest whilst you're here. You look worn out.'

Katharine smiled wanly, only too happy to comply.

As always, Flora was the perfect hostess.

Nothing was too much trouble and Katharine was left free to do exactly as she pleased.

Flora asked no questions and Katharine felt under no pressure. And gradually, as the days drifted slowly by, Ardnakil wound its spell around her. She relaxed and a semblance of peace flowed back into her tired, overwrought body and aching heart.

It was the week before Christmas when she arrived.

She didn't know how she was going to cope with the celebrations after the hopes she had had for their first Christmas together.

Ashley's present, her father's beautiful gold cufflinks engraved with the Montval family crest, which she had discovered in one of the trunks, still lay festively wrapped in her drawer at Group R.

And she wondered what his gift to her would have been.

Katharine had intended buying a folding leather photograph frame to accompany the cufflinks, so that Ashley could have a picture of the baby alongside the one of her which he always carried with him.

Where was that photograph now?

'Along with his "personal effects" I suppose,' she thought grimly.

And the words made her shudder. They had a sinister connotation.

As with so many things one dreads, the days running up to Christmas were the most difficult for Katharine.

Little Cristobel's first birthday just a few days before, was a forefunner to the festivities. So that once the dreaded day actually arrived, she was caught up in the merry whirl. The childrens' excitement and happiness, drinks with the "occupying forces" in the Ardnakil drawing-room, which had now become part of the officers' quarters. And Christmas Day spent with Ashley's cousins, the Farquharsons.

In the end, for a few short hours, she had ceased to

think of the present or the future and had just given herself over to the joyful celebration.

Both Dorothy Farquharson and Flora had their husbands overseas. It would have been churlish to have allowed her own aching misery to surface when everyone was making such an effort to ensure that the day was a happy one for all the children.

It would also, she reasoned, be insensitive and selfish to even allow herself to be miserable, faced with the cheerfulness of the officers' convalescing at Ardnakil. Some had been terribly badly wounded. And many were also refugees from occupied countries without news of their families and their loved ones.

As she and Flora sat together in Flora's little sitting room after the children had gone to bed on Christmas night, Katharine began to feel that she could cope. The rest and the peace had restored her health, brought colour to her cheeks and she was beginning to regain some of the weight she had lost. She no longer dreaded the end of the month when she had to return to Group R.

'I'm delighted to see you looking so much better,' Flora said fondly as they sat in the flickering firelight, sipping sherry and trying to decide whether they had any appetite for the cold supper which had been left for them.

'If I am, it's thanks to you,' Katharine replied.

Flora gazed absently into the leaping flames, a smile on her lips.

'I wonder if now might not be the time to ask you a question,' she mused, talking half to herself. 'You looked so exhausted when you arrived, I thought it best to wait.'

Katharine looked up enquiringly.

'Cristobel hasn't been christened yet,' Flora went on. 'I want to wait till Robert comes home.'

She put her glass down on a small carved table at her side.

'But when he does . . . would you be her godmother?'

Katharine's eyes filled with tears.

'Please,' Flora hurriedly broke in. 'If it upsets you . . . after what has just happened . . . we'll talk about it another time.'

'It doesn't upset me,' Katharine said quietly. 'I feel honoured. Thank you Flora.'

She fished blindly in her pocket and pulled out a wisp of hankie.

'Please don't misunderstand me,' she went on, dabbing at the corners of her eyes. 'I'd be delighted.'

'I'm *so* pleased, Flora said softly. 'I wasn't sure how you'd feel about it, or even if this was the right time to ask you . . . A miscarriage is a very traumatic affair. I know, I had one and it took me a long time to get over it. One's body is all expectant, prepared and ready to nurture this life which is just beginning. And then, suddenly, everything stops.'

'The doctors said they weren't sure I was pregnant,' Katharine demurred.

She paused and her lips trembled.

'They seemed to think it was my imagination.'

Flora looked into the fire.

'I have great admiration for doctors,' she said at last. 'But most of them are men and can't know how women feel. We're instinctive creatures. A woman knows if there's a child beginning to grow inside her, in spite of what they say.'

She looked across at Katharine with a smile.

'Did *you* think you were pregnant.'

Katharine slowly inclined her head, her heart too full to speak.

'Then you most probably were.'

At that, the floodgates opened and tears which Katharine had not shed since Ashley left burst forth. She knew she was crying for the child she had lost. But she was also crying for the husband she longed to have in her arms.

Wisely Flora did not attempt to stop her or try to comfort her. She just waited till the flow dried up naturally.

'I know Ashley has had to go away,' she said tactfully. 'But . . . did you tell him you thought you were pregnant before he left?'

'I meant to,' Katharine choked.

She blew her nose loudly.

'What happened?' Flora asked gently.

'The last time we met,' Katharine confided, 'was on Victoria Station, in an air-raid. Some bombs exploded not far away and Ashley made me put on a tin hat.'

She wiped her eyes.

'I looked like a comic turn in a pantomine.'

But Flora didn't laugh.

She waited while Katharine sat gazing miserably into the fire, trying to find her words, the tears once again streaming down her cheeks.

'We should have spent the night together,' she whispered. 'I'd planned it all, how I was going to break the news to him . . .'

She stopped and her shoulders heaved with sobs.

'How *could* I tell him, standing in a filthy doorway wearing a tin hat!'

She expected Flora to laugh. But she didn't. She crossed over to where Katharine was sitting and put an arm around her shoulders.

'Of course you couldn't darling,' she said quietly, holding her close. 'Neither could I.'

Katharine reached up and touched her hand.

'Thank you Flora,' she whispered brokenly. 'I knew you'd understand.'

* * *

After her time with Flora, Katharine returned to Group R refreshed and strengthened, feeling that she could cope.

She had no direct news from Ashley, but she knew better than to expect any. Every so often she received an official letter informing her that he was well. And with that she had to be content.

January slipped by and February crept in.

Katharine felt herself becoming tense again. She did not want to forget, yet she dreaded reliving those precious moments they had shared just twelve months before.

It was leap year and her first wedding anniversary fell on a Monday. Unusually, after a hectic morning, she had the afternoon free. Throwing on her greatcoat and winding her woolly scarf several times around her neck she plunged out of the cottage and tramped through the woods till night began to fall.

She had no desire to return to the laughter and chatter at the cottage and would have stayed out indefinitely, walking mechanically, blindly into the biting wind: anything to keep her mind from dwelling on the past. But she knew that Rickie would very quickly have sounded the alarm and a search party would have set out to find her.

And that was the last thing she wanted.

Everyone was extremely busy. As Ashley had predicted when he had tried to explain his reasons for leaving, 'things were happening'. More and more agents were being sent into the field and an air of suppressed excitement hovered over their outpost in the woods. No one knew for sure what was going to happen in the next few months: but many made very shrewd guesses.

Rickie looked at her strangely as she lifted the latch and walked back into the cosy little cottage.

'Would you like a cup of tea?' she enquired. 'I was just going to make one for myself.'

Katharine knew it wasn't true.

It was well past teatime and Rickie was already in the throes of preparing dinner. She smiled at her and Rickie noticed the strain on her face. Her eyes had lost their tawny sheen and changed to a dull brown. She couldn't help contrasting it with Katharine's radiant face just one year ago today. Rickie hadn't forgotten the date. And she wondered whether to mention it.

But Katharine turned and made for the stairs.

'I've got a bit of a headache,' she lied. 'I think I'll go up to bed and sleep it off. It could be the beginnings of a cold. I'll take some aspirin and nip it in the bud, then I'll be all right in the morning.'

She paused on the top step and looked down at Rickie, standing plump and motherly, gazing anxiously up at her from below.

'Don't wake me for dinner,' Katharine smiled. 'I'm not very hungry.'

Rickie's face was grim as she returned to the kitchen.

She knew that last statement wasn't true.

The war had been on for four and a half years. Rationing had become more and more stringent and they were all of them hungry most of the time.

Katharine kicked off her shoes and flopped back on the bed in the small blacked-out room.

The hard physical exercise in the numbing cold had tired her body. But it had not stopped her mind from working. Had not enabled her to shut out the past, to wrap a blanket of forgetfulness over her emotions and her memories.

She didn't turn on the little lamp beside her. She didn't want to see Ashley's face smiling up at her from the silver frame on her bedside table. She put her hands over her ears to shut out his voice, his laughter which seemed to be echoing round the room, trying to reach her from every corner.

As she had done on that early June morning after he had left her to return to Scotland, Katharine rolled over on to her side and, clutching a pillow tightly to her, rocked miserably backwards and forwards.

'Ashley, Ashley,' she called into the darkness. 'Where are you? Why did you leave me?'

Without realising it she was using the same gestures, the same words. Only this time there was an added poignancy because now she did not know where he was. And although her head understood why he had left her, her heart could not accept it.

She heard the sitting-room door open and strains of 'What'll I do when you are far away . . .' floated up the stairs.

The door closed cutting off the singer's voice. But it had been enough to dredge up memories which she had been trying all day to keep hidden. Memories of Ashley holding her in his arms as they danced. Gazing into her eyes, rubbing his cheek gently against hers. Whispering the words of the tune in her ear as they swayed together, oblivious of everyone else.

Once again she called his name into the darkness.

But there was no reply.

With a heart-rending sob she buried her face in the pillow and wept.

When she awoke, the house was quiet and the room cold. A chilling damp hung over everything.

Half-drugged with sleep, Katharine got stiffly off the bed and, groping blindly for her nightie, left her uniform in a crumpled heap on the floor and crawled back into bed

'Better?' Rickie remarked as she walked into the dining-room next morning. 'You managed to ward it off?'

'I think so,' Katharine replied non-committally.

The long sleep had not refreshed her. But emotionally she felt better. More able to cope. The day she had dreaded had passed. All she now wanted to do was plunge back into the work and get this war over as quickly as possible.

From what she had been able to gather from the rumours which ran around, everyone seemed to think that it wouldn't be much longer. Ashley had survived up till now. There was no reason why he shouldn't survive for the rest of the time. He had said he didn't expect to be away for long. Perhaps he'd be back for his birthday in May.

Hugging this hope to her, it sustained her during the hectic, action-filled weeks which followed.

But Ashley did not return for his birthday.

One beautiful May evening Katharine was perched on her bedroom window sill breathing in the variegated scents rising up from the damp earth below. Watching the birds as they twittered in and out of the blossom-laden branches or drowsed contentedly on a bough, waiting for night to fall.

It was the third springtime she had spent at Group R. And each year she marvelled afresh at the beauty of the blossoming countryside. The shaded greens of the woods, the hedgerows bursting into flower and the glory of the enormous rhododendron bushes which surrounded the cottage.

She felt particularly privileged to be living in such secluded beauty when so many FANYs were sweating it out in Baker Street, spending their days in dark dusty offices, the windows boarded up or criss-crossed with strips of ugly brown paper. And their nights in an underground shelter.

And she wondered why she had been chosen to come down here. Why, in time, she hadn't been briefed with another identity and sent into the field. But deep down inside her she knew that since she had met Ashley she had lost all desire to go.

She smiled to herself.

How much she had changed!

Two years ago she had been furious, frustrated by this imposed exile.

But now she simply didn't care.

She was Ashley's wife and that was all she ever wanted to be.

Remembering that Sunday afternoon with her husband in the Buckinghamshire woods, a warm glow swept through her, fanning out into every part of her body.

And she felt safe and at peace.

Ashley had promised to serve God once the war was over. He believed in him, trusted him. God wouldn't let him down. She had no need to worry. After such a promise, he would surely bring him safely back.

It was the 7th of May. Tomorrow was his birthday. Perhaps next year they would spend it together.

Katharine positively glowed as she turned from the window and skipped happily down to dinner, wrapped in this warm comforting assurance.

Chapter 21

What on earth's Lawrence Masters doing down here?' Katharine frowned, glancing out of the office window the following morning.

'He seems to be in an awful hurry. His car pulled up with a skid and now he's roaring up the steps two at a time.'

Tatiana coloured slightly, but said nothing.

Katharine grinned mischievously.

Lawrence Masters had shown more than a professional interest in Tatiana since they had been best man and bridesmaid at her wedding.

'You wouldn't know by any chance?' she teased.

'I've no idea,' Tatiana replied hastily, getting to her feet and shuffling some papers together to hide her embarrassment.

Only Katharine knew that she and Lawrence had been meeting in London during her weekends off.

'He's a bit of all right,' Anne winked, strolling over to the window. 'Let's have a look.'

'Too late,' Katharine laughed. 'He's disappeared inside in a cloud of dust. Never seen him in such a state. Looked as if all the devils in hell were after him.'

'I'd be after him if I thought I should half a chance,' Anne yawned. 'Isn't it nearly lunchtime, I'm starving.'

Katharine glanced at her watch.

'Another half hour. I've got to pop back to my room: left a file there last night and I need it. Won't be a sec.'

She had hardly left when the telephone rang.

It was the Colonel wanting Katharine to come to his office.

'She's just gone over to the cottage,' Nicola answered. 'She won't be long. I'll tell her to come as soon as she gets back.'

'Yes, do that,' the Colonel replied. 'No, wait a minute . . . What did you say Lawrence?'

There was a pause.

'Yes, very well, if you think that would be best. Don't bother to ask her to come,' he ended.

'Shall I come then?' Nicola queried. 'Or Anne or Tatiana?'

'No, no, it's quite all right.'

He sounded flustered.

'Never mind.'

And he rang off.

Nicola put down the receiver with a shrug.

Completely potty, was her only comment.

Katharine was on her way back from the cottage, the file in her hand, when she saw Masters coming towards her. His head was down and he looked preoccupied.

'Good morning Lawrence,' she said brightly as he walked straight past her, deep in thought.

He started. Then slowly turned round.

Katharine turned round too, dimpling in amusement. Then she saw the expression on his face. And stood stock-still.

His usually suave features were drawn. His face greyish white in the spring sunshine. There was a taut anguished look about him, as if every nerve in his body was being stretched to its limit.

As they stared at each other, their eyes met and

Katharine felt the blood slowly drain out of her face too. Out of her whole body. The file she was holding trembled and fell to the grass, scattering its contents. But she scarcely noticed. She couldn't take her eyes off Lawrence Masters' face which she instinctively knew now mirrored her own.

'Lawrence,' she said, and her voice seemed to come from far away, like the croak of a frog at the bottom of a pond.

He took a step towards her.

She could see a muscle working in his left cheek. His hands clenching and unclenching at his sides.

She didn't move, she couldn't. A heavy dead-weight was anchoring her to the ground, tugging at her feet and refusing to let them go forward to meet him. As she watched, helpless, he slowly covered the few yards which separated them, like a man dragging his feet to meet the executioner.

'Katharine,' he began, his eyes on the ground.

He took her arm. But she shrugged him away and forced him to look at her.

'It's Ashley . . . isn't it?'

That tell-tale muscle twitched. But he didn't speak.

'He's . . .'

But she couldn't pronounce the word. Couldn't bear to hear it out in the open, floating away on the air with all its finality. All it implied.

He slowly nodded.

Suddenly the blood which had drained out of Katharine as she watched him walk towards her roared back, beating in her head, her ears, throbbing in her chest as it frantically pumped at her heart. She felt blinded by it, choked by it as it rushed into her throat and gurgled round, threatening to suffocate her.

He took her arm again but she blazed round at him.

'Say it's not true,' she cried.

'Katharine,' he pleaded.

'Say it's not true Lawrence. He's not dead, he's only missing, wounded, anything . . .'

He stood motionless.

'But not that,' she pleaded.

She suddenly crumpled and he caught her as she fell.

Her eyes were black with fear and pain as she grabbed the lapels of his jacket.

'Lawrence . . . please.'

It was the cry of a hunted fawn, desperate, lost, abandoned, with no strength left to go on.

He put his arm round her and half-carried her the few steps back to the cottage.

'Eleanor,' he called sharply as he lifted the latch. 'Can you bring some brandy.'

Eleanor Ricks was out of the kitchen and into the hall in a flash.

She took one look at Katharine and, putting her shoulder beneath her other arm, helped her into the sitting-room.

'It's all right Lawrence,' she gasped, as between them they managed to get Katharine on to the sofa. 'You leave her to me.'

'But you don't know . . .' he began.

'I don't need to know,' she said tartly. 'It's obvious.'

She gently lifted Katharine's feet on to the sofa and dragging a tartan rug off one of the armchairs covered her trembling body.

'Off you go Lawrence and do what you have to do. You might suggest the three girls have lunch over there. Katharine needs peace.'

'Of course,' he said meekly, capitulating beneath Eleanor's business-like efficiency.

He looked helplessly down at Katharine.

'I'll be over to see you before I go back to London,' he said diffidently. 'Try to sleep.'

Katharine gave him a venemous look.

'Please don't bother,' she spat bitterly. 'I'm not interested in hearing you pontificate about the nobility of sacrifice. Especially when it's someone else's.'

She took a sharp intake of breath, letting it out in a sound that was almost a hiss.

'You can go to hell for all I care.'

It was so unlike Katharine to be even unpleasant, let alone downright rude, that both Eleanor and Lawrence were momentarily taken back. But Rickie recovered first.

She jerked her head in the direction of the door.

'Don't take any notice,' she whispered as he passed her on tiptoe. 'She's had a terrible shock and she's not herself.'

He bent over and kissed her cheek.

'Dear Eleanor,' he murmured, and glided through the door.

Rickie slipped out of the room and came back with a glass in her hand.

'Drink this,' she said, gently raising Katharine's head.

Katharine pressed her lips tightly together.

'I don't want it,' she hissed.

'I'm not asking you what you want,' Rickie replied equably, totally unperturbed by Katharine's unpleasant manner. 'I'm telling you to drink it. Now come along and let's have no more nonsense.'

To her surprise Katharine took the glass and downed the brandy in one gulp, grimacing as the fiery liquid shot through her body.

Rickie gently eased her back on to the sofa, plumping the cushion behind her head and settling her as comfortably as possible.

'Now,' she said, sitting down beside her. 'Would you like to go to bed, to sleep here, or do you want to talk?'

For a moment Katharine lay back with closed eyes, saying nothing. Then she opened them, her full gaze hitting Rickie like a dagger. There was no longer any light in them. Rickie was left gazing into two dark black cavernous hollows from which all life seemed to have been extinguished.

Katharine reached out a hand and grasped Rickie's plump fingers, squeezing them so tightly she thought the joints must surely break.

'Dear Rickie,' she whispered, releasing the pressure slightly only to reinforce it once again, as if she were a lifeline to which the drowning Katharine could cling. 'If you can bear it, I'd like to talk.'

'I can bear it,' Rickie said gently, smoothing the hair back from Katharine's damp forehead.

She released her hand and unlaced Katharine's shoes, dropping them one by one on to the floor beside the sofa.

'You don't need to tell me anything you don't want to,' she went on. 'But if it helps, we'll talk all afternoon.'

Katharine sat up and hugged her, then clung to her warm ample bosom.

'It's Ashley,' she whispered. 'Lawrence says he's dead.'

Her voice broke.

'But he's not, he's not . . .'

She looked up pleadingly. But Rickie only shook her head sorrowfully.

'If Lawrence says he is, then, my dear, I'm afraid you have to accept it. I'm sure he'd have preferred to give you any news but that.'

Rickie looked down at her, her hazel eyes full of compassion.

'You can wait for official notification if you don't believe him.'

Katharine said nothing. She knew Rickie was right. She knew, in her heart, that Lawrence was right. But the rest of her refused to believe it.

Rickie took her icy hand in both of hers.

'Lawrence made the journey from London when he's very busy, using his precious petrol, so as to tell you himself. He wanted to spare you hearing it from an impersonal piece of paper.'

Katharine looked down at the criss-cross on the blanket. But she didn't reply.

In spite of what Ashley had told her at their last meeting, she still felt that Lawrence Masters was responsible for her husband returning to the field.

'Perhaps he only came to salve his conscience,' she said bitterly.

'Katharine,' Rickie chided. 'You know that's not true.'

'I don't,' Katharine replied stubbornly. 'Ashley was blown, he should never have returned to the field. Why didn't Lawrence go himself?'

Rickie got up.

'That sort of talk won't get us anywhere,' she said equably. 'And it's not fair. You don't know the circumstances.'

'I only know that Ashley's dead and *he's* here,' Katharine cut in angrily. 'Sitting safely in a chairborne job.'

Rickie sighed.

'How can I help you if you close your mind like that.'

Katharine's soft lips shut in a hard line.

'No one can help me,' she said bitterly. 'I've got everything I didn't want. Beginning with a dead hero for a husband.'

She turned her blank, lifeless eyes full on Rickie.

'They sent him back into that murderous hell for a false ideal,' she whispered brokenly. 'For some stupid idea of patriotism spawned by loud-mouthed politicians sitting safely in Whitehall chanting "It's a glorious thing to die for your country!"'

Her hands clenched tightly together until the knuckles showed white.

'I only have to wait for an official box with a medal inside. And letters of sympathy from people who never left the War Office!'

Her eyes, now blazing with a terrible anger, pierced through Rickie.

'Where is this God everyone keeps talking about? Where is he? Tell me that!'

'Don't blame God, Katharine,' Rickie said quietly, her eyes steadily returning Katharine's gaze. 'It was men who killed Ashley, not God.'

Katharine crumpled. All resistance gone.

She felt completely cut off from reality. As if she had been transported to another planet and was looking impersonally down on her own tortured body.

Rickie sat quietly beside her, saying nothing. Making no attempt to comfort or even touch her. Waiting until the terrible storm had passed.

The mellow chimes of the grandfather clock in the hall rang out the half hour.

Katharine looked up.

'Half-past twelve?' she queried.

'Half-past one,' Rickie replied.

Katharine threw aside the blanket.

'I must go,' she cried. 'The car is leaving in a quarter of an hour. We've got an exercise this afternoon. James and I are decoys for the new students. Got to leave a message in the telephone box near the Winter Gardens . . . have tea in the cinema café . . . see if they can detect us . . . try to throw them off.'

Her speech was rambling and disjointed.

Rickie gently urged her back on to the sofa.

'Don't worry Katharine, Nicola is going in your place.'

'But . . .'

'Try to sleep,' Rickie soothed. 'I know it sounds trite, but grief is exhausting and one can't think clearly. Let me help you up to bed and we'll see how you feel in an hour or two.'

* * *

When Katharine awoke, the late afternoon sun was streaming in through her bedroom window.

Lawrence Masters was sitting on the sill, idly gazing down into the garden below.

Katharine frowned, momentarily lost.

What was she doing in bed in the middle of the afternoon? And why was Lawrence here?

Then, as the clouds of sleep drifted away and consciousness flooded back, she remembered. And suddenly the sun was extinguished, the sky grew black and all colour vanished from the beautiful May day.

'It's Ashley's birthday,' she murmured, sitting up and pushing her hair away from her face.

Her hand sought her husband's last present to her, the little regimental brooch pinned to the pocket of her khaki shirt. And she clutched it desperately.

Lawrence Masters turned round.

'I know,' he said softly.

She lay back on the pillows, her hand idly stroking the small hard diamonds.

'I'm sorry Lawrence.'

His face cleared and he came quickly towards her.

She patted the bed and he gingerly sat down.

'Don't worry,' she smiled. 'I don't bite.'

He smiled back tautly.

'I probably would in your shoes.'

'It was the shock,' she explained.

'I know. I thought by coming to tell you myself I could cushion it a little.'

He passed his hand wearily across his immaculate dark hair. 'But perhaps I did more harm than good.'

'No,' she said gently. 'I'm grateful to you for coming. I'm just sorry I was so awful.'

'Oh that's all right,' he smiled.

And finally relaxed.

'I rather held you responsible,' Katharine murmured. 'Thought it was you who pushed Ashley to go back, even though he was blown.'

'On the contrary,' Lawrence cut in. 'I was *against* it, in spite of his experience.'

He smiled sadly down at Katharine.

'Your husband was one of our crack agents. Been in the racket since the very beginning and had a wealth of experience behind him. That's why the powers-that-be decided to send him back, despite the odds.'

His handsome face hardened momentarily.

'But I felt the risk was too great.'

He looked thoughtfully down at his finger nails.

'I'm only sorry I was proved right.'

He sighed deeply

'No, the whole thing was out of my hands. The decision was taken at a much higher level.'

'So Ashley told me'

Katharine paused and took a deep breath, as if summoning all her courage.

'What happened?' she asked at last.

'Do you really want to know?'

'Wouldn't you?'

'I don't know. Yes, I suppose so.'

He got up and, thrusting his hands deep into his trouser pockets, strolled over to the little casement window and stood looking out once more.

'Ashley didn't go into the field alone. There were four of them. He was in charge of the mission.'

He looked round to where she was following him with her eyes, hanging on his every word.

'You must know that things are about to happen. Ashley and his team went as an advance guard, to prepare the way. There's been a lot of sabotage lately, especially in the north and west of France. He was responsible for a great deal of it. And for organising others. The object of the operation was to blow up railway lines and cut communications so that when the Allied landing actually happens, the Germans won't be able to immediately rush troops and supplies to the battle zone. And we shall be able to get a good spearhead.'

Lawrence sighed.

'Unfortunately, the last one went wrong. Well, that's not strictly true. The operation was successful. But they were discovered.'

'How many of them?' Katharine enquired.

'Only Ashley was arrested. He was in charge and he held the fort so that the others could get away. They were picked up in the early hours of this morning by Dakota.'

Katharine raised her eyebrows in surprise.

'We couldn't get a Lysander at such short notice,' Lawrence explained, 'so the Americans, God bless 'em, lent us one of theirs. I was at the airfield when they landed. That's how I got the news.'

'And Ashley? If he was arrested, perhaps he's still alive somewhere. Perhaps there's still hope.'

She sat up eagerly, her eyes pleading, willing him to say yes.

He walked slowly towards her and sat heavily down on the bed once again.

'If that were the case,' he said brokenly, 'I wouldn't be here. I'd be raising heaven and earth to get him freed.'

Katharine's eyes wandered to the whitewashed walls where late sunbeams were dancing up and down, forming ever-changing patterns.

'You haven't answered my question,' she said steadily. 'How do you know Ashley's not a prisoner?'

He looked around the room, as if seeking a way out.

Then his eyes locked with hers. And he knew there was no escape.

Taking both her hands he held them tightly in his own.

'We had a quick Y9 at Orchard Court as soon as the others landed this morning.'

He breathed deeply, struggling to find his words. And the pressure on her hands increased.

'And?'

Lawrence looked at her and then looked quickly away, the pain he saw in her eyes reflected in his own.

'They told us that Ashley was shot last night in the prison yard.'

She stared at him, stunned.

'Katharine,' he said helplessly.

But she remained motionless, her mind whirling round and round like a revolving door.

Last night!

Perhaps even when she had been sitting on the window-sill in the evening sunshine exulting in the fact that the God he wished to serve for the rest of his life would surely protect him . . . he had already been lying in a crumpled heap in a French prison yard.

'How can you be sure it was Ashley?'

And once again her voice came out like a croak.

'Maybe it was someone else.'

'It was Ashley,' he said quietly. 'One of our men is working in the prison. He took a tremendous risk, but he got the news to the others just before they left . . .'

Lawrence's voice broke.

'He saw his body . . .'

His voice ended in a strangled choke.

Katharine's normally pale face was suddenly drained of all colour. Only her eyes still seemed alive, burning in a parchment frame.

'Katharine,' he pleaded helplessly.

But she remained staring, her hands limp and lifeless in his own.

He got up and strode over to the door.

'Eleanor,' he called. 'Can you come.'

The sitting-room door opened and a snatch of music drifted up the stairs.

'What'll I do when you are far away . . .'

The door closed cutting the music off. She heard Rickie running up the stairs.

But the music had sprung the coil on Katharine's taut nerves.

As Rickie entered the little room, the floodgates opened. With a heart-rending shriek, Katharine buried her face in her pillow and wept.

But tears, which had eased many a broken heart, could not touch this one. Every part of her body agonised and ached with the love she could no longer give to the man who had died.

* * *

That night, after Lawrence left, she tried to sleep.

But whenever she closed her eyes she could see him, standing, sometimes blindfolded, sometimes tied to a stake, in a bare prison yard. And, in the distance, she heard the sharp crack of rifle fire.

'It's not guns which kill,' Ashley had once said when she had remarked on the rifles soldiers so nonchalantly carried around with them. 'It's men.'

How true it had proved in his case.

Had it just been guns, lying idle on a table, Ashley would still be alive. But it was the hands which held them which had killed him.

Her moods during that first terrible, sleepless night alternated between passive despair and boiling fury against the people who had torn her husband away from her. And heartlessly extinguished his life.

'It was a summary execution,' Lawrence had said. 'The Germans are panicking and there a lot of them in France at the moment.'

She tried to put herself in Ashley's place. To wonder what had gone through his mind. How he had felt when he knew that there was no longer any hope, that they were never going to be together again.

But she couldn't.

Her own misery was so overpowering that she was unable to think of anything else. Ashley was dead. And with his death everything had gone. There was nothing left to live for. Only a bleak succession of days and weeks and months, even years, which stretched pointlessly ahead of her.

A grey fog of utter hopelessness imprisoned her, as he had been imprisoned. And she felt amputated.

Part of herself, without which she would never be whole again, was no longer there. It had been brutally cut away leaving her torn and bleeding. Like an amputee, she still felt the pain in the vital missing part. And she knew that she would go through life on crutches.

The dark hours of the endless night wore on, punctuated only by the chimes of the clock in the hall below. Yet, although incoherent with pain and grief, out of the charred and battered remnants of her mind one assurance rose crystal clear in her mind. No matter what she did or where she went, Ashley would always be there beside her, sending life pulsating through her tired, aching body.

And, momentarily, it calmed her.

As birds began to twitter, the darkness of night gradually lifted, turning from the pallid cloak of dawn to the clear glow preceding sunrise, and a new day dawned, so did that terrible blackness lift from her heart.

She relived the tender moments of their short time together, recalled their ever-deepening love. Clutching the little Pegasus brooch in her hand until the diamonds bit into her palm, Katharine turned her aching head and gazed into her husband's face, smiling down at her from its silver frame.

And she could find nothing to regret.

Chapter 22

Katharine was given five days compassionate leave.

But she didn't know what to do or where to go.

For the past year her life had been bound up in Ashley. When he wasn't with her she felt that she no longer existed, and had just lived for their next meeting.

She shuddered at the thought of going to Goudhurst and seeing, every time she left the house, the little church where they had been married. But worse, she dreaded having to face the funeral expressions and combined wailing of Elsie and Myrtle. Especially Myrtle, who thrived on bad news. And the air of genteel mourning which they would spread throughout the house.

Then she remembered Flora.

And a sudden longing for her and for Ardnakil, where war seemed remote and far away and the days drifted by like a soft Highland mist, overwhelmed her.

But another thought struck her.

Her last visit had been at Christmas time and the garden had been deserted. But now, with the beautiful summer weather, it would be strewn with wheelchairs and the walking wounded, with men on crutches being helped across the lawns by VADs. Officers who had survived.

And her courage failed her.

Katharine felt that there was no one with whom she could share the deep pain of Ashley's death. No one who would really understand.

As if a light dawned in her brain, she suddenly realised that *she* was now Ashley's next of kin. Her father-in-law would not have been informed.

Packing a bag, she left immediately for the Rectory.

With the dawn, Katharine had reached some sort of truce with her emotions and the anger and bitterness had momentarily dissipated. But as the train chunted through the battered north London suburbs, she wondered if the terrible aching void which was left behind was not worse.

Anger she could fight.

But this sense of nothingness, of wandering alone in a long black tunnel with no light at either end; floating in a kind of limbo cut off from reality; isolated from every other human being by a vast sea of pain and grief, was worse than anything she had ever experienced.

The straggling suburbs gave way to lacy fields of buttercups and daisies, their pale delicate faces raised upwards to catch the teasing rays of the sun. It kept peeping, like a mischievous child, then disappearing behind the endlessly shifting clouds: gliding across tiny fields enclosed by hedgerows, then darting into dark expanses of woodland.

Gazing numbly at the changing lights of the passing countryside, Katharine remembered the pain of her mother's death, the injustice of it. But it was different. Life had still gone on in a strange, remote kind of way. She had been young. Her whole life before her. And she had known that one day she would come out of it, be able to laugh again.

But not so with Ashley's death. Part of herself had

stood in that prison yard with him. Part of herself had crumpled and died.

She covered her ears with her hands as the sound of shots rang out again. And she felt suddenly weary and very old.

A portly man sitting in the opposite seat glanced curiously at her over the top of *The Times*.

Katharine slowly removed her hands from her ears, feeling slightly foolish.

When she arrived, the clouds had dispersed and it was another sunny May day.

'It's Mrs Ashley,' the housekeeper called, as Katharine walked out to join her father-in-law.

He was in the garden tying back the rose bushes which wandered in rich profusion all over the old stone walls of the Rectory in summer.

Putting down his shears he turned to greet her. But something in her face, or perhaps Mrs Miles' tone of voice, must have warned him that this was not just a social visit.

Taking her gently by the arm he led her to a seat under the weeping-willow.

'What is it Katharine?' he said gently as they sat down side by side.

She looked up at him, her eyes bleak and lifeless, wondering whether or not to tell him the whole truth.

He waited patiently, his arm lying along the back of the bench behind her.

'Ashley's dead,' she said at last.

And her voice sounded dead too.

For a few minutes William Paget didn't speak. Just sat gazing through the swaying leaves as they dipped around them, fighting to gain control of his voice.

'When I saw your face I guessed it was bad news,' he said at last. 'But I hoped it wasn't as bad as that.'

He looked down at her, compassion mirrored in his violet-blue eyes.

'And something in you has died too.'

A deep silence fell between them. The only sound came from the birds fluttering in and out of the blossom-laden trees, the gentle sigh of the willow as a soft breeze stroked its leaves.

He put his arm round her shoulders and she leaned against him, hungry for comfort and reassurance.

'Don't you want to know what happened?' she asked at last.

'Of course I want to know,' he murmured. 'What father wouldn't. But what I want to avoid at the moment is hurting you even more.'

He absently stroked her hair, just as Ashley had so often done.

'Would it help you to tell me?'

Katharine didn't immediately answer.

'I don't know,' she said slowly at last.

And she wondered whether she had been right to insist when Lawrence had hesitated to give her the horrible details. Her knowing hadn't helped Ashley. He was beyond helping. And it certainly hadn't helped her.

Then she looked up into his father's face and saw the love and concern for her etched with his own pain. And she suddenly realised that it would help. It wouldn't change anything. It wouldn't bring Ashley back. But the burden was too great for her to carry alone.

She turned to his father.

'He was doing undercover work in France.'

'I guessed as much,' William Paget replied. 'Though I didn't know where.'

Katharine took a deep breath in an effort to control

herself. Then, in a voice choked with sobs, told him the whole gruesome story.

He sat very still for a long time after she had finished, his eyes fixed on the old stone wall at the end of the garden.

Katharine looked up at him, her own eyes dark with pain.

'How can you sit there as if nothing had happened,' she whispered brokenly. 'How can you be so calm? You've lost *everything*. Your wife, both your sons . . .'

And she burst into tears.

'We've *both* lost everything,' he said softly when the storm of weeping began to abate. 'But I think it is worse for you Katharine than it is for me. You and Ashley had such a short time together. You had so many hopes and plans for the future.'

He sighed.

'A future which now has been blotted out.'

Noticing the sodden scrap of linen in her hand, he passed her a handkerchief.

'Most of my plans had already been accomplished when tragedy struck. It's not quite the same. But it still hurts. It hurts most dreadfully. And I imagine it will go on hurting for the rest of my life.'

Katharine scrubbed the hankie round her swollen face.

'I wish I knew where Ashley was,' she said miserably.

'I can tell you,' he replied without looking round. 'He's with his Heavenly Father and with Guy and his mother. He'll be there waiting for us when our time comes to join him.'

'But how can you be so *sure*,' Katharine blurted out.

He turned and looked at her.

Despite the pain in his eyes, Katharine could also see

a deep peace. His features were drawn, but not tortured. His smile gentle, without bitterness.

'Because Ashley was prepared,' he replied. 'Like Guy was prepared. He told me the last time I saw him, when you were both here in October, that he had spoken with you and that you were in agreement for him to take Holy Orders once the war was over.'

Katharine gave a shuddering sob.

So many plans, so much happiness in store . . . now shattered.

Tears filled her eyes and blurred her vision. No longer able to control them they forced their way through her tightly-closed lids and burned hot furrows down her sore cheeks.

She wondered where they could possibly come from, all those tears. Where they had been stored. In the past twenty-four hours she seemed to have shed enough to last a lifetime. And still they kept flowing.

'I'm afraid I don't have another handkerchief on me,' William Paget said. 'Shall I go into the house and get one for you?'

She shook her head, rubbing her arm across her face.

'No, please go on.'

'We discussed it at length when you and Hope were bathing the boys. From what Ashley told me then I'm convinced that he had a real conversion when he was in prison.'

'Conversion?' Katharine frowned. 'What do you mean? I thought Ashley was brought up as a Christian?'

'He was. But, like everyone else, he had to find his faith for himself. Up till then he'd been living on his mother's faith, and mine.'

Katharine's eyes followed his gaze.

He was watching two chattering sparrows hopping on the old stone birdbath in the middle of the lawn.

He smiled as a starling swooped down and, jabbering angrily, the sparrows flew away.

'It's a personal thing Katharine, faith in a loving Heavenly Father. And Ashley didn't really find it until he was face to face with death two years ago.'

Katharine shuddered. For a brief moment, over preoccupied with the sparrows, she had forgotten.

'Then why didn't God look after him?' she cut in belligerently. 'Surely he'd have been more use to him alive than dead. Especially as he intended going into the church.'

The starling flew off.

William Paget's eyes followed it as it rose and disappeared among the leaves of a spreading oak tree.

'Look at it this way Katharine.'

He turned towards her. And once again Katharine noticed the sweetness of his smile. She wondered what he found to smile about.

'God gives us free will. Ashley chose to do this dangerous work . . . I'm sure God protected him. And maybe his death was a kind of protection, even a deliverance.'

Katharine opened her mouth to protest, but he silenced her.

'He died quickly, didn't he?'

Once again her tears overflowed.

'Would you rather he had fallen into the hands of the Gestapo?'

Katharine choked.

'At least there'd have been a chance of his coming out alive,' she said miserably at last.

'Perhaps,' he answered drily. 'But at what cost? I think, considering the circumstances, God *did* look after him.'

'But why didn't he *rescue* him, if he's all-powerful.'

William Paget thoughtfully stroked his chin.

'I don't know Katharine. I wish I did. If I did know, I'd be God.'

He sighed deeply.

'Death and suffering are two of life's great unsolved mysteries to which we will never have the answer this side of heaven.'

A wasp hovered, buzzing dangerously near Katharine's tear-stained face. She flapped at it with her hand and it angrily flew away.

'The one thing that keeps me going is that I know that those people I loved most in the world, my wife Catriona, Guy and Ashley believed in God. And because they believed, they are now with him. For me death is not a final parting but only, as you say in French, an adieu, till we meet again.'

He looked down at her, his eyes warm and understanding.

'Can you believe that too Katharine?'

She didn't return his gaze. Just sat staring straight ahead of her at the old stone wall where her father-in-law's eyes had so recently rested. She wondered whether he had seen something there. Some sign which she couldn't see.

But there were only the clustered rose bushes waiting to burst into bloom.

'I don't know,' she said at last.

He placed his hand over hers.

'That's the first step to faith,' he said gently.

He got up and stretched down his hand to her.

'My dear,' he said contritely. 'I didn't even ask you whether you had had lunch, and now it's almost teatime. Let's go into the house, Hope will soon be back. She went to attend a local firewatchers' meeting and is picking the boys up from school on her way home.'

He linked his arm affectionately in hers, as Ashley had so often done. A lump rose in her throat once again. But she managed to stem the tears.

'You don't have to rush away I hope. You can stay a little while with us?'

'I've got five days compassionate leave,' she said flatly as they walked together across the lawn.

'Good,' he said. 'I'll ask Mrs Miles to make up the bed in the spare room.'

Katharine looked up at him gratefully.

When she had stayed before, she had occupied Ashley's old room. All his things were still there. His trophies, his mementos, his school and college photographs. She didn't think she could face it just at the moment.

'Thank you Father,' she said, calling him that for the first time.

Up till then she had been embarrassed and avoided calling him anything.

He squeezed her arm against his side.

'You see,' he smiled. 'God is good. I've lost two sons, but he has given me two beautiful daughters.'

As they went through the sidedoor into the hall, the front door burst open and Ben and Philip shot through it, ties round the backs of their necks and grey socks concertinaed. Their raised voices echoed round the quiet house, their exhuberant high spirits causing instant chaos.

Her father-in-law grabbed Ben as he attempted to butt him in the midriff.

'I'm sure you and Hope would like to have a chat together,' he gasped, above Ben's butting head. 'I'll look after these two monsters. They can have tea with me in my study.'

Ben stopped butting immediately.

'But you've got to wash those filthy hands first,' his grandfather warned.

The two boys dashed off in the direction of the downstairs cloakroom as Hope walked into the hall.

Her face lit with pleasure when she saw Katharine.

Then her eyes took in her sister-in-law's wan cheeks, her red swollen eyes and abruptly her smile faded. With a cry she ran across the hall and flung her arms around her.

The tears welled up again. There didn't seem to be any way of stopping them. But Katharine's cold almost lifeless body suddenly felt warmer. She felt loved. She felt she had come home.

* * *

The few days which Katharine spent at the Rectory were like a balm to her aching heart and weary spirit.

Unlike Elsie and Myrtle, Mrs Miles did not droop around the house spreading gloom, nor assume a funereal expression the minute Katharine walked into a room. She carried on usual. But, in her own quiet way, through little acts of kindness, she showed Katharine that she cared.

William Paget remained an enigma to his daughter-in-law.

Even after their conversation on the day of her arrival she still could not understand how, in spite of his deep grief, he had this peace about him. A stillness which came from within. It wasn't the empty blankness which she felt. It was a well of quiet which rose up and surrounded him.

Yet she knew that he felt and understood the enormity of her loss. Because it was also his own.

'I know that death is not the end,' he had said to her

gently one evening when she had broken down in front of Ashley's photograph smiling at her from the top of the grand piano. 'And I know that I shall see him again.'

He had looked at her his blue eyes, so like Ashley's, kindly yet piercing.

'Do you Katharine?' he had ended kindly.

But she had been unable to answer him.

In her heart she wanted to believe. Sometimes, on sunny afternoons, when she walked in the woods with Hope she almost did believe. Then this dreadful question-mark 'why' would rise up and dangle mockingly in front of her eyes.

And in the long sleepless nights when she tossed and turned, lived and relived the events of the past few days she knew that she didn't want a future heaven where Ashley would be waiting for her.

She wanted him now, warm and passionate in her arms. She wanted the reassurance of his hard muscular body close to hers, his hands caressing her, the lingering odour of his haircream on her pillow. She wanted to be able to reach out in the night and touch him. To wake in the morning and know that he was there.

In her anguish she cried out in anger against this God whom he had worshipped. And who had not saved him.

On the Saturday afternoon, as she and Hope sat together in the shade of the weeping willow, idly flipping through some family photograph albums, smiling at snapshots of Guy and Ashley as tousle-haired little boys, their clarity muddied by the old-fashioned sepia colour, Hope reached out a hand and touched hers.

'It does get better Katharine,' she said gently. 'I promise you it does. It's almost four years now since Guy was killed and when it happened I thought my life had ended. But the hackneyed old saying is true. Time *is* a great healer. One just has to be patient.'

She lay back in her deckchair, her eyes on the blurr of roses meandering over the old stone wall.

'I'm not saying it's easy. It isn't. I still ache for Guy, more so at some times than at others. And I ache for the boys.'

She smiled sadly at Katharine, who was drinking in her every word.

'What can one say to one's children when they cry out for their Daddy in the night, as Philip did that first year? Ben was only two when Guy was killed. Sometimes I wonder whether he really remembers him. But he knows there's something missing in his life.'

Hope paused.

'It's easier at the moment because so many fathers are away. But, once the war's over, hopefully many of them will come back. But their Daddy won't.'

She sat up and shaded her eyes, looking for her sons whose shouts had abruptly ceased. But they reappeared round the side of the house, pushing bicycles. And she leant back again, reassured.

'One swears one will never forget,' Hope went on pensively. 'And, of course, one never does.'

She smiled to herself.

'But after a while, one doesn't remember *all* the time. Sensations *do* grow dim, however much one vows they never will. Memory doesn't fade, it just becomes a little blurred. The pain stops being a knife turning constantly in a jagged open wound and gradually becomes a nagging ache.'

She smiled at Katharine.

'In the end I imagine it goes away altogether. And one is able to live again.'

She sighed deeply.

'I haven't quite got to that stage yet. But I know I will.'

'If one has faith?' Katharine queried.

Hope smiled.

'Even if one doesn't have faith. No one can go on for ever hurting like that all the time. Either the pain dies or you die.'

She took hold of Katharine's hand and cradled it in her own.

'But yes, if one *does* have faith it makes it easier. That's what Father was trying to tell you at your wedding service. No matter *what* happens, nothing can ever separate us from the love of God. And if we believe that, we *are* able to cope.'

Katharine looked down, avoiding Hope's clear gaze.

'Perhaps it's easier for Father,' she reflected. 'He's nearing the end of his life. He knows he doesn't have to suffer this agony for very much longer.'

'I don't think it's easy for him at all,' Hope cut in. 'He's bleeding inside.'

'Do you really think so?' Katharine asked. 'He seems sometimes to be floating above everything in a kind of no-man's-land of his own, where nothing can touch him.'

'He *is* bleeding,' Hope assured her. 'Didn't you see his face when you broke down the other evening?'

Katharine shook her head.

'His eyes were full of tears. He had difficulty controlling himself. No, he's hurting all right.'

She spread her hands and looked thoughtfully down at her fingernails.

'But he has this hope, this assurance, that death is not the end.'

She lay back once again, watching the leaves stirring lazily in the soft spring breeze. And for a few minutes the two women sat together in a warm, companionable silence.

Mrs Miles came to the side door agitating a huge handbell.

'Tea,' Hope said lazily as the boys, who had been furiously cycling round and round the garden, suddenly dropped their bicycles as if they had become red-hot, and raced towards the kitchen.' Shall we have ours out here? It will be so much more peaceful than watching Ben and Philip wolfing down everything in sight.'

She laughed.

'Especially Ben!'

And, in spite of the memories the afternoon had brought flooding back, Katharine laughed with her.

Chapter 23

That evening Lawrence Masters telephoned.

'Don't bother to rush back on a crowded train tomorrow afternoon,' he said. 'Come up on Monday morning.'

'Oh Lawrence, will that be all right?' Katharine asked anxiously, knowing how busy everyone was at Group R and not wanting to put a further load on the other three.

'Quite all right,' he affirmed. 'I've looked up the times. Catch the train which gets in at 12.06. I'll meet you and take you out to lunch, then you can get back to base late afternoon.'

Katharine had been grateful for the respite.

She didn't know how she was going to face Group R and all the people who had known Ashley. And the longer the dreaded moment could be put off, the better.

It meant too that she could accompany Hope to Evensong.

In spite of her reticence, her doubts about this loving God William talked about with such ease, she was nonetheless curious. And, without realising it, hungry to know more.

When her father-in-law announced the hymn, 'The King of love my shepherd is' and the congregation rose, so did the memory of her wedding day.

And Katharine's tears flowed again.

But the only person to be embarrassed was herself.

At the end of the service, William asked her to stand in the old stone porch with him and greet the departing worshippers.

Although tears kept gathering behind her eyes, and occasionally spilling over, she had been touched and warmed by the many people who came up to her. They had all known Ashley. But there had been no forced funereal expressions, no embarrassed clichés. Each person who had spoken to her had done so out of genuine love and concern.

And, although her heart was aching when they returned to the Rectory, she also felt it was cleansed. As though someone had poured healing oils on her gaping wound and then wrapped it in fresh clean bandages.

'*Do* come again whenever you wish,' Hope said, standing with her on the station platform as the train puffed round the bend and whistled to a standstill. 'We're the only immediate family Father has now.'

She tugged open a door, then turned and hugged Katharine warmly.

'Don't forget what I said,' she whispered. 'It *will* get better. I promise you.'

Katharine returned Hope's embrace then climbed into the compartment. She smiled down at her sister-in-law through the open window, and a warm feeling enveloped her.

A whistle blew, the train gave a piercing shriek and began to pull away from the station.

Katharine leant out and waved. Hope ran a few steps along the platform, but a light breeze carried the engine's smoke backwards and they were each lost from view. Flopping down in her seat, Katharine felt comforted. She was still part of Ashley's family.

* * *

Lawrence Masters was standing at the barrier when the train arrived at Euston, his eyes scanning the crowd of alighting passengers. Katharine waved and he walked swiftly down the platform towards her, taking her case from her hand.

He didn't ask her how she was.

For which she was grateful.

'London's been devilishly hot these past few days,' he said, removing his cap and wiping his brow as the taxi bowled along Tottenham Court Road, heading for Upper Grosvenor Street. 'What's it been like in Buckinghamshire?'

'Blissful,' she replied. 'Beautiful weather, beautiful countryside. Everything one needs for a perfect holiday.'

He looked at her sharply, but her face was turned away from him, watching the crowds strolling along Oxford Street.

As they sat facing each other in the dining-room of the United Hunts Club she looked across the table at him and smiled.

'Isn't this where we came in?'

He rutted his brow.

'I don't understand.'

'We seem to have come full circle. This is where we had lunch the day you more or less recruited me into the racket in January '41.'

His brow cleared.

'Yes, of course, I remember now.'

He looked anxiously at her.

'Katharine, I'm so sorry, we can go somewhere else . . .'

'But you've just given the order.'

'Damn the order,' he exclaimed.

He half rose but Katharine laid a restraining hand on his arm and pulled him down.

'Don't be silly Lawrence,' she smiled. 'I don't mind at all. Sit down and tell me why you wanted to see me.'

'Well, if you're quite sure.'

He hesitantly regained his seat.

'Of course I'm sure. Now, what's all this about?'

He cleared his throat as the waiter placed a small serving table beside them.

'I was wondering,' he began, flicking out his table-napkin and placing it carefully on his knees, 'whether you'd like a change?'

It was Katharine's turn to look puzzled.

'Whatever do you mean,' she asked. 'What kind of change?'

As the words left her lips, a strange look came over her face. And she smiled. Perhaps this was the answer, a way out of her terrible misery. A legitimate way to end her life.

'Are you thinking of sending me into the field?' she enquired.

'No,' he interrupted quickly. 'Not that sort of change.'

His piercing eyes bored through her.

'If I did,' he said laconically, 'you'd be going for all the wrong reasons.'

Katharine sat back, feeling deflated.

'Well what then?'

He laid down his knife and fork.

'I don't want to upset you, but it had occurred to me that it might be difficult for you to go back to Group R. Everyone there knew Ashley, some had worked with him . . .'

She raised her eyebrows in surprise.

'Oh yes,' he replied in answer to her unspoken question. 'All part of our watertight system. Charlie Mann, amongst others, was in the field with him until he was blown and had to come back.'

He paused, seeing a look of pain cross Katharine's features.

'If this conversation is difficult for you,' he began diffidently, 'let's drop it.'

'No,' she said, taking a sip of the excellent wine he had chosen. 'Say what's on your mind.'

'Well,' he went on. 'I was wondering whether you'd like to work in Baker Street for a while? Everything's coming to a head and I imagine the flow of bods will greatly lessen in the next few months . . . even weeks. Hopefully, there'll be no more need of them. So the pressure will be off Group R.'

She raised her eyebrows enquiringly.

But he didn't clarify his statement.

'Cristina, who took over from Tatiana when she joined you, would be invaluable to the Poles. They're desperate for people at the moment.'

'In the shop or on the field?' Katharine cut in.

'Both,' he replied laconically.

'Cristina is of Polish origin and she speaks perfect German. I was thinking you might come up and take her place. You'd be up to your neck in work which, in the circumstances, might not be a bad thing. And it would release Cristina.'

He looked at her enquiringly.

'I think Nadine would be pleased to have you too,' he went on when she didn't reply. 'Hugh's on the run, no one knows where he is at the moment.'

Nadine and Hugh Barrington had been married by special licence, on a forty-eight-hour leave pass, the previous summer.

'Only forty-eight hours,' Katharine had exclaimed when they met shortly afterwards. 'You poor darling.'

'You can live a lifetime in forty-eight hours,' the indomitable Nadine had grinned. 'Providing you don't sleep.'

Hugh had been dropped into France shortly afterwards.

'I think she's pretty down,' Masters went on. 'Though she doesn't show it.'

'Not like me,' Katharine remarked.

'Oh come, Katharine,' he chided. 'That's all forgotten.'

His suave face broke into one of his rare smiles.

'It might help you both to be working with someone who knows how the other's feeling.'

Katharine crumbled a roll thoughtfully.

Perhaps it *would* be good to be with Nadine. To be in London. A complete break from all she had known with Ashley.

'Sounds as if all your bods are on the run,' she remarked drily.

'Far from it,' Masters replied. 'There's a lot of splendid work being done. But, unfortunately, Hugh's circuit was infiltrated. He's probably in hiding waiting to escape across the Pyrenees.'

A shadow crossed Katharine's face. That was the way Ashley had escaped.

She leant back in her chair as the waiter removed their plates.

'Do I have to give you an answer now Lawrence?' she enquired.

'No,' he said. 'But don't leave it too long. I'd like to know before Friday. And, if possible, have you installed by the beginning of next week.'

Katharine looked at him in amazement.

'You don't waste much time, do you?'

He leant forward earnestly.

'Katharine, there *isn't* much time.'

She smiled to herself, watching him from beneath her eyelashes.

'Wouldn't you rather have Tatiana back?' she enquired archly.

For a moment he seemed to lose his composure, then quickly regaining his self-control he stared icily across at her.

'I'm asking you Katharine,' he replied.

And a heavy silence fell between them.

Lawrence produced a gold monogrammed cigarette-case and, snapping it open, offered her one.

She shook her head.

'You still don't?. . . May I?'

She smiled her assent.

'Lawrence,' she said hesitantly, as he flicked his lighter into action.

He paused and looked at her, the flame quivering between them.

'Have you never wanted to go into the field yourself? I've always thought you'd be the perfect undercover agent.'

He bent his head to the flame before replying.

'There's nothing I'd have liked more,' he said at last. 'If liked is the right word to use.'

He drew deeply on his cigarette then placed it in the ashtray.

'But I can't.'

She looked at him enquiringly.

'I'm diabetic,' he said shortly.

Katharine's eyes widened.

'Oh Lawrence . . . I'm *so* sorry. I should never have asked.'

'Please don't pity me,' he cut in curtly. 'There are

worse things in life than that. I should have gone into the field but it was discovered when I was in training. Well, before real training actually began. Right at the very beginning, after the Battle of Britain, when the Racket was being dreamed up.'

He flicked ash into the ashtray, then sat staring at the glowing tip of his cigarette.

'That's probably why I'm here and Ashley's not.'

Katharine looked down at the tablecloth remembering her outburst and the hateful remark she had made on the day Lawrence had brought news of Ashley's death. And Rickie's reaction. She had said that there were circumstances which Katharine knew nothing about.

'Does Rickie know by any chance?'

Masters looked across at her in surprise and that rare smile lit his face again.

'Yes, as a matter of fact she does. What makes you ask?'

'Just something she said the day you brought me the news of Ashley's death.'

She didn't elaborate and he didn't question her further.

'You and she are among the very few people who *do* know, apart from the authorities. And I want it to stay that way. But you can see now why I didn't go into the field. I'd have been more of a liability than anything else.'

She nodded.

'And Tatiana?'

Katharine knew she was sticking her neck out by mentioning Tatiana's name, especially after the snub she had received earlier on. But she took the risk.

There was a moment's hesitation on his part.

Then his dark eyes softened and his lips parted in a

way that robbed his high cheekbones of their sharpness. That rare smile, now glowing with an extraordinary sweetness, spread slowly across his lean features.

Glancing up, Katharine saw a look on his face she had never seen there before. Never ever expected to see. His whole expression had mellowed and become warm and tender.

'Yes,' he said softly. 'And Tatiana.'

'So it's serious then?'

He nodded and his complexion darkened slightly in what could only be described as a blush.

'Oh Lawrence,' she said breathlessly, her eyes shining. 'I'm *SO* pleased . . . for both of you.'

'Thank you,' he murmured. 'I've waited a long time for the right woman. Now I've found her, I'll do my very best to make her happy.'

He placed his cigarette thoughtfully in the ashtray.

'I'm almost thirty-five, eleven years older than Tatiana . . .'

'But it doesn't matter,' Katharine broke in. 'There was ten years between my parents. And one of my dearest friends, Flora Hamilton, you met her at our wedding, married a man twenty-seven years her senior.'

Lawrence frowned.

'The beautiful lady in the large red hat?'

Katharine nodded.

'They have four lovely children and a wonderful marriage.'

He seemed reassured.

'It's not age which matters,' she said, leaning earnestly across the table towards him. 'It's the people themselves.'

Lawrence selected another cigarette and sat tapping it absently on the top of its case. Katharine sensed he had something to tell her but didn't know how to begin.

'Katharine,' he ventured diffidently, the cigarette remaining unlit between his fingers. 'Don't think I'm heartless.'

She started to protest. But he stopped her.

'I haven't said much about Ashley . . . This awful British reserve I suppose.'

He raised his dark eyes and looked across at her.

'But I didn't know whether you wanted me to or not. It's very early days and an emotional subject . . . for both of us.'

Katharine looked at him in surprise. Until a few minutes ago she had not realised that he was capable of feeling any emotion, much less expressing it.

'He was your husband,' he went on quietly, absently replacing the unsmoked cigarette in the slim gold case. 'But he was also my friend . . . we'd known each other for years.'

He raised his eyes and gave her a sad smile. So unlike the sardonic twist which usually flitted across his lips.

'I was his rugger captain at school.'

Katharine's eyes widened.

She knew that Ashley had played rugger. But she simply couldn't imagine the debonair Lawrence even dirtying his hands, let alone his whole body.

Katharine shook her head in amazement. Suddenly realising how little we really know about the people we come in contact with. How easy it is to get a false impression and make hasty erroneous judgements.

And, remembering the cruel remark she had spat out at Rickie on the day he had brought her the news of Ashley's death, she coloured with shame. A Lawrence she had never known existed behind that caustic, self-confident exterior.

'I just want you to know that I'm here,' he ended

lamely, further revealing his sensibility, his vulnerability.

'If ever you want to talk . . . or a shoulder to cry on . . .'

Tears rushed to her eyes and glistened like sparkling dewdrops on her long curling lashes.

'Thank you Lawrence,' she choked.

Suddenly realising that he had uncovered too much of himself, shown his humanity, he looked hastily down at his watch.

'I'm afraid Katharine,' he said, his old authoritative self once more, 'we're going to have to get moving. I've told them at Group R you'll be catching the 3.24 and it's almost three o'clock now. If we don't grab a cab immediately, you'll never make it.'

As they walked through the door into Upper Grosvenor Street, he anchored his cap firmly on his abundant dark hair, and hailed a taxi.

It cruised to a standstill beside them.

'You'll let me have your answer by Friday?' he asked, holding the cab door open for her.

She smiled at him as he climbed in and sat down beside her.

'You can have it now,' she whispered conspiratorially. 'It's yes.'

Chapter 24

Tatiana was standing at the cottage door when the jeep drew up. Katharine scarcely had time to alight before she rushed out and threw her arms round her.

'*Katharine*,' she cried brokenly.

And in her warm embrace Katharine felt her friend's tears scalding her own cheeks.

'It's all right Tat,' she soothed, gently disentangling herself.

Tatiana looked at her, her eyes swimming.

'Come on,' Katharine chided, picking up her suitcase. 'Let's go in.'

But inside, it was no better.

Popular music from the Forces Programme had been drifting through the open window as the car approached the house. But the minute the engine stopped, the wireless was quickly switched off. And an eerie hush fell over the usually animated household.

Rickie was in the kitchen preparing dinner. She popped her head round the door and embraced Katharine warmly, but not tragically as Tatiana had done, before offering her the British panacea for all ills. A cup of tea.

'No thank you Rickie,' Katharine smiled. 'I had tea on the train.'

Rickie returned her smile.

'Dinner won't be long,' she announced over her shoulder, bustling back into the kitchen.

Katharine walked into the sitting-room.

Anne and Nicola quickly stubbed out their cigarettes and stood up, not knowing what to do or say.

'Not too rushed off your feet?' Katharine remarked, in an effort to break the awkward silence.

They looked at each other.

'It *has* been a bit hectic,' Nicola ventured.

Then, afraid that she might have said the wrong thing, implied that Katharine's absence had put an extra load on their shoulders, she hastened to make amends.

And only made things worse.

Katharine realised that the best thing she could do would be to disappear until dinner in the hope that the tension would ease in her absence. But even if it didn't, she knew that with Rickie presiding over the table, her practical good sense would soon restore normality and, hopefully, banish the gloom.

'I'm off upstairs to unpack,' she said over-brightly. 'No, don't bother to come with me Tat. I can manage.'

She caught a glimpse of Tatiana's woebegone face.

'I'm all right,' she whispered, squeezing her arm reassuringly. 'Really I am.'

As she walked into her little room, Ashley's photograph smiled up at her from the bedside table.

Dropping her suitcase she picked up the oval frame and stood gazing down at it.

But there was no reaction, no lump in her throat, no rush of tears splashing down her face like a heavy shower of rain. Just a terrible sense of emptiness and loss.

With a sigh, she put it carefully back in its place and sat down heavily on the bed.

She felt as she had done on the station that morning

when she and Ashley had said goodbye after their honeymoon. All passion spent. The difference was that now the passion which was momentarily spent was no longer love but grief.

She could cry no more.

There were no tears left.

On that cold March morning, little more than a year ago, she had felt desolate at parting from her bridegroom. But there had been hope. This time there was no hope. The passion would return, she knew that her grief was far from over. But it would be a passion of weeping, not a passion born of love.

As she sat there, empty and drained of all feeling, the shadows of the beautiful spring evening flitted across the bed, darting up and down the whitewashed walls. She looked through the window at the blossom-laden trees, the cloudless blue sky, the shimmer of gnats dancing on the sunbeams.

And she couldn't believe that it was only a week ago, only eight short days since she had sat curled up on the sill on such an evening, dreaming of Ashley. Convinced that the God he wished to serve would preserve his life and allow them to fulfil their plans.

She seemed to have lived a whole life since then.

From below, in the hall, the telephone rang.

'It's Lavinia,' Tatiana said, cautiously putting her head round the door, uncertain what she would find.

Katharine heaved herself from the bed.

'Please Tat,' she said picking up the receiver as Tatiana walked mournfully back down the stairs. 'Don't look so tragic. It doesn't help.'

'Darling,' Lavinia said. 'Why didn't you let me know? Just that scribbled note from the Rectory. I only received it this morning. And when I telephoned your father-in-law you'd already left.'

There was a gentle reproach in her voice.

'Tamara rang me on Wednesday after Tatiana told her the dreadful news. But nobody seemed to know where you'd gone.'

'Good for Rickie,' Katharine thought.

She'd been the only person Katharine had told.

'I left immediately I heard,' she said. 'I didn't want Ashley's father to hear about it from anyone else.'

'I do understand. But I'd have come with you,' Lavinia exclaimed. 'You shouldn't have been alone at such a time.'

There was a pause.

'I kept expecting you to arrive here. It was rather worrying having no idea where you were.'

'I'm sorry darling,' Katharine breathed. 'I really am. It was such a shock I didn't stop to think . . . But I'm all right now Lavinia, I promise.'

There was another pause.

'What happened?' Lavinia asked at last. 'Was it an accident?'

Katharine bit her lip.

She had been cocooned during the past week. Not realising what it would be like once she was back in circulation and questions, to which she couldn't give answers, would be asked by everyone.

'Not exactly,' she said. 'I'd rather tell you some other time if you don't mind. I'm still feeling pretty raw.'

'I can well imagine.'

Lavinia sighed.

'But you say you're all right?. . . I'm not so sure.'

Katharine forced a laugh.

'I'm as all right as any other woman whose husband's been killed in action.'

That seemed to be the best explanation.

'I didn't realise Ashley *was* in action,' Lavinia went

on. 'I thought he was in Scotland. But of course you don't want to have to answer a lot of questions now.'

She paused.

'When shall I see you? When are you coming home?'

'On my next weekend leave,' Katharine replied. 'I . . . won't be down here much longer. I'm being transferred to London at the end of the week.'

'Isn't that a bit hard?' Lavinia queried. 'After what's happened?'

'As a matter of fact, I think it's probably a good thing,' Katharine replied. 'A complete change . . . And there's a lot of work to do up there, it'll keep me from brooding.'

'But where will you stay?' Lavinia went on. 'Will you go to Tamara's?'

Katharine hadn't even thought about it.

But hearing Lavinia's question she suddenly realised that this change she was about to make had to be drastic. A complete cut with the past. And she silently thanked Lawrence Masters for his insight.

When she had arrived at Group R, two years before, she had been a young girl of twenty. Since then she had run through the whole gamut of human emotions. Love marriage, motherhood and death.

She was no longer the same person.

She couldn't go back to living her former sheltered existence. She must now assume her new status. That of a war widow. And attempt to remake her life. Alone. It was her only chance of survival.

'I don't know yet darling,' she answered cautiously. 'But don't worry, I'll let you know as soon as I get to London.'

'Yes, please do.' Lavinia answered. 'And Katharine . . .'

'Yes?'

'You know I'm here, don't you?'

Katharine thought she detected a catch in her aunt's voice.

'I know,' she replied softly. 'And . . . thank you Lavinia, for everything.'

The following morning Nadine rang.

'I hear you're coming to work with us next week. Have you anywhere to stay?'

Katharine demurred.

'It's just a thought,' Nadine rattled on. 'But accommodation isn't easy to find in London at the moment and there's room in my flat. The girls I had from the Min. of Ag. and Fish were transferred last year and I've been on my own ever since. Quite enjoyed it actually, but now that Hugh's missing I sometimes find it a bit difficult.'

She sighed.

'You know what I mean, don't you Katharine?'

There was a slight pause.

'Only it's different for me,' she said contritely, almost guiltily, 'because I've still got hope. But all the same I don't feel like sharing with girls who're racing off to Milroy's or the Nuthouse every evening. (The Nuthouse was a night club which had recently opened in London and become very popular.) On the other hand, it would be nice to have company occasionally. When you can't sleep it gets a bit lonely drinking tea in the kitchen all by yourself at three in the morning.'

Nadine laughed suddenly. But her former bubbling gaiety was missing.

'So the offer's there if you want it,' she ended. 'I won't batter your door down if you want to bawl your eyes out all alone. But if you do feel like a friendly shoulder to cry on, I'll lend you mine from time to time. As long as you promise to lend me yours.'

Katharine rutted her brows.

This was not at all what she had envisaged for herself. But it was kind of Nadine to offer.

'Can I ring you back?' she hesitated.

'Oh sure,' Nadine replied. 'Don't even need to bother. Just turn up if you want to. I'm on duty this weekend so you know where to find me.'

Katharine left Group R the following Saturday and went straight to Nadine's, full of good intentions. Determined to look forwards and not backwards.

It was only when she awoke on Sunday morning in the unfamiliar surroundings that she fully understood the complete about-turn her life had taken.

She had cut her ties with the past. And was now completely on her own to start this new life she had so bravely proclaimed. And she wasn't sure that she wanted it.

Pulling on her dressing-gown she walked across to the little kitchen and began opening and shutting cupboard doors in an attempt to make herself some breakfast. Nadine had already left for Baker Street and the silence was oppressive.

As she sat at the kitchen table scraping a slither of margarine on to a piece of toast, the air-raid siren began to wail.

It was the time of the doodlebugs, those deadly unmanned missiles which hummed in, wave after wave, over London during that hot summer of 1944.

They were inoffensive as long as they could be heard. But when the hum stopped, it was time to race madly for shelter. The few minutes, sometimes seconds, between their automatic switch-off and the shattering noise of their explosion, when they were cruising silently, lethally across the sky before plunging with their load of death and destruction, were eerie and menacing. Everyone held their breath until the thundering crash split the air. Then sighed with relief knowing that this time they had been spared . . . until the next deadly hum abruptly ceased.

Katharine heard the hum and waited.

Suddenly it stopped and she made to dive under the Morrison table which almost filled the sitting-room. Then, she flopped back on to her chair, the toast uneaten on her plate.

And she knew she simply didn't care whether the bomb hit her or not.

The shock she had received two weeks before, and now the sharp separation from everything familiar suddenly proved too much for her. And a terrible listless depression set in. She wandered back to her littered room and sat wearily on the bed surrounded by unpacked suitcases.

There was an ear-splitting explosion followed by the sound of splintering glass. The windows of the flat rattled and the whole building shook. But it remained standing. The bomb had fallen on an adjacent street.

Immediately the screech of ambulances and the fire engines' bells mingled with the overhead hum of the next unmanned missile.

Kicking off her slippers, Katharine crawled back into bed and pulled the covers over her head just as the menacing hum stopped.

* * *

Katharine had scarcely been in London two weeks when a bomb of another kind exploded.

The Allied invasion of France.

Everybody had been expecting it and longing for it for years. And even though, when she had lunched with him three weeks before, Lawrence Masters had hinted at something momentous on the very near horizon, when it actually happened it left most people with a feeling of stunned disbelief. Until realisation set in and another explosion, not only of joy but of frenzied activity, broke out.

When she had agreed to stay with Nadine, Katharine had wondered whether both living and working with someone might not prove too much of a strain. But, in his wisdom, Lawrence had not based her permanently with the French Section in Baker Street. For most of the time, she was at Orchard Court, taking down the reports of agents on their return from the field.

At first she was afraid.

She didn't want to meet those who had survived, hear the often gruesome stories they had to tell.

But as the weeks flew by and the skills in shorthand and typing which she had learned at Mrs Hosters during that first year of the war, and never used since, became less rusty, and her confidence in her ability to read back the hieroglyphics she had jotted down increased, she found it therapeutic.

And once again, she silently saluted Lawrence's insight.

Listening first hand to what actually happened in the field, occasionally meeting those who had trained with Ashley or who had known him over there helped her to gain an insight into a side of her husband's life which she had not been able to share. And, no longer in ignorance, she found that she was gradually starting along the long road to accepting what had happened.

At Group R she had been working with agents on their last lap before being dropped into enemy territory. Eager often idealistic young men and women, with a wide experience in what might happen, but no experience of life in the field as it actually was.

She rarely heard what became of them after they left. She only knew the bitter disappointment of those who were refused at this very last fence. And often, as in the case of the young Dane, their anger against her.

At Orchard Court she was dealing with reality after the fact.

And she came to understand that there was no glamour to being an undercover agent. There was not even the remotest connection between the lifestyle of exotic spies portrayed in popular fiction and the lives of the men she met on their return from the field.

It was a lonely, dangerous, sometimes even a monotonous life they lived in occupied territory. But always a life of terrible strain.

They needed to be armed with an unconditional commitment to the belief, with no compromise, in each man's right to be free, not subjugated to the tyranny of a cruel dictator. To the intrinsic value of each human life. And a willingness to fight for, even to die for, those beliefs.

As a picture of her husband's life in the field unfolded before her, she began to understand what he had meant that sunny autumn afternoon when they had discussed their future in the Buckinghamshire woods. And to realise the truth of his words. That we are impotent when faced with the really important issues of life. And can become pompous, until life cuts us down to size.

* * *

The liberation of Paris in August was greeted by all with jubilation. And when, shortly afterwards, news came through that Hugh Barrington was alive and would soon be on his way home, Katharine knew that it was time for her to move.

'I don't suppose you know of a flat in London I could rent, do you Eddie?' Katharine enquired one evening in late September.

The interrogating officers had left to return to Baker Street and, tired and dispirited, Katharine had sought out Eddie's company.

Eddie Field was a middle-aged Englishman who had spent most of his life in Paris, but had been obliged to flee in 1940. He had been sent to Orchard Court as a glorified caretaker and general factotum when the organisation was set up. And many an agent, both leaving or returning, had been grateful for his welcoming smile, his calm and his unfailing cheerfulness.

Katharine had always found him a sympathetic listener on days when everything had seemed to go wrong. But, most important for her, he had known Ashley. And remembered the grim determination with which he had set off on that last fatal mission.

Seeing her tired, woebegone face, without wasting words he had rustled up an omelette which they shared sitting companionably together at the kitchen table.

'Your husband was a fine man,' he remarked sadly. 'But then they all are.'

He smiled his gentle smile. Yet his eyes had a mischievous glint in them.

'The others get themselves nice cushy jobs at home . . . like me.'

'Oh Eddie,' Katharine protested, knowing that he was well beyond the age for active service. 'You're doing a wonderful job here. Look how delighted all the bods are to see you when they get back.'

Her brow puckered.

'How *did* they pick you? You're absolutely perfect for the job.'

Eddie smiled, that mischievous twinkle still dancing in his light-grey eyes.

'The General said it was because I could keep my mouth shut!'

And they both laughed.

'What was that you were saying about a flat?' he went on, clearing up the plates and piling them in the sink.

Katharine shrugged.

'Oh nothing. It's just that Nadine's husband is coming back. He was missing when I moved in with her. She says she doesn't mind my staying on, but they haven't seen each other since their honeymoon so I'm sure they won't want me hanging around when he gets back.'

She smiled sadly to herself.

'I know I wouldn't.'

Eddie put a coffee-pot on the table and sat down again.

'Don't worry Eddie,' she concluded. 'It was just a thought. As you seem to be the universal provider for everybody, I wondered whether you might not have a little flat up your sleeve. They're like gold dust in London at the moment.'

His brow puckered.

'I know,' he said, thoughtfully stroking his chin. 'How long would you want it for?'

Katharine shrugged.

'I've no idea; until the war's over I suppose, and I decide what to do with the rest of my life.'

'Give me a few days. I know that Miss Harrison-Clarke is going over to France with a delegation very shortly. She might just be willing to rent her flat till she comes back.'

Miss Harrison-Clarke was a FANY bigwig, known unofficially as a Queen Bee.

He picked up the coffee-pot and poured her a cup.

'Leave it to me,' he smiled giving her a conspiratorial wink.

Two weeks later Katharine was putting Ashley's photograph on the small period table beside the satin-covered bed in Miss Harrison-Clarke's little mews flat just off Harley Street. And this time it was with pleasure that she unpacked her suitcases and arranged her belongings in the small tastily-furnished rooms overlooking the cobbled courtyard.

As she sat that first evening in the little sitting-room listening to the news on the wireless, she realised that each successive move was bringing with it its own healing. Taking her a step further along that road to wholeness which, five months ago, she had never thought she would achieve.

At first, she had felt angry and resentful every time she heard that the Allies were advancing deeper into France. Unable to rejoice as towns were liberated and people, who after more than four years under the German jackboot, were finally regaining their freedom.

All she had been able to think was that it had come too late. Too late to save Ashley.

Yet that mild October evening, sitting in the comfortable armchair, watching the curtains gently float in and out of the open window on the light breeze, she realised that she had finally come to some sort of compromise with life. And with what had happened.

What was it her father-in-law had said on her last visit to Buckingham?

'We must rejoice with those who rejoice and weep with those who mourn.'

She had certainly wept enough, and she knew it was not over. This was just a remission.

But that early autumn evening, she found herself able to rejoice with those in her father's country who were at this moment rejoicing.

Chapter 25

In early November three days of impenetrable fog, which smothered London like a thick yellow blanket, proved to be too much for Prince Voronovsky's now fragile lungs. He caught pneumonia. And, two days after it lifted, he died.

Although both Tamara and Tatiana knew that at ninety-four death was a constant threat, when it actually happened, they were both shattered with grief. And Katharine found herself in the role of comforter instead of the one being comforted.

The effect was therapeutic.

But, even so, the Prince's death, coming so soon after Ashley's, dealt her a hard blow.

Ever since that evening of the ball almost four years before, when he had unofficially adopted her as his granddaughter, there had been a special bond between them. He had been a rock she knew she could cling to when her life was floundering in deep waters. Often she had noticed his eyes on her questioningly. She knew that he could penetrate her hidden thoughts, her deepest emotions. And the knowledge had given her a sense of belonging, of peace.

Now he was gone.

And Katharine felt herself lost and anchorless, floundering in deep waters once again.

On that grey November afternoon when his extraordinarily long coffin, on which his general's hat and sword together with his many decorations had been placed, was carried into the ornate Russian church, the realisation that another chapter in her life had now closed hit Katharine with full force.

His funeral in no way resembled the splendid ceremony it would have been, had times been different. But the church was crowded. The Metropolitan in his robes which matched his flowing beard, was there. And a choir of Russian émigrés had sung the Kontakion for the dead.

While the beautiful, mournful notes rose and fell on the incense-laden air, Katharine's eyes lingered on the coffin. And she realised that it was a goodbye in all its splendour, a final tribute to this incredible old man, before the damp earth of an alien soil received the Prince's earthly remains.

And she wondered where Ashley's body was.

She still was not sure whether she believed in an after-life. But she wished she had been able to seal the brief chapter of their life together with a final salute.

As the service ended and the bearers prepared to remove the coffin from its trestles, Tamara stumbled forward, her face damp with tears.

'Otets!' she whispered brokenly, placing her hand lovingly on the coffin's shiny surface. Lavinia, struggling to control her own emotions, caught her sister-in-law's arm and held her in a steady grip.

Through brimming eyes, Katharine looked at Tamara and understood that for her it was the end of an era. The final break with her past. With Russia.

Otets, her father, had always been there. The buffer between his family and the world. But now that he was gone Tamara, for the first time in her life, was truly alone. And Katharine knew from bitter experience the terrible feeling of isolation death left in its wake.

When Lavinia walked slowly past the coffin, Katharine saw her aunt's lips quiver.

'Do Svedanya Nikolai Andreivitch,' she murmured. Then added brokenly, 'Otets!'

And Katharine realised that for Lavinia also it was the end of an era. The final parting from the man who for so many years had been not only Tamara's father, but also hers. Now she and Tamara had lost their rock. And had abruptly become the older generation.

Shortly after her grandfather's death Tatiana was transferred to London.

Work at Group R had greatly slowed down since the liberation of Paris. And, although the war was by no means over by Christmas, as so many hopefuls had predicted, the urgent need to send agents into the field had greatly diminished.

Caroline having finally realised that, in spite of all her efforts, her hopes of capturing Lawrence Masters were nil had opted to join Miss Harrison-Clarke and the delegation to France. And Tatiana was brought back to replace her.

The end being in sight Lawrence Masters now felt free to bring his feelings for Tatiana out into the open. And that Christmas she and Tamara travelled with him to York to meet his mother. Their engagement was announced on New Year's Eve.

Katharine declined Lawrence's invitation to accompany them, as she had declined every invitation they had made during the months she had been living in London.

'I don't understand you,' Tatiana had so often protested. 'Lawrence and I would *like* you to come out to dinner with us.'

'I know you would,' Katharine had always replied. 'But I also know how precious those moments I had alone with Ashley were. However fond I am of you, I really didn't want you there as well.'

'It's not the same,' Tatiana had pleaded.

But Katharine had remained adamant.

'I feel almost guilty,' Tatiana groaned, the week before she left on Christmas leave.

'Whatever for?' Katharine enquired.

It was Sunday afternoon and they were having tea together in Katharine's little flat.

'Being so happy,' Tatiana mused.

Her expression changed and her face became luminous.

'You really do love him, don't you,' Katharine murmured.

Tatiana's light green eyes misted into turquoise with emotion.

'I didn't know it was possible to love anyone as much as I do Lawrence,' she whispered. 'When he's with me . . . When he takes me in his arms the whole world stops. It's as if nothing existed outside the two of us.'

Her voice faltered and became low and vibrant as a faint shudder went through her slim body.

'I can hardly breathe, the rush of feelings is so strong. Sometimes I think I can't bear it.'

She stopped abruptly and looked in anguish at Katharine.

'Oh *Katharine*, how could I be so cruel after . . .'

But Katharine cut her short.

'It's all right, Tatiana. It doesn't hurt me. In a way, it helps. Makes me realise that the kind of love we both know can't be destroyed by death. Because I love Ashley so much, he will go on living in me. I *do* know what you mean. You've entered the enchanted garden like I did on my wedding night.'

Tatiana blushed.

'I've wanted to, Katharine. In the night I long to feel Lawrence beside me, to know that he is wholly mine. But . . .'

'But what?' Katharine gently prompted.

'It's Lawrence,' Tatiana said, her voice almost inaudible. 'He seems to think I'm an angel or a piece of priceless porcelain, too fragile to be handled.'

She twisted a scrap of hankie between her fingers, her eyes hurt and bewildered.

'I thought it was always the man who couldn't wait, and the woman who held back. But with us, it's the opposite. I ache for Lawrence, but he insists on waiting. Maybe it's his Christian upbringing surfacing. He hasn't gone to church for years, but his mother is apparently very devout. Lawrence says he wants to show me how much he loves me by waiting until we're married. I'm too precious to him to be cheapened and tarnished by a hole-and-corner affair.'

Tatiana smiled shyly.

'He says I'm different from all the others.'

Katharine raised her eyebrows in surprise but didn't comment. She hadn't realised that with the distant, aloof Lawrence Masters there had been others. But again acknowledged how wrong one can be when judging by appearances.

'Have there been others for you?' she enquired gently.

Tatiana shook her head.

'Same as me. I was so glad I'd waited for Ashley. But it was different for us it all happened so quickly. We didn't have to wait.'

'Lawrence says the war won't last much longer and as soon as it's over we'll be married.'

'And until you're married *he won't make love to you?'*

No.

'He's right you know. There's something very special about having made that commitment, for better for worse, and then to discover the depths of love together, knowing that it's for ever.'

She leant back in her chair gazing across the room at nothing in particular.

'At least one hopes it is.'

Tatiana looked at her sharply. But a sweet smile was playing around Katharine's lips. There was no bitterness. And she knew she was remembering.

'I think that's what Lawrence means,' she went on diffidently. 'He's so strong. And I'm so weak. Sometimes I feel like slut wanting him so badly.'

'He wants you just as badly.'

'Yes, I know. Sometimes when we're alone together I think he'll capitulate. But he never does. Says he's waited thirty-five years for me; he can wait a few months longer however hard it may be.'

'Don't worry, Tat,' Katharine soothed. 'It can't be long now. And then you'll have the rest of your lives to prove how much you love each other.'

'I don't think a lifetime is long enough for me to show Lawrence how much I love him,' Tatiana exulted, her eyes shining. 'Just his touch sends bolts of lightning shooting through my body. And when he kisses me it's as if the heavens had opened and all the stars rained down on us.'

She looked across at Katharine, and it seemed to her friend that those stars had fixed themselves in her gaze.

'Oh Katharine,' she whispered. 'I never knew that falling in love was like this. That it was so wonderful, so breathtaking, so . . . so *earth shattering*. And yet at times so painful. I can't find words to describe what I mean. But you understand, don't you?'

She looked appealingly across at her.

'And . . . you don't think I'm a slut?'

Katharine laughed softly.

'Of *course* I don't. You're just a very normal young woman deeply in love for the first time.'

'It's just,' Tatiana began.

She stopped, searching for words. Then it all came out in a rush.

'I'm afraid,' she cried. 'I'm so afraid of losing him. I couldn't bear it if anything happened to Lawrence and I'd never know him as my husband. Even if I didn't have a ring on my finger and a certificate to prove it.'

'Don't be silly,' Katharine chided. 'What *could* happen to Lawrence?'

'What happened to you,' Tatiana whispered.

Katharine got up and walked over to the fire, mechanically turning the gas tap, sending the dancing flames hissing to a bright orange glow.

'There's no comparision,' she answered quietly. 'Lawrence is here. Don't look for trouble, Tat. You've got a beautiful future ahead of you.'

Katharine sat down and smiled across at her friend.

'Don't you agree?'

She nodded. And a comfortable silence fell between them.

'There is just one thing,' Tatiana ventured as the ornate marble clock on the mantelpiece gave six tinkling chimes. 'You've suffered so much these past few months. Ever since Ashley left for the field in fact. I wondered, do you have any regrets?'

She paused diffidently.

'Would you rather that evening at the Vineyard hadn't happened. That Ashley had never come back into your life?'

Katharine's face turned deathly pale, and for a few minutes there was an electric silence in the room. Tatiana moved uneasily in her chair, regretting having brought the subject up. Then, a tinge of magnolia crept up Katharine's ashen cheeks.

'Someone once said,' she murmured softly, 'I don't remember who but I understand now what they meant: "One crowded hour of glorious life is worth an age without a name."'

'That just about sums it up, Tat. What I feel. For nothing in the world would I rather the last couple of years had never happened. And, in spite of the pain, if I could choose to go back and live it all again, I'd happily do so. I wouldn't change one single hour. The times I spent with Ashley were the most precious moments of my life. No matter what happens, no one can take them away from me.'

Tatiana looked intently at her hands and a lone tear crept down her cheek.

'I can understand now why you don't want to come to York with us,' she whispered. 'After what you've gone through, it would be too painful.'

Katharine smiled across at her.

'Tat darling, it's not that at all,' she said gently. 'I'm delighted for you and Lawrence, honestly I am. But . . . three has never been much company.'

'And anyway,' she ended, making a snap decision. 'I want to spend Christmas with Hope and Ashley's father.'

She knew there could be no argument with that.

Lavinia agreed to join her. And two days before Christmas they travelled to Buckinghamshire in an overcrowded train. Katharine managed to secure a seat for her aunt. But she spent the entire journey sitting on her suitcase in the corridor, chatting with cheerful but war-weary soldiers on their way home for a few days respite.

Twice during the long, slow journey the train was halted by the air-raid siren. They heard the drone of enemy aircraft overhead and crouched on the dirty floor, their hands covering their heads in an attempt to protect not only their ear drums from the terrible blasts but also their bodies from splintering glass which rained in on them through the gaps in the taped-up windows.

By the time the train finally arrived, almost two hours late, Katharine had her thick woollen scarf wound like a yashmak round her nose and mouth and her greatcoat tightly buttoned up. But she was still chilled to the bone from the damp cold which seeped in through the broken windows.

Although each one in their hearts had dreaded the festivities, with the painful memories they could not help but invoke, when Christmas Eve arrived the boys' enthusiasm and excitement made them put aside their own feelings and determine to make this Christmas a happy one which Ben and Philip would remember.

As Katharine stood in her chilly bedroom on Christmas morning in the cold half-light of a winter's dawn, she unwrapped the blue leather box containing her father's gold cuff-links. The present she had intended to give Ashley at this very moment last year.

She wondered why she had brought them with her. Looking down at them, nestling on their bed of faded blue velvet, a lump rose in her throat. It was the first time she had felt any emotion of any kind for several months.

Carefully taking them out of the box she held them against her cheek. The metal was hard and cold and she shivered at its touch. It was as if she were holding Ashley himself, stiff and cold and lifeless against her.

She whispered his name, but there was no reply. She called again, urgently, pleadingly, but the only sound came from the wind sighing in the trees outside her window. It seemed to be mocking her, echoing her voice as she brokenly called Ashley once more.

There was a knock on the door and Hope walked in.

She looked at Katharine strangely. And she wondered whether Hope had heard her calling in the half-light for her dead husband.

'Lavinia's downstairs,' she announced. 'We're ready if you are.'

Katharine quickly put the leather box into the dressing-table drawer as Hope crossed the room and linked her arm in hers. She had seen the gesture, but she made no comment.

'Better put on all the warm clothes you've got,' she smiled, it can be pretty cold in the church.

On Christmas morning, during that early communion service, something broke inside Katharine.

She told herself it was the mesmeric effect of the candles, shimmering and flickering in the still frosty air, their pale-gold flames haloed by the cold. But she knew it was more than that. It was something which came from deep within herself. Something which she had never really acknowledged or come to terms with.

As she knelt at the altar-rail in that old stone church which had witnessed many a heartache, many a final parting, Ashley's father handed her the silver chalice softly murmuring the words: 'The blood of our Lord Jesus Christ which was shed for you', Katharine seemed to completely lose control.

A great well of anger, bitterness and despair rose up in her like a tidal flood and just poured out. And with the flood came the tears.

Looking up, as he held the chalice to her lips, she saw

that tears were also streaming down William Paget's face.

He carefully wiped the edge with a white napkin and, placing his hand gently on her head, passed the cup to Hope, kneeling beside her.

Katharine remained on her knees, her head bowed, those poignant words ringing in her ears.

She felt weak and helpless but at the same time cleansed. As if a great festering wound inside her had suddenly burst releasing its poisonous contents. And the blood of Jesus had entered, cleansed the wound and brought his healing power to work.

She realised at that moment what her father-in-law had meant when she had angrily asked him where God had been when Ashley stood before a firing squad.

'Exactly where he was when *his* son was executed,' William had quietly replied.

It didn't make her husband's death any easier to bear. But as if a light had suddenly been switched on illuminating a part of her brain hitherto left in darkness, it helped her to see beyond the immediate present into a future which lay beyond.

And she knew that death was not the end: that one day she would see Ashley again.

Hope gently touched her elbow and drew her to her feet.

Katharine had meant to tell William what she had experienced in church that morning. But, her few days' leave passed and the opportunity didn't arise.

After breakfast on the day that she was to return to London he suggested they go for a walk.

It was the first chance they had had to be alone together. But, as they were about to set off, the telephone rang.

It was a parishioner who had just received news

that her son had been killed in action in the Western Desert. William left immediately to be with her and didn't return until they were halfway through lunch.

Katharine had to catch her train immediately afterwards and the moment almost passed.

But, as they stood together on the bleak station platform he put his arm around her shoulders.

'I know what you've been through Katharine,' he said gently. 'What you are still going through. And the questions which are tormenting you.'

He looked at her and his beautiful smile lit his tired face.

'I wish we could have had some time alone. I want so much to help you.'

Katharine looked down at the platform, her lip trembling.

'I understand your anger with God for not saving Ashley. But, do you remember at your wedding service I said that all things work for good for those who love the Lord? Those words are written in the New Testament.'

William Paget sighed.

'I don't know how he will do it. But some good will come out of Ashley's death. I promise you.'

His grip tightened on her shoulder, and he drew her close to him.

'Can you try to believe that?'

Katharine looked up at him, her eyes blurred by tears. Through the mist his face vanished and it was as if Ashley were standing in his father's place. As if he had spoken those words to her. And she knew that she must hold the cleansing experience she had had in the church on Christmas morning tightly to her. Not let it escape. Never forget.

'I'll try,' she whispered brokenly.

She reached into the pocket of her greatcoat and

drew out the worn leather box containing her father's cufflinks.

'I had intended to give these to Ashley last Christmas,' she began.

A lump rose in her throat.

'I'd like you to have them,' she choked. 'A bond between us. In memory of my husband and your son, whom we both loved so much.'

The snaking line of the train appeared in the distance.

'My dear child,' he said, smiling gently down at her. 'We neither of us need a bond to remind us of Ashley.'

William looked down at the little square box lying in the palm of his hand.

'But, thank you Katharine. I shall treasure them.'

The shrill, lonely whistle of the train rushed past them. And it screeched to a halt.

'There's a Bible verse I particularly love,' he said quietly. 'It's in Ecclesiastes. "He has made everything beautiful in his time." He will do it for you Katharine, if you will let him.'

Katharine reached up on tiptoe to kiss his cold cheek.

'I think he's already started,' William whispered, as he opened a carriage door and helped her find a seat.

Katharine hoped he was right.

But she returned to London not really understanding.

When they said goodbye she had promised William to come again soon. But once back in the hectic whirl of the final race to wind down the war in Europe, she had little time for long weekends or contemplation or for anything at all other than the work in hand.

At the end of February she began to feel the strain of long hours under great tension and very little time away from the job. So she telephoned Lavinia.

'I'll be down tomorrow evening for the weekend. And, hopefully, if I can get an early enough train on Monday morning I won't have to rush back on Sunday night.'

There was a slight pause at the other end of the line.

'Is something the matter?' Katharine enquired.

'Well, no, not really. I can always cancel. But it would be rather rude.'

'Oh, don't cancel anything for me,' Katharine broke in. 'Were you going to Tamara's? I can still come down to Goudhurst on Friday and we'll come up together on Sunday morning and both have lunch with her.'

Since the Prince's death Lavinia had often lunched with Tamara on Sundays.

Lavinia didn't immediately reply. She seemed slightly embarrassed.

'William has invited me to go to Buckingham for the weekend,' she said at last.

Katharine was stunned.

'But darling,' she cried, when she regained her breath. 'Of course you must go. Don't worry about me, I'll come some other time.'

'If you're quite sure,' Lavinia demurred.

'Don't give it another thought,' Katharine assured her. 'I'll try to make it the following weekend, then you can give me all the news.'

'Yes, do that,' Lavinia said. 'I'll look forward to seeing you then.'

Katharine put down the 'phone, feeling slightly bewildered.

Although Hope telephoned her regularly, she had not been able to keep the promise made at Christmas to return very soon. And the news that Lavinia had been invited back by her father-in-law intrigued her.

It was probably that weekend when she felt most alone.

Tatiana was now spending every available spare minute with Lawrence making plans for their wedding, which was to take place as soon as possible after hostilities ceased.

Hugh had finally returned. So Nadine, who previously had always been ready for a visit to a cinema or supper and a chat by the fire, was out of circulation. And now Lavinia, who up till then had been there whenever Katharine needed her, seemed to be taking on a life of her own.

That evening, as she sat alone by the sitting-room fire, she idly flicked on the wireless. The silvery sounds of a tenor saxophone playing 'All the things you are' floated over the waves.

Memories of Ashley asking the saxophonist at Group R to play the tune, the one he called 'their tune', especially for her, flooded her mind.

As Carroll Gibbons' fingers ran nimbly up and down the keyboard, his slow, lazy voice announced that the broadcast was coming from the Savoy Ballroom.

Katharine's eyes misted over, remembering the last night of her honeymoon. Dancing with Ashley to the music of this very same band. The melody changed. But she hardly noticed it. Then the crooner's voice struck a plaintive note. 'Just to feel in the night the nearness of you,' he whispered throatily.

And suddenly it was more than she could bear.

The memories which she had been trying all day to push to the back of her mind surged in a triumphant, mounting crescendo. And throbbed agonisingly through her frail body.

In a gesture of utter hopelessness, Katharine put her head in her hands and wept.

It was her second wedding anniversary.

Chapter 26

Suddenly it was all over.

The long struggle had ended.

Nearly six years of anger and hunger, of pain and heartache, of patriotic songs and frantic flag-waving, of tearful goodbyes and joyful reunions, of blackouts and ration-cards, gas masks, tin hats and convoys of soldiers being shipped to some unknown destination, many never to return. It was in the past, finished.

Now all that remained was to build the land fit for heroes which had been promised so many times during the long hard struggle.

Norgeby House was almost deserted that beautiful May morning as Katharine stood in front of the wide-open office window listening to the church bells ringing out over the battered remains of London.

In the distance she could hear people cheering.

She imagined the flags waving, the sailors' hats being thrown into the air, the vast crowds stretching down the Mall, milling round Buckingham Palace, shouting hysterically for the King, for the Queen, for the Princesses, for any member of the Royal Family who cared to appear on the balcony and acknowledge their cheers.

They were singing the National Anthem, 'Land of Hope and Glory,' 'Run, rabbit, run,' 'We're gonna hang out the washing on the Siegfried line.' Any patriotic song which came into their heads.

She smiled as the noise rose and mingled with the joyful bells.

It was over.

And she couldn't believe it.

War had been so much part of her life, part of everyone's life that it was difficult suddenly to realise that there would be no more blackout, no more wailing sirens, no more devastating bombing, no more heaps of fresh rubble each morning, where the night before a block of flats or a row of houses or shops had stood.

It was difficult to suddenly come to terms with peace.

As she stood there listening to the sounds of rejoicing, Katharine realised that for her a chapter had now closed.

Since she had returned to London after Ashley's death she had cruised along, not thinking about tomorrow, not thinking about anything but the job in hand. But very soon, there would no longer be a job in hand. And she would have to decide what to do with her life.

All her props seemed to have been removed from under her.

Since Lavinia's startling announcement that she was going to spend the weekend at the Rectory with William Paget, the friendship between these two people whom Katharine loved so dearly had grown. She knew that her father-in-law was only waiting for the war to end, and the young chaplains to return, in order to retire. Then he would leave Buckinghamshire. He, too, would have to decide where to go and what to do with the rest of his life.

Hope and the boys would go back to her family in Boston for an extended stay and most probably for good.

And William would be alone. Katharine wondered what would happen then. Perhaps he would settle near Lavinia. Continue their friendship. She fervently hoped so.

Tatiana's wedding was fixed for September at the latest. Lawrence would soon be demobilised from the Army and return to the Foreign Office. They could be posted anywhere in the world.

And Tamara was considering returning to Nice.

Since the Allies had liberated virtually the whole of France and begun their push into Germany there had been no news at all of Louis. Unconventional to the end, he had disappeared. And no one knew whether he was alive or dead.

Katharine's thoughts turned to Flora and Ardnakil.

Since Ashley's death Flora had never stopped pleading with her to go back to Scotland and rest, recuperate and take stock of her life. To stay as long as she wished, even to make her home there. Up until now even a short visit had been impossible. There simply hadn't been time.

Katharine knew that very soon she would have all the time in the world. And she longed, at that moment, to drop everything and fly back to the warmth of Flora's friendship and the security she always found between those old stone walls.

But she knew it wouldn't be an answer, much less a solution to her problem. And she wondered if there was a solution. Life without Ashley presented just a long, bleak road with no turnings.

As the bells clanged round the empty room and the shouts of the crowd rose and fell, Katharine fondled the little Pegasus brooch, winking on the pocket of her shirt in the morning sunshine. And she suddenly felt lost. And very alone.

For perhaps the first time since Ashley's death she realised what it meant to be truly alone. And she longed to feel his strong arms around her, the tickle of his moustache as he rubbed his face against hers and bent to kiss her lips.

She wondered whether it was possible to remake her life without him. To live alone after having known the pure joy, the complete happiness of living with him however brief their marriage had been. And loving someone as deeply as she had loved him.

'Ashley,' she murmured as tears began to trickle down her face, unconsciously repeating the words she had cried out many times before. 'Why did you have to leave me? Why did you have to go?'

Katharine looked at the ugly calendar hanging on the wall, though she didn't need any reminder of the date. It had been screaming at her ever since she awoke. And no matter what she did she could not forget it. Today was the anniversary of the day Lawrence Masters had come down to Group R with the news which had shattered her hopes and obliterated her future.

It was also Ashley's birthday.

He would have been thirty-two.

The door opened and someone entered.

Katharine didn't look round. She just stood there, as if in a dream or rather a nightmare from which she longed to awake, listening to the sounds of rejoicing from the distant crowds. Her hand desperately clutching her brooch.

There was a thud. Something heavy had been dropped on the floor.

But it didn't matter what it was. Nothing was urgent any more. Nothing was important. It was all over.

A man's footsteps sounded behind her, then stopped.

She stiffened, swayed, not daring to move as she heard his voice call her name.

For a few seconds the street below swam before her eyes, turning crazy somersaults, round and round. Then slowly, her tear-stained face deathly white, she turned to face him.

He smiled and held out his arms.

With a strangled cry, her eyes wide with unbelief, she stumbled across the few yards which separated them and fell sobbing against his broad chest.

Gathering her to him he held her tightly, murmuring endearments until her storm of weeping ceased. Then, gently releasing her arms from around his neck, he held her at arm's length and looked tenderly down at her.

He seemed taller, but that was because he was so much thinner. Deep furrows creased his forehead and ran sharply down from his nose to his chin. His thick hair was flecked with grey. But his eyes were still the same. Piercing, laughing, full of changing moods and expressions.

Katharine looked up at him.

He smiled and gently dried her tears.

'I've come to take you home Kate,' he said softly.

Hearing his words she suddenly remembered other words. The last words her mother had spoken to her as she lay dying, almost five years before. Words which, at the time had sounded nonsensical.

'Go to your grandmother,' Rowena had whispered. 'To Paris, rue de la Faisanderie.'

As they clicked into the jigsaw puzzle of her mind, other words followed. Those which William had quoted on the station platform that cold December afternoon. 'He has made everything beautiful in his time.'

Katharine felt a warm glow rush through her. And she knew that, in spite of everything, he had.

She gazed into his face, her beautiful tawny eyes shining golden with unshed tears.

'We've wasted enough time,' she whispered. 'Let's go.'

He bent to pick up his heavy bag from the floor where he'd dropped it. Throwing an arm lightly across her shoulders, they walked together out of the office, along the empty corridor and down the stairs. Their footsteps echoed as they crossed the deserted hall and stepped out into the sunshine of Victory morning.

As the door of Norgeby House swung-to behind them, Katharine realised that she had come full circle.

She looked up and smiled through her tears. Then linked her arm in her father's.

Zag had come to take her home.

Glossary of Terms Used

Ack-ack fire	Anti-aircraft fire.
All clear	Siren signalling the end of an air-raid.
ARP Post	Air Raid Precautions Post. Manned by civilian men and women volunteers who patrolled the streets herding people to safety and public shelters when the air-raid siren sounded, and checking that no chink of light showed.
ATS	Auxilliary Territorial Service (Women's Corps of the Army).
Balaclava helmet	Knitted cap, resembling a chainmail helmet, first worn by soldiers during the Crimean War and in successive wars since.
Barnyard, Wanderer, etc.	Code names given to different circuits.
Blown	Agents whose identity had become known to the enemy.
Bod	Agent in the field.
British warm	Greatcoat worn by British Army Officers.
Bush House	Location of BBC World Service.
Circuit	An area where agents were operating in enemy territory.
Courier	An agent, usually a woman, carrying messages from the

	organiser to the W/T operator for coding and transmission to London, and vice versa.
Cover story	False identity, including false name and life story, given to every agent prior to being infiltrated.
Croix de Lorraine	Emblem of the Free French during World War II.
Crosse and Blackwell Brigade	General List. Officers not attributed to any specific regiment. Familiar nickname given to the Intelligence Service.
Demarcation Line	The frontier between German-occupied France and the 'Zone Libre' or so-called free zone.
Dropped	Parachuted.
FANY	(Women's Corps of the Army). Field Army Nursing Yeomanry, founded during World War 1.
The Field	Enemy territory into which agents were infiltrated.
Ginette Leblond	Name by which Katharine would be known to those she met once dropped into enemy territory. Name which would appear on the identity papers, together with false place of birth and CV.
Gisèle	Katharine's code name by which she would be referred to in HQ, London and in any coded messages passing between HQ and enemy territory.
Group R	Final training school for prospective agents before being infiltrated into enemy territory.
Mrs Hosters	An exclusive secretarial college in London run by Mrs Hoster.

Jeu de Paume	Art gallery, part of the Louvre in Paris where Impressionist paintings were housed.
LMS	London Midland and Scottish branch of the railway.
Lysander	Plane used to land or pick up agents in the field.
Mata Hari	Woman spy, working for the Germans, executed by the French during World War I.
Messages Personnels	Non-coded, seemingly meaningless, pre-arranged messages announcing a drop of supplies or drop or pick-up of agents in the field. Transmitted by BBC World Service.
Min. of Ag. and Fish	Ministry of Agriculture and Fisheries.
M15	Military Intelligence.
Montague Mansions	Part of the SOE HQ.
Morrison shelter	A cast-iron table set up on the ground floor or in the cellar of a house under which several people could sleep in comparative safety during an air-raid. Named after the MP Herbert Morrison.
Norgeby House	In Baker Street, HQ of SOE.
Orchard Court	Flat where agents were briefed prior to being infiltrated, prepared for drops and interrogated upon their return.
Organiser	Person, usually a British officer, in charge of a circuit.
Otets	Russian for father. Pronounced 'Atiets'.
Pères Blancs	A Roman Catholic order, working with the underprivileged in Africa

	and elsewhere. So named because of the white habit they wear.
Quad	Prison.
Racket	In-house nickname for SOE.
Reseau	Specified area under the control of an organiser.
Sam Browne	Special leather belt, invented by General Sam Browne after he lost his left arm in the Indian Mutiny. Worn ever since by British Army Officers.
Siegfried Line	German fortification line between France and Germany.
Signal	Coded message sent or received by W/T operator.
Sked	Each W/T operator was assigned a special time, known as a sked, when he could send and receive messages from London. Should he not come up on his sked for several days, it alerted HQ to the fact that he had been captured or was in hiding.
SOE	Special Operations Executive. Created during World War 2 to infiltrate agents into enemy-occupied territory.
Students	Prospective agents in training.
VAD	Voluntary Aid Detachment.
Wavy Navy	Name given by regular Naval officers to wartime volunteers, who wore 'wavy' stripes on their cuff to denote rank, instead of straight ones.
Wrens	WRNS, Womens' Royal Naval Service.

W/T operator	An agent coding, transmitting, receiving and decoding messages to and from HQ in London.
WVS	Womens' Voluntary Service.
Y9	Code name given to the interrogation of agents returning from the field.